# SCOOBY-DOO

# RUH-ROH!

**WRITTEN BY:**
CHRIS DUFFY
TERRANCE GRIEP
MICHAEL KRAIGER
MICHAEL KUPPERMAN
MATT WAYNE

**ILLUSTRATED BY:**
ERNIE COLÓN
TIM HARKINS
ANDREW PEPOY
BOB SMITH
JOE STATON

**COLORED BY:**
PATRICIA MULVIHILL

**LETTERED BY:**
JOHN COSTANZA
TIM HARKINS
KEN LOPEZ
CLEM ROBINS

Dan DiDio
VP-Editorial

Bronwyn Taggart
Editor-original series

Scott Nybakken
Editor-collected edition

Robbin Brosterman
Senior Art Director

John J. Hill
Art Director

Paul Levitz
President & Publisher

Georg Brewer
VP-Design & Retail Product
Development

Richard Bruning
Senior VP-Creative Director

Patrick Caldon
Senior VP-Finance & Operations

Chris Caramalis
VP-Finance

Terri Cunningham
VP-Managing Editor

Alison Gill
VP-Manufacturing

Lillian Laserson
Senior VP & General Counsel

Jim Lee
Editorial Director-WildStorm

David McKillips
VP-Advertising & Custom Publishing

John Nee
VP-Business Development

Cheryl Rubin
VP-Brand Management

Bob Wayne
VP-Sales & Marketing

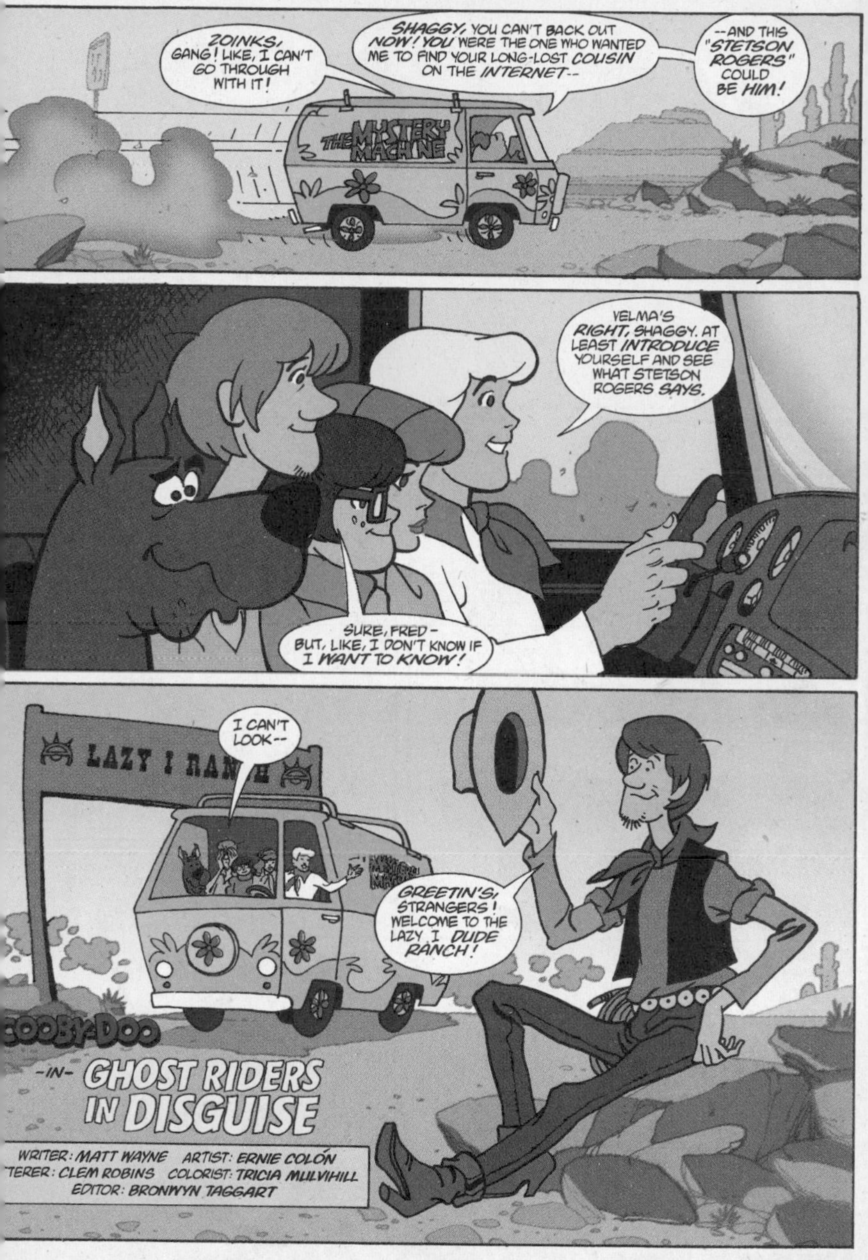
ZOINKS, GANG! LIKE, I CAN'T GO THROUGH WITH IT!
SHAGGY, YOU CAN'T BACK OUT NOW! YOU WERE THE ONE WHO WANTED ME TO FIND YOUR LONG-LOST COUSIN ON THE INTERNET--
--AND THIS "STETSON ROGERS" COULD BE HIM!
THE MYSTERY MACHINE
VELMA'S RIGHT, SHAGGY. AT LEAST INTRODUCE YOURSELF AND SEE WHAT STETSON ROGERS SAYS.
SURE, FRED - BUT, LIKE, I DON'T KNOW IF I WANT TO KNOW!
LAZY I RAN
I CAN'T LOOK--
GREETIN'S, STRANGERS! WELCOME TO THE LAZY I DUDE RANCH!
COOBY-DOO
-IN- GHOST RIDERS IN DISGUISE
WRITER: MATT WAYNE ARTIST: ERNIE COLÓN
TERER: CLEM ROBINS COLORIST: TRICIA MULVIHILL
EDITOR: BRONWYN TAGGART

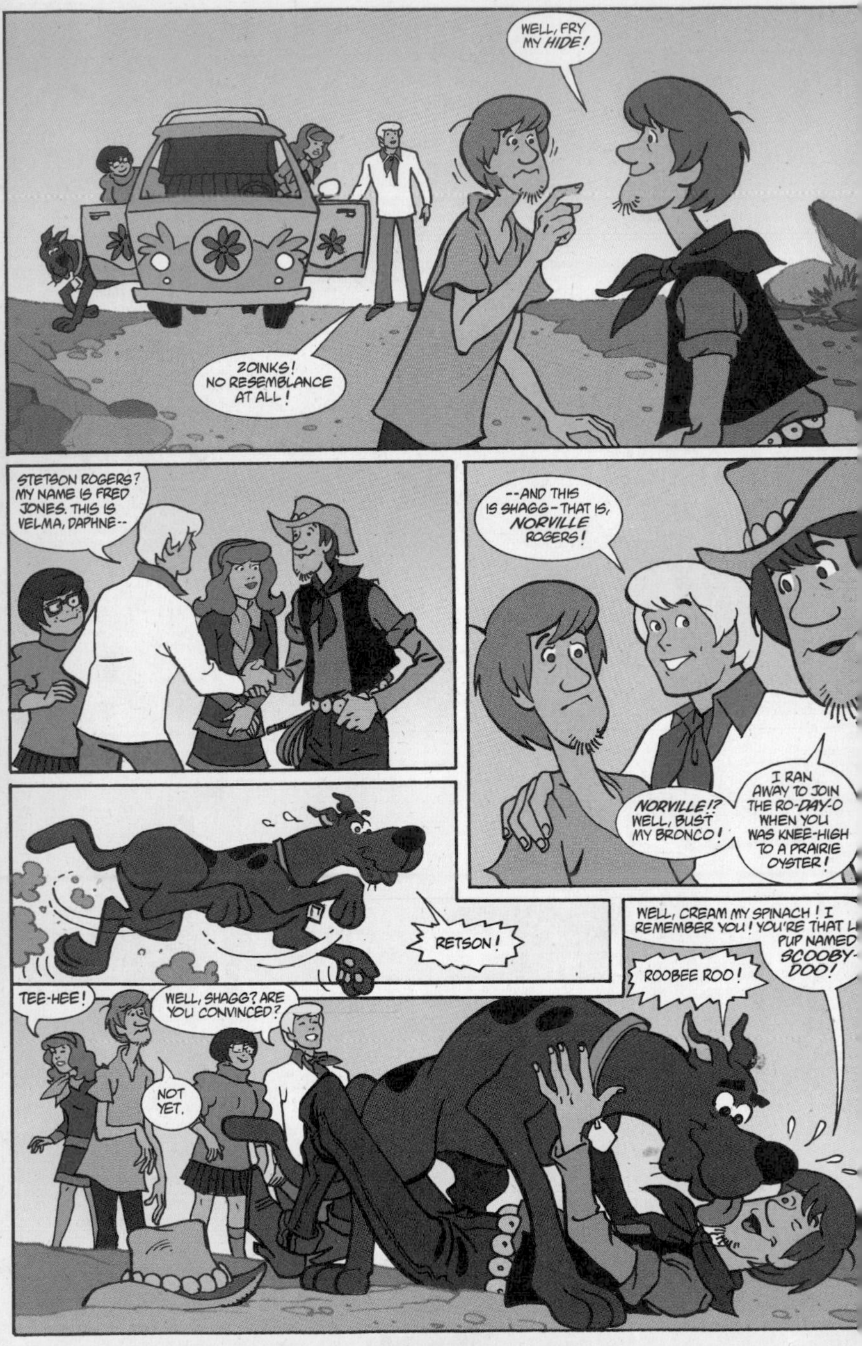
WELL, FRY MY HIDE!
ZOINKS! NO RESEMBLANCE AT ALL!
STETSON ROGERS? MY NAME IS FRED JONES. THIS IS VELMA, DAPHNE--
--AND THIS IS SHAGG-THAT IS, NORVILLE ROGERS!
NORVILLE!? WELL, BUST MY BRONCO!
I RAN AWAY TO JOIN THE RO-DAY-O WHEN YOU WAS KNEE-HIGH TO A PRAIRIE OYSTER!
RETSON!
WELL, CREAM MY SPINACH! I REMEMBER YOU! YOU'RE THAT L PUP NAMED SCOOBY-DOO!
ROOBEE ROO!
TEE-HEE!
WELL, SHAGG? ARE YOU CONVINCED?
NOT YET.

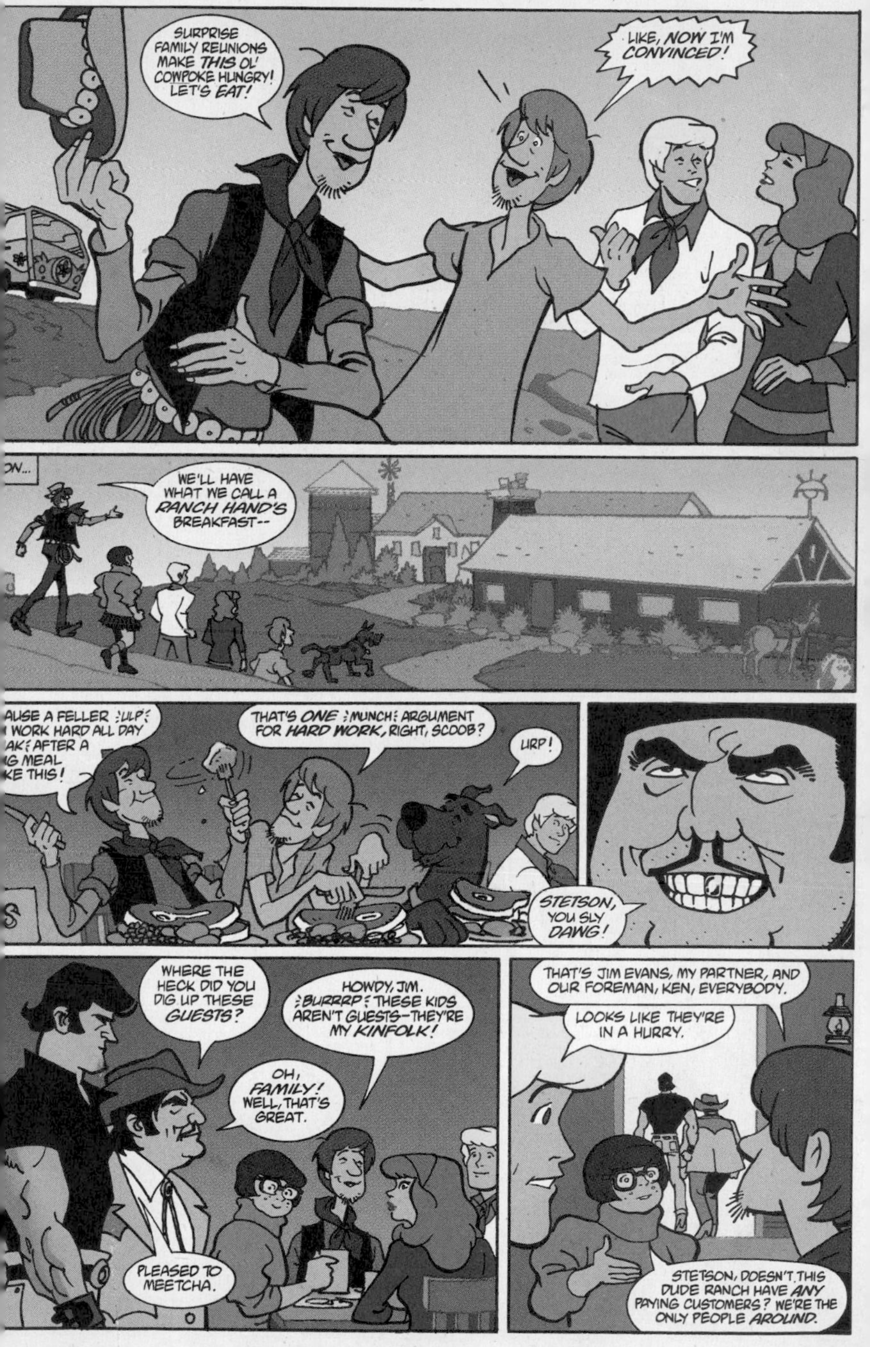
SURPRISE FAMILY REUNIONS MAKE THIS OL' COWPOKE HUNGRY! LET'S EAT!
LIKE, NOW I'M CONVINCED!
ON...
WE'LL HAVE WHAT WE CALL A RANCH HAND'S BREAKFAST--
AUSE A FELLER ;ULP; WORK HARD ALL DAY AK; AFTER A G MEAL KE THIS!
THAT'S ONE ;MUNCH; ARGUMENT FOR HARD WORK, RIGHT, SCOOB?
URP!
STETSON, YOU SLY DAWG!
WHERE THE HECK DID YOU DIG UP THESE GUESTS?
HOWDY, JIM. ;BURRRP; THESE KIDS AREN'T GUESTS—THEY'RE MY KINFOLK!
OH, FAMILY! WELL, THAT'S GREAT.
PLEASED TO MEETCHA.
THAT'S JIM EVANS, MY PARTNER, AND OUR FOREMAN, KEN, EVERYBODY.
LOOKS LIKE THEY'RE IN A HURRY.
STETSON, DOESN'T THIS DUDE RANCH HAVE ANY PAYING CUSTOMERS? WE'RE THE ONLY PEOPLE AROUND.

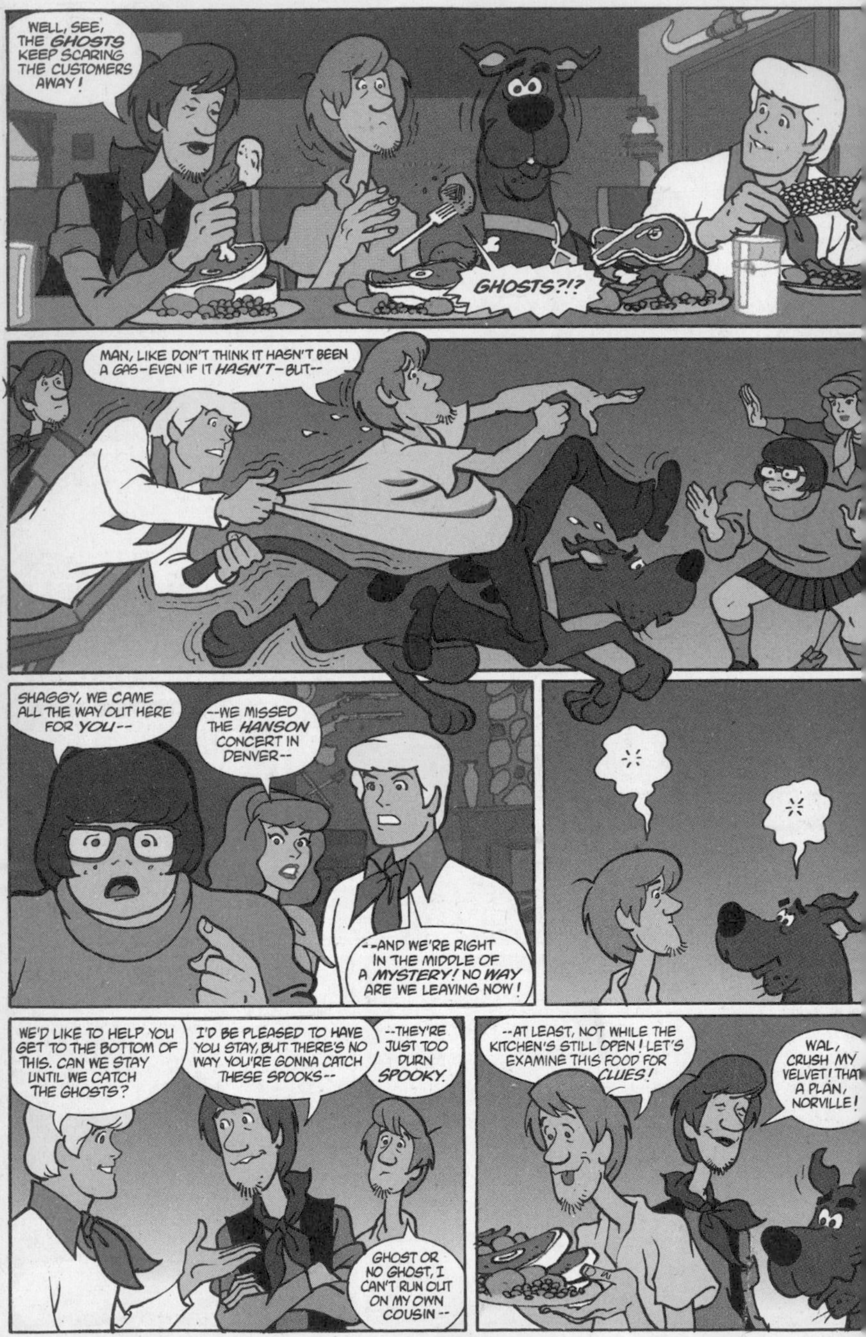
WELL, SEE, THE GHOSTS KEEP SCARING THE CUSTOMERS AWAY!
GHOSTS?!?
MAN, LIKE DON'T THINK IT HASN'T BEEN A GAS--EVEN IF IT HASN'T--BUT--
SHAGGY, WE CAME ALL THE WAY OUT HERE FOR YOU--
--WE MISSED THE HANSON CONCERT IN DENVER--
--AND WE'RE RIGHT IN THE MIDDLE OF A MYSTERY! NO WAY ARE WE LEAVING NOW!
WE'D LIKE TO HELP YOU GET TO THE BOTTOM OF THIS. CAN WE STAY UNTIL WE CATCH THE GHOSTS?
I'D BE PLEASED TO HAVE YOU STAY, BUT THERE'S NO WAY YOU'RE GONNA CATCH THESE SPOOKS--
--THEY'RE JUST TOO DURN SPOOKY.
GHOST OR NO GHOST, I CAN'T RUN OUT ON MY OWN COUSIN--
--AT LEAST, NOT WHILE THE KITCHEN'S STILL OPEN! LET'S EXAMINE THIS FOOD FOR CLUES!
WAL, CRUSH MY VELVET! THAT'S A PLAN, NORVILLE!

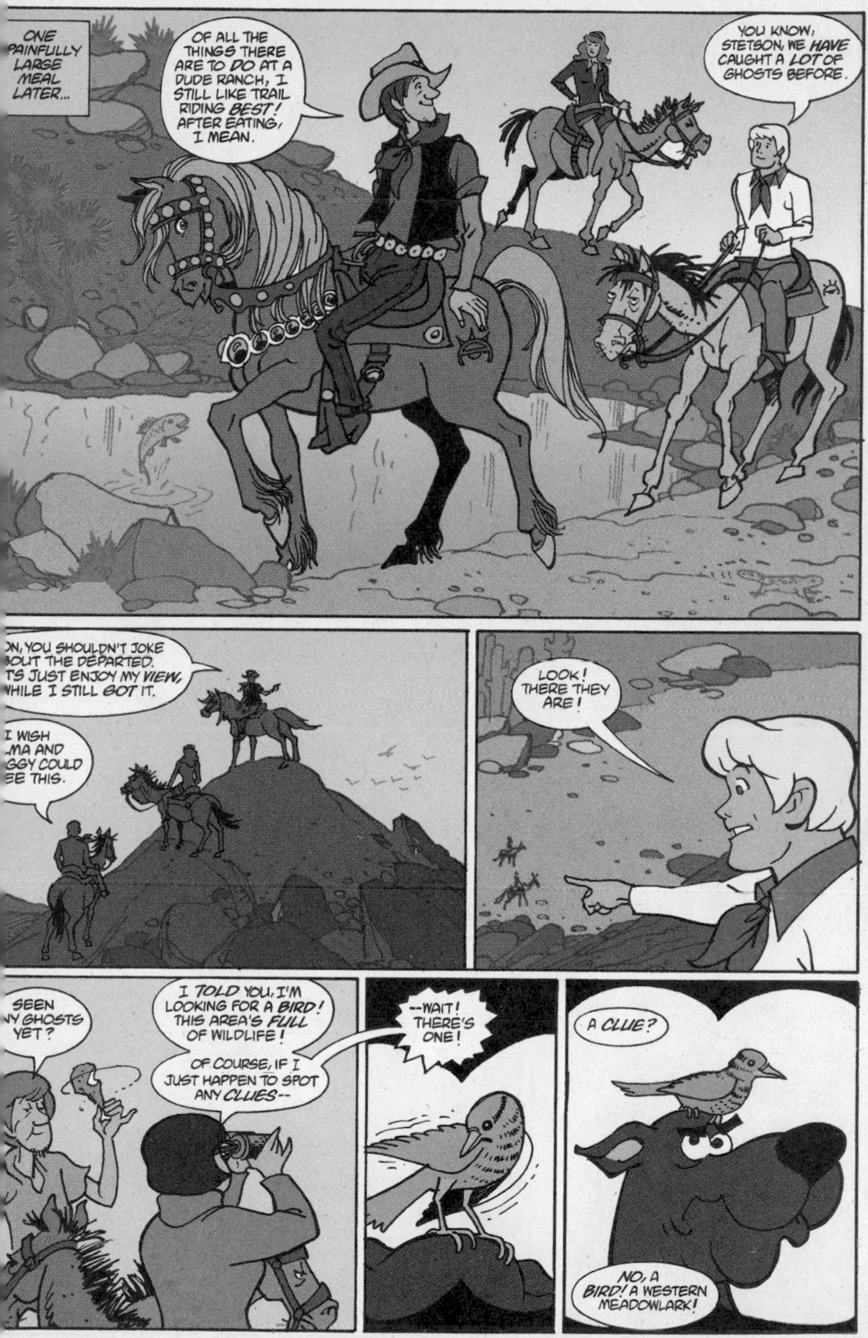
ONE PAINFULLY LARGE MEAL LATER...
OF ALL THE THINGS THERE ARE TO DO AT A DUDE RANCH, I STILL LIKE TRAIL RIDING BEST! AFTER EATING, I MEAN.
YOU KNOW, STETSON, WE HAVE CAUGHT A LOT OF GHOSTS BEFORE.
ON, YOU SHOULDN'T JOKE BOUT THE DEPARTED. T'S JUST ENJOY MY VIEW, WHILE I STILL GOT IT.
I WISH LMA AND GGY COULD EE THIS.
LOOK! THERE THEY ARE!
SEEN NY GHOSTS YET?
I TOLD YOU, I'M LOOKING FOR A BIRD! THIS AREA'S FULL OF WILDLIFE!
OF COURSE, IF I JUST HAPPEN TO SPOT ANY CLUES--
--WAIT! THERE'S ONE!
A CLUE?
NO, A BIRD! A WESTERN MEADOWLARK!

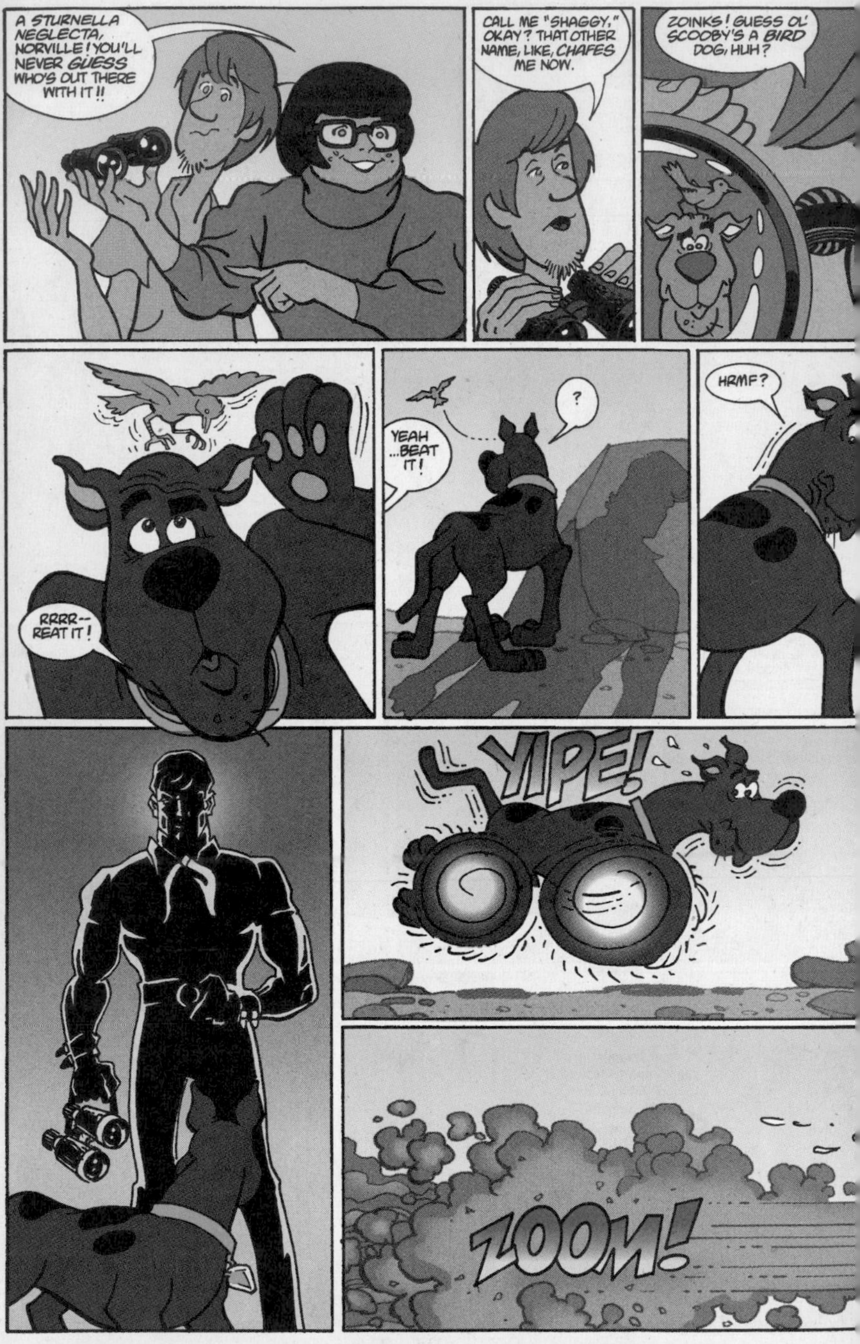
A STURNELLA NEGLECTA, NORVILLE! YOU'LL NEVER GUESS WHO'S OUT THERE WITH IT!!
CALL ME "SHAGGY," OKAY? THAT OTHER NAME, LIKE, CHAFES ME NOW.
ZOINKS! GUESS OL' SCOOBY'S A BIRD DOG, HUH?
RRRR--REAT IT!
YEAH ...BEAT IT!
?
HRMF?
YIPE!
ZOOM!

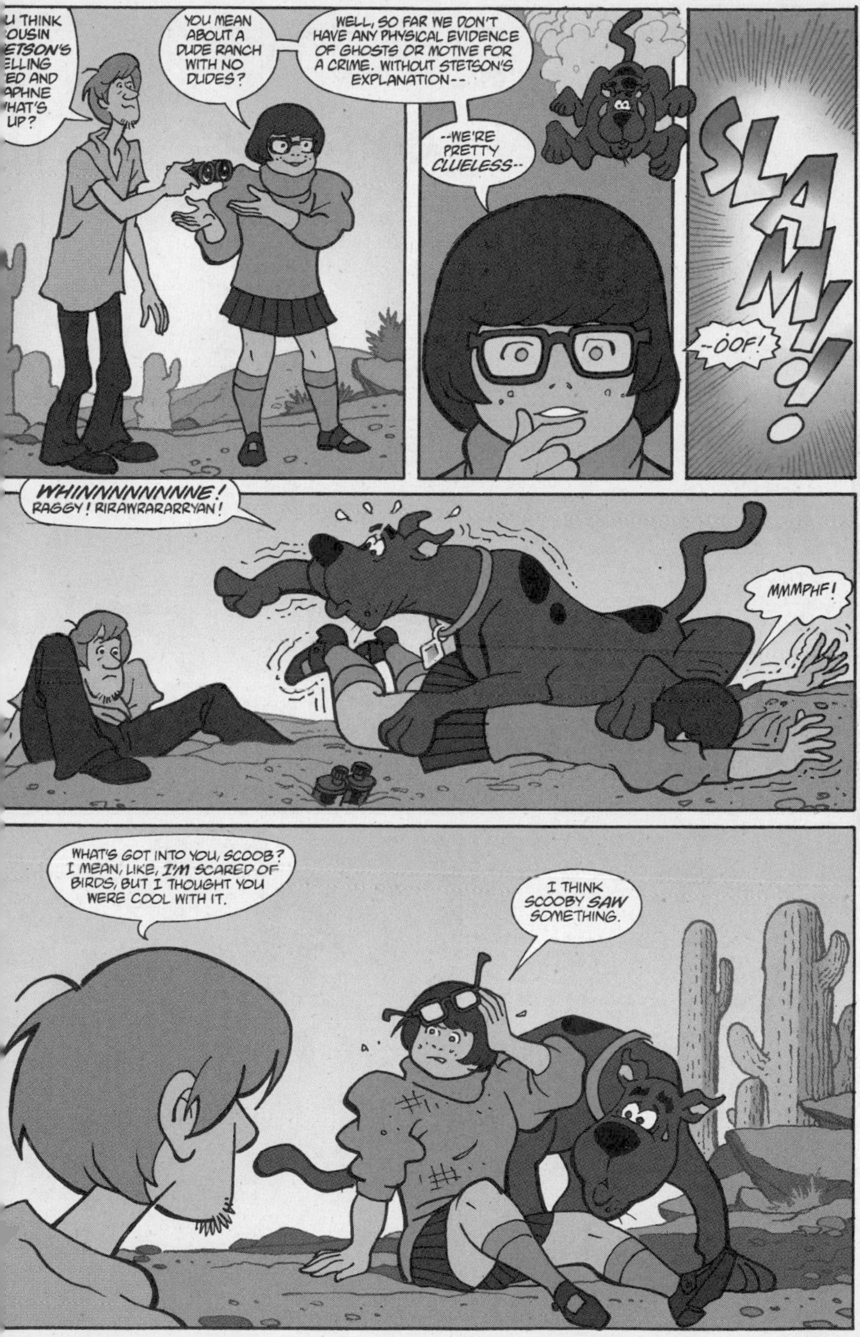
U THINK COUSIN STETSON'S ELLING ED AND APHNE WHAT'S UP?
YOU MEAN ABOUT A DUDE RANCH WITH NO DUDES?
WELL, SO FAR WE DON'T HAVE ANY PHYSICAL EVIDENCE OF GHOSTS OR MOTIVE FOR A CRIME. WITHOUT STETSON'S EXPLANATION--
--WE'RE PRETTY CLUELESS--
SLAM!!
--OOF!
WHINNNNNNNNNE! RAGGY! RIRAWRARARRYAN!
MMMPHF!
WHAT'S GOT INTO YOU, SCOOB? I MEAN, LIKE, I'M SCARED OF BIRDS, BUT I THOUGHT YOU WERE COOL WITH IT.
I THINK SCOOBY SAW SOMETHING.

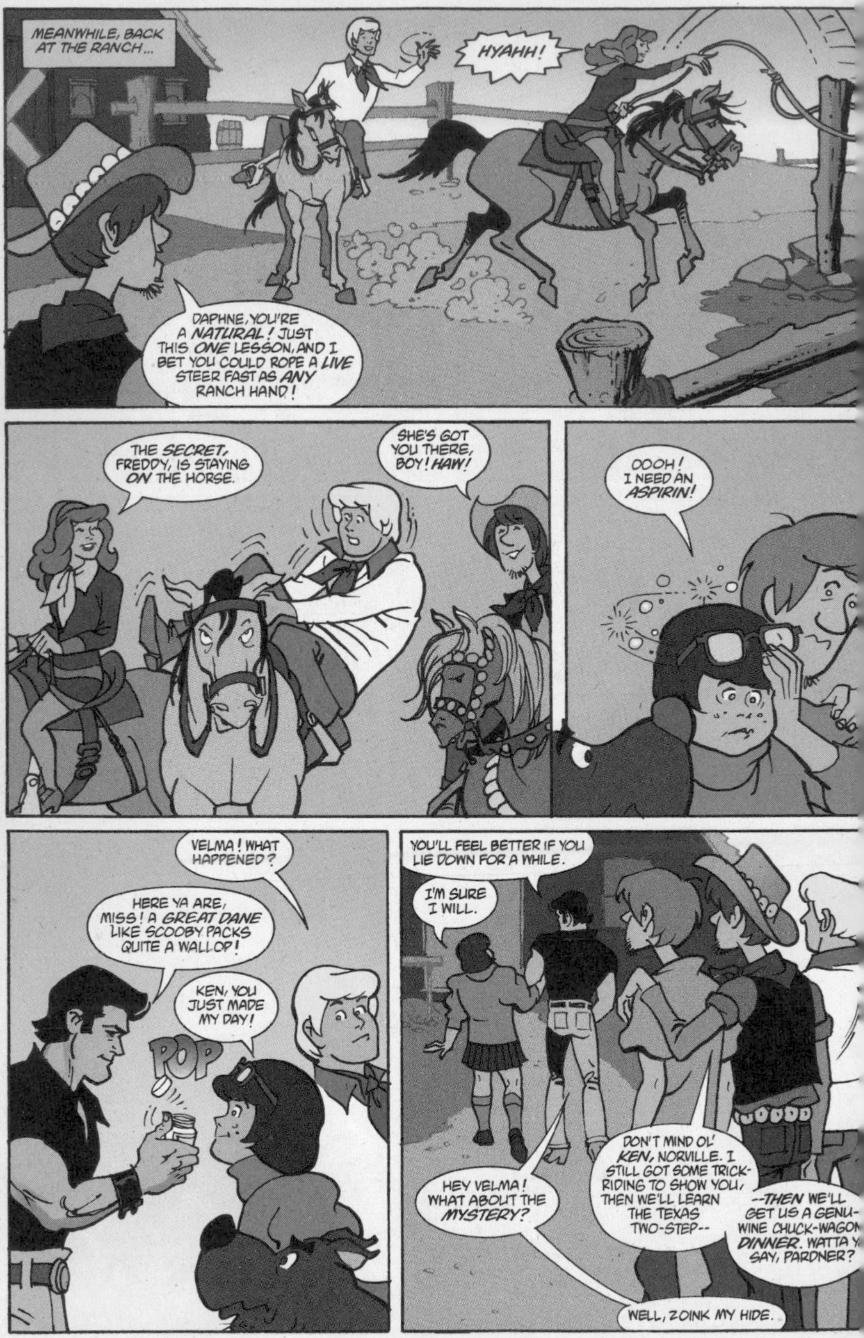
MEANWHILE, BACK AT THE RANCH...
HYAHH!
DAPHNE, YOU'RE A NATURAL! JUST THIS ONE LESSON, AND I BET YOU COULD ROPE A LIVE STEER FAST AS ANY RANCH HAND!
THE SECRET, FREDDY, IS STAYING ON THE HORSE.
SHE'S GOT YOU THERE, BOY! HAW!
OOOH! I NEED AN ASPIRIN!
VELMA! WHAT HAPPENED?
HERE YA ARE, MISS! A GREAT DANE LIKE SCOOBY PACKS QUITE A WALLOP!
KEN, YOU JUST MADE MY DAY!
POP
YOU'LL FEEL BETTER IF YOU LIE DOWN FOR A WHILE.
I'M SURE I WILL.
HEY VELMA! WHAT ABOUT THE MYSTERY?
DON'T MIND OL' KEN, NORVILLE. I STILL GOT SOME TRICK-RIDING TO SHOW YOU, THEN WE'LL LEARN THE TEXAS TWO-STEP--
--THEN WE'LL GET US A GENU-WINE CHUCK-WAGON DINNER. WATTA YA SAY, PARDNER?
WELL, ZOINK MY HIDE.

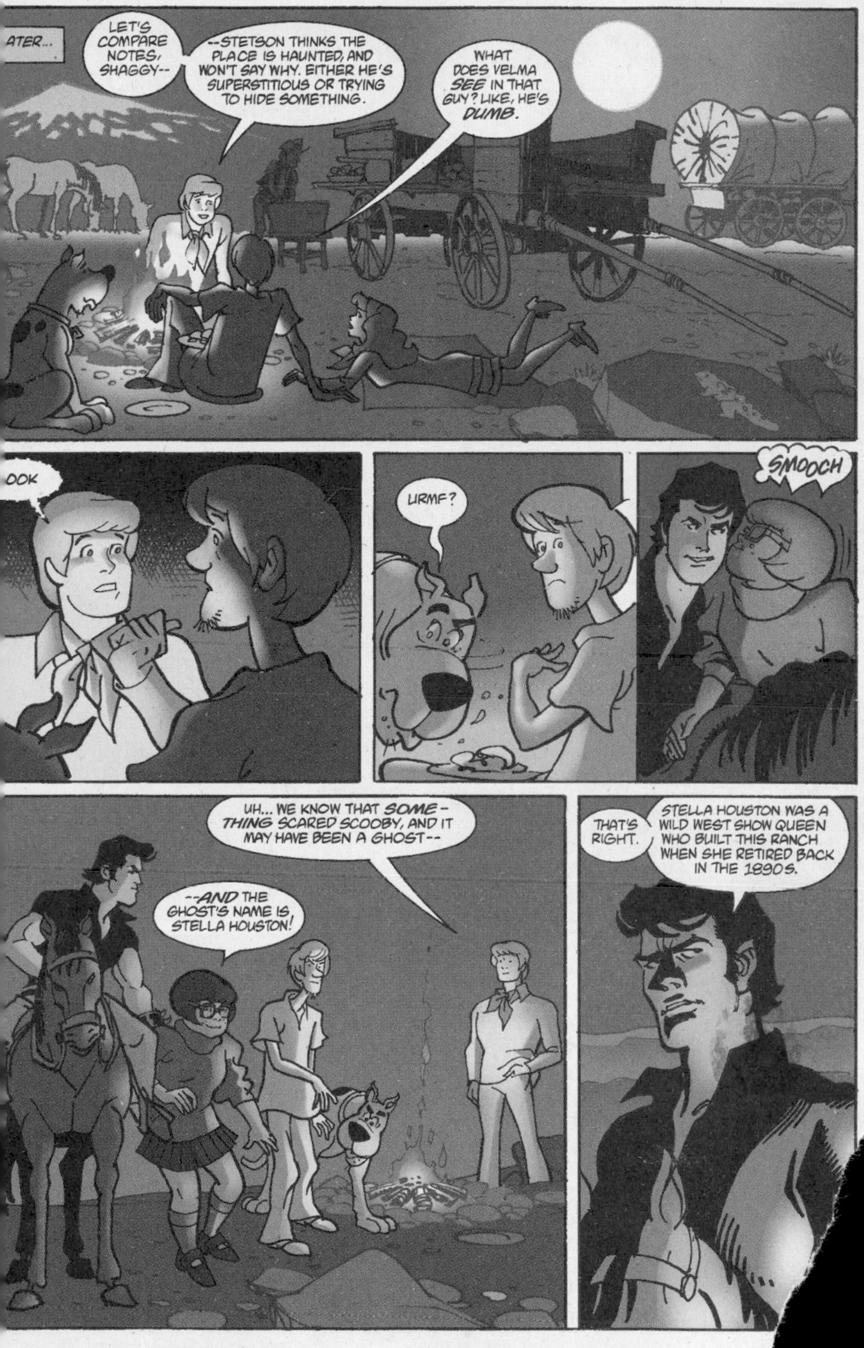

ATER...
LET'S COMPARE NOTES, SHAGGY--
--STETSON THINKS THE PLACE IS HAUNTED, AND WON'T SAY WHY. EITHER HE'S SUPERSTITIOUS OR TRYING TO HIDE SOMETHING.
WHAT DOES VELMA SEE IN THAT GUY? LIKE, HE'S DUMB.
OOK
URMF?
SMOOCH
UH... WE KNOW THAT SOME-THING SCARED SCOOBY, AND IT MAY HAVE BEEN A GHOST--
--AND THE GHOST'S NAME IS STELLA HOUSTON!
THAT'S RIGHT.
STELLA HOUSTON WAS A WILD WEST SHOW QUEEN WHO BUILT THIS RANCH WHEN SHE RETIRED BACK IN THE 1890S.

"STELLA AND HER HORSE, ZENOBIA, USED TO PERFORM RIDING TRICKS FOR THE CUSTOMERS HERE.

"HER BUSINESS PARTNER, SISSY HAWGSHANK, WAS MIGHTY SMART--

"--SHE EVEN MADE UP A SPECIAL SHOE FOR ZENOBIA, WITH TWO BARS RUN ACROSS IT TO HELP THE HORSE CLIMB STAIRS IN THEIR ACT--

DAGNABIT, KEN! DON'T GO TELLING OUR PROBLEMS TO MY FRIENDS! CAN'T YOU LEAVE WELL ENOUGH ALONE?

NO STETSON EXPECT CAN"

NOW WE'RE GETTING SOMEWHERE! GOOD GOING, VELMA.

YEAH, NICE INTERROGATION TECHNIQUE!

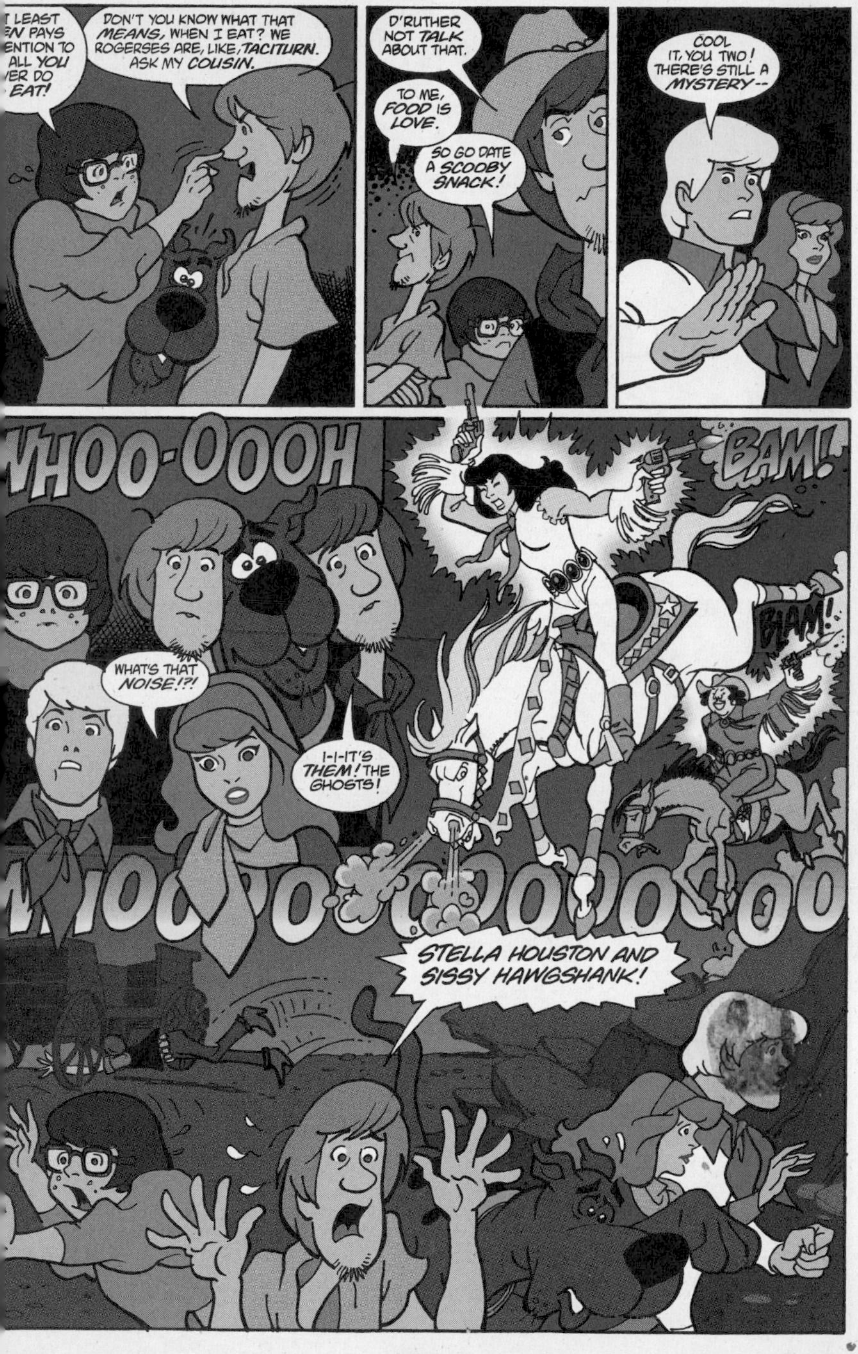

T LEAST
EN PAYS
ENTION TO
ALL YOU
ER DO
EAT!
DON'T YOU KNOW WHAT THAT MEANS, WHEN I EAT? WE ROGERSES ARE, LIKE, TACITURN. ASK MY COUSIN.
D'RUTHER NOT TALK ABOUT THAT.
TO ME, FOOD IS LOVE.
SO GO DATE A SCOOBY SNACK!
COOL IT, YOU TWO! THERE'S STILL A MYSTERY--
WHOO-OOOH
BAM!
BLAM!
WHAT'S THAT NOISE!?!
I-I-IT'S THEM! THE GHOSTS!
STELLA HOUSTON AND SISSY HAWGSHANK!

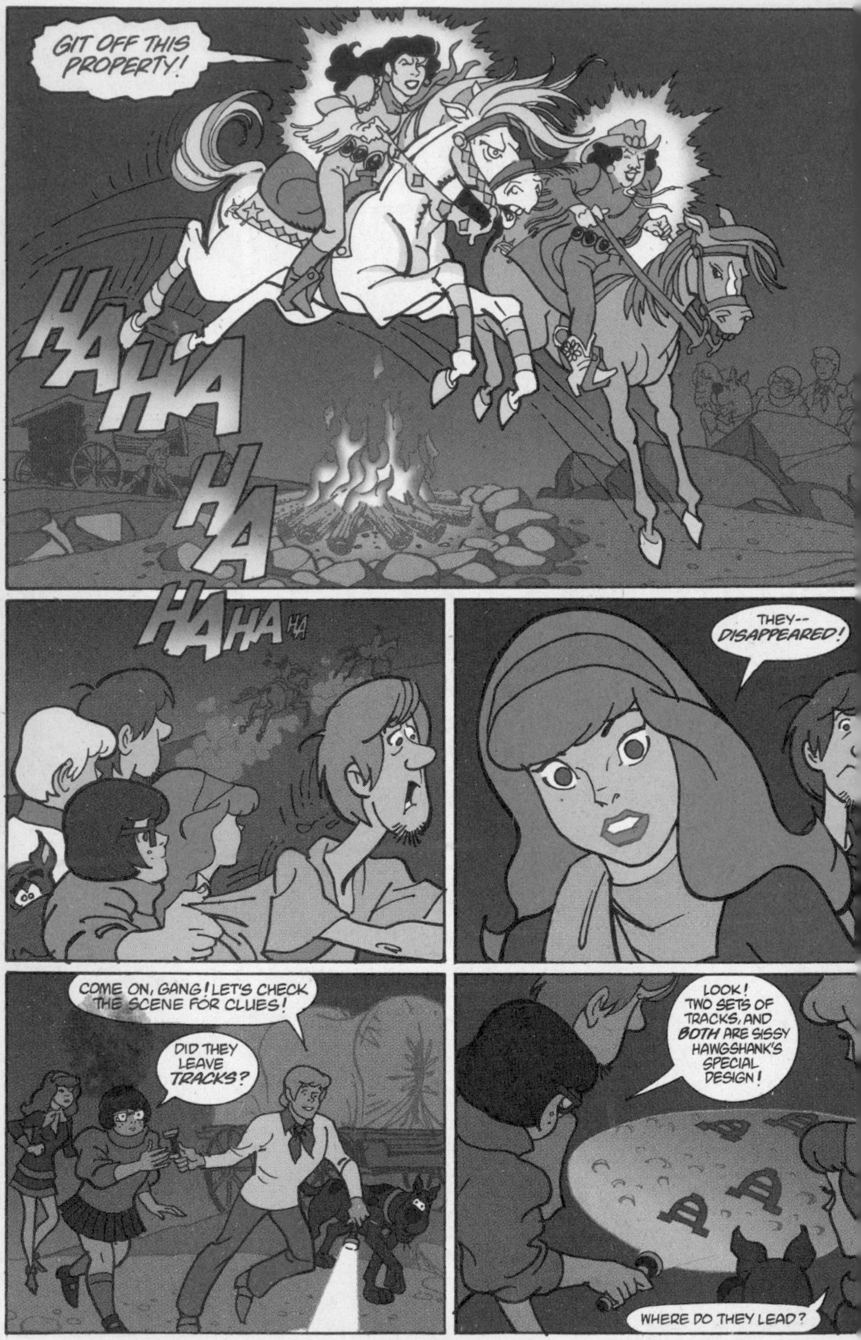

GIT OFF THIS PROPERTY!
HAHAHA
HA
HA
HAHA
HA
THEY-- DISAPPEARED!
COME ON, GANG! LET'S CHECK THE SCENE FOR CLUES!
DID THEY LEAVE TRACKS?
LOOK! TWO SETS OF TRACKS, AND BOTH ARE SISSY HAWGSHANK'S SPECIAL DESIGN!
WHERE DO THEY LEAD?

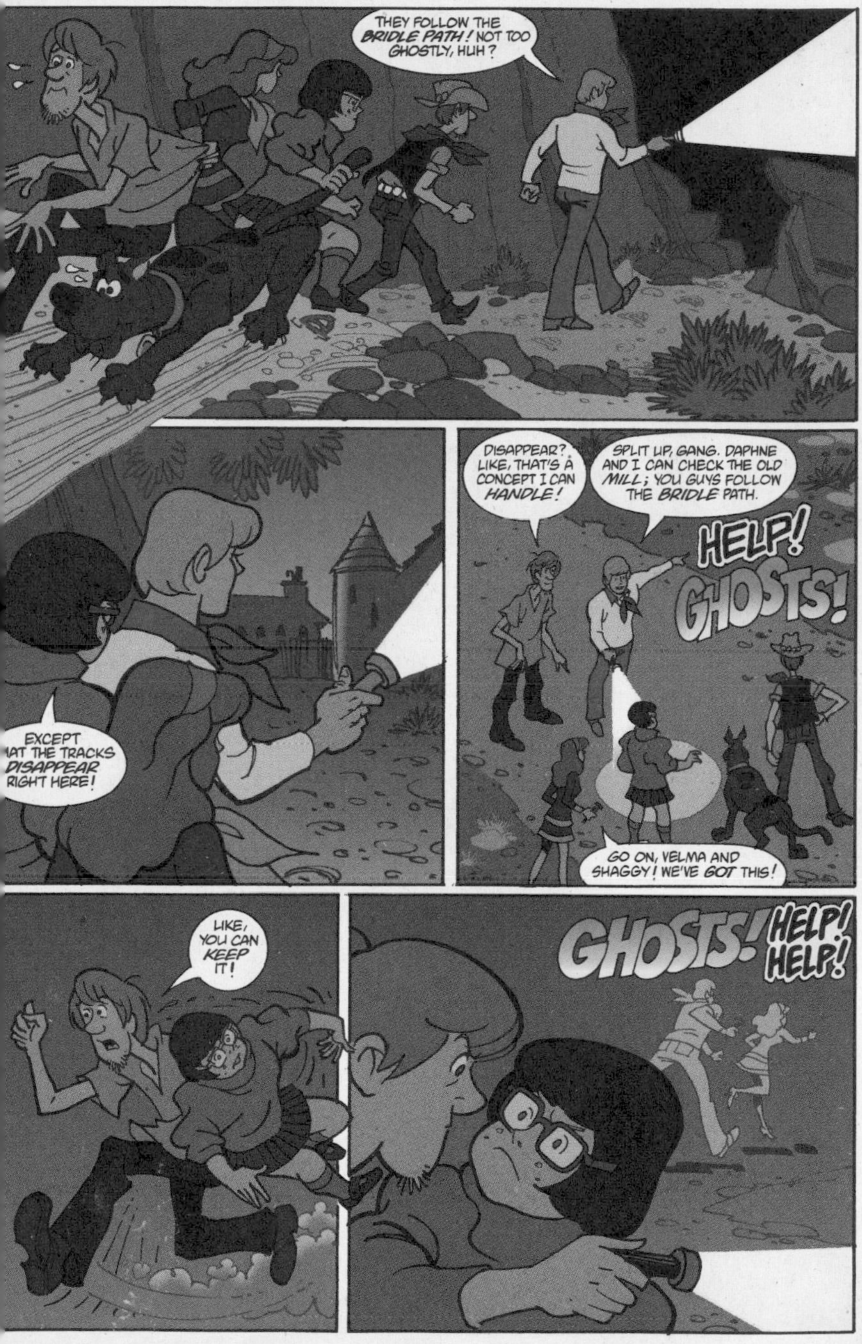
THEY FOLLOW THE BRIDLE PATH! NOT TOO GHOSTLY, HUH?
EXCEPT THAT THE TRACKS DISAPPEAR RIGHT HERE!
DISAPPEAR? LIKE, THAT'S A CONCEPT I CAN HANDLE!
SPLIT UP, GANG. DAPHNE AND I CAN CHECK THE OLD MILL; YOU GUYS FOLLOW THE BRIDLE PATH.
HELP! GHOSTS!
GO ON, VELMA AND SHAGGY! WE'VE GOT THIS!
LIKE, YOU CAN KEEP IT!
GHOSTS! HELP! HELP!

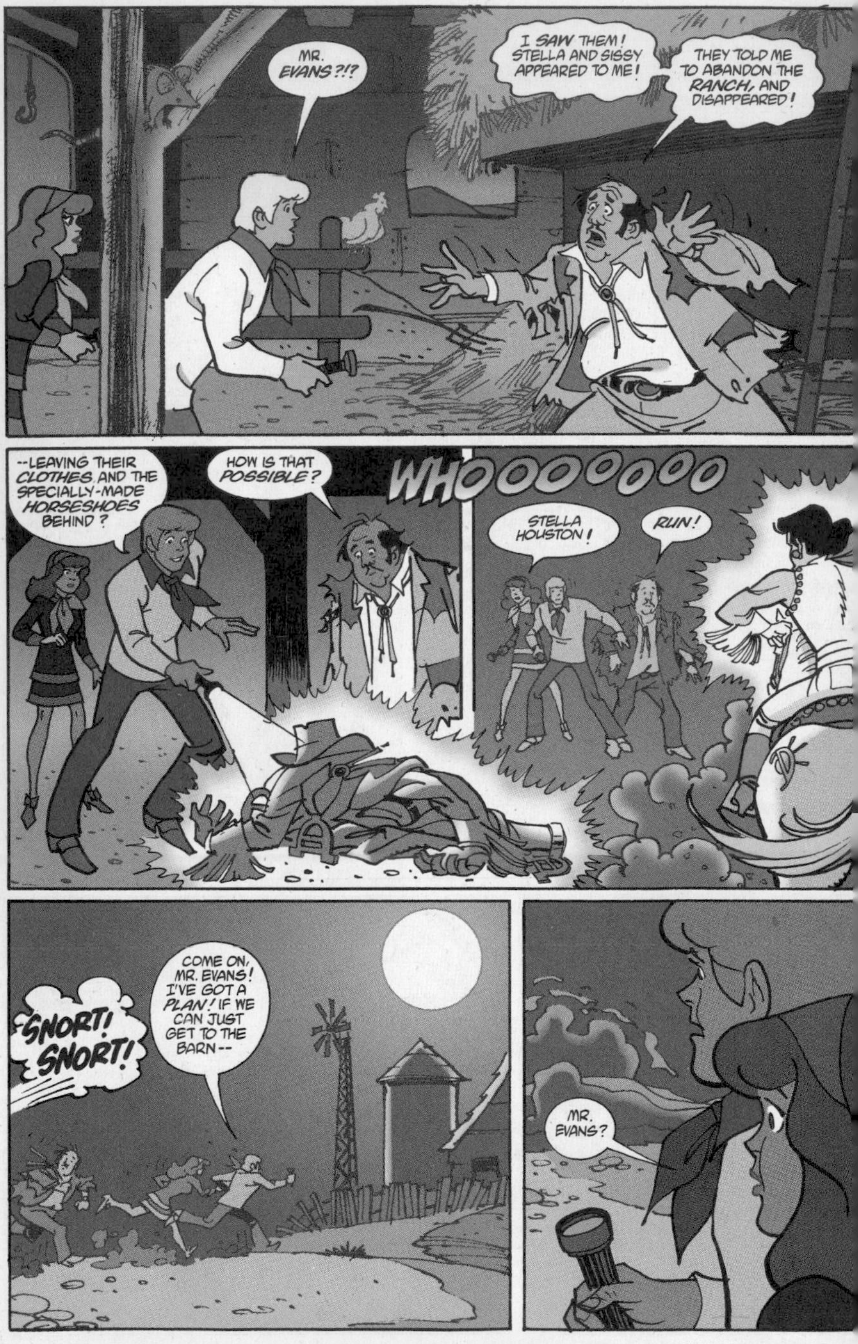
MR. EVANS?!?
I SAW THEM! STELLA AND SISSY APPEARED TO ME!
THEY TOLD ME TO ABANDON THE RANCH, AND DISAPPEARED!
--LEAVING THEIR CLOTHES AND THE SPECIALLY-MADE HORSESHOES BEHIND?
HOW IS THAT POSSIBLE?
WHOOOOOOOO
STELLA HOUSTON!
RUN!
SNORT! SNORT!
COME ON, MR. EVANS! I'VE GOT A PLAN! IF WE CAN JUST GET TO THE BARN--
MR. EVANS?

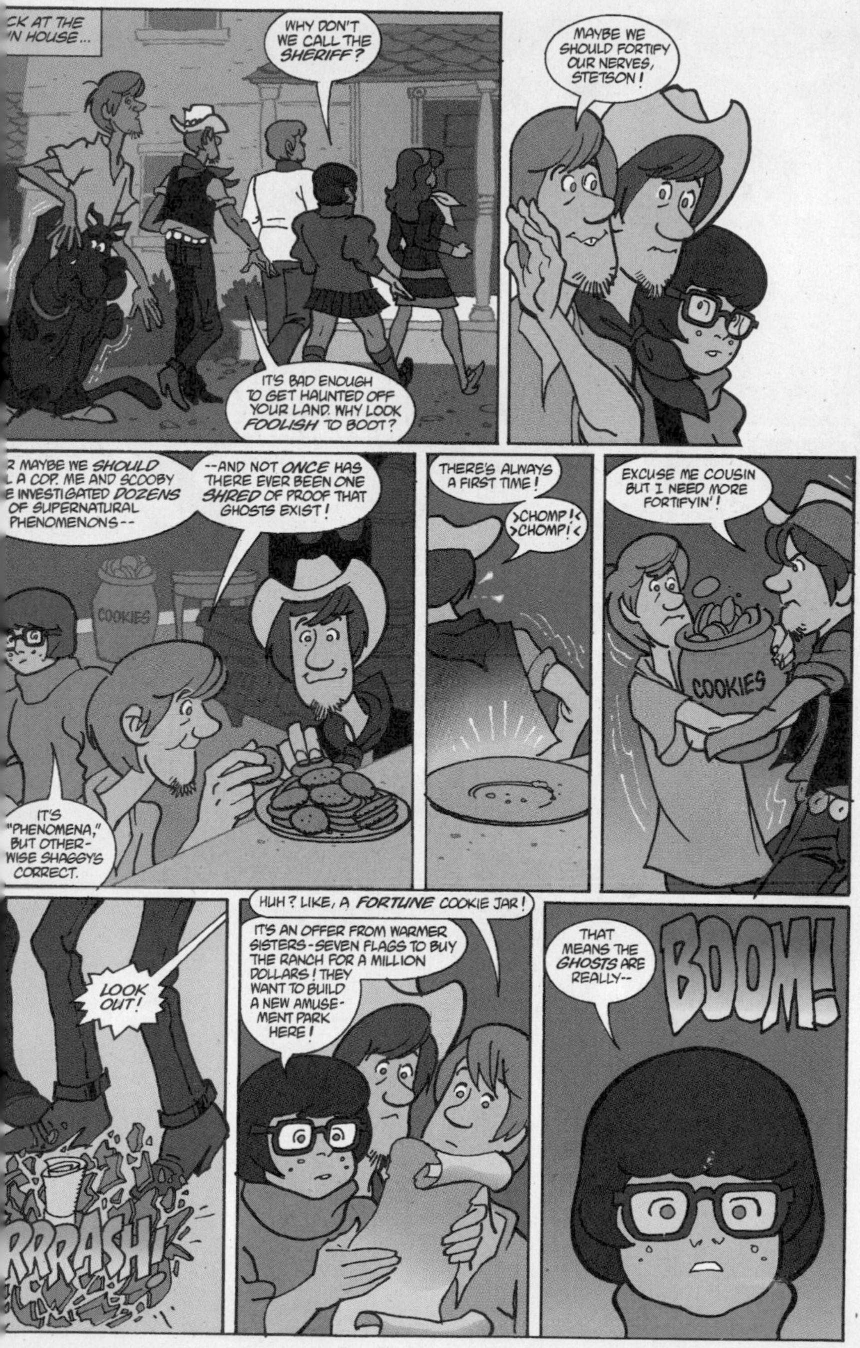
CK AT THE
N HOUSE...
WHY DON'T WE CALL THE SHERIFF?
IT'S BAD ENOUGH TO GET HAUNTED OFF YOUR LAND. WHY LOOK FOOLISH TO BOOT?
MAYBE WE SHOULD FORTIFY OUR NERVES, STETSON!
R MAYBE WE SHOULD L A COP. ME AND SCOOBY E INVESTIGATED DOZENS OF SUPERNATURAL PHENOMENONS--
--AND NOT ONCE HAS THERE EVER BEEN ONE SHRED OF PROOF THAT GHOSTS EXIST!
COOKIES
IT'S "PHENOMENA," BUT OTHER-WISE SHAGGY'S CORRECT.
THERE'S ALWAYS A FIRST TIME!
>CHOMP!<
>CHOMP!<
EXCUSE ME COUSIN BUT I NEED MORE FORTIFYIN'!
COOKIES
LOOK OUT!
RRRASH!
HUH? LIKE, A FORTUNE COOKIE JAR!
IT'S AN OFFER FROM WARMER SISTERS-SEVEN FLAGS TO BUY THE RANCH FOR A MILLION DOLLARS! THEY WANT TO BUILD A NEW AMUSE-MENT PARK HERE!
THAT MEANS THE GHOSTS ARE REALLY--
BOOM!

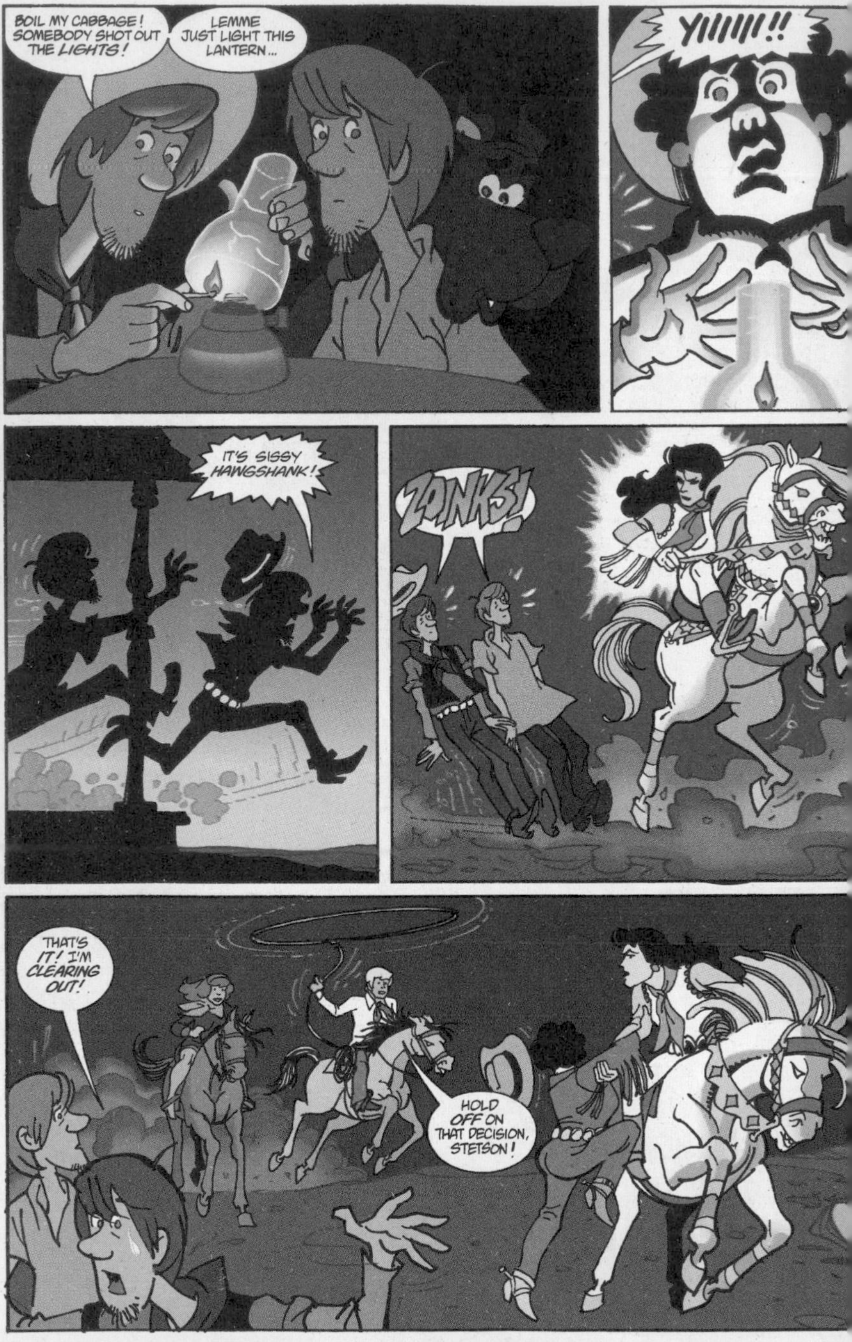
BOIL MY CABBAGE! SOMEBODY SHOT OUT THE *LIGHTS*!
LEMME JUST LIGHT THIS LANTERN...
YIIIIII!!
IT'S SISSY HAWGSHANK!
ZOINKS!
THAT'S *IT!* I'M *CLEARING OUT!*
HOLD *OFF* ON THAT DECISION, STETSON!

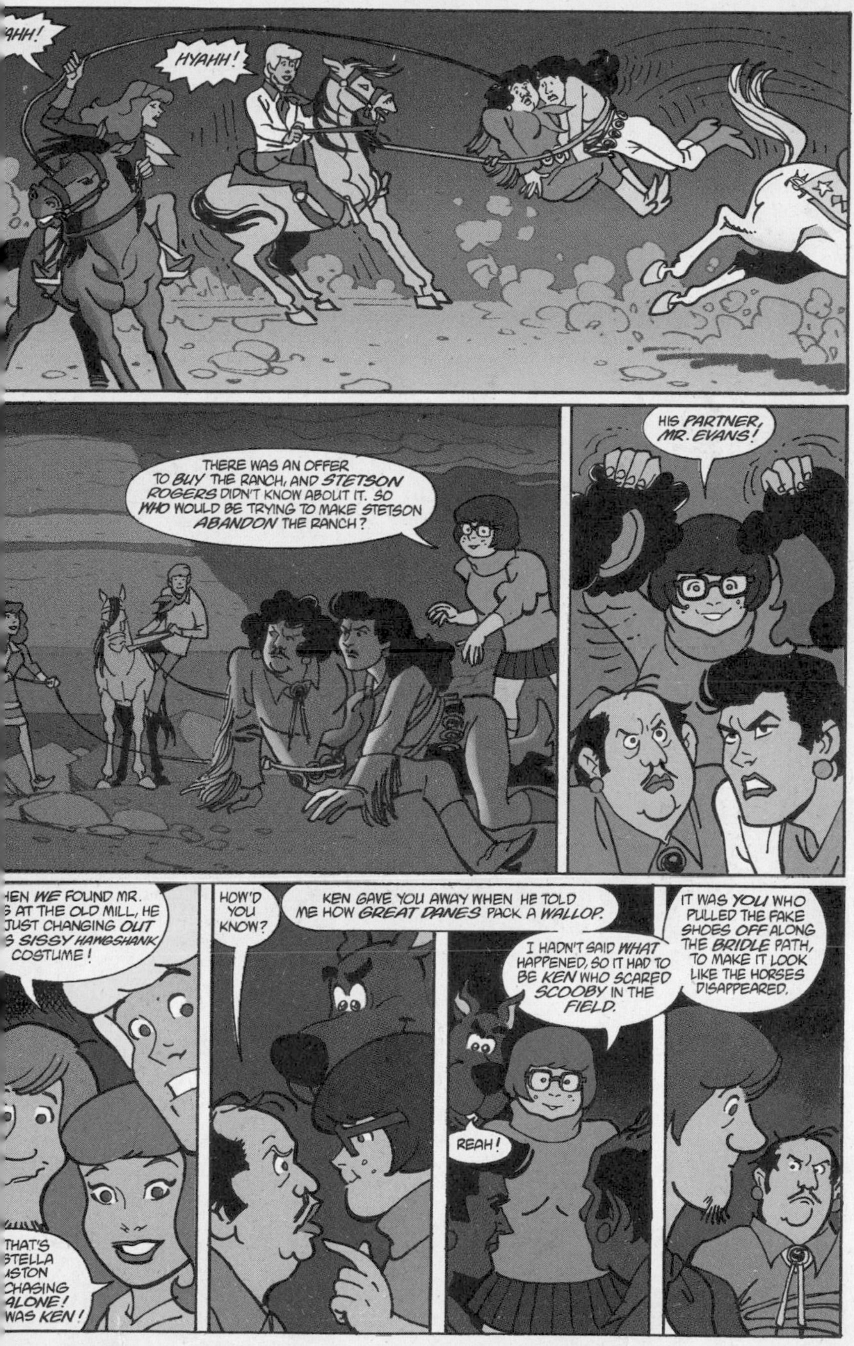

...AHH!
HYAHH!
THERE WAS AN OFFER TO BUY THE RANCH, AND STETSON ROGERS DIDN'T KNOW ABOUT IT. SO WHO WOULD BE TRYING TO MAKE STETSON ABANDON THE RANCH?
HIS PARTNER, MR. EVANS!
...HEN WE FOUND MR. ...S AT THE OLD MILL, HE ...JUST CHANGING OUT ...S SISSY HAWGSHANK COSTUME!
THAT'S ...STELLA ...USTON ...CHASING ...ALONE! ...WAS KEN!
HOW'D YOU KNOW?
KEN GAVE YOU AWAY WHEN HE TOLD ME HOW GREAT DANES PACK A WALLOP.
I HADN'T SAID WHAT HAPPENED, SO IT HAD TO BE KEN WHO SCARED SCOOBY IN THE FIELD.
REAH!
IT WAS YOU WHO PULLED THE FAKE SHOES OFF ALONG THE BRIDLE PATH, TO MAKE IT LOOK LIKE THE HORSES DISAPPEARED.

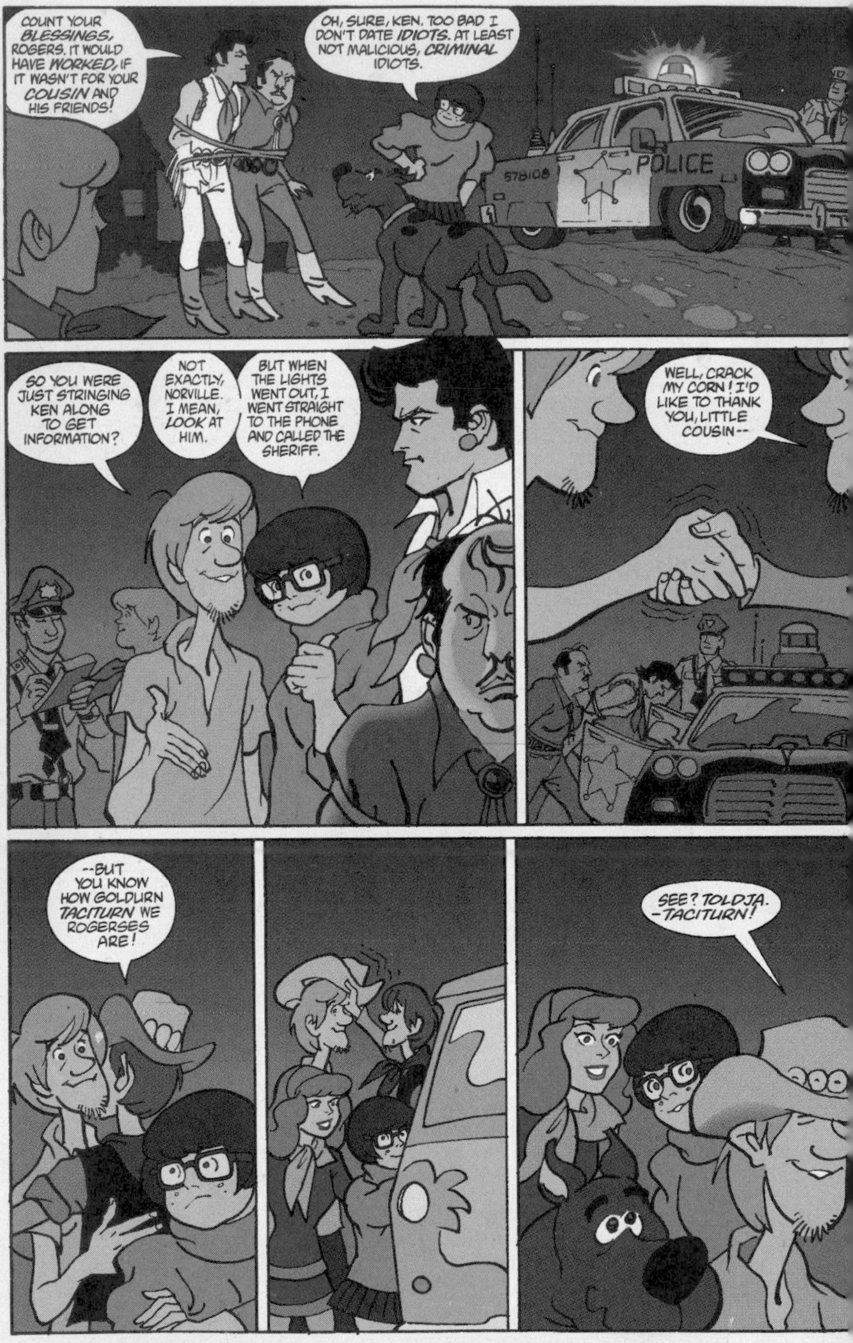
COUNT YOUR BLESSINGS, ROGERS. IT WOULD HAVE WORKED, IF IT WASN'T FOR YOUR COUSIN AND HIS FRIENDS!
OH, SURE, KEN. TOO BAD I DON'T DATE IDIOTS. AT LEAST NOT MALICIOUS, CRIMINAL IDIOTS.
POLICE
578108
SO YOU WERE JUST STRINGING KEN ALONG TO GET INFORMATION?
NOT EXACTLY, NORVILLE. I MEAN, LOOK AT HIM.
BUT WHEN THE LIGHTS WENT OUT, I WENT STRAIGHT TO THE PHONE AND CALLED THE SHERIFF.
WELL, CRACK MY CORN! I'D LIKE TO THANK YOU, LITTLE COUSIN--
--BUT YOU KNOW HOW GOLDURN TACITURN WE ROGERSES ARE!
SEE? TOLDJA. -TACITURN!

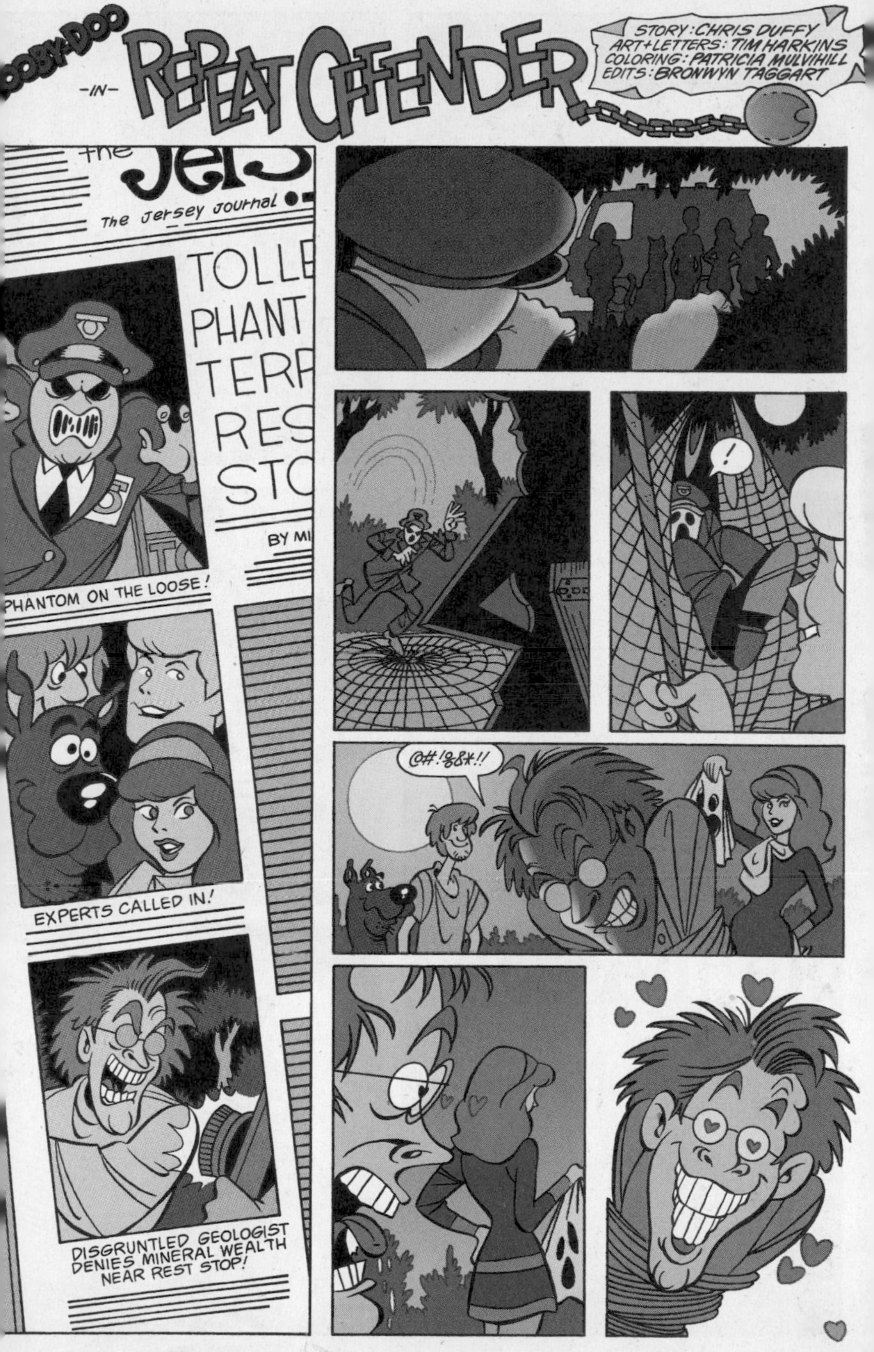

SCOOBY-DOO
-IN-
REPEAT OFFENDER
STORY: CHRIS DUFFY
ART+LETTERS: TIM HARKINS
COLORING: PATRICIA MULVIHILL
EDITS: BRONWYN TAGGART
the Jers
The Jersey Journal
TOLLE
PHANT
TERR
RES
STO
BY MI
PHANTOM ON THE LOOSE!
EXPERTS CALLED IN!
DISGRUNTLED GEOLOGIST DENIES MINERAL WEALTH NEAR REST STOP!
!
@#!%&*!!

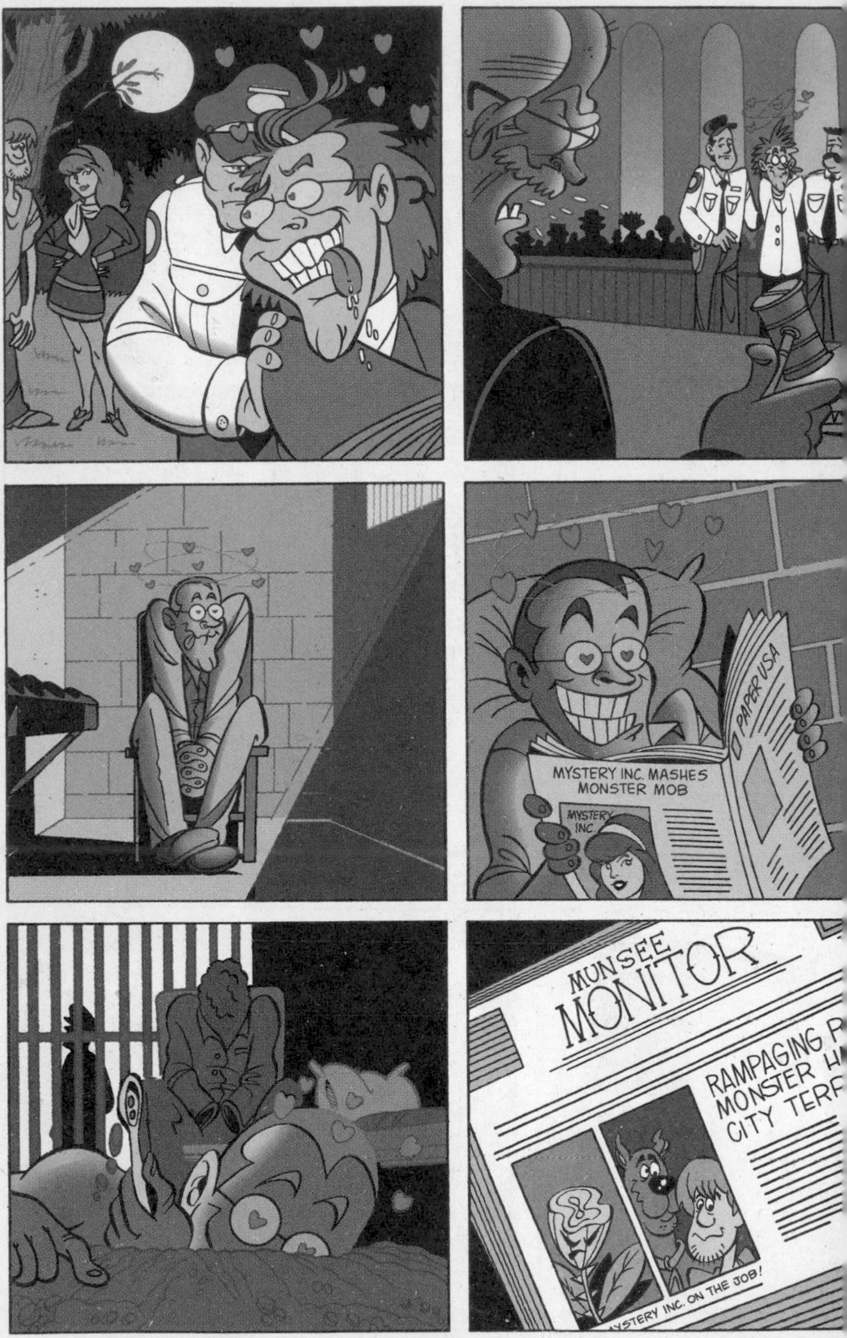
PAPER USA
MYSTERY INC. MASHES MONSTER MOB
MYSTERY INC.
MUNSEE MONITOR
RAMPAGING
MONSTER
CITY
INC. ON THE JOB!

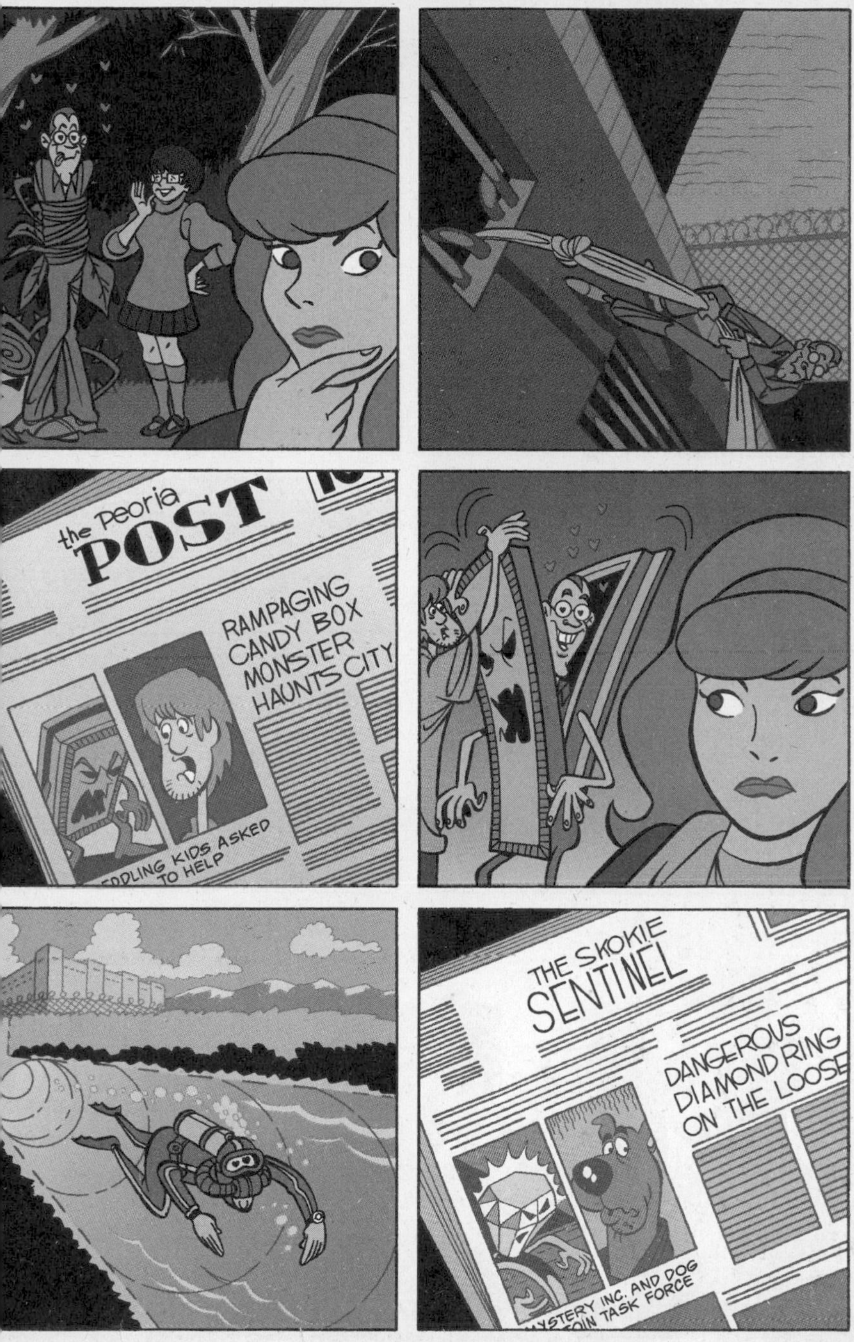
the Peoria POST
RAMPAGING CANDY BOX MONSTER HAUNTS CITY
EDDLING KIDS ASKED TO HELP
THE SKOKIE SENTINEL
DANGEROUS DIAMOND RING ON THE LOOSE
MYSTERY INC. AND DOG
OIN TASK FORCE

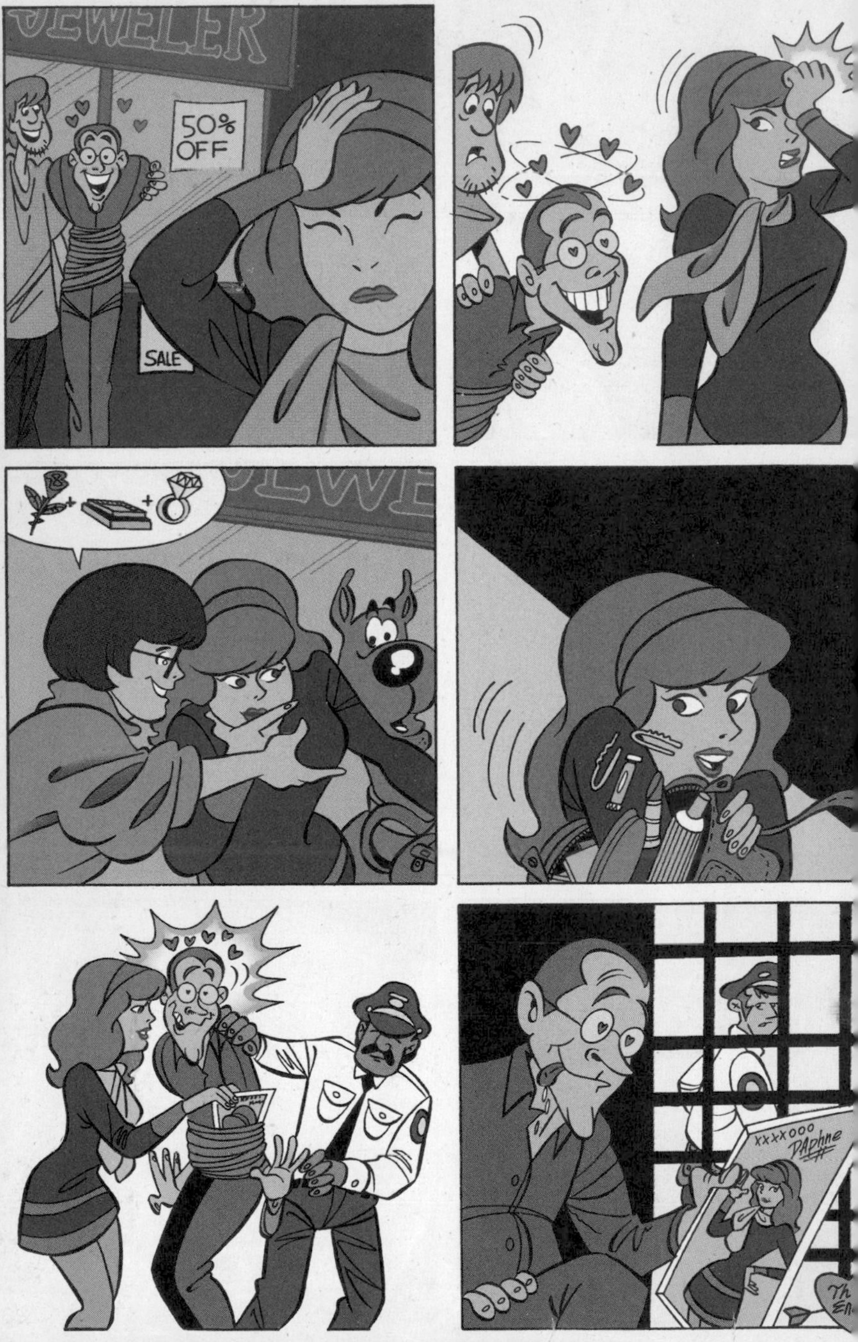
JEWELER
50% OFF
SALE
XXXXOOO
DAphne

THE WEATHER STATION AT CHICAGO'S O'HARE AIRPORT...

THAT'S IT! MY NERVOUS BREAKDOWN HAS BEEN CLEARED FOR TAKE-OFF!

AW, C'MON, MISTER BUSSEL. COOL YOUR JETS.

YEAH, BOSS. KOVALCHEK'S RIGHT. TAKE IT EASY.

SCOOBY-DOO -IN-

THE OGRE OF O'HARE

TERRANCE GREIP, Jr.—writer / BOB SMITH—artist
JOHN COSTANZA— letterer
TRISHA MULVIHILL—colorist / BRONWYN TAGGART—editor

OL YOUR JETS!" YOU PAID MORE TENTION TO WHAT U WERE DOING, UR PRECIOUS RGO WOULDN'T MISSING, CRASH!

I TOLD YOU NOT TO CALL ME THAT!

AND YOU, ECKBLAD! YOU'RE AN AIR TRAFFIC CONTROLLER, NOT A METEOROLOGIST! WHY AREN'T YOU UP IN THE TOWER?

THE AIRPORT'S CLOSED DUE TO THE WEATHER, BOSS. THERE'S NOT MUCH FOR ME TO DO.

25

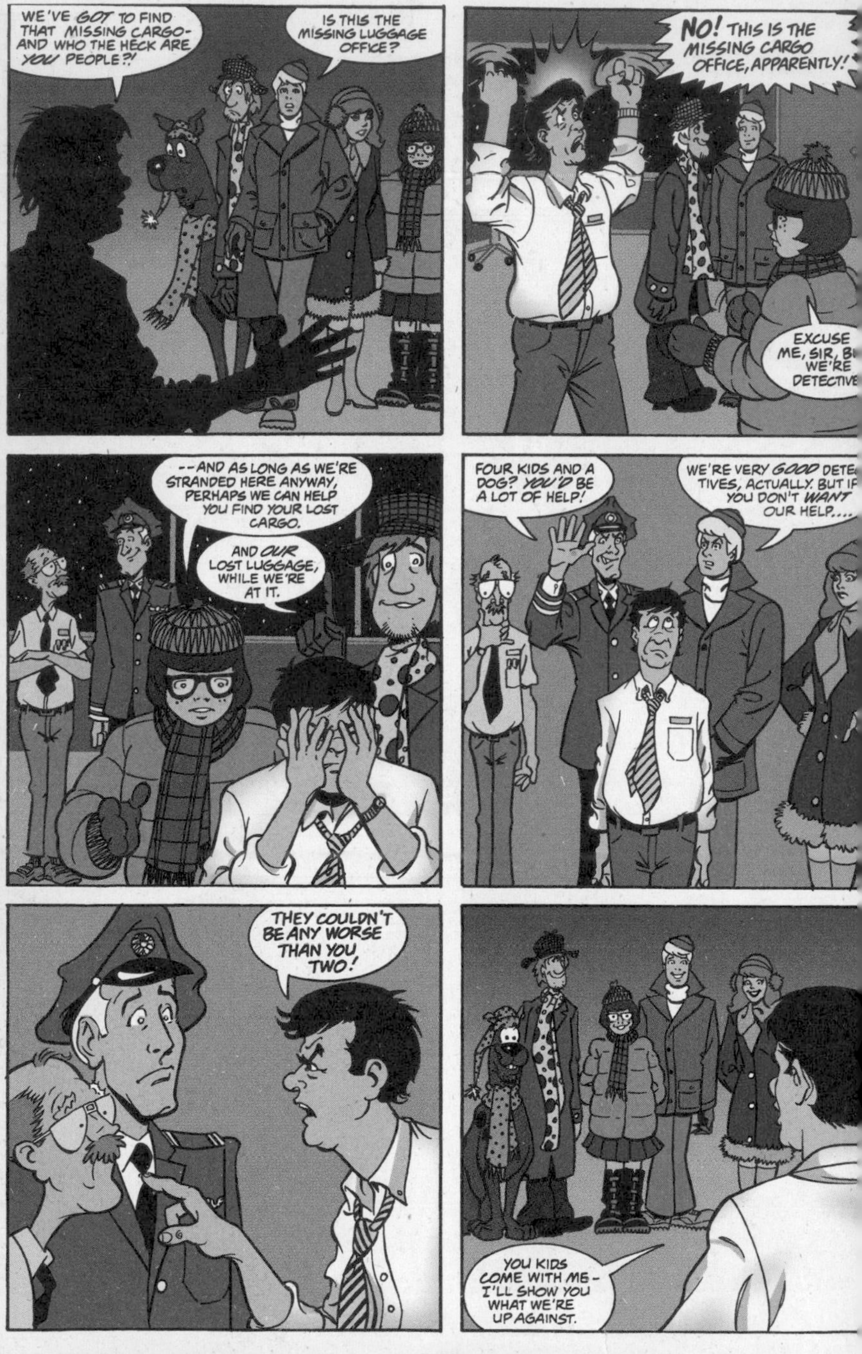
WE'VE GOT TO FIND THAT MISSING CARGO- AND WHO THE HECK ARE YOU PEOPLE?!
IS THIS THE MISSING LUGGAGE OFFICE?
NO! THIS IS THE MISSING CARGO OFFICE, APPARENTLY!
EXCUSE ME, SIR, B WE'RE DETECTIVE
--AND AS LONG AS WE'RE STRANDED HERE ANYWAY, PERHAPS WE CAN HELP YOU FIND YOUR LOST CARGO.
AND OUR LOST LUGGAGE, WHILE WE'RE AT IT.
FOUR KIDS AND A DOG? YOU'D BE A LOT OF HELP!
WE'RE VERY GOOD DETE TIVES, ACTUALLY. BUT IF YOU DON'T WANT OUR HELP....
THEY COULDN'T BE ANY WORSE THAN YOU TWO!
YOU KIDS COME WITH ME- I'LL SHOW YOU WHAT WE'RE UP AGAINST.

SOON, ON A SNOW-PAVED RUNWAY...

DOES THIS HAVE SOMETHING TO DO WITH THE MYSTERY OF YOUR MISSING CARGO?

MMM... YES, YOUNG LADY.

LIKE MOST MAJOR AIRPORTS, O'HARE HAS SEPARATE TERMINALS RESERVED SPECIFICALLY FOR CARGO PLANES. WE WERE SUPPOSED TO GET A VERY SPECIAL SHIPMENT, BUT ALL WE RECEIVED WAS *THIS.*

AN EMPTY CAGE!

IT WOULD HELP IF YOU COULD TELL US EXACTLY WHAT HAPPENED.

YES. JUST START AT THE BEGINNING.

ALL RIGHT. *FIRST,* A LEOPARD WAS TAKEN FROM THE *KANHIROBA HIMAL* IN NEPAL AND LOADED ONTO THIS PLANE.

*NEXT,* THE LEOPARD IN THIS C PLANE

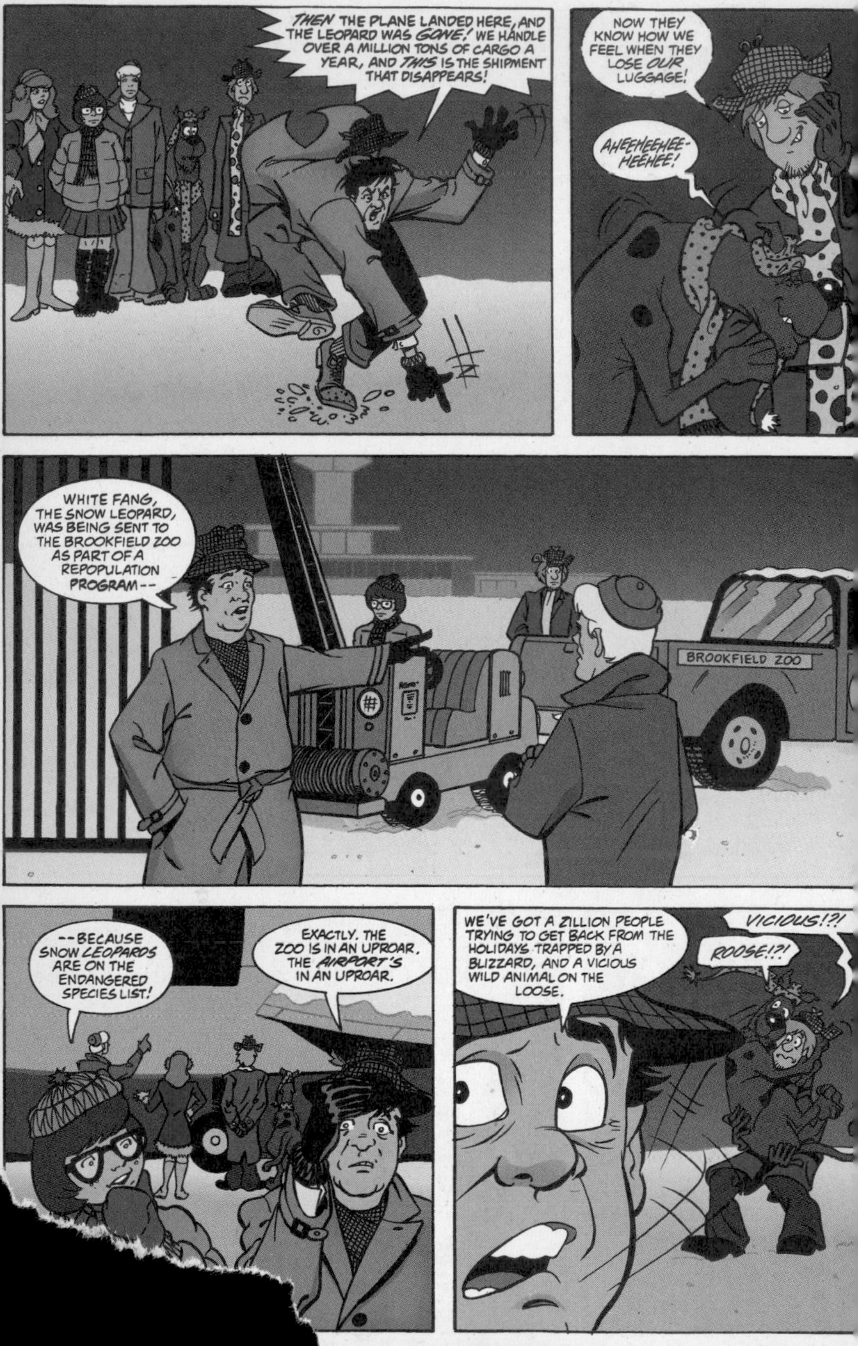
THEN THE PLANE LANDED HERE, AND THE LEOPARD WAS GONE! WE HANDLE OVER A MILLION TONS OF CARGO A YEAR, AND THIS IS THE SHIPMENT THAT DISAPPEARS!
NOW THEY KNOW HOW WE FEEL WHEN THEY LOSE OUR LUGGAGE!
AHEEHEEHEE-HEEHEE!
WHITE FANG, THE SNOW LEOPARD, WAS BEING SENT TO THE BROOKFIELD ZOO AS PART OF A REPOPULATION PROGRAM--
BROOKFIELD ZOO
--BECAUSE SNOW LEOPARDS ARE ON THE ENDANGERED SPECIES LIST!
EXACTLY. THE ZOO IS IN AN UPROAR. THE AIRPORT'S IN AN UPROAR.
WE'VE GOT A ZILLION PEOPLE TRYING TO GET BACK FROM THE HOLIDAYS TRAPPED BY A BLIZZARD, AND A VICIOUS WILD ANIMAL ON THE LOOSE.
VICIOUS!?!
ROOSE!?!

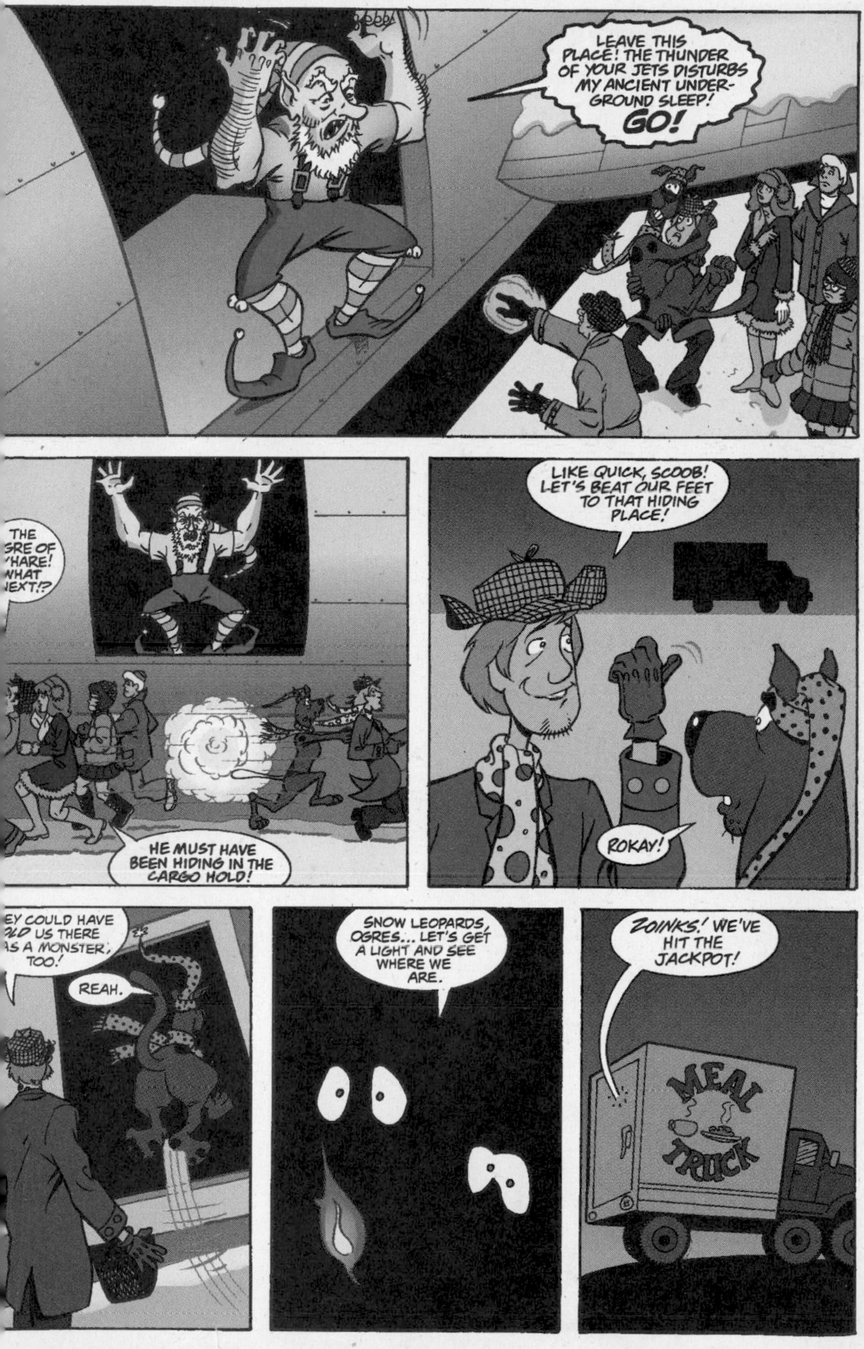

LEAVE THIS PLACE! THE THUNDER OF YOUR JETS DISTURBS MY ANCIENT UNDER-GROUND SLEEP! GO!
THE GRE OF HARE! WHAT NEXT!?
HE MUST HAVE BEEN HIDING IN THE CARGO HOLD!
LIKE QUICK, SCOOB! LET'S BEAT OUR FEET TO THAT HIDING PLACE!
ROKAY!
EY COULD HAVE OLD US THERE AS A MONSTER, TOO!
REAH.
SNOW LEOPARDS, OGRES... LET'S GET A LIGHT AND SEE WHERE WE ARE.
ZOINKS! WE'VE HIT THE JACKPOT!
MEAL TRUCK

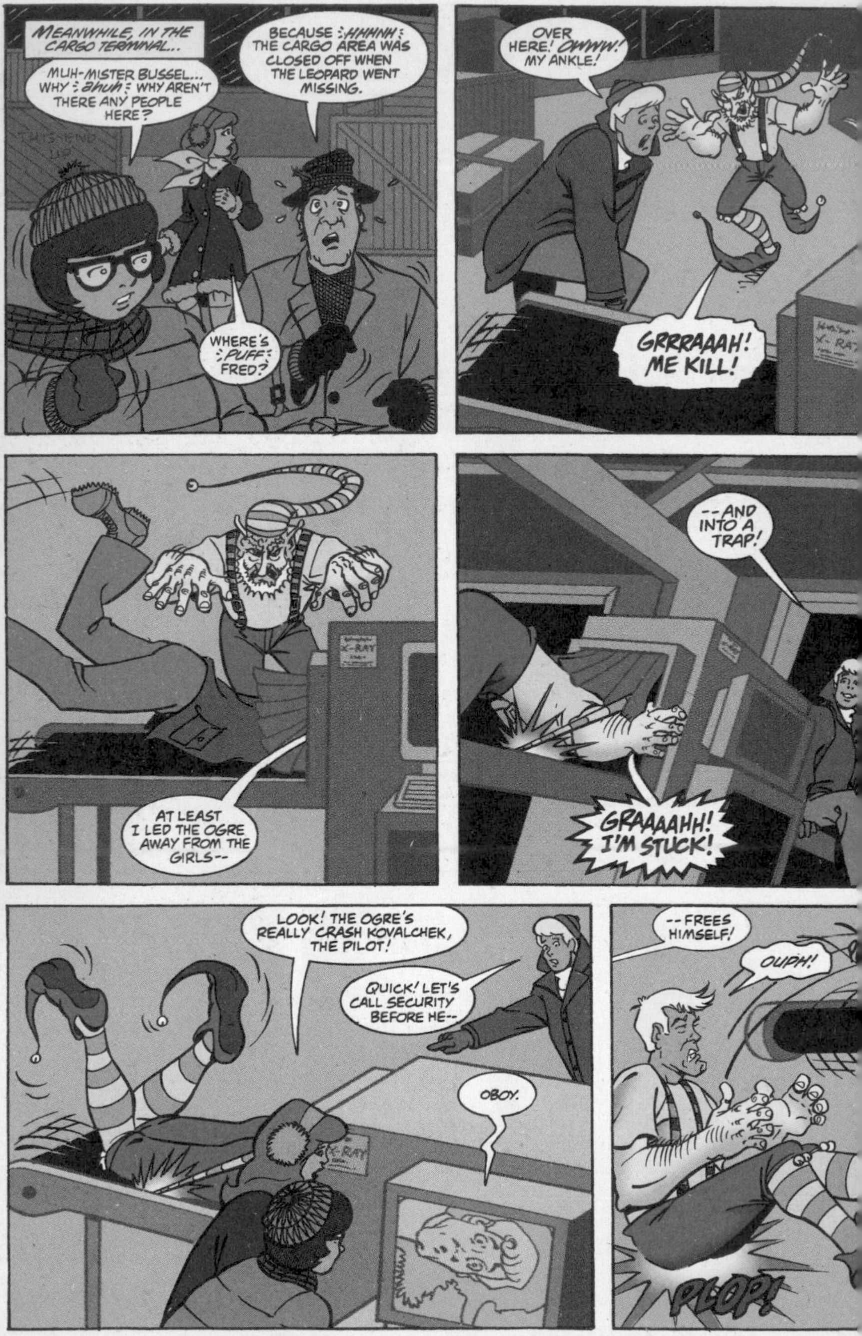
MEANWHILE, IN THE CARGO TERMINAL...
MUH-MISTER BUSSEL... WHY ahuh WHY AREN'T THERE ANY PEOPLE HERE?
BECAUSE HHHNH THE CARGO AREA WAS CLOSED OFF WHEN THE LEOPARD WENT MISSING.
WHERE'S PUFF FRED?
OVER HERE! OWWW! MY ANKLE!
GRRRAAAH! ME KILL!
X-RAY
AT LEAST I LED THE OGRE AWAY FROM THE GIRLS--
--AND INTO A TRAP!
GRAAAAHH! I'M STUCK!
LOOK! THE OGRE'S REALLY CRASH KOVALCHEK, THE PILOT!
QUICK! LET'S CALL SECURITY BEFORE HE--
OBOY.
--FREES HIMSELF!
OUPH!
PLOP!

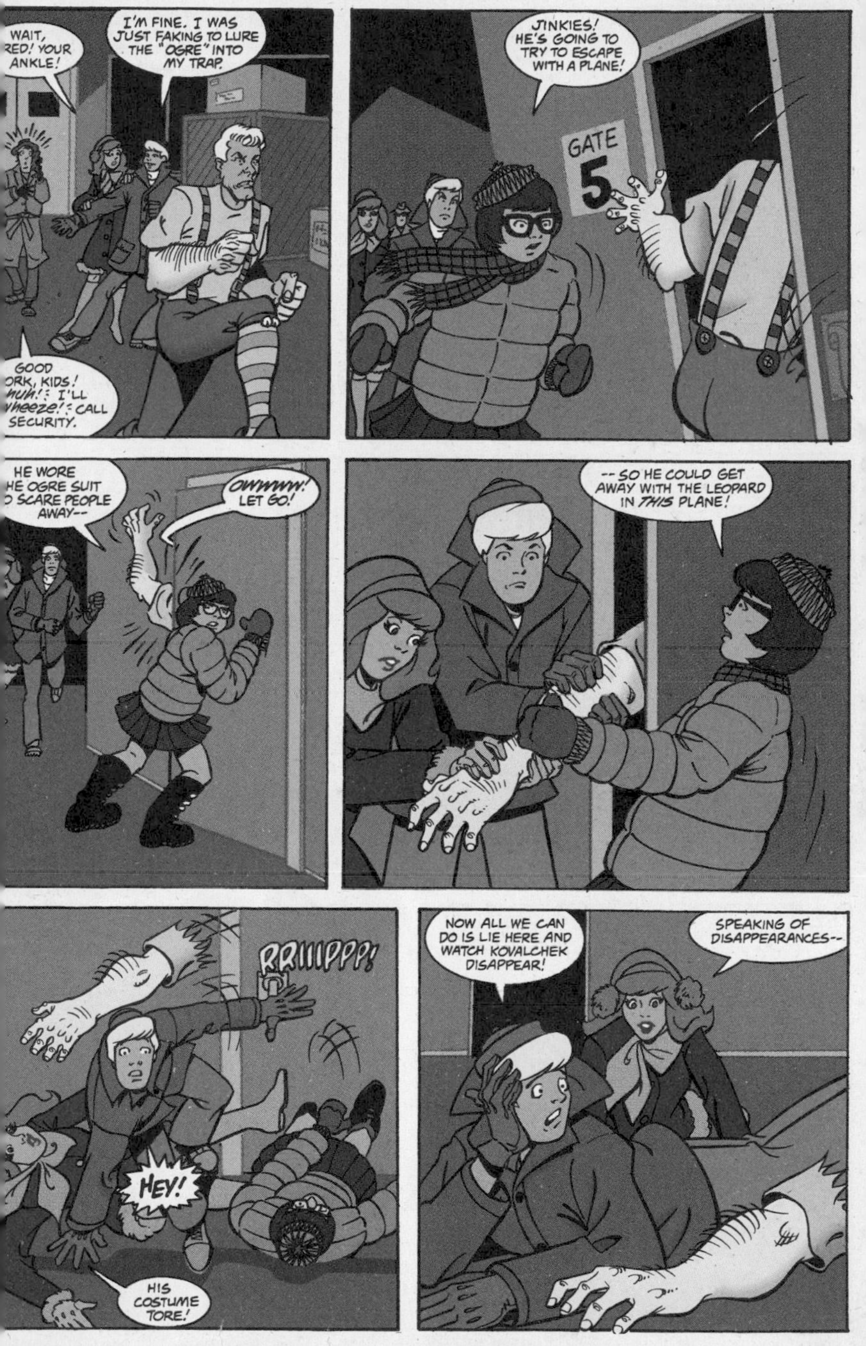
WAIT, RED! YOUR ANKLE!
I'M FINE. I WAS JUST FAKING TO LURE THE "OGRE" INTO MY TRAP.
GOOD ORK, KIDS! huh! I'LL wheeze! CALL SECURITY.
JINKIES! HE'S GOING TO TRY TO ESCAPE WITH A PLANE!
GATE 5
HE WORE HE OGRE SUIT O SCARE PEOPLE AWAY--
OWWWW! LET GO!
--SO HE COULD GET AWAY WITH THE LEOPARD IN THIS PLANE!
RRIIIPPP!
HEY!
HIS COSTUME TORE!
NOW ALL WE CAN DO IS LIE HERE AND WATCH KOVALCHEK DISAPPEAR!
SPEAKING OF DISAPPEARANCES--

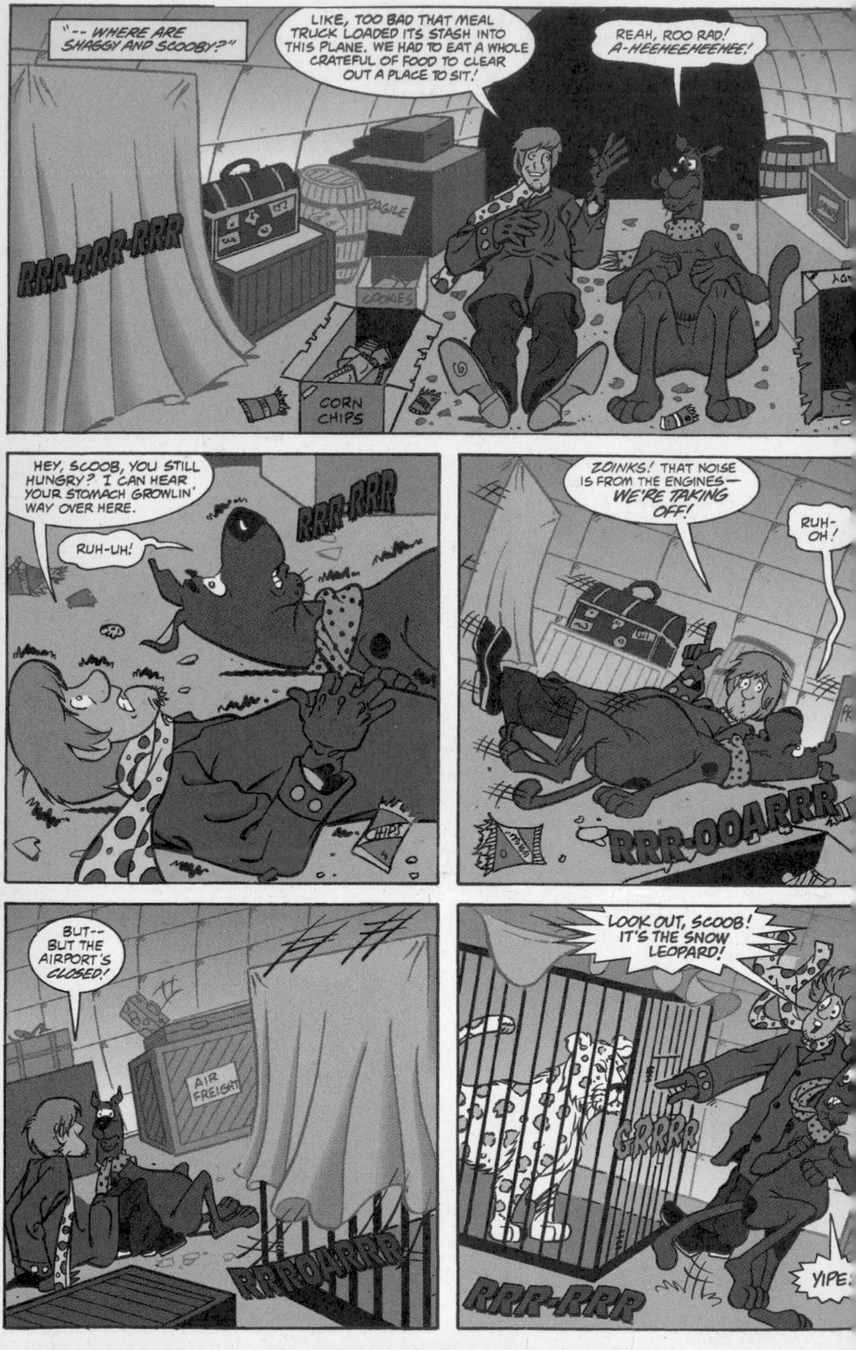

"-- WHERE ARE SHAGGY AND SCOOBY?"
LIKE, TOO BAD THAT MEAL TRUCK LOADED ITS STASH INTO THIS PLANE. WE HAD TO EAT A WHOLE CRATEFUL OF FOOD TO CLEAR OUT A PLACE TO SIT!
REAH, ROO RAD! A-HEEHEEHEEHEE!
RRR-RRR-RRR
FRAGILE
COOKIES
CORN CHIPS
HEY, SCOOB, YOU STILL HUNGRY? I CAN HEAR YOUR STOMACH GROWLIN' WAY OVER HERE.
RUH-UH!
RRR-RRR
CHIPS
ZOINKS! THAT NOISE IS FROM THE ENGINES-- WE'RE TAKING OFF!
RUH-OH!
RRR-OOARRR
BUT--BUT THE AIRPORT'S CLOSED!
AIR FREIGHT
RRROARRR
LOOK OUT, SCOOB! IT'S THE SNOW LEOPARD!
GRRRR
YIPE!
RRR-RRR

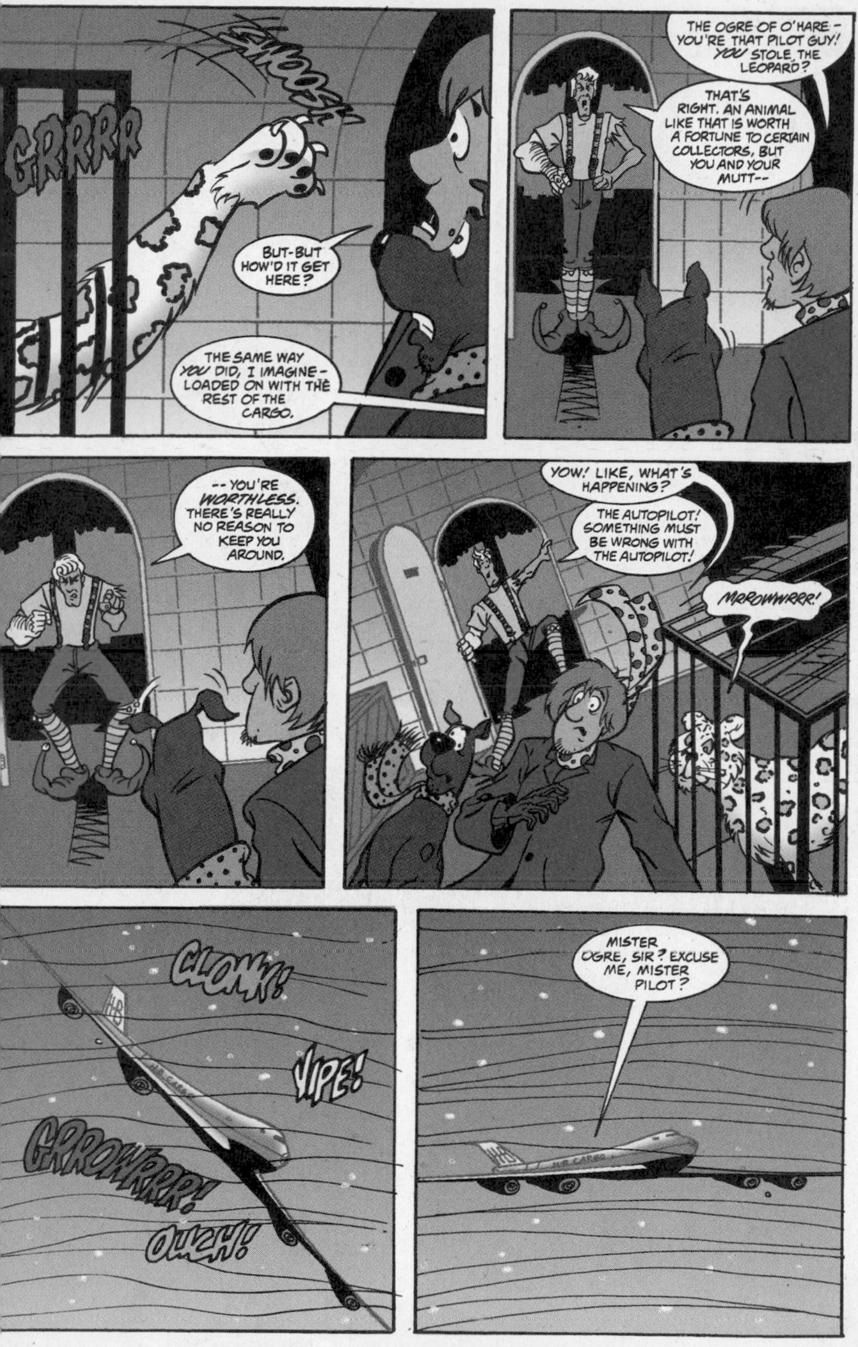
SHOOOSH!
GRRRR
BUT-BUT HOW'D IT GET HERE?
THE SAME WAY YOU DID, I IMAGINE-LOADED ON WITH THE REST OF THE CARGO.
THE OGRE OF O'HARE - YOU'RE THAT PILOT GUY! YOU STOLE THE LEOPARD?
THAT'S RIGHT. AN ANIMAL LIKE THAT IS WORTH A FORTUNE TO CERTAIN COLLECTORS, BUT YOU AND YOUR MUTT--
--YOU'RE WORTHLESS. THERE'S REALLY NO REASON TO KEEP YOU AROUND.
YOW! LIKE, WHAT'S HAPPENING?
THE AUTOPILOT! SOMETHING MUST BE WRONG WITH THE AUTOPILOT!
MRROWWRRR!
CLONK!
YIPE!
GRROWRRR!
OUCH!
MISTER OGRE, SIR? EXCUSE ME, MISTER PILOT?

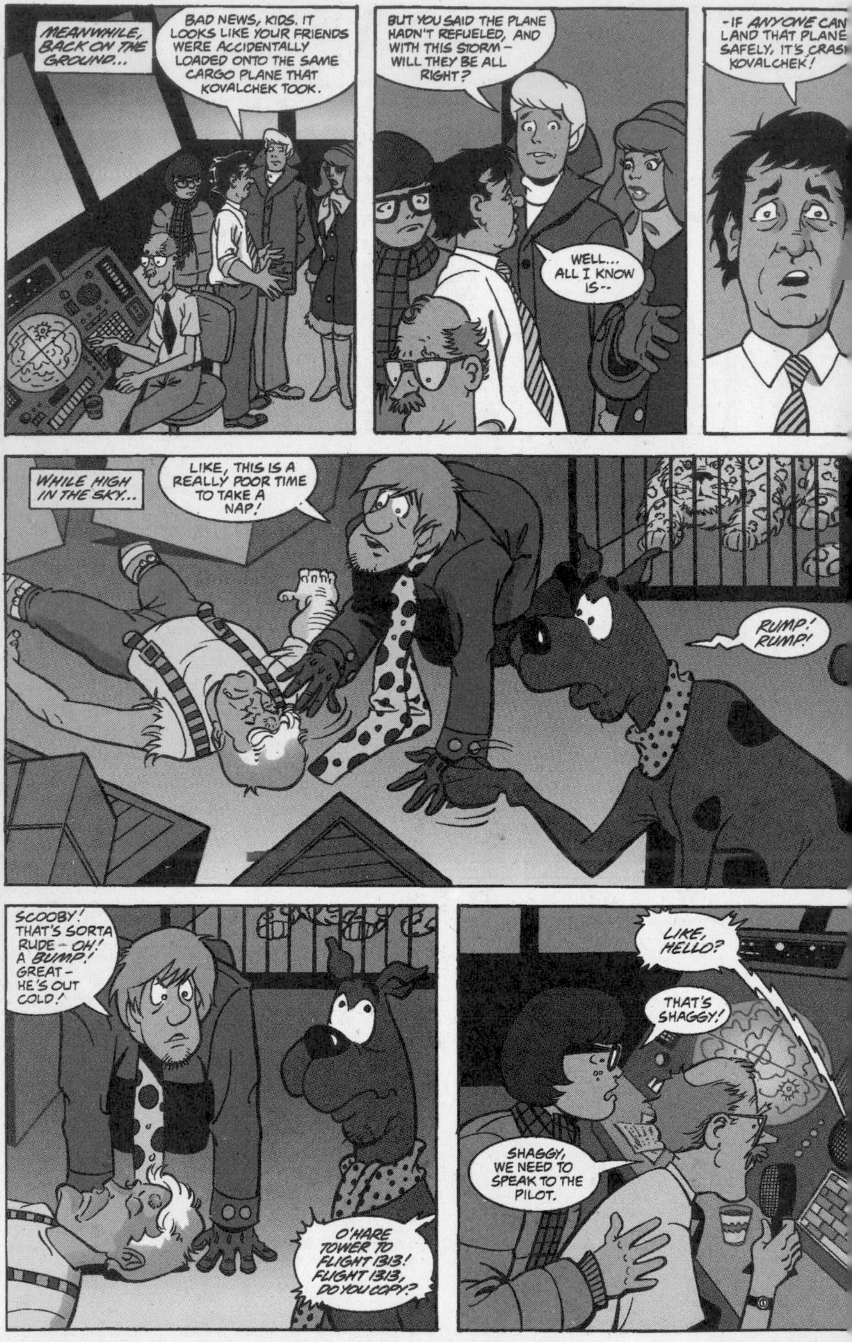
MEANWHILE, BACK ON THE GROUND...
BAD NEWS, KIDS. IT LOOKS LIKE YOUR FRIENDS WERE ACCIDENTALLY LOADED ONTO THE SAME CARGO PLANE THAT KOVALCHEK TOOK.
BUT YOU SAID THE PLANE HADN'T REFUELED, AND WITH THIS STORM-- WILL THEY BE ALL RIGHT?
WELL... ALL I KNOW IS--
-IF ANYONE CAN LAND THAT PLANE SAFELY, IT'S CRASH KOVALCHEK!
WHILE HIGH IN THE SKY...
LIKE, THIS IS A REALLY POOR TIME TO TAKE A NAP!
RUMP! RUMP!
SCOOBY! THAT'S SORTA RUDE-- OH! A BUMP! GREAT-- HE'S OUT COLD!
O'HARE TOWER TO FLIGHT 1313! FLIGHT 1313, DO YOU COPY?
LIKE, HELLO?
THAT'S SHAGGY!
SHAGGY, WE NEED TO SPEAK TO THE PILOT.

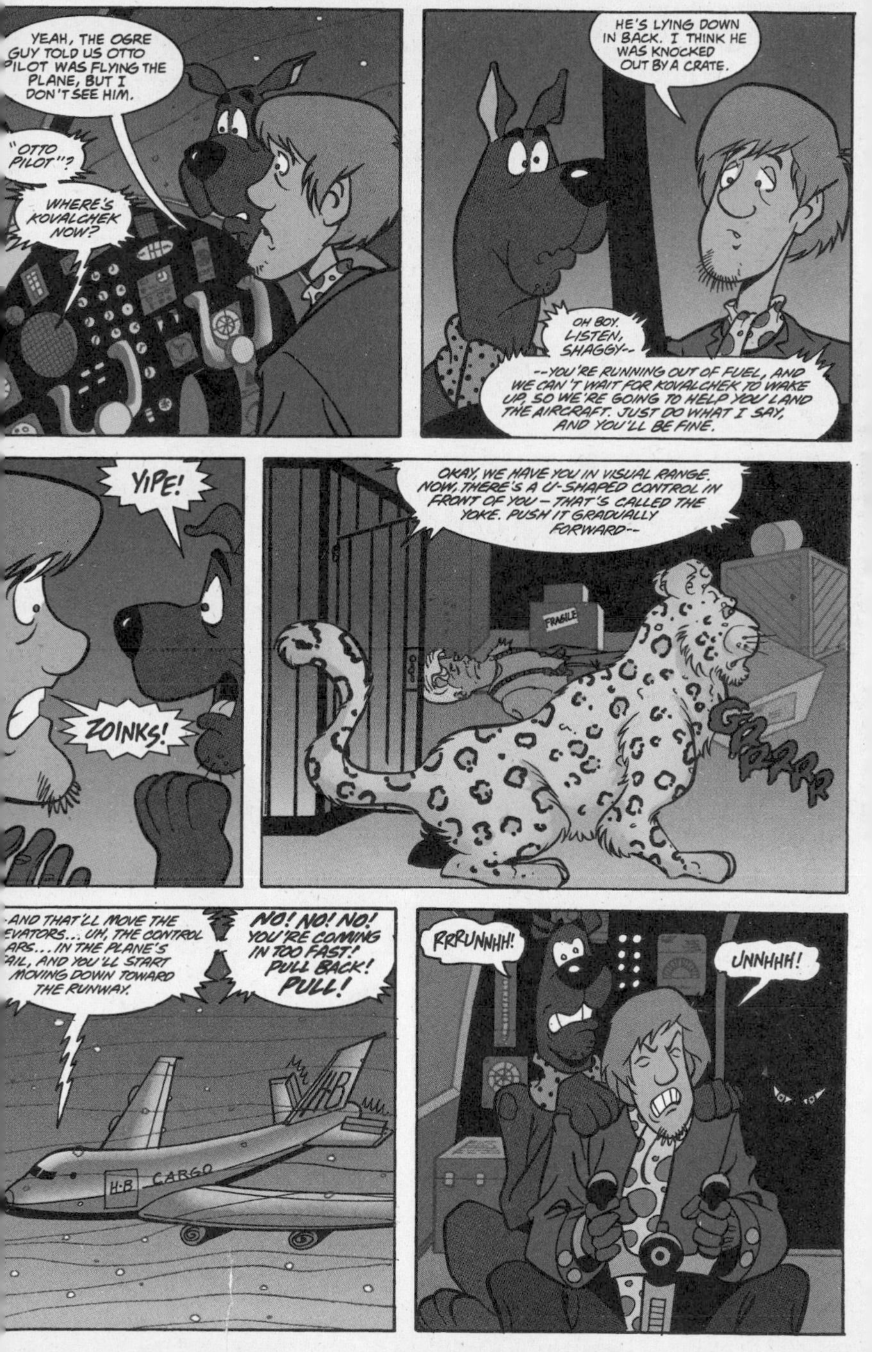
YEAH, THE OGRE GUY TOLD US OTTO PILOT WAS FLYING THE PLANE, BUT I DON'T SEE HIM.
"OTTO PILOT"?
WHERE'S KOVALCHEK NOW?
HE'S LYING DOWN IN BACK. I THINK HE WAS KNOCKED OUT BY A CRATE.
OH BOY. LISTEN, SHAGGY--
--YOU'RE RUNNING OUT OF FUEL, AND WE CAN'T WAIT FOR KOVALCHEK TO WAKE UP, SO WE'RE GOING TO HELP YOU LAND THE AIRCRAFT. JUST DO WHAT I SAY, AND YOU'LL BE FINE.
YIPE!
ZOINKS!
OKAY, WE HAVE YOU IN VISUAL RANGE. NOW, THERE'S A U-SHAPED CONTROL IN FRONT OF YOU -- THAT'S CALLED THE YOKE. PUSH IT GRADUALLY FORWARD--
FRAGILE
GRRRRR
-AND THAT'LL MOVE THE EVATORS... UH, THE CONTROL ARS... IN THE PLANE'S AIL, AND YOU'LL START MOVING DOWN TOWARD THE RUNWAY.
NO! NO! NO! YOU'RE COMING IN TOO FAST! PULL BACK! PULL!
H-B CARGO
RRRUNNHH!
UNNHHH!

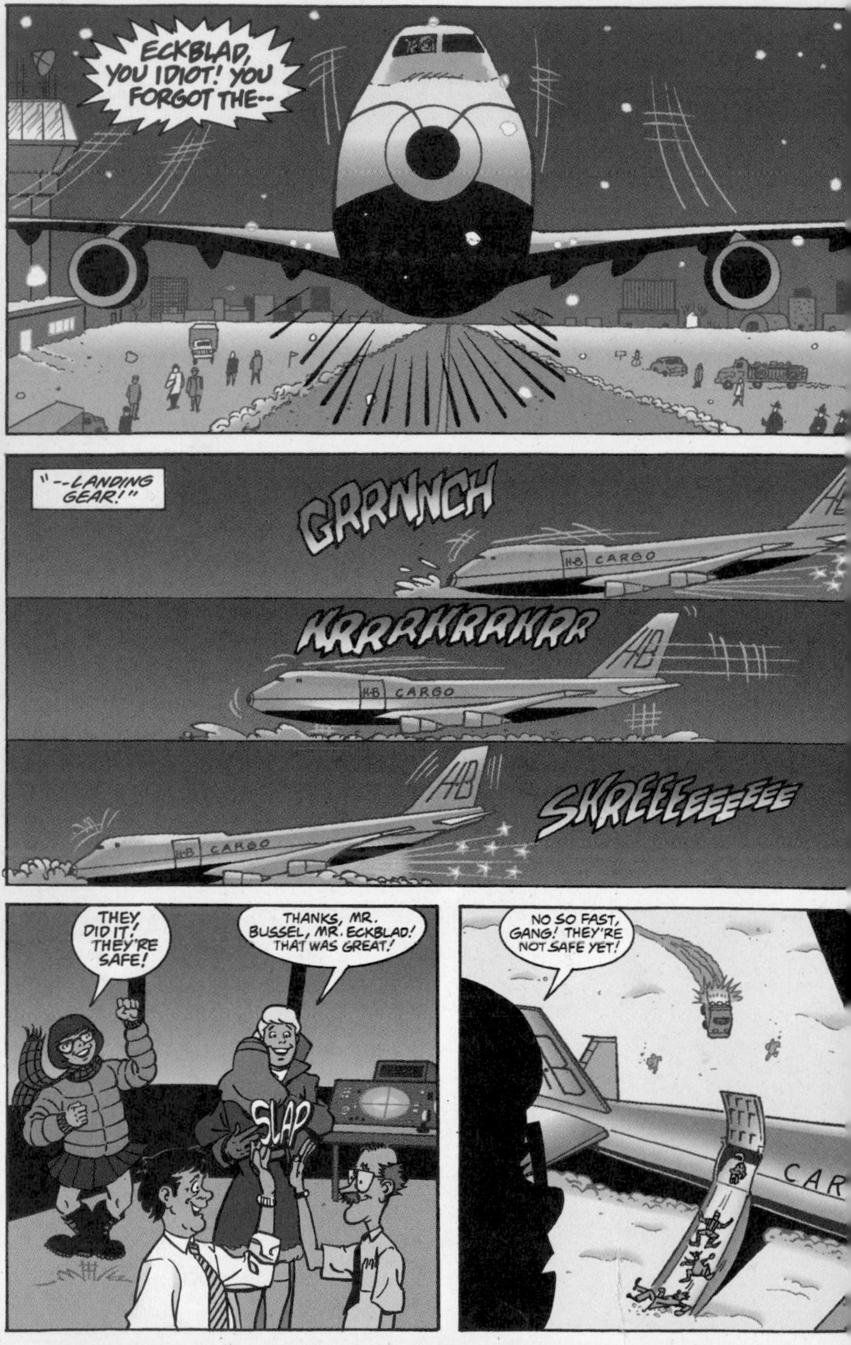
ECKBLAD, YOU IDIOT! YOU FORGOT THE--
"--LANDING GEAR!"
GRRNNCH
H-B CARGO
KRRRKRRKRR
H-B CARGO
SKREEEEEEEEE
H-B CARGO
THEY DID IT! THEY'RE SAFE!
THANKS, MR. BUSSEL, MR. ECKBLAD! THAT WAS GREAT!
SLAP
NO SO FAST, GANG! THEY'RE NOT SAFE YET!
CAR

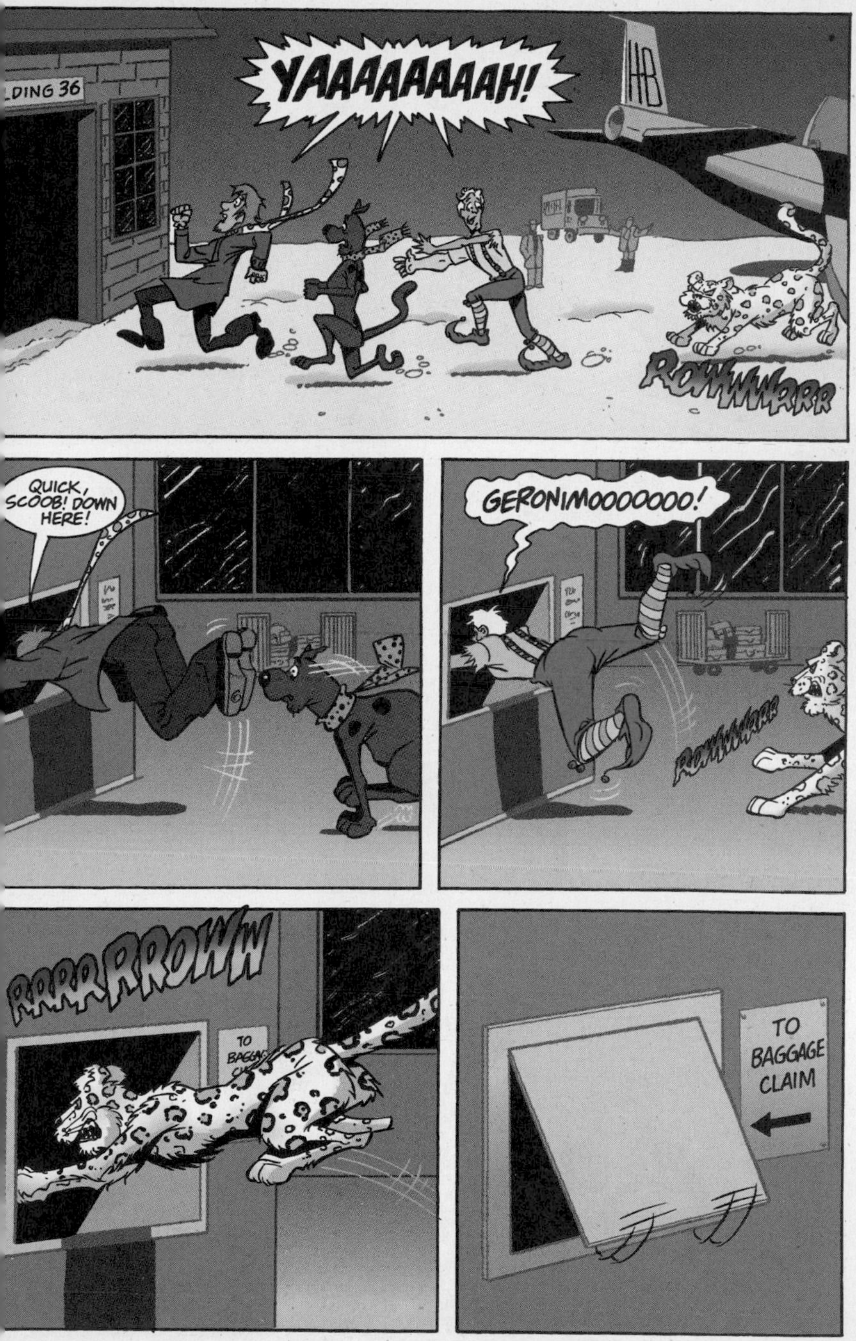

LDING 36
YAAAAAAAAH!
HB
ROWWWRRR
QUICK, SCOOB! DOWN HERE!
GERONIMOOOOOOO!
RRRRROWW
TO BAGGAGE CLAIM

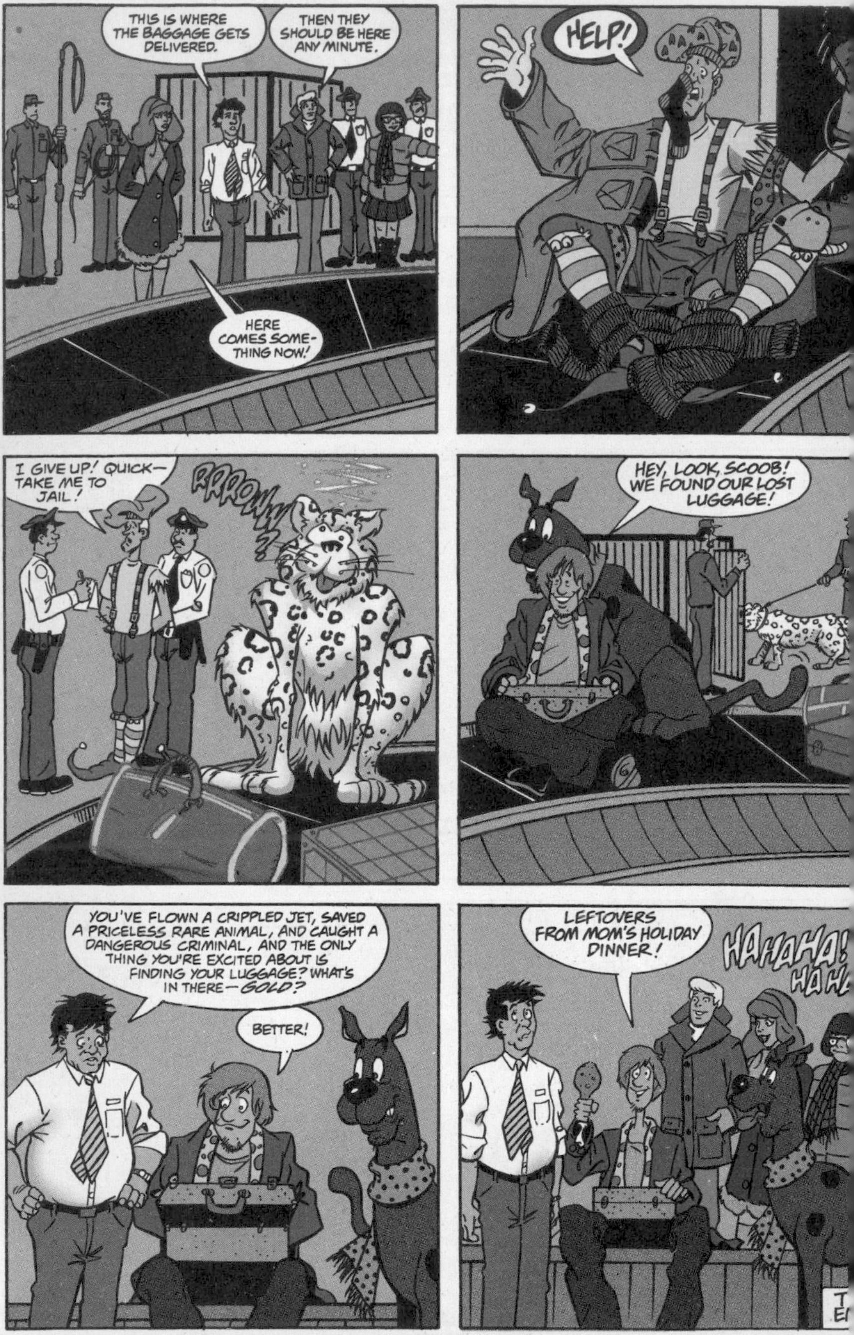

THIS IS WHERE THE BAGGAGE GETS DELIVERED.
THEN THEY SHOULD BE HERE ANY MINUTE.
HERE COMES SOME-THING NOW!
HELP!
I GIVE UP! QUICK— TAKE ME TO JAIL!
RRROWW
HEY, LOOK, SCOOB! WE FOUND OUR LOST LUGGAGE!
YOU'VE FLOWN A CRIPPLED JET, SAVED A PRICELESS RARE ANIMAL, AND CAUGHT A DANGEROUS CRIMINAL, AND THE ONLY THING YOU'RE EXCITED ABOUT IS FINDING YOUR LUGGAGE? WHAT'S IN THERE—GOLD?
BETTER!
LEFTOVERS FROM MOM'S HOLIDAY DINNER!
HAHAHA!

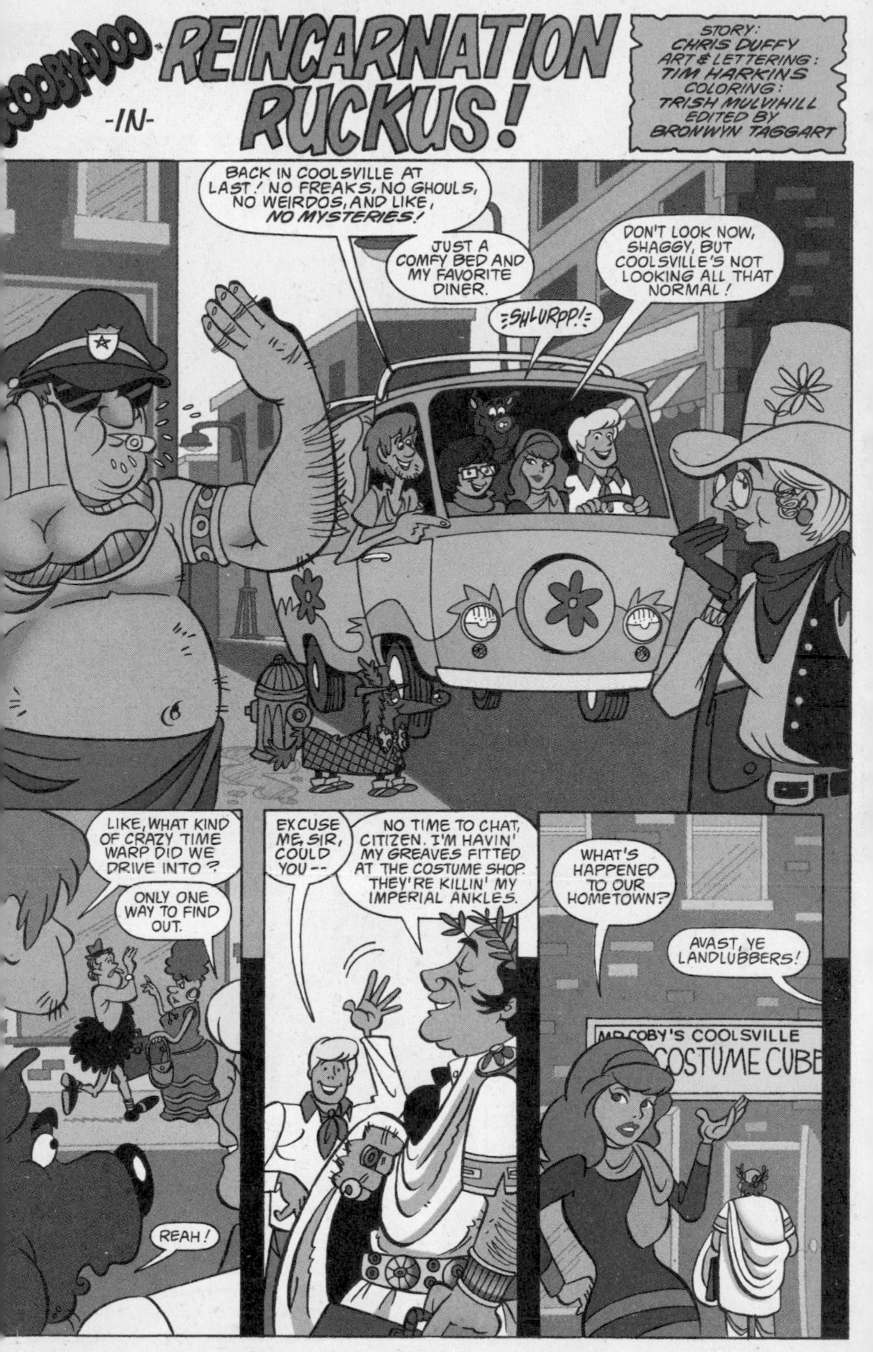
SCOOBY-DOO
-IN-
REINCARNATION RUCKUS!
STORY: CHRIS DUFFY
ART & LETTERING: TIM HARKINS
COLORING: TRISH MULVIHILL
EDITED BY BRONWYN TAGGART
BACK IN COOLSVILLE AT LAST! NO FREAKS, NO GHOULS, NO WEIRDOS, AND LIKE, NO MYSTERIES!
JUST A COMFY BED AND MY FAVORITE DINER.
SHLURPP!
DON'T LOOK NOW, SHAGGY, BUT COOLSVILLE'S NOT LOOKING ALL THAT NORMAL!
LIKE, WHAT KIND OF CRAZY TIME WARP DID WE DRIVE INTO?
ONLY ONE WAY TO FIND OUT.
REAH!
EXCUSE ME, SIR, COULD YOU --
NO TIME TO CHAT, CITIZEN. I'M HAVIN' MY GREAVES FITTED AT THE COSTUME SHOP. THEY'RE KILLIN' MY IMPERIAL ANKLES.
WHAT'S HAPPENED TO OUR HOMETOWN?
AVAST, YE LANDLUBBERS!
MR. COBY'S COOLSVILLE COSTUME CUBE

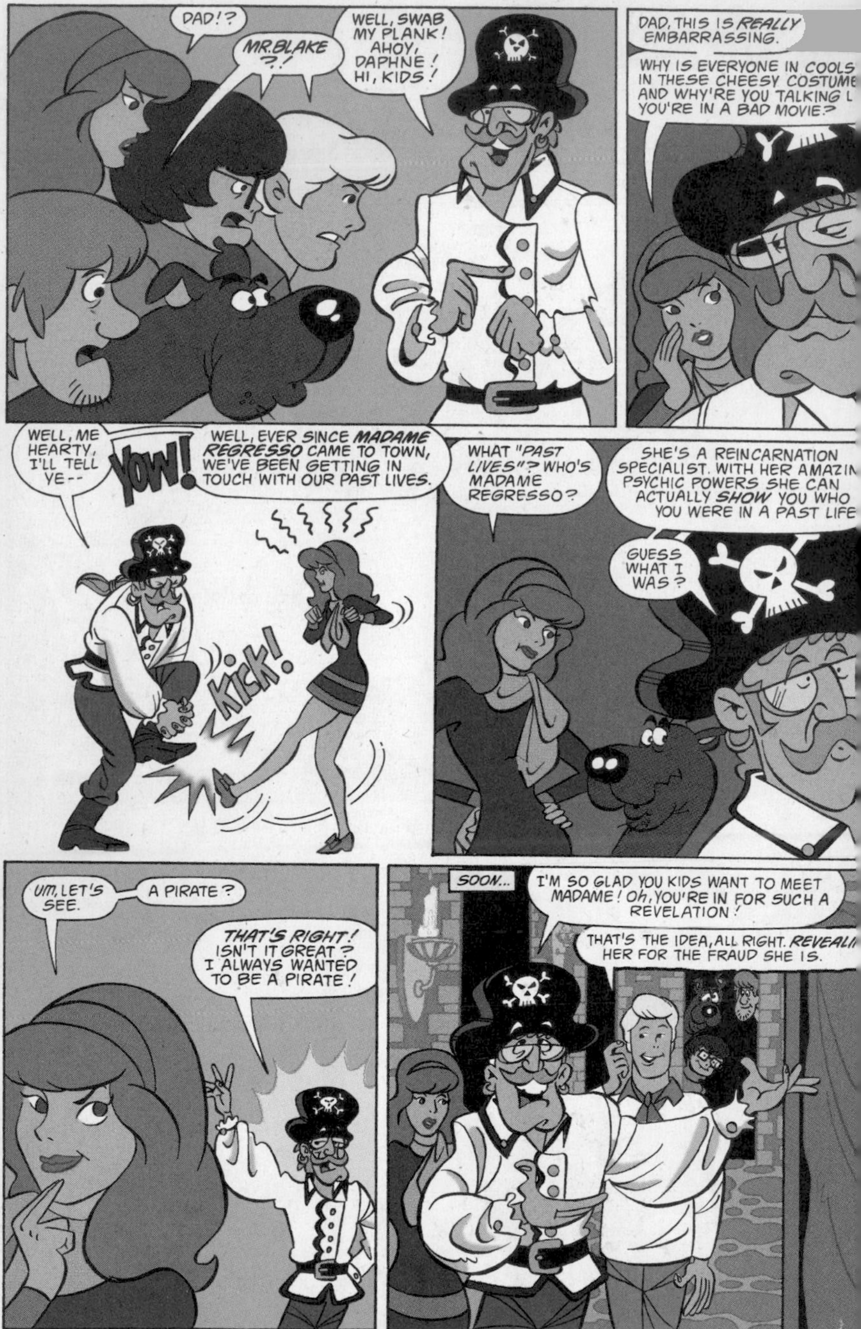

DAD!?
MR.BLAKE ?!
WELL, SWAB MY PLANK! AHOY, DAPHNE! HI, KIDS!
DAD, THIS IS REALLY EMBARRASSING.
WHY IS EVERYONE IN COOLS IN THESE CHEESY COSTUME AND WHY'RE YOU TALKING L YOU'RE IN A BAD MOVIE?
WELL, ME HEARTY, I'LL TELL YE--
YOW!
KICK!
WELL, EVER SINCE MADAME REGRESSO CAME TO TOWN, WE'VE BEEN GETTING IN TOUCH WITH OUR PAST LIVES.
WHAT "PAST LIVES"? WHO'S MADAME REGRESSO?
SHE'S A REINCARNATION SPECIALIST. WITH HER AMAZIN PSYCHIC POWERS SHE CAN ACTUALLY SHOW YOU WHO YOU WERE IN A PAST LIFE
GUESS WHAT I WAS?
UM, LET'S SEE.
A PIRATE?
THAT'S RIGHT! ISN'T IT GREAT? I ALWAYS WANTED TO BE A PIRATE!
SOON...
I'M SO GLAD YOU KIDS WANT TO MEET MADAME! Oh, YOU'RE IN FOR SUCH A REVELATION!
THAT'S THE IDEA, ALL RIGHT. REVEALI HER FOR THE FRAUD SHE IS.

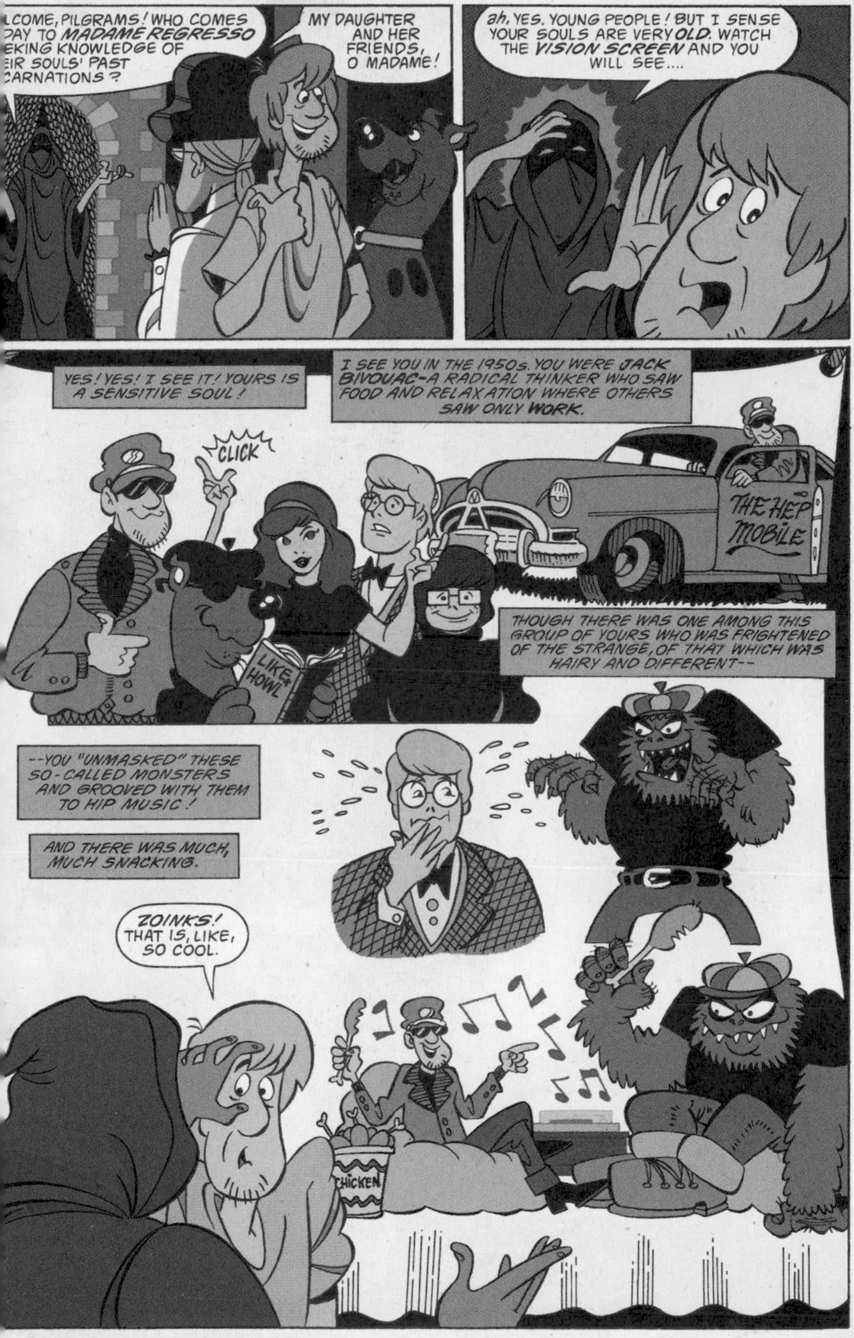

LCOME, PILGRAMS! WHO COMES
DAY TO MADAME REGRESSO
EKING KNOWLEDGE OF
EIR SOULS' PAST
CARNATIONS?
MY DAUGHTER AND HER FRIENDS, O MADAME!
ah, YES. YOUNG PEOPLE! BUT I SENSE YOUR SOULS ARE VERY OLD. WATCH THE VISION SCREEN AND YOU WILL SEE....
YES! YES! I SEE IT! YOURS IS A SENSITIVE SOUL!
I SEE YOU IN THE 1950s. YOU WERE JACK BIVOUAC--A RADICAL THINKER WHO SAW FOOD AND RELAXATION WHERE OTHERS SAW ONLY WORK.
CLICK
LIKE, HOWL
THE HEP MOBILE
THOUGH THERE WAS ONE AMONG THIS GROUP OF YOURS WHO WAS FRIGHTENED OF THE STRANGE, OF THAT WHICH WAS HAIRY AND DIFFERENT--
--YOU "UNMASKED" THESE SO-CALLED MONSTERS AND GROOVED WITH THEM TO HIP MUSIC!
AND THERE WAS MUCH, MUCH SNACKING.
ZOINKS! THAT IS, LIKE, SO COOL.
CHICKEN

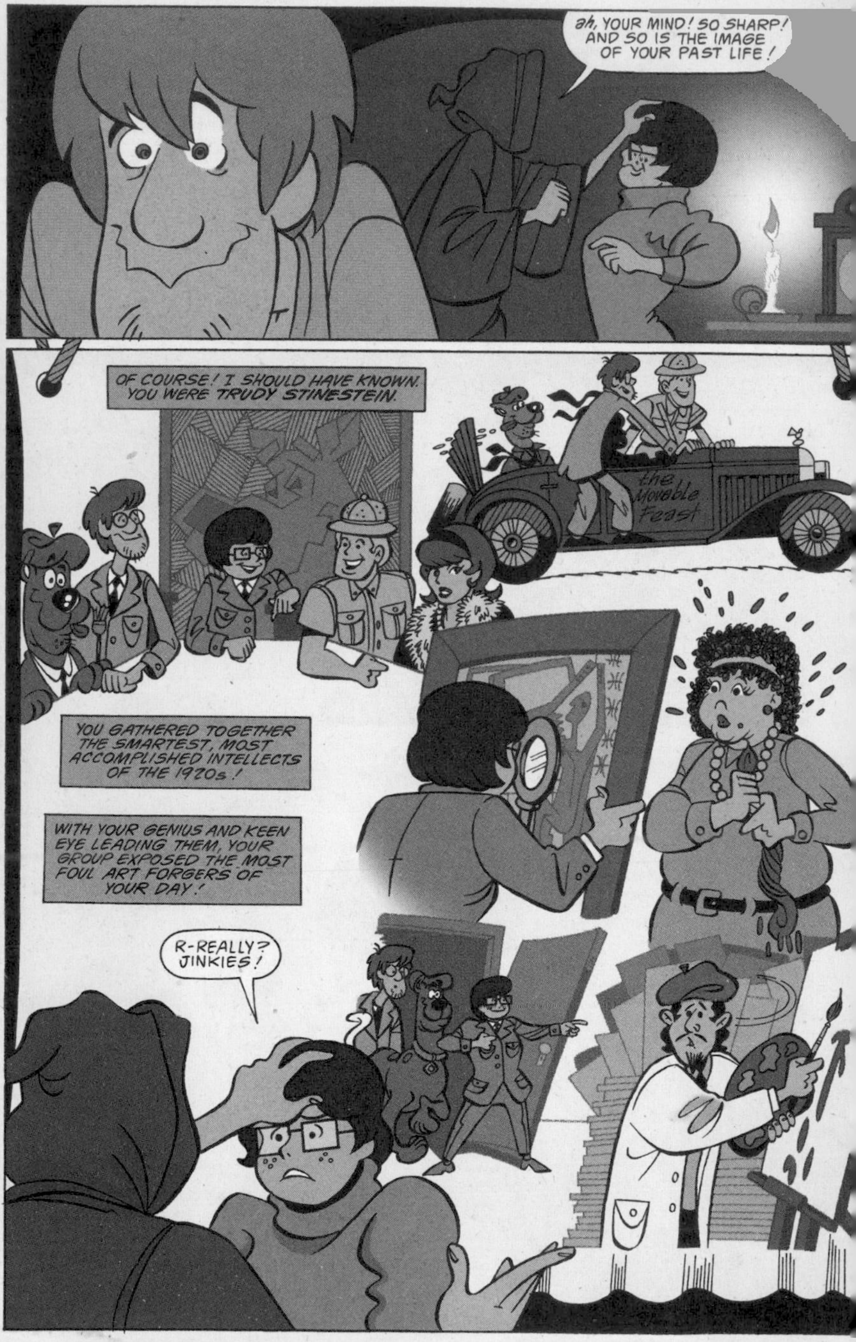
ah, YOUR MIND! SO SHARP! AND SO IS THE IMAGE OF YOUR PAST LIFE!
OF COURSE! I SHOULD HAVE KNOWN. YOU WERE TRUDY STINESTEIN.
the Movable Feast
YOU GATHERED TOGETHER THE SMARTEST, MOST ACCOMPLISHED INTELLECTS OF THE 1920s!
WITH YOUR GENIUS AND KEEN EYE LEADING THEM, YOUR GROUP EXPOSED THE MOST FOUL ART FORGERS OF YOUR DAY!
R-REALLY? JINKIES!

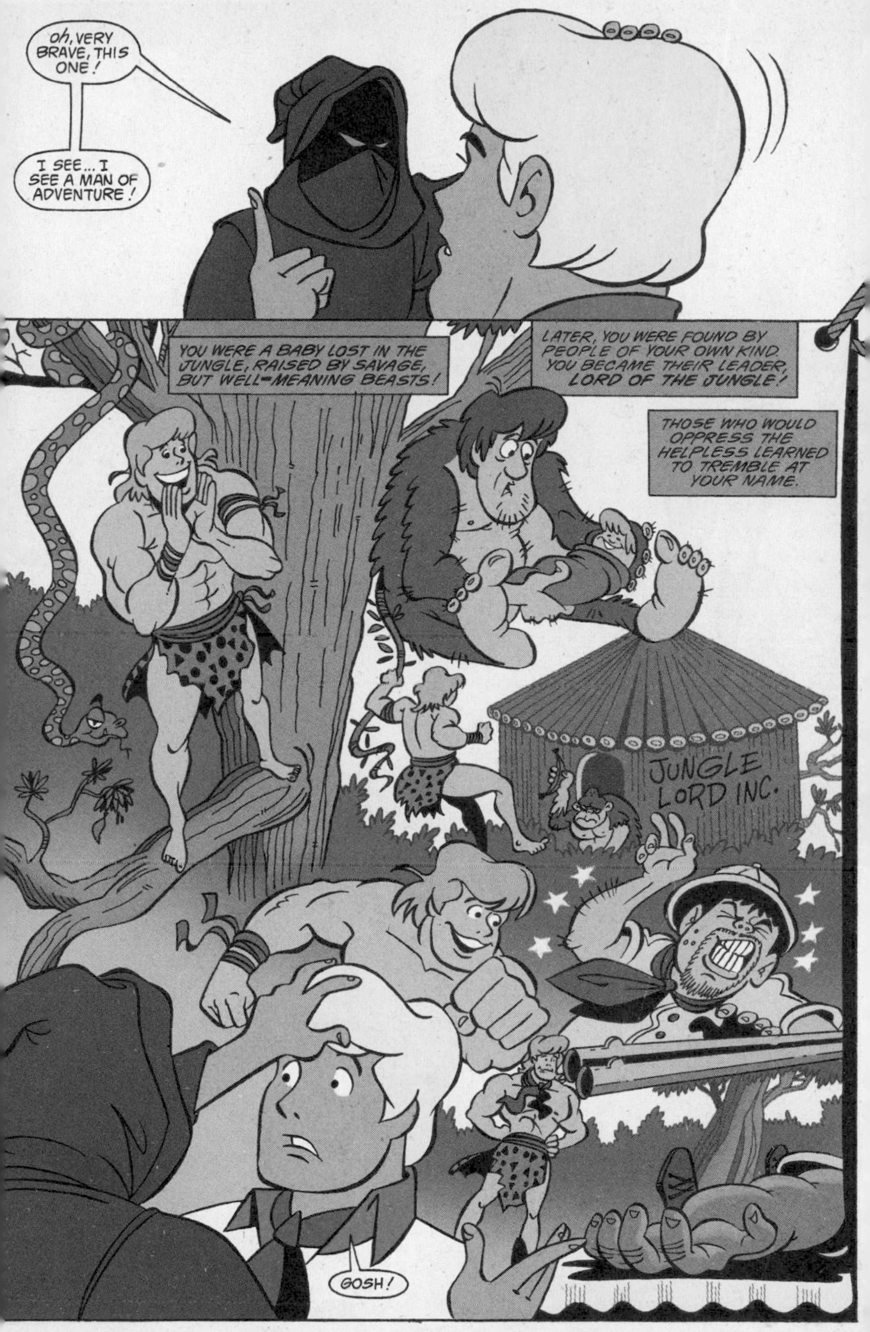

OH, VERY BRAVE, THIS ONE!
I SEE... I SEE A MAN OF ADVENTURE!
YOU WERE A BABY LOST IN THE JUNGLE, RAISED BY SAVAGE, BUT WELL-MEANING BEASTS!
LATER, YOU WERE FOUND BY PEOPLE OF YOUR OWN KIND. YOU BECAME THEIR LEADER, LORD OF THE JUNGLE!
THOSE WHO WOULD OPPRESS THE HELPLESS LEARNED TO TREMBLE AT YOUR NAME.
JUNGLE LORD INC.
GOSH!

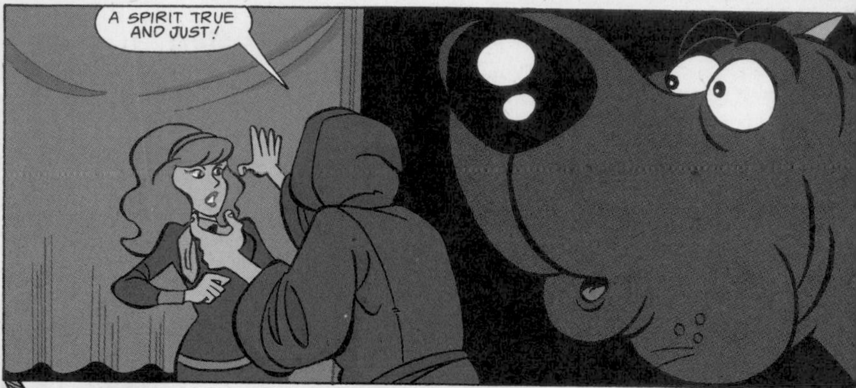
A SPIRIT TRUE AND JUST!

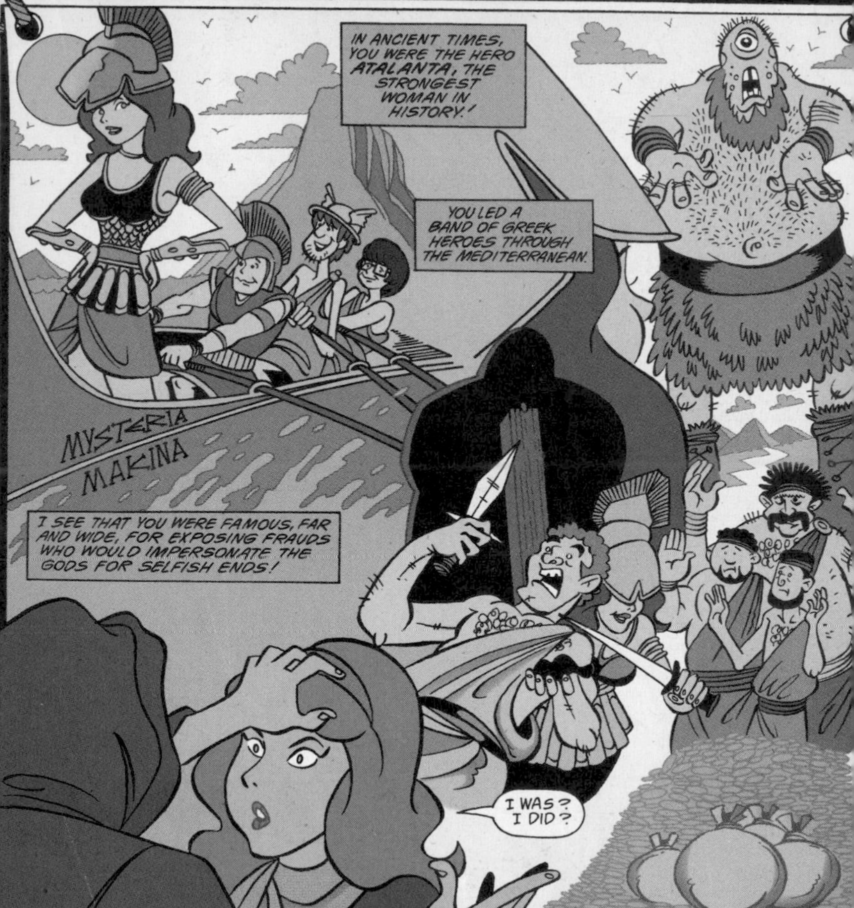
IN ANCIENT TIMES, YOU WERE THE HERO ATALANTA, THE STRONGEST WOMAN IN HISTORY!
YOU LED A BAND OF GREEK HEROES THROUGH THE MEDITERRANEAN.
MYSTERIA
MAKINA
I SEE THAT YOU WERE FAMOUS, FAR AND WIDE, FOR EXPOSING FRAUDS WHO WOULD IMPERSONATE THE GODS FOR SELFISH ENDS!
I WAS? I DID?

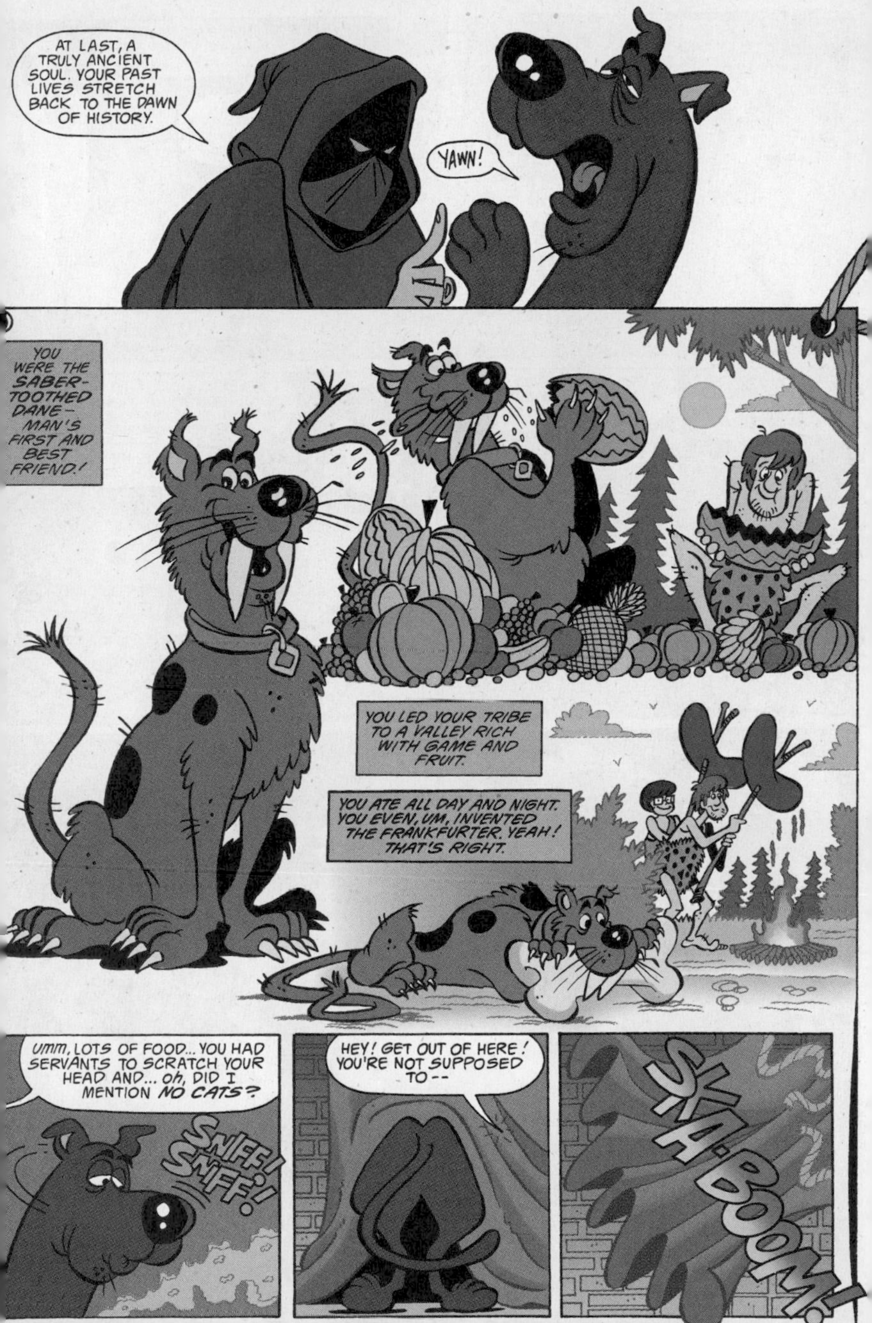

AT LAST, A TRULY ANCIENT SOUL. YOUR PAST LIVES STRETCH BACK TO THE DAWN OF HISTORY.
YAWN!
YOU WERE THE SABER-TOOTHED DANE— MAN'S FIRST AND BEST FRIEND!
YOU LED YOUR TRIBE TO A VALLEY RICH WITH GAME AND FRUIT.
YOU ATE ALL DAY AND NIGHT. YOU EVEN, UM, INVENTED THE FRANKFURTER. YEAH! THAT'S RIGHT.
UMM, LOTS OF FOOD... YOU HAD SERVANTS TO SCRATCH YOUR HEAD AND... OH, DID I MENTION NO CATS?
SNIFF! SNIFF!
HEY! GET OUT OF HERE! YOU'RE NOT SUPPOSED TO --
SKA-BOOM!

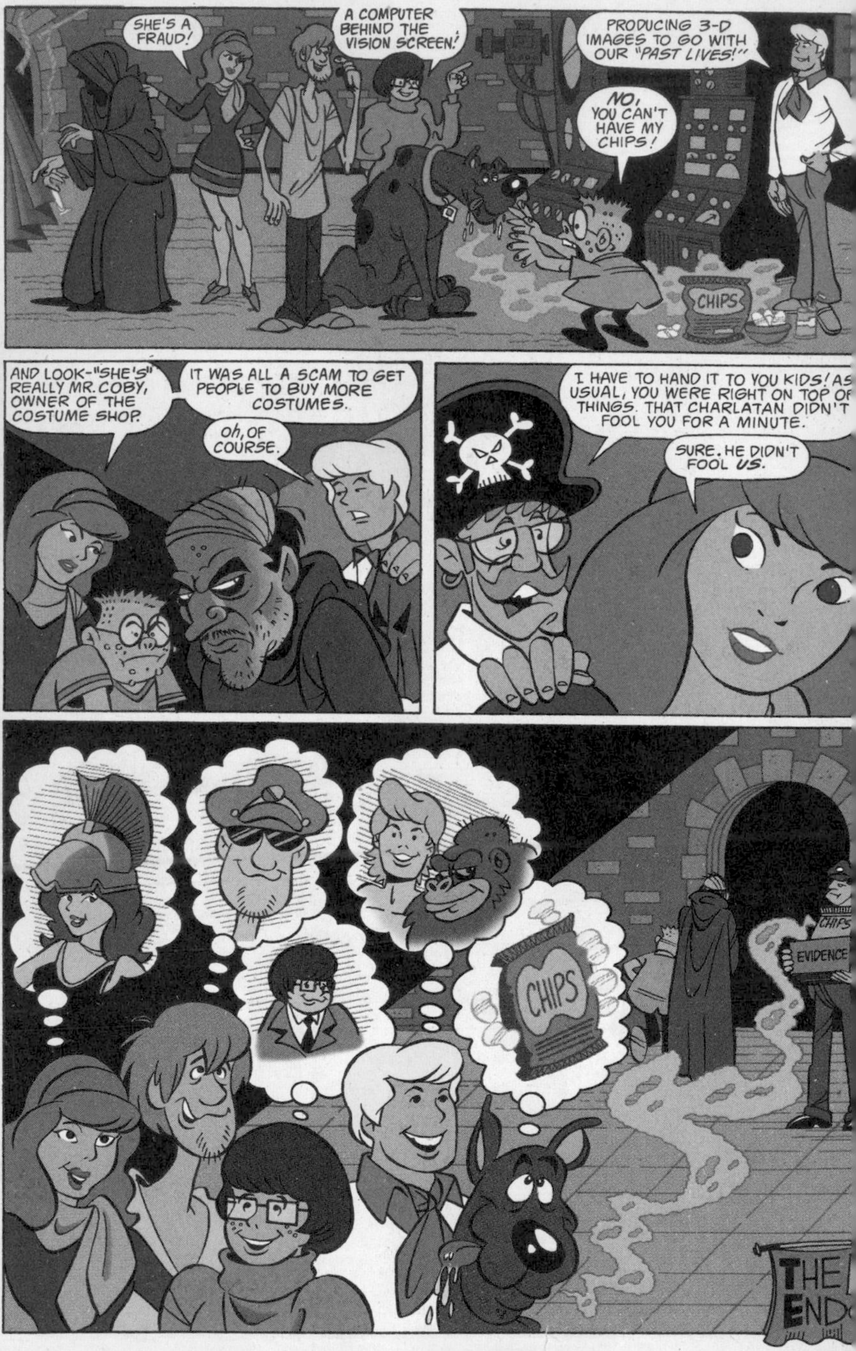

SHE'S A FRAUD!
A COMPUTER BEHIND THE VISION SCREEN!
PRODUCING 3-D IMAGES TO GO WITH OUR "PAST LIVES!"
NO, YOU CAN'T HAVE MY CHIPS!
CHIPS
AND LOOK-"SHE'S" REALLY MR. COBY, OWNER OF THE COSTUME SHOP.
IT WAS ALL A SCAM TO GET PEOPLE TO BUY MORE COSTUMES.
Oh, OF COURSE.
I HAVE TO HAND IT TO YOU KIDS! AS USUAL, YOU WERE RIGHT ON TOP OF THINGS. THAT CHARLATAN DIDN'T FOOL YOU FOR A MINUTE.
SURE. HE DIDN'T FOOL US.
CHIPS
CHIPS
EVIDENCE
THE END

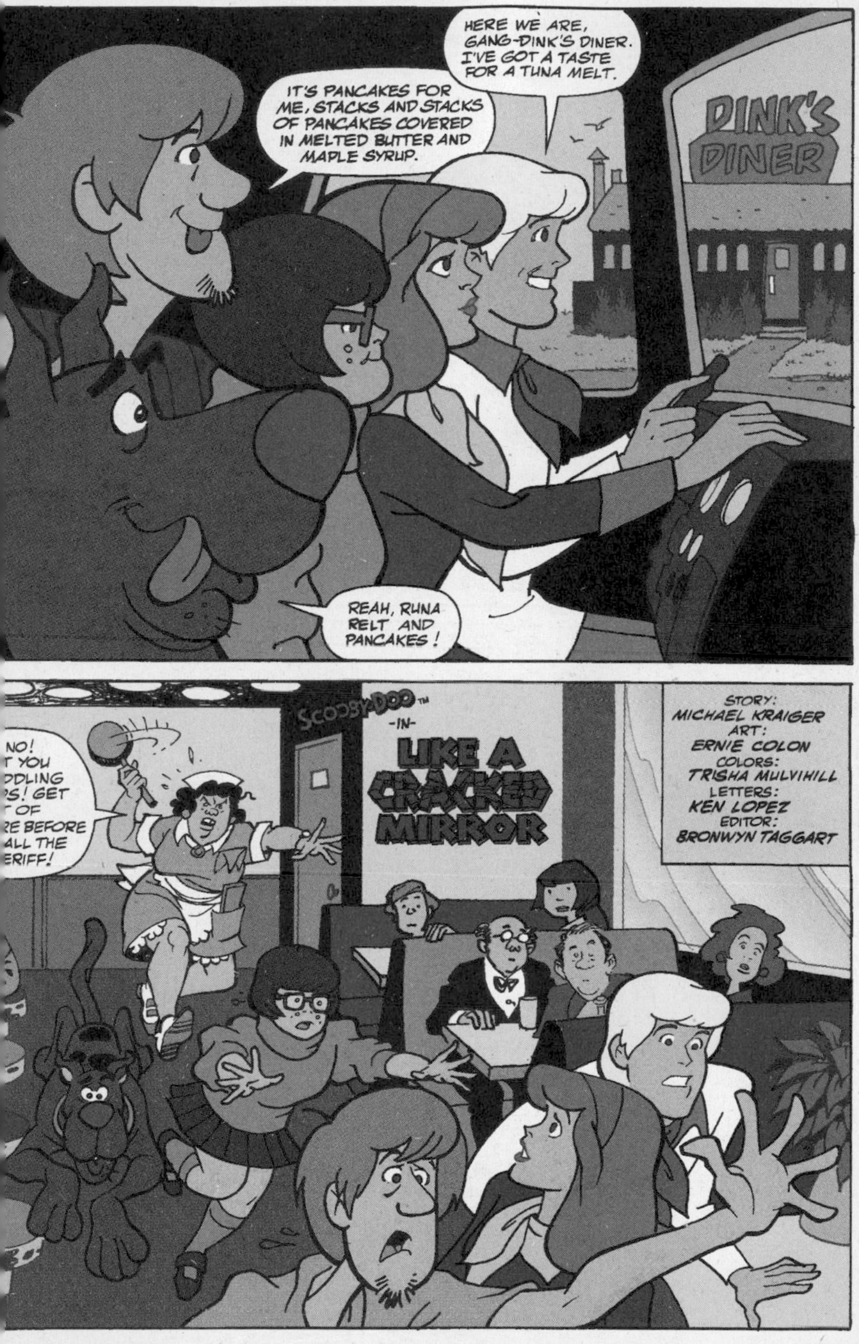
DINK'S DINER
IT'S PANCAKES FOR ME, STACKS AND STACKS OF PANCAKES COVERED IN MELTED BUTTER AND MAPLE SYRUP.
HERE WE ARE, GANG--DINK'S DINER. I'VE GOT A TASTE FOR A TUNA MELT.
REAH, RUNA RELT AND PANCAKES!
SCOOBY-DOO™ -IN- LIKE A CRACKED MIRROR
STORY: MICHAEL KRAIGER
ART: ERNIE COLON
COLORS: TRISHA MULVIHILL
LETTERS: KEN LOPEZ
EDITOR: BRONWYN TAGGART
NO!
T YOU
DDLING
PS! GET
T OF
RE BEFORE
ALL THE
ERIFF!

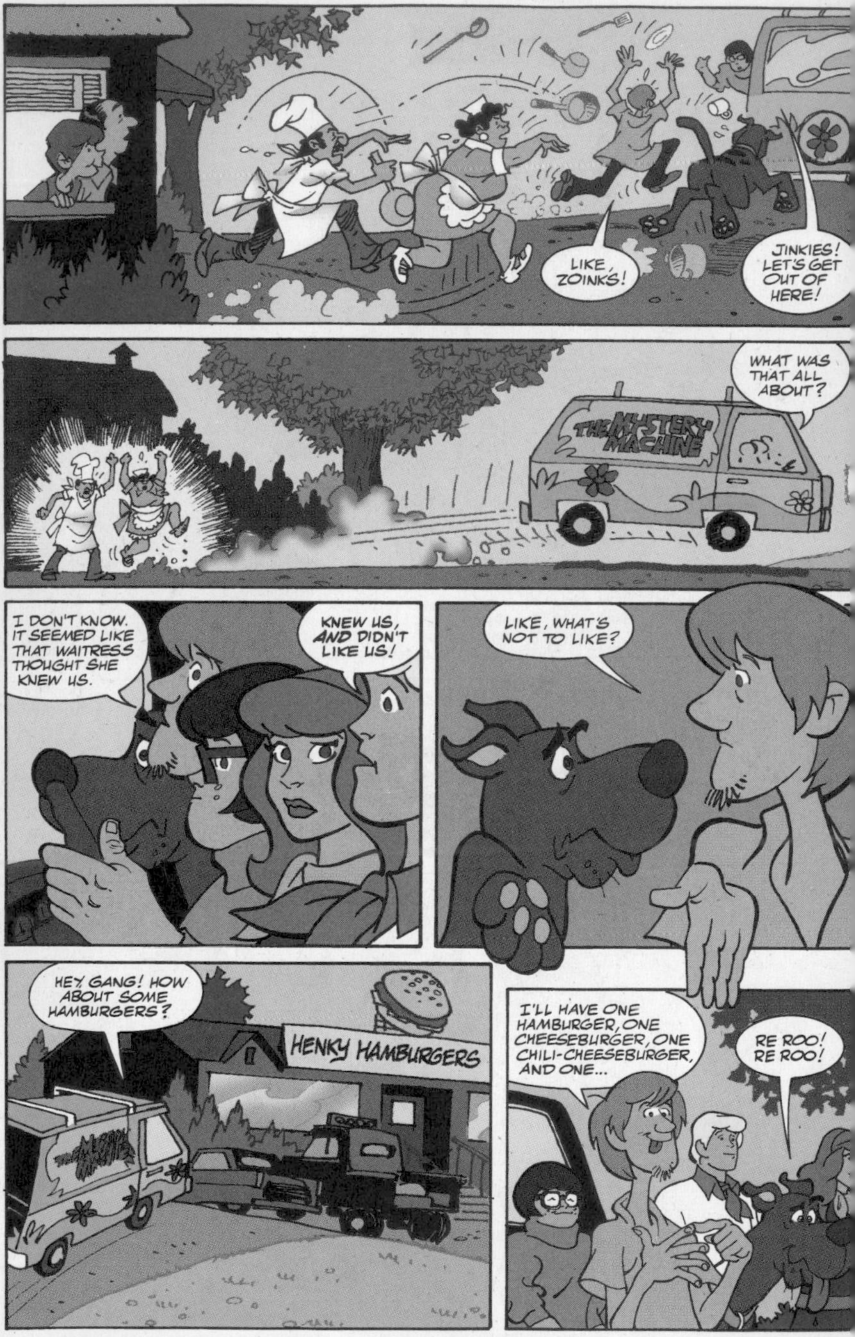
LIKE, ZOINKS!
JINKIES! LET'S GET OUT OF HERE!
WHAT WAS THAT ALL ABOUT?
THE MYSTERY MACHINE
I DON'T KNOW. IT SEEMED LIKE THAT WAITRESS THOUGHT SHE KNEW US.
KNEW US, AND DIDN'T LIKE US!
LIKE, WHAT'S NOT TO LIKE?
HEY, GANG! HOW ABOUT SOME HAMBURGERS?
HENKY HAMBURGERS
I'LL HAVE ONE HAMBURGER, ONE CHEESEBURGER, ONE CHILI-CHEESEBURGER, AND ONE...
RE ROO! RE ROO!

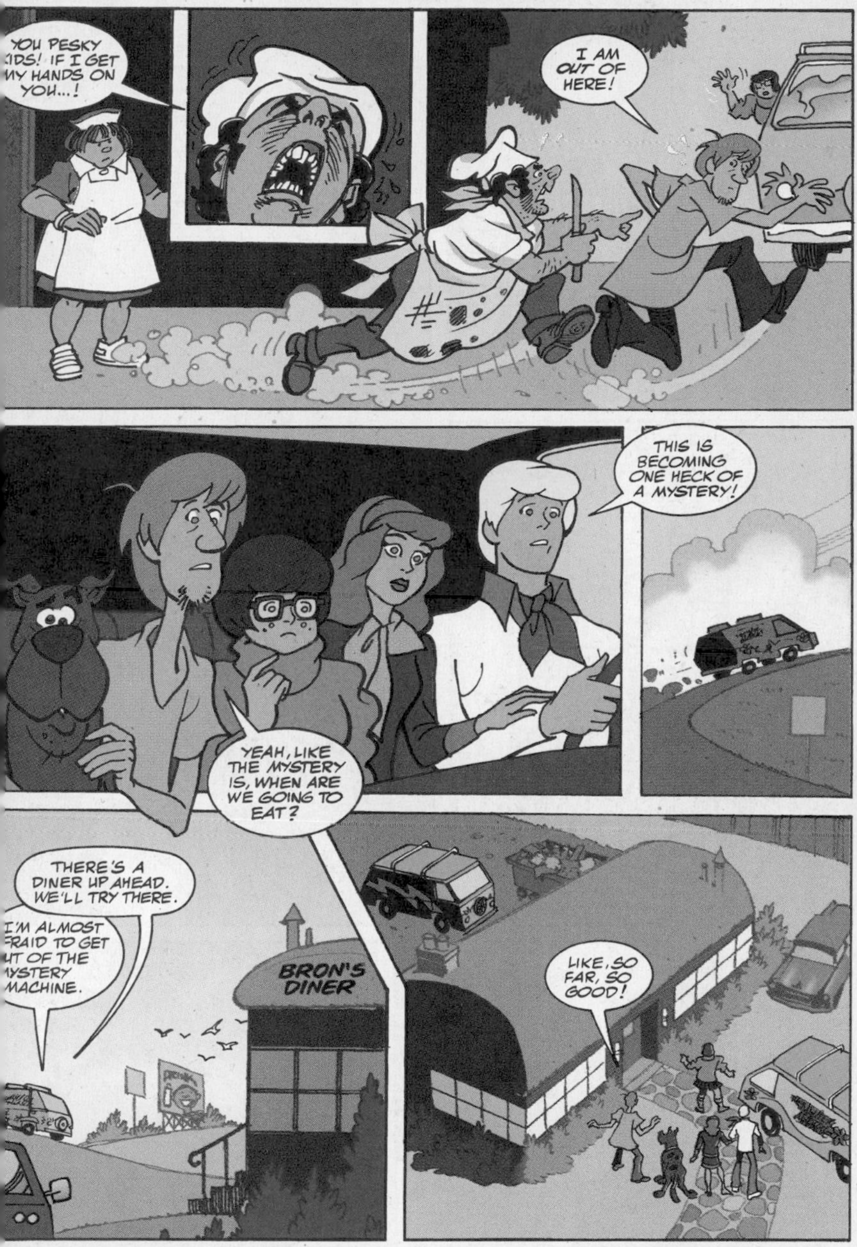
YOU PESKY KIDS! IF I GET MY HANDS ON YOU...!
I AM OUT OF HERE!
THIS IS BECOMING ONE HECK OF A MYSTERY!
YEAH, LIKE THE MYSTERY IS, WHEN ARE WE GOING TO EAT?
THERE'S A DINER UP AHEAD. WE'LL TRY THERE.
I'M ALMOST FRAID TO GET UT OF THE YSTERY MACHINE.
BRON'S DINER
LIKE, SO FAR, SO GOOD!

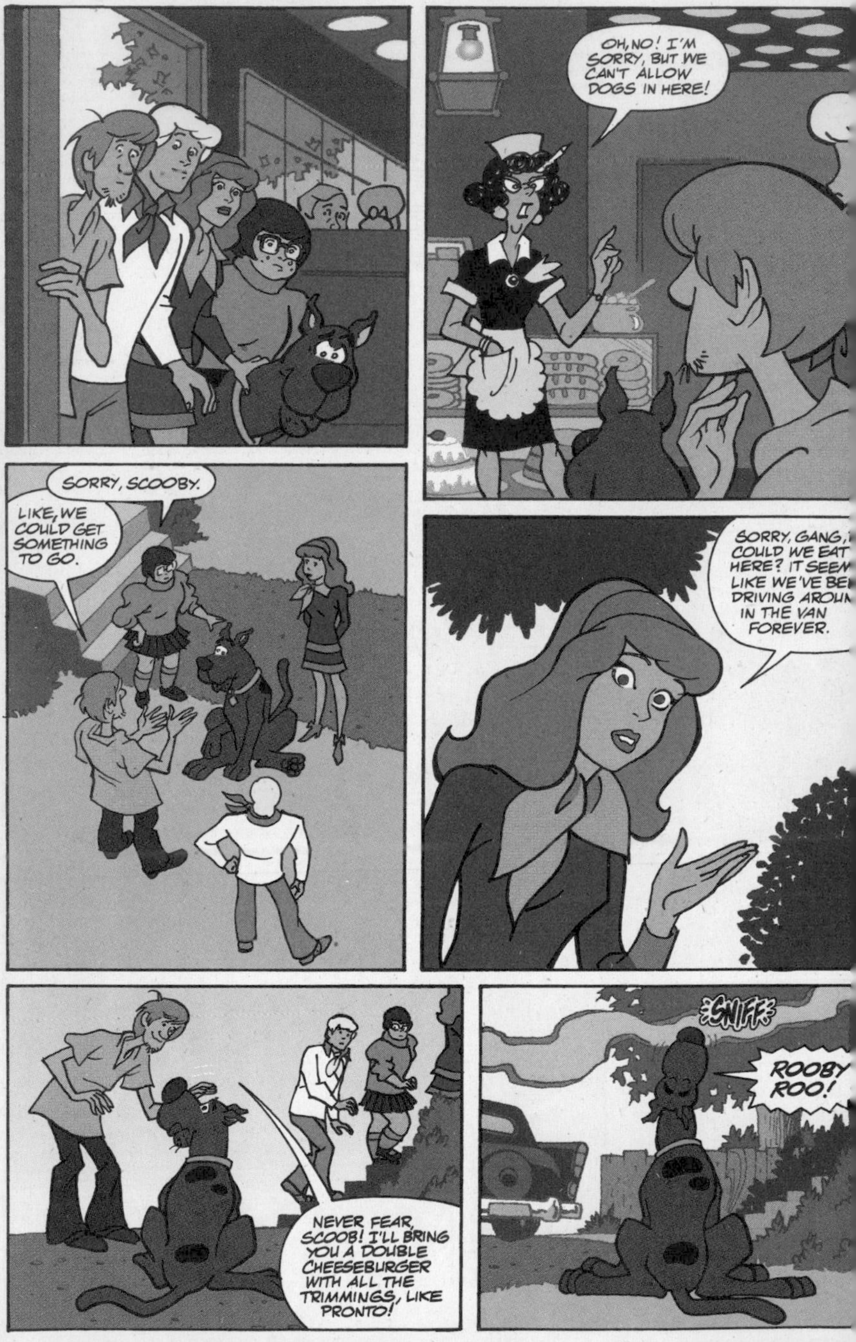
OH, NO! I'M SORRY, BUT WE CAN'T ALLOW DOGS IN HERE!
SORRY, SCOOBY.
LIKE, WE COULD GET SOMETHING TO GO.
SORRY, GANG, COULD WE EAT HERE? IT SEEM LIKE WE'VE BE DRIVING AROU IN THE VAN FOREVER.
NEVER FEAR, SCOOB! I'LL BRING YOU A DOUBLE CHEESEBURGER WITH ALL THE TRIMMINGS, LIKE PRONTO!
SNIFF
ROOBY ROO!

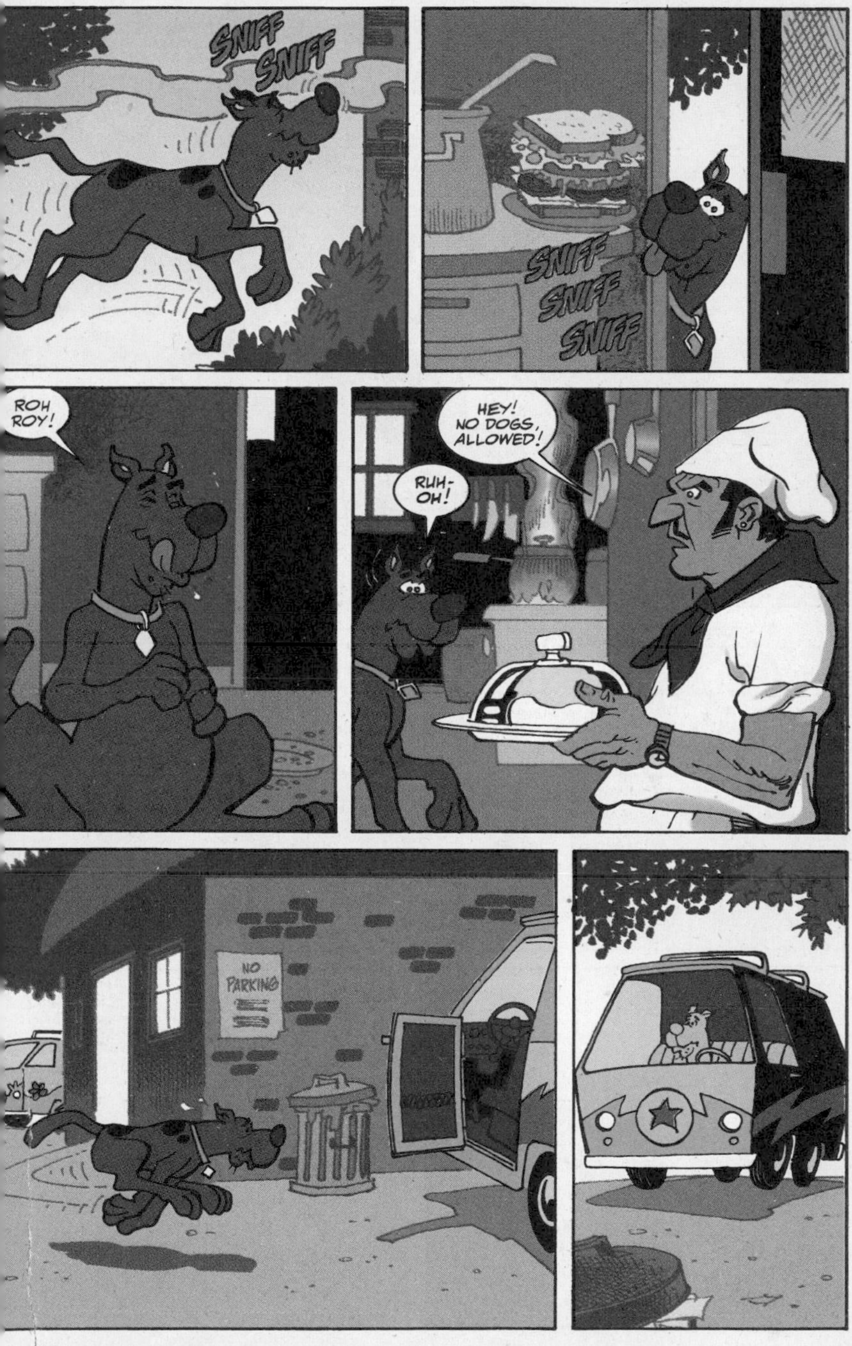
SNIFF SNIFF
SNIFF SNIFF SNIFF
ROH ROY!
HEY! NO DOGS ALLOWED!
RUH-OH!
NO PARKING

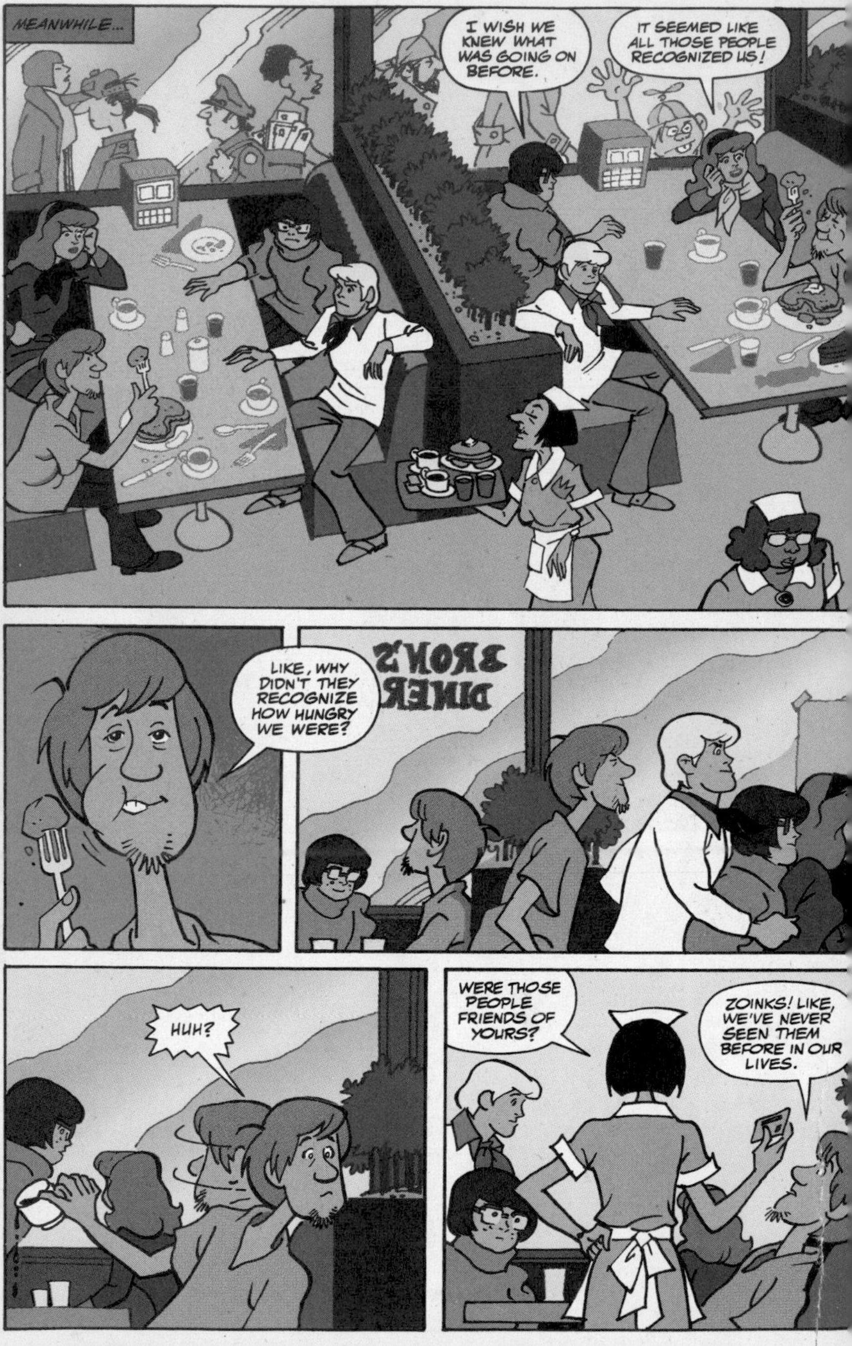
MEANWHILE...
I WISH WE KNEW WHAT WAS GOING ON BEFORE.
IT SEEMED LIKE ALL THOSE PEOPLE RECOGNIZED US!
LIKE, WHY DIDN'T THEY RECOGNIZE HOW HUNGRY WE WERE?
HUH?
WERE THOSE PEOPLE FRIENDS OF YOURS?
ZOINKS! LIKE, WE'VE NEVER SEEN THEM BEFORE IN OUR LIVES.

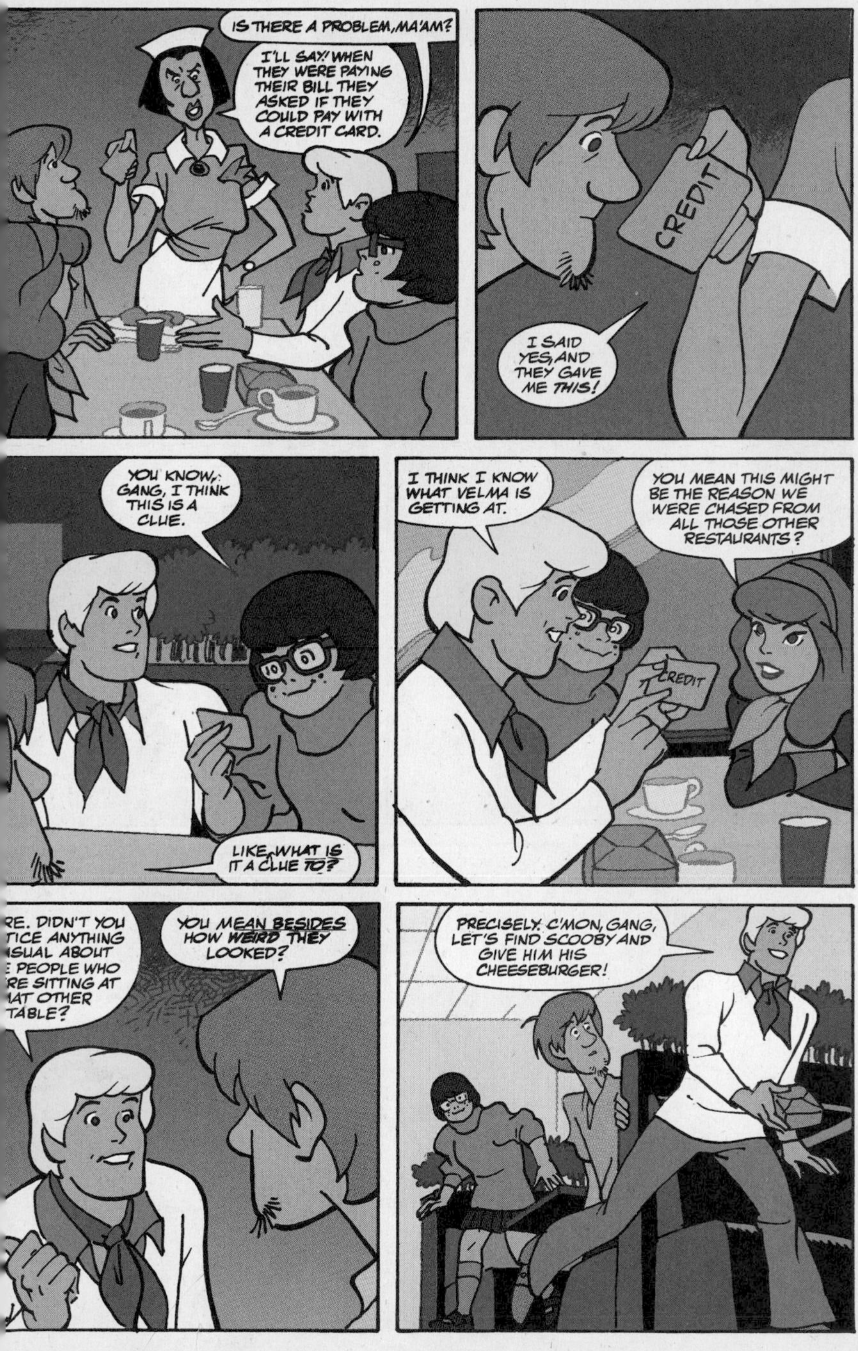
IS THERE A PROBLEM, MA'AM?
I'LL SAY! WHEN THEY WERE PAYING THEIR BILL THEY ASKED IF THEY COULD PAY WITH A CREDIT CARD.
CREDIT
I SAID YES, AND THEY GAVE ME THIS!
YOU KNOW, GANG, I THINK THIS IS A CLUE.
LIKE, WHAT IS IT A CLUE TO?
I THINK I KNOW WHAT VELMA IS GETTING AT.
YOU MEAN THIS MIGHT BE THE REASON WE WERE CHASED FROM ALL THOSE OTHER RESTAURANTS?
CREDIT
RE. DIDN'T YOU TICE ANYTHING ISUAL ABOUT E PEOPLE WHO RE SITTING AT IAT OTHER TABLE?
YOU MEAN BESIDES HOW WEIRD THEY LOOKED?
PRECISELY. C'MON, GANG, LET'S FIND SCOOBY AND GIVE HIM HIS CHEESEBURGER!

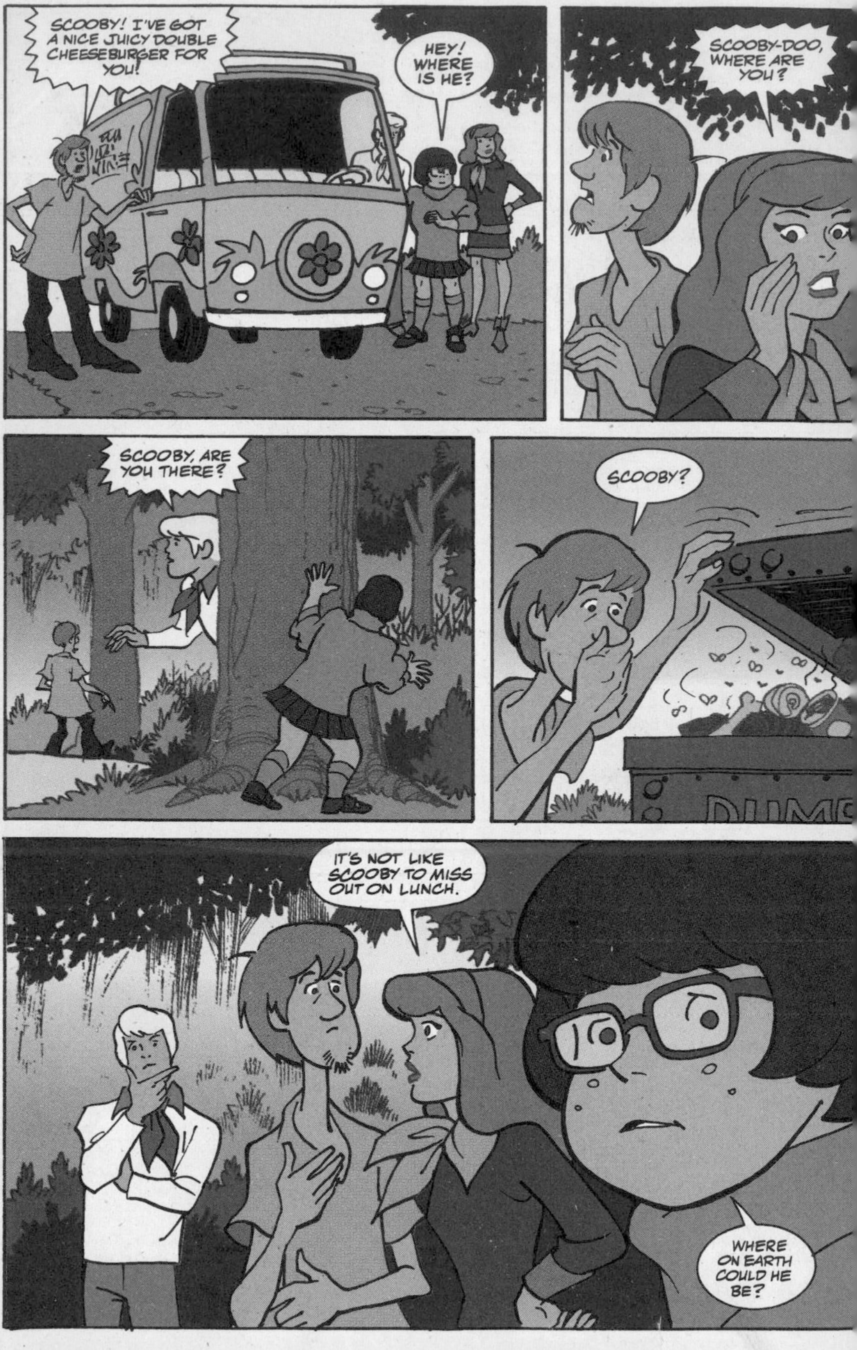
SCOOBY! I'VE GOT A NICE JUICY DOUBLE CHEESEBURGER FOR YOU!
HEY! WHERE IS HE?
SCOOBY-DOO, WHERE ARE YOU?
SCOOBY, ARE YOU THERE?
SCOOBY?
IT'S NOT LIKE SCOOBY TO MISS OUT ON LUNCH.
WHERE ON EARTH COULD HE BE?

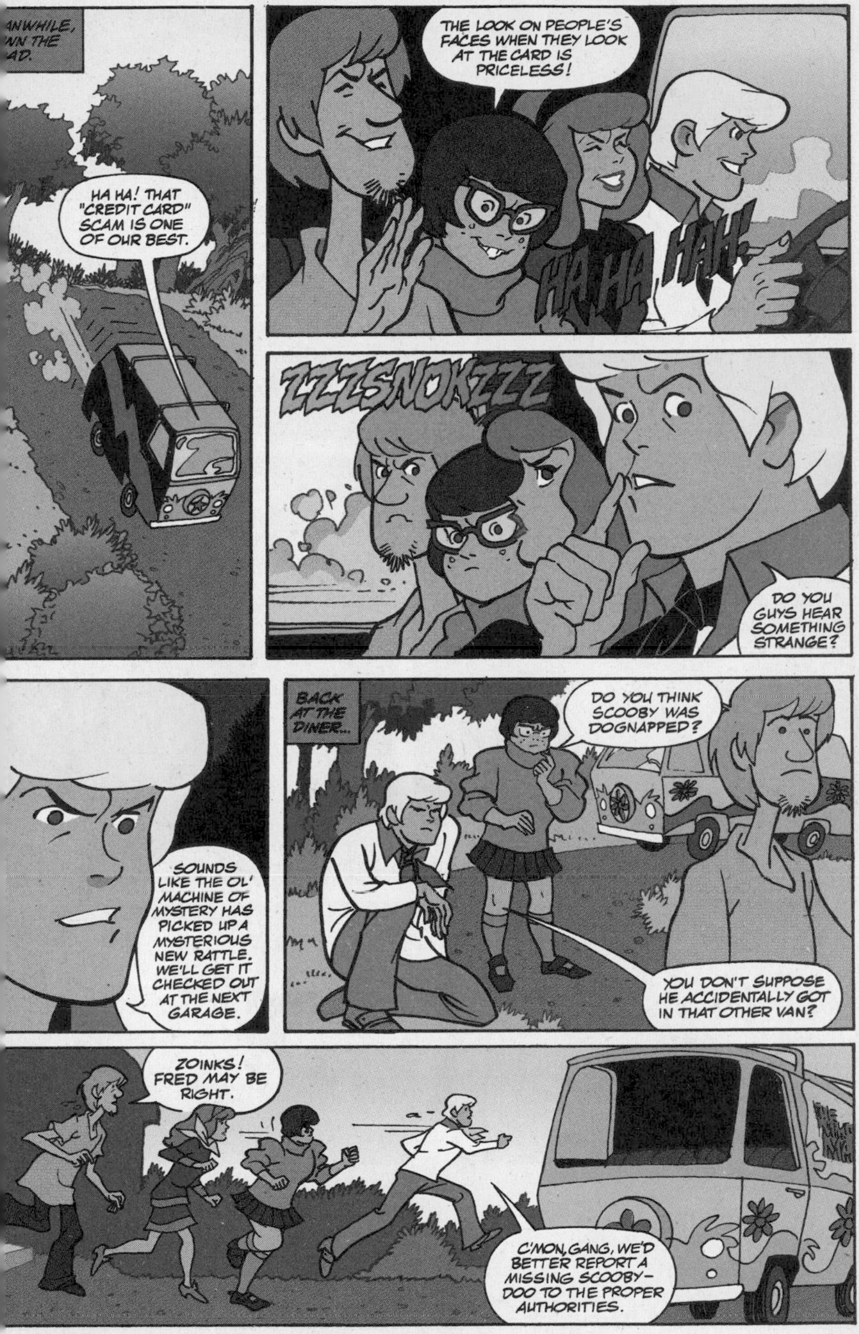

...ANWHILE, ...WN THE ...AD.
HA HA! THAT "CREDIT CARD" SCAM IS ONE OF OUR BEST.
THE LOOK ON PEOPLE'S FACES WHEN THEY LOOK AT THE CARD IS PRICELESS!
HA HA HAH!
ZZZSNOKZZZ
DO YOU GUYS HEAR SOMETHING STRANGE?
SOUNDS LIKE THE OL' MACHINE OF MYSTERY HAS PICKED UP A MYSTERIOUS NEW RATTLE. WE'LL GET IT CHECKED OUT AT THE NEXT GARAGE.
BACK AT THE DINER...
DO YOU THINK SCOOBY WAS DOGNAPPED?
YOU DON'T SUPPOSE HE ACCIDENTALLY GOT IN THAT OTHER VAN?
ZOINKS! FRED MAY BE RIGHT.
C'MON, GANG, WE'D BETTER REPORT A MISSING SCOOBY-DOO TO THE PROPER AUTHORITIES.

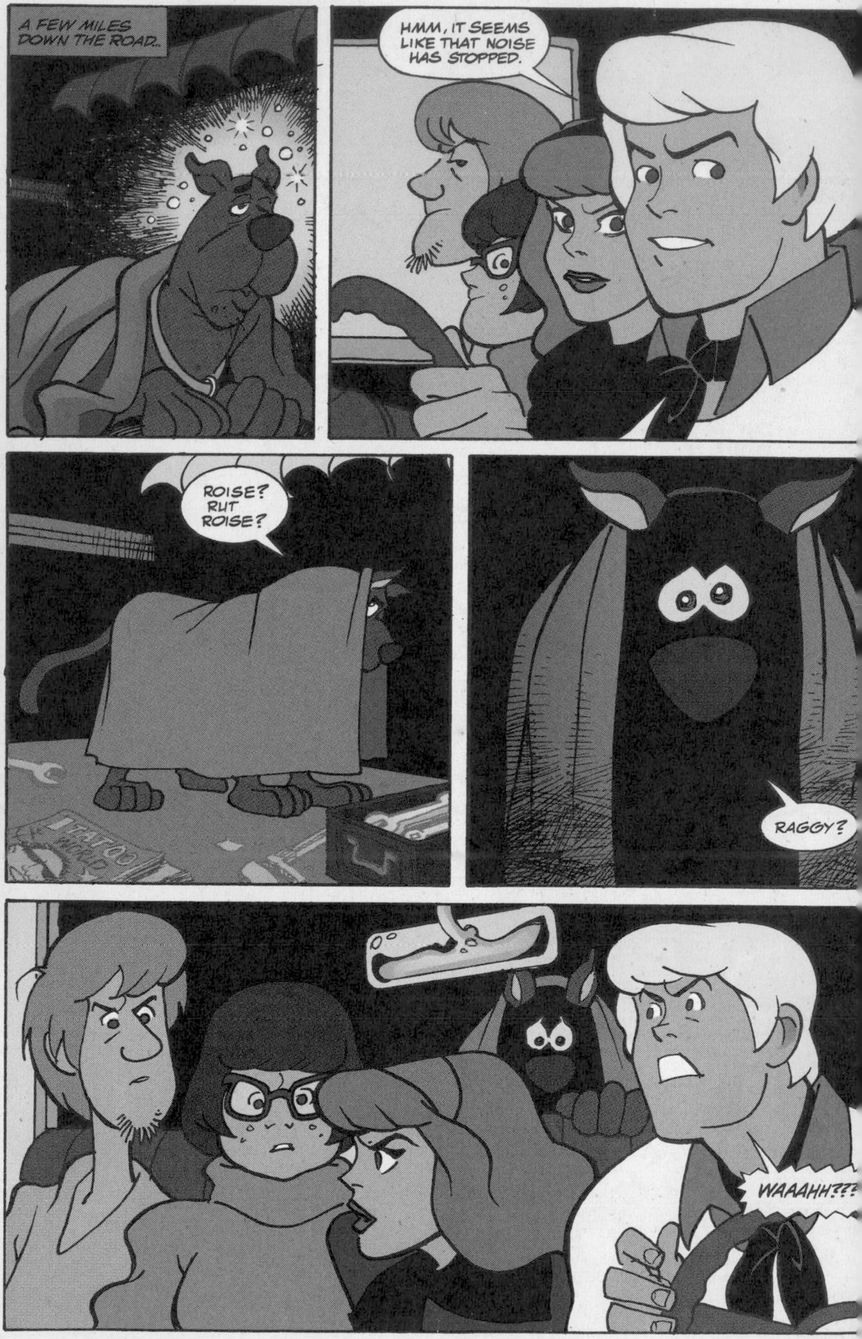
A FEW MILES DOWN THE ROAD...
HMM, IT SEEMS LIKE THAT NOISE HAS STOPPED.
ROISE? RUT ROISE?
RAGGY?
WAAAHH???

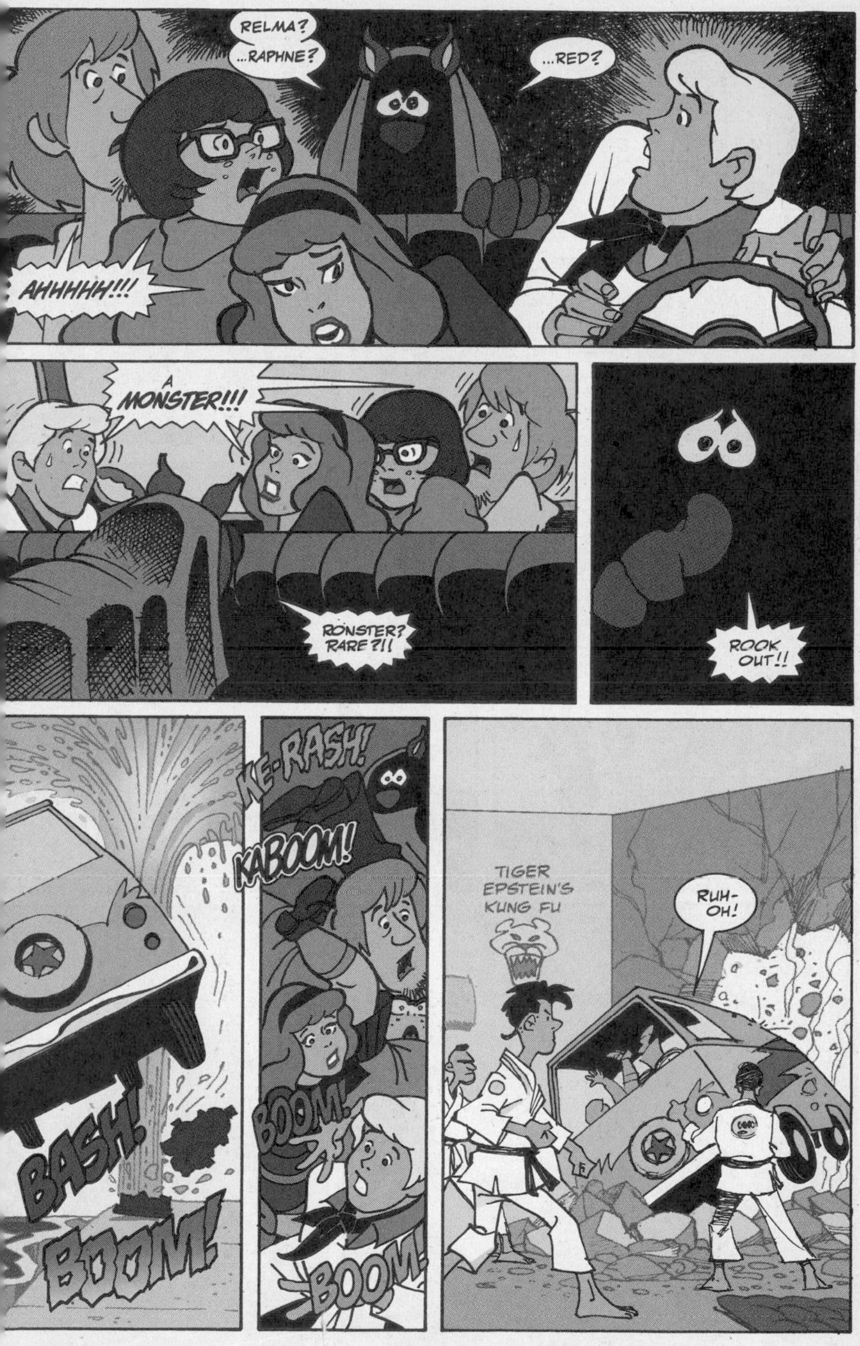
RELMA?
...RAPHNE?
...RED?
AHHHHH!!!
A MONSTER!!!
RONSTER? RARE?!!
ROOK OUT!!
BASH!
BOOM!
KE-RASH!
KABOOM!
BOOM!
BOOM!
TIGER EPSTEIN'S KUNG FU
RUH-OH!

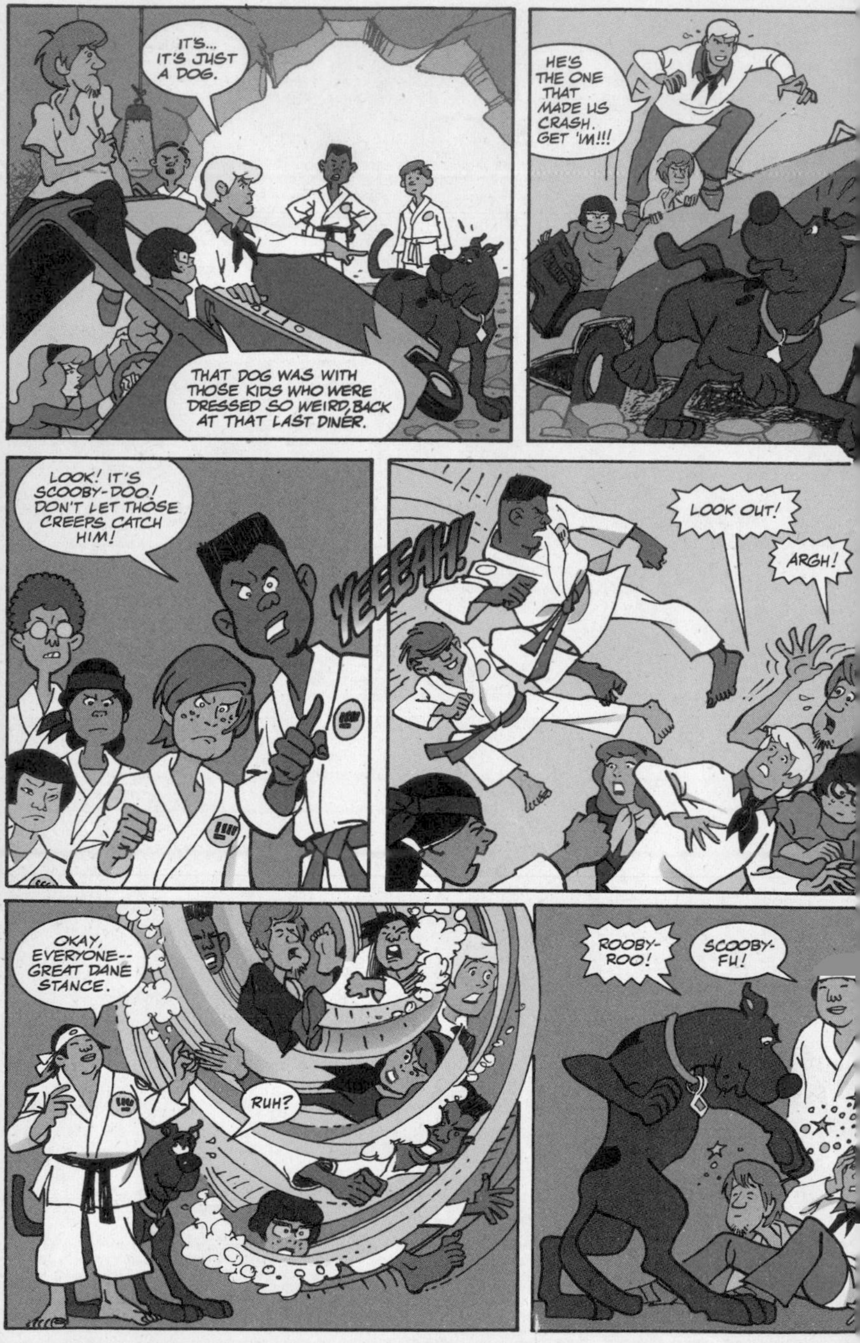
IT'S... IT'S JUST A DOG.
THAT DOG WAS WITH THOSE KIDS WHO WERE DRESSED SO WEIRD, BACK AT THAT LAST DINER.
HE'S THE ONE THAT MADE US CRASH. GET 'IM!!!
LOOK! IT'S SCOOBY-DOO! DON'T LET THOSE CREEPS CATCH HIM!
YEEEAH!
LOOK OUT!
ARGH!
OKAY, EVERYONE-- GREAT DANE STANCE.
RUH?
ROOBY-ROO!
SCOOBY-FU!

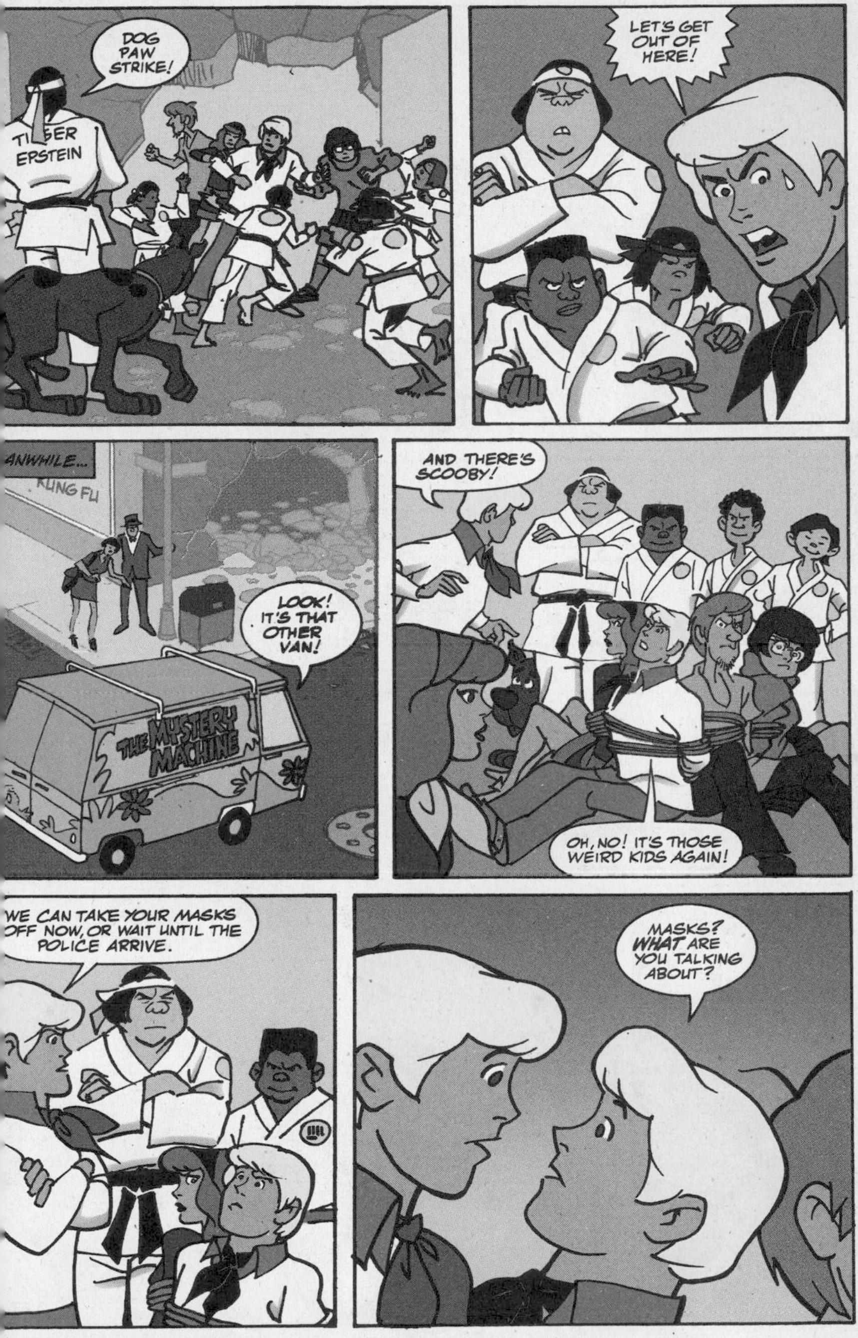

DOG PAW STRIKE!
TIGER EPSTEIN
LET'S GET OUT OF HERE!
...ANWHILE...
KUNG FU
LOOK! IT'S THAT OTHER VAN!
THE MYSTERY MACHINE
AND THERE'S SCOOBY!
OH, NO! IT'S THOSE WEIRD KIDS AGAIN!
WE CAN TAKE YOUR MASKS OFF NOW, OR WAIT UNTIL THE POLICE ARRIVE.
MASKS? WHAT ARE YOU TALKING ABOUT?

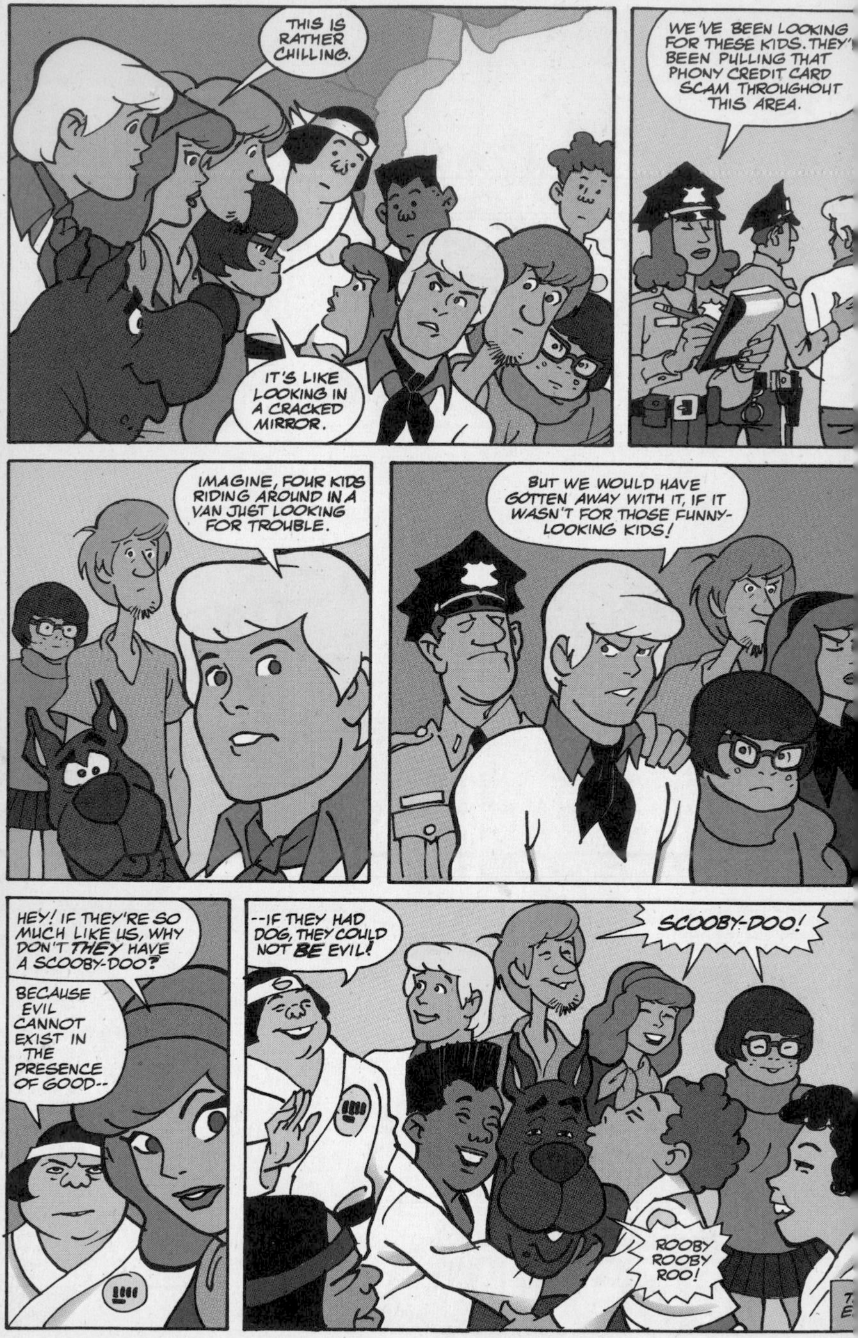
THIS IS RATHER CHILLING.
IT'S LIKE LOOKING IN A CRACKED MIRROR.
WE'VE BEEN LOOKING FOR THESE KIDS. THEY' BEEN PULLING THAT PHONY CREDIT CARD SCAM THROUGHOUT THIS AREA.
IMAGINE, FOUR KIDS RIDING AROUND IN A VAN JUST LOOKING FOR TROUBLE.
BUT WE WOULD HAVE GOTTEN AWAY WITH IT, IF IT WASN'T FOR THOSE FUNNY-LOOKING KIDS!
HEY! IF THEY'RE SO MUCH LIKE US, WHY DON'T *THEY* HAVE A SCOOBY-DOO?
BECAUSE EVIL CANNOT EXIST IN THE PRESENCE OF GOOD--
--IF THEY HAD DOG, THEY COULD NOT *BE* EVIL!
SCOOBY-DOO!
ROOBY ROOBY ROO!

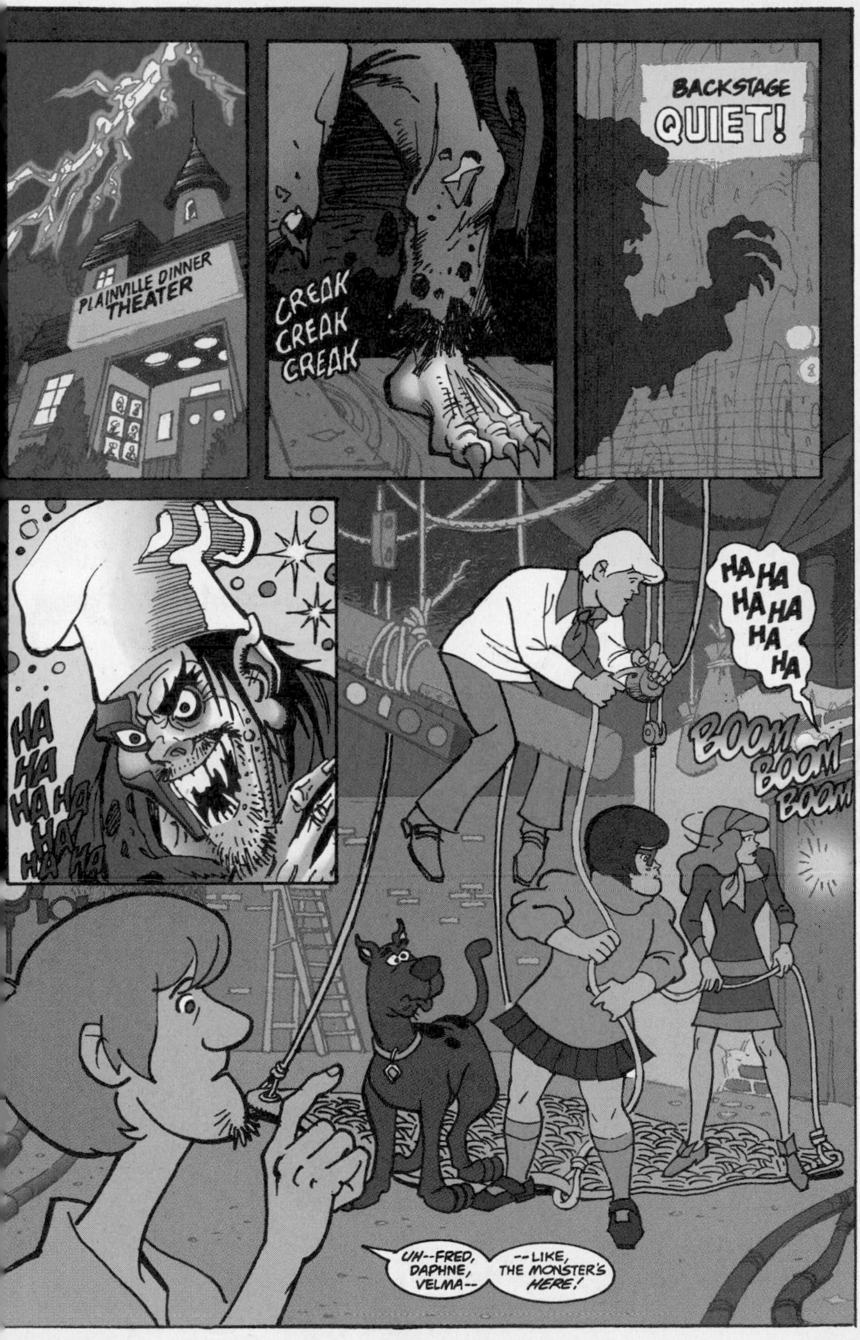
PLAINVILLE DINNER THEATER
CREAK
CREAK
CREAK
BACKSTAGE
QUIET!
HA HA HA HA HA HA HA
HA HA HA HA HA HA HA
BOOM BOOM BOOM
UH--FRED, DAPHNE, VELMA--
--LIKE, THE MONSTER'S *HERE!*

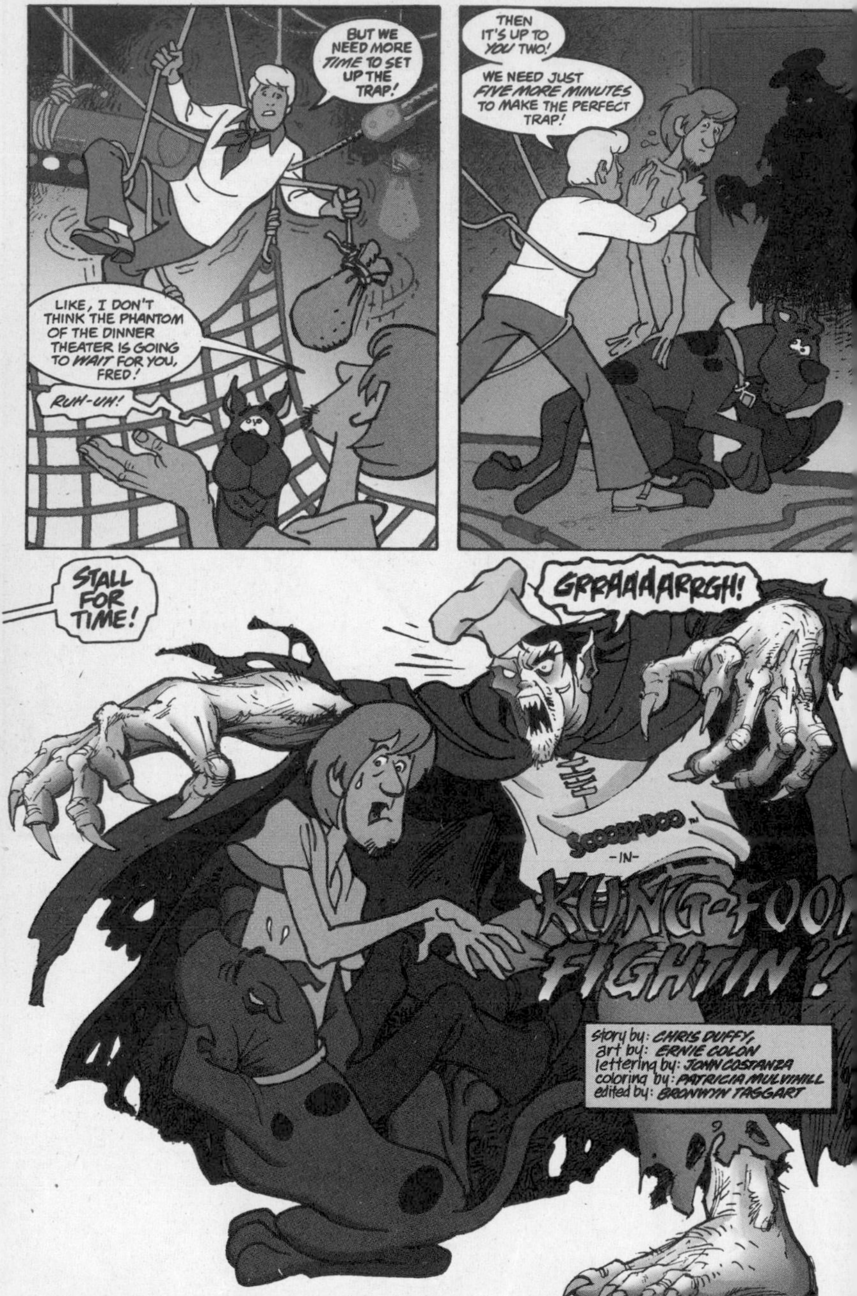
BUT WE NEED MORE TIME TO SET UP THE TRAP!
LIKE, I DON'T THINK THE PHANTOM OF THE DINNER THEATER IS GOING TO WAIT FOR YOU, FRED!
RUH-UH!
THEN IT'S UP TO YOU TWO!
WE NEED JUST FIVE MORE MINUTES TO MAKE THE PERFECT TRAP!
STALL FOR TIME!
GRRAAAARRGH!
SCOOBY-DOO™
-IN-
KUNG-FOOD FIGHTIN'!
story by: CHRIS DUFFY,
art by: ERNIE COLON
lettering by: JOHN COSTANZA
coloring by: PATRICIA MULVIHILL
edited by: BRONWYN TAGGART

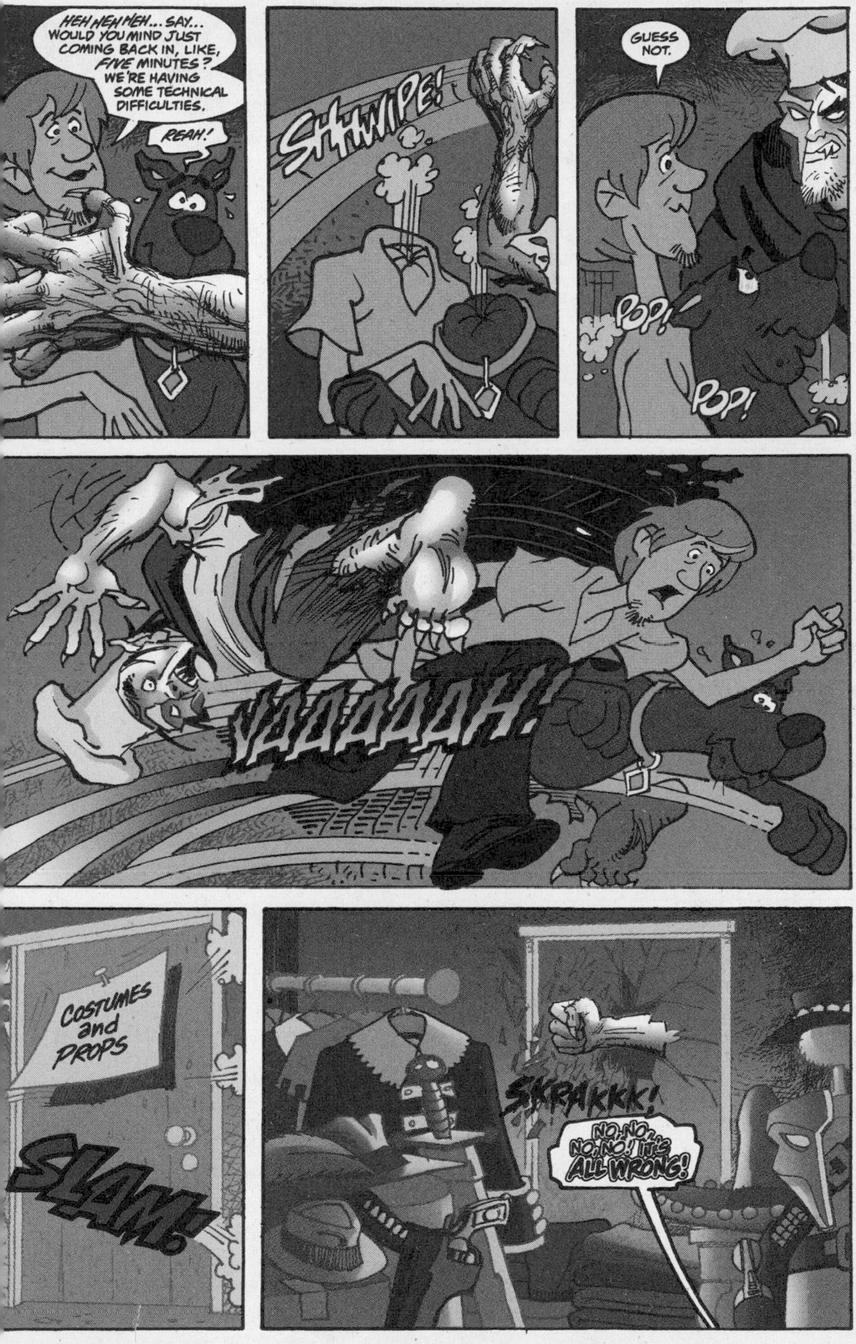
HEH HEH HEH... SAY... WOULD YOU MIND JUST COMING BACK IN, LIKE, FIVE MINUTES? WE'RE HAVING SOME TECHNICAL DIFFICULTIES.
REAH!
SHHWIPE!
GUESS NOT.
POP!
POP!
YAAAAAH!
COSTUMES and PROPS
SLAM!
SKRAKKK!
NO, NO, NO, NO! IT'S ALL WRONG!

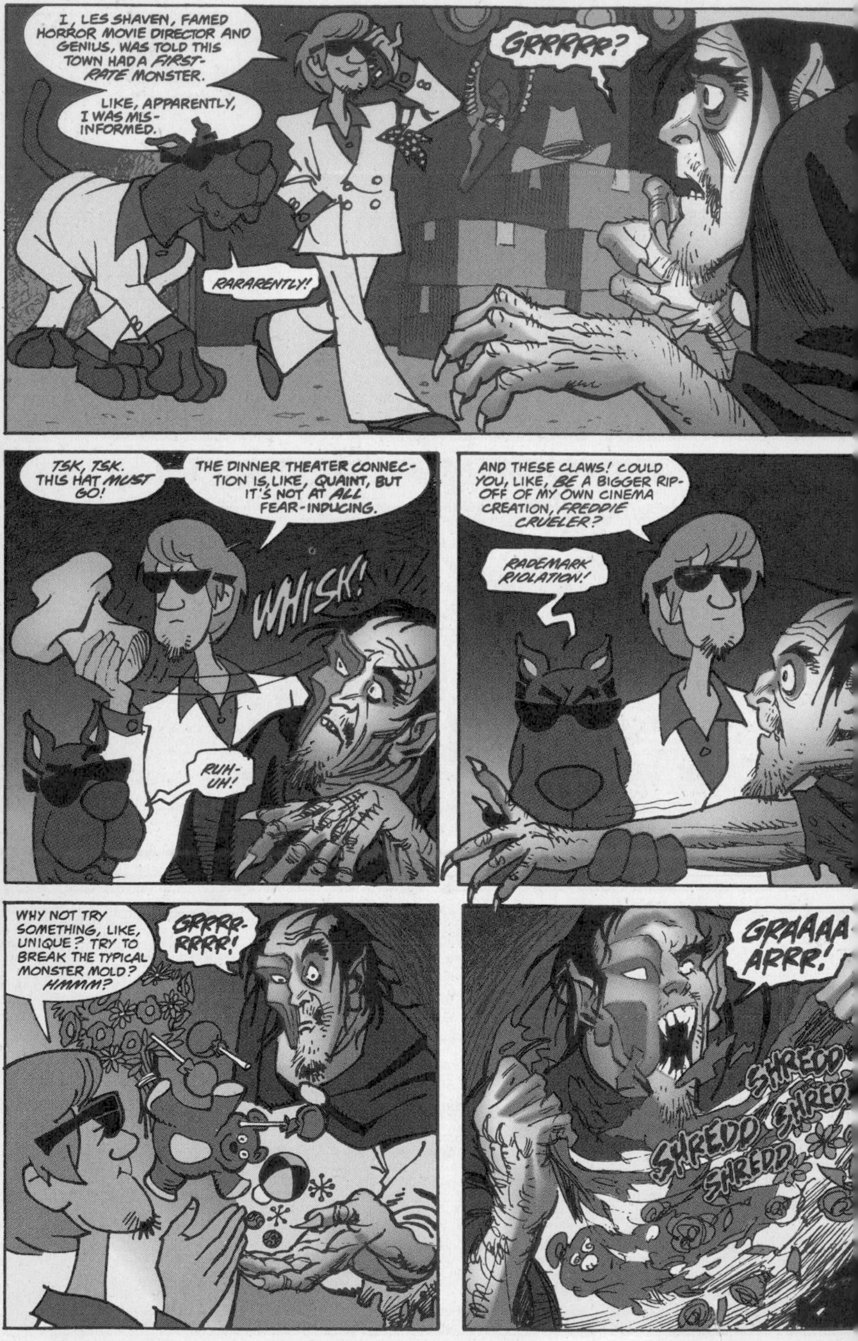
I, LES SHAVEN, FAMED HORROR MOVIE DIRECTOR AND GENIUS, WAS TOLD THIS TOWN HAD A FIRST-RATE MONSTER.
LIKE, APPARENTLY, I WAS MIS-INFORMED.
GRRRRR?
RARARENTLY!
TSK, TSK. THIS HAT MUST GO!
THE DINNER THEATER CONNECTION IS, LIKE, QUAINT, BUT IT'S NOT AT ALL FEAR-INDUCING.
WHISK!
RUH-UH!
AND THESE CLAWS! COULD YOU, LIKE, BE A BIGGER RIP-OFF OF MY OWN CINEMA CREATION, FREDDIE CRUELER?
RADEMARK RIOLATION!
WHY NOT TRY SOMETHING, LIKE, UNIQUE? TRY TO BREAK THE TYPICAL MONSTER MOLD? HMMM?
GRRRR-RRRR!
GRAAAA ARRR!
SHREDD
SHRED
SHREDD
SHREDD

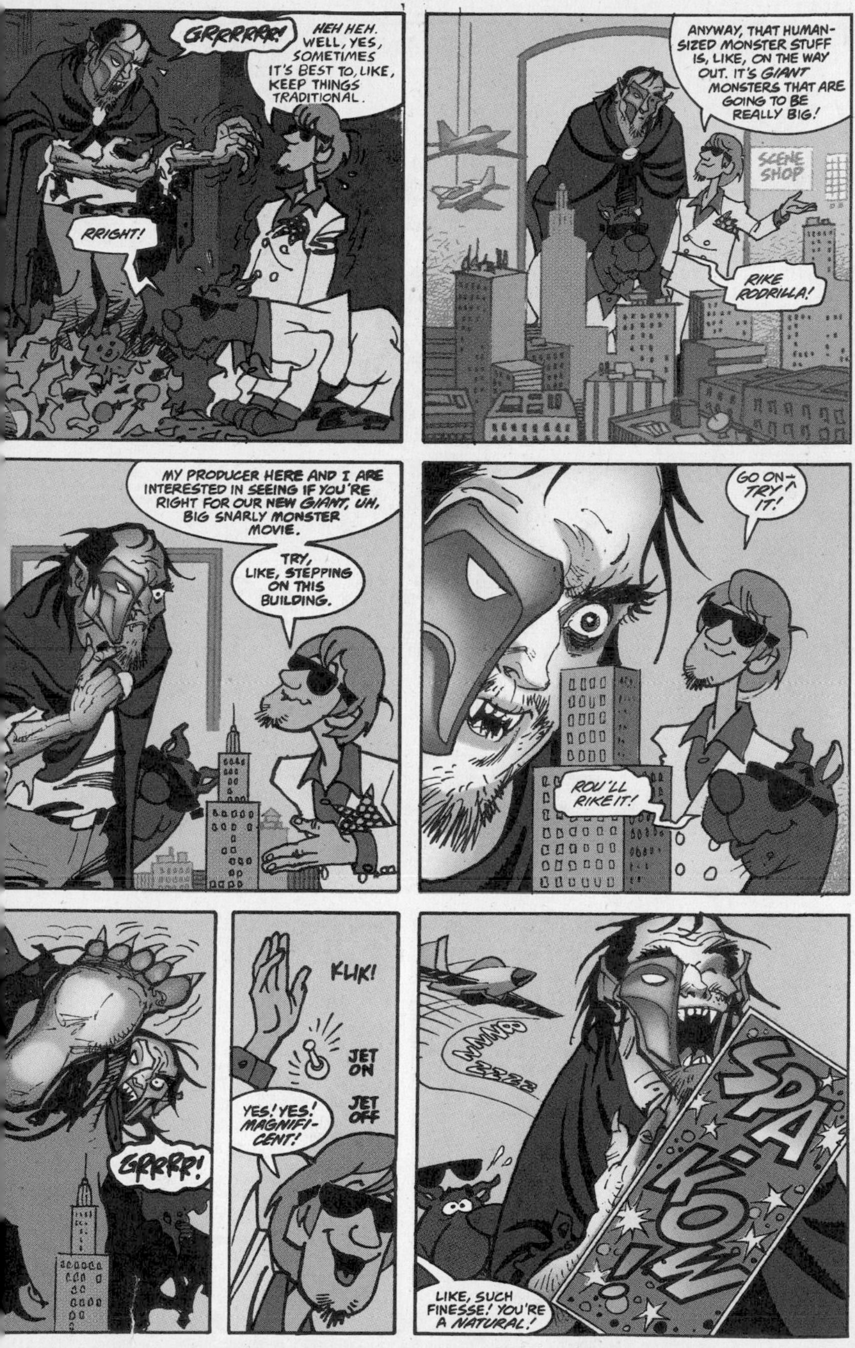
GRRRRRR!
HEH HEH. WELL, YES, SOMETIMES IT'S BEST TO, LIKE, KEEP THINGS TRADITIONAL.
RRIGHT!
ANYWAY, THAT HUMAN-SIZED MONSTER STUFF IS, LIKE, ON THE WAY OUT. IT'S GIANT MONSTERS THAT ARE GOING TO BE REALLY BIG!
SCENE SHOP
RIKE RODRILLA!
MY PRODUCER HERE AND I ARE INTERESTED IN SEEING IF YOU'RE RIGHT FOR OUR NEW GIANT, UH, BIG SNARLY MONSTER MOVIE.
TRY, LIKE, STEPPING ON THIS BUILDING.
GO ON-- TRY IT!
ROU'LL RIKE IT!
GRRRR!
KLIK!
JET ON
JET OFF
YES! YES! MAGNIFI-CENT!
SPA-KOOM!
LIKE, SUCH FINESSE! YOU'RE A NATURAL!

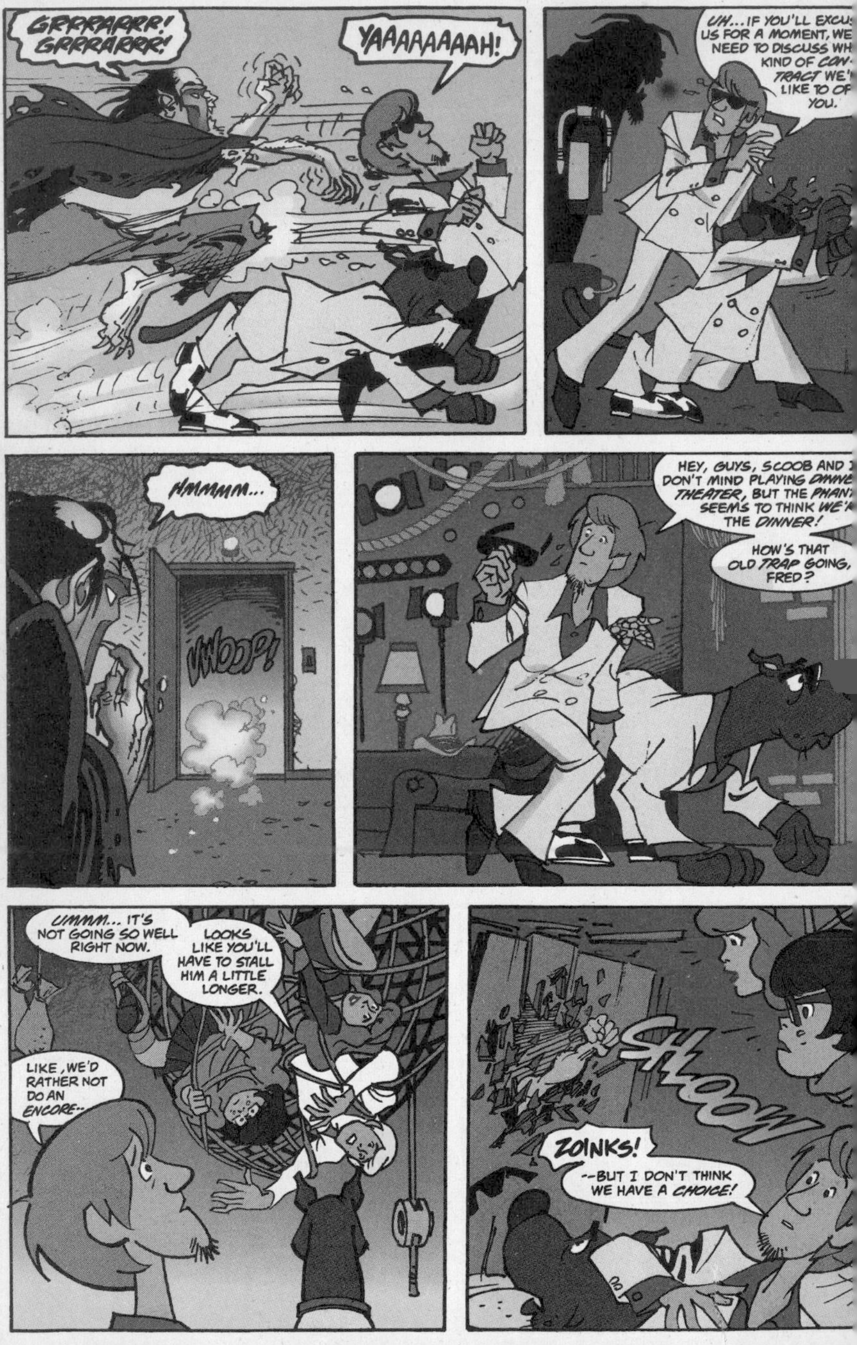
GRRRARRR! GRRRARRR!
YAAAAAAAAH!
UH... IF YOU'LL EXCUS US FOR A MOMENT, WE NEED TO DISCUSS WH KIND OF CON- TRACT WE' LIKE TO OF YOU.
HMMMM...
WHOOP!
HEY, GUYS, SCOOB AND I DON'T MIND PLAYING DINNE THEATER, BUT THE PHAN SEEMS TO THINK WE' THE DINNER!
HOW'S THAT OLD TRAP GOING, FRED?
UMMM... IT'S NOT GOING SO WELL RIGHT NOW.
LOOKS LIKE YOU'LL HAVE TO STALL HIM A LITTLE LONGER.
LIKE, WE'D RATHER NOT DO AN ENCORE--
SHOOM
ZOINKS!
--BUT I DON'T THINK WE HAVE A CHOICE!

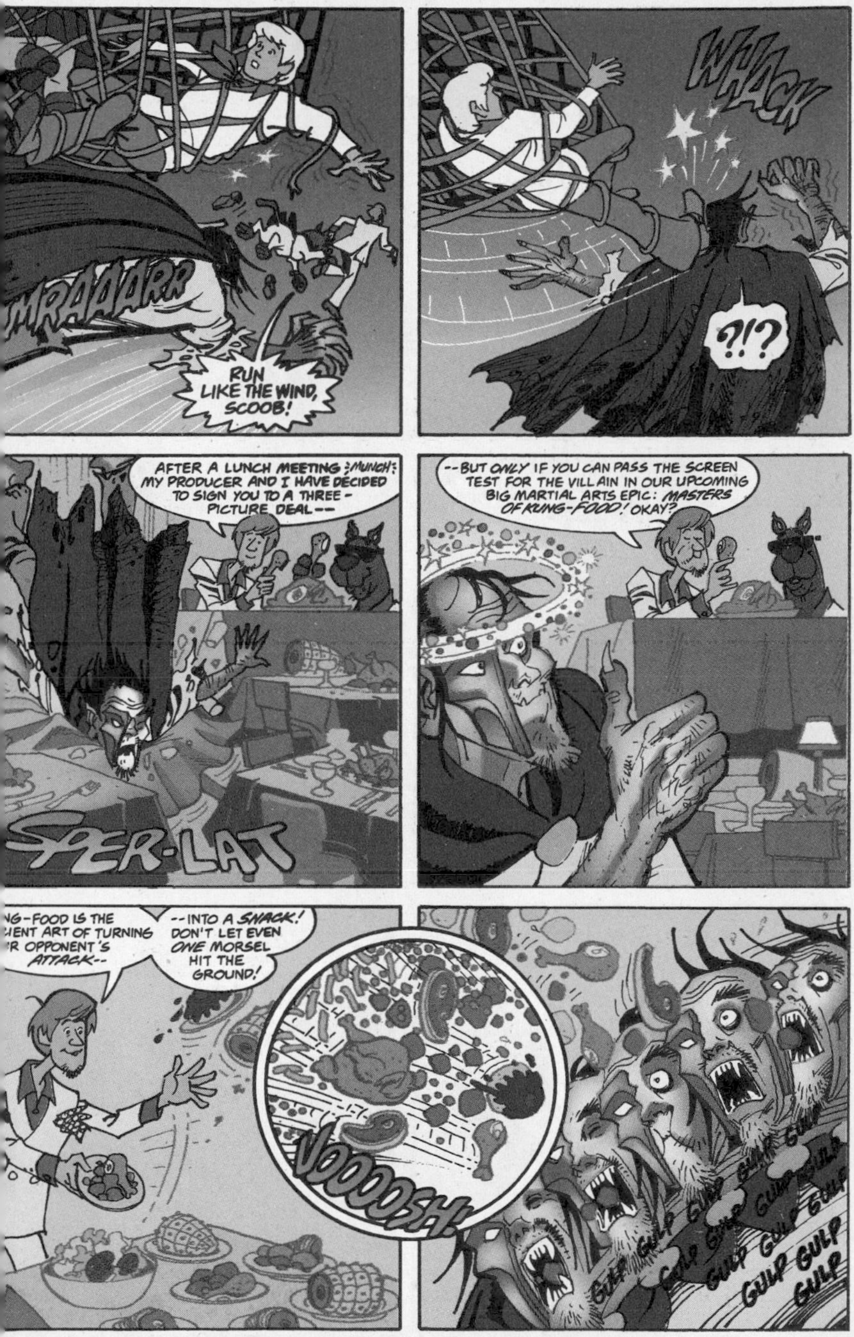
MRAAAARR
RUN LIKE THE WIND, SCOOB!
WHACK
?!?
AFTER A LUNCH MEETING :MUNCH: MY PRODUCER AND I HAVE DECIDED TO SIGN YOU TO A THREE-PICTURE DEAL--
SPER-LAT
--BUT ONLY IF YOU CAN PASS THE SCREEN TEST FOR THE VILLAIN IN OUR UPCOMING BIG MARTIAL ARTS EPIC: MASTERS OF KUNG-FOOD! OKAY?
NG-FOOD IS THE
CIENT ART OF TURNING
R OPPONENT'S
ATTACK--
--INTO A SNACK! DON'T LET EVEN ONE MORSEL HIT THE GROUND!
VOOOOSH
GULP GULP GULP GULP GULP GULP GULP GULP GULP GULP GULP GULP GULP GULP

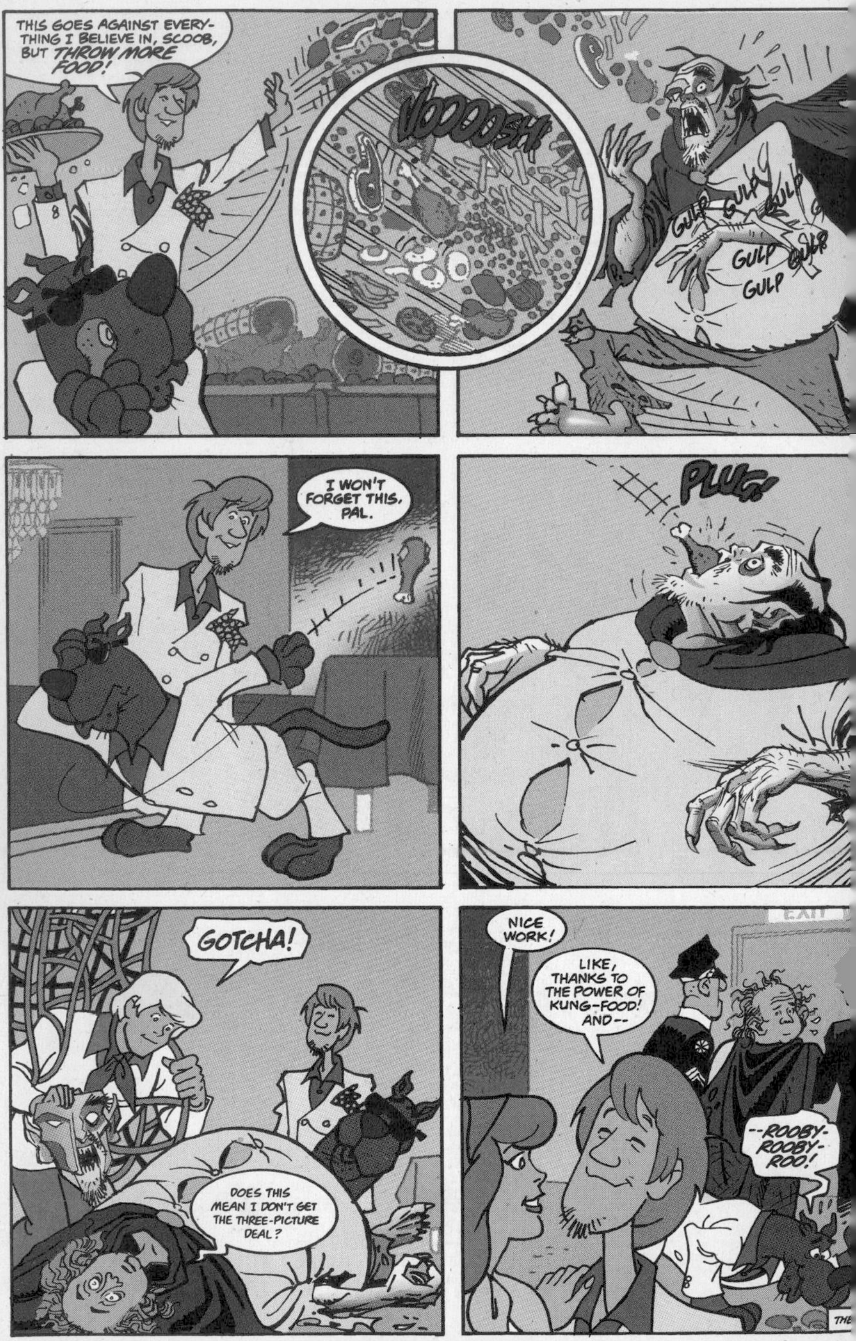
THIS GOES AGAINST EVERYTHING I BELIEVE IN, SCOOB, BUT THROW MORE FOOD!
VOOOOOSH!
GULP GULP GULP GULP GULP GULP
I WON'T FORGET THIS, PAL.
PLUG!
GOTCHA!
DOES THIS MEAN I DON'T GET THE THREE-PICTURE DEAL?
NICE WORK!
LIKE, THANKS TO THE POWER OF KUNG-FOOD! AND--
--ROOBY-ROOBY-ROO!
THE

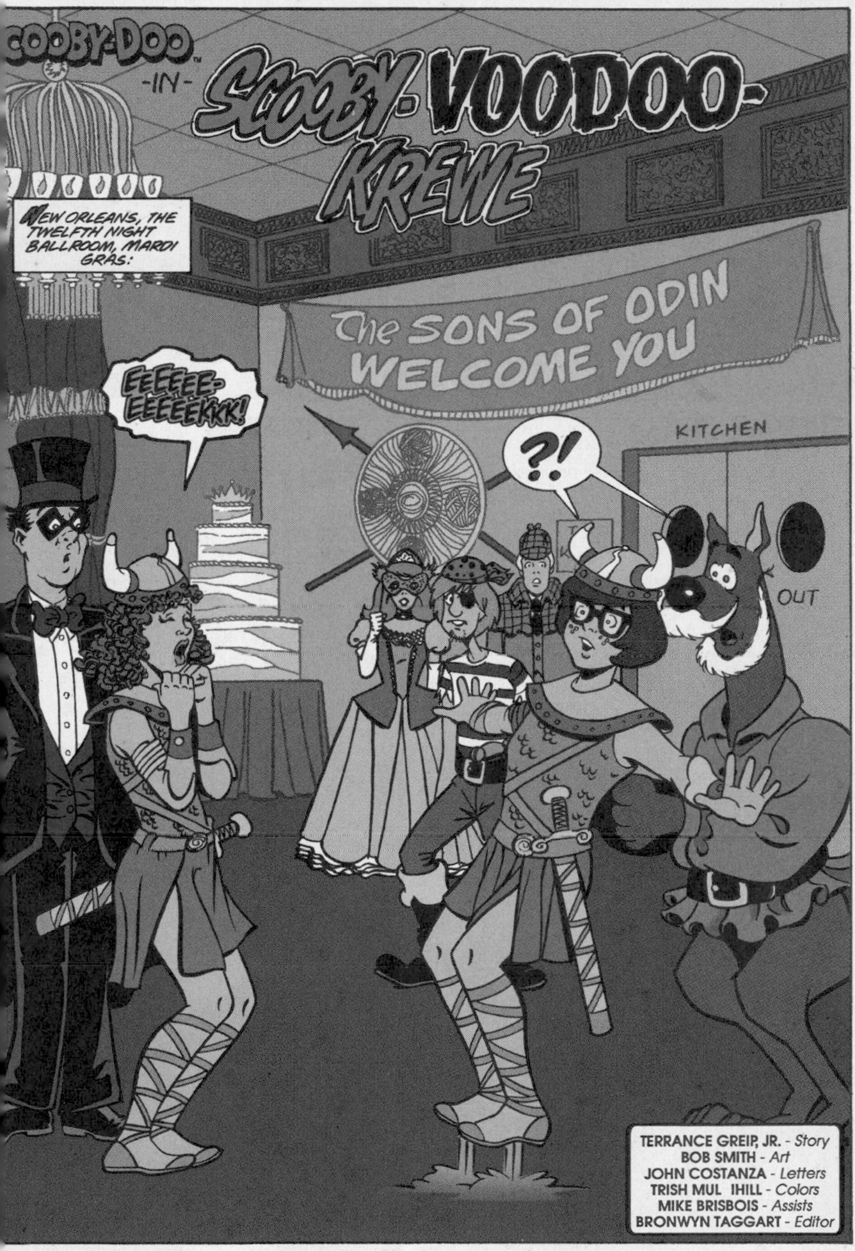
SCOOBY-DOO™
-IN-
SCOOBY-VOODOO-KREWE
NEW ORLEANS, THE TWELFTH NIGHT BALLROOM, MARDI GRAS:
The SONS OF ODIN WELCOME YOU
EEEEEE-EEEEEKKK!
KITCHEN
?!
OUT
TERRANCE GREIP, JR. - Story
BOB SMITH - Art
JOHN COSTANZA - Letters
TRISH MUL IHILL - Colors
MIKE BRISBOIS - Assists
BRONWYN TAGGART - Editor

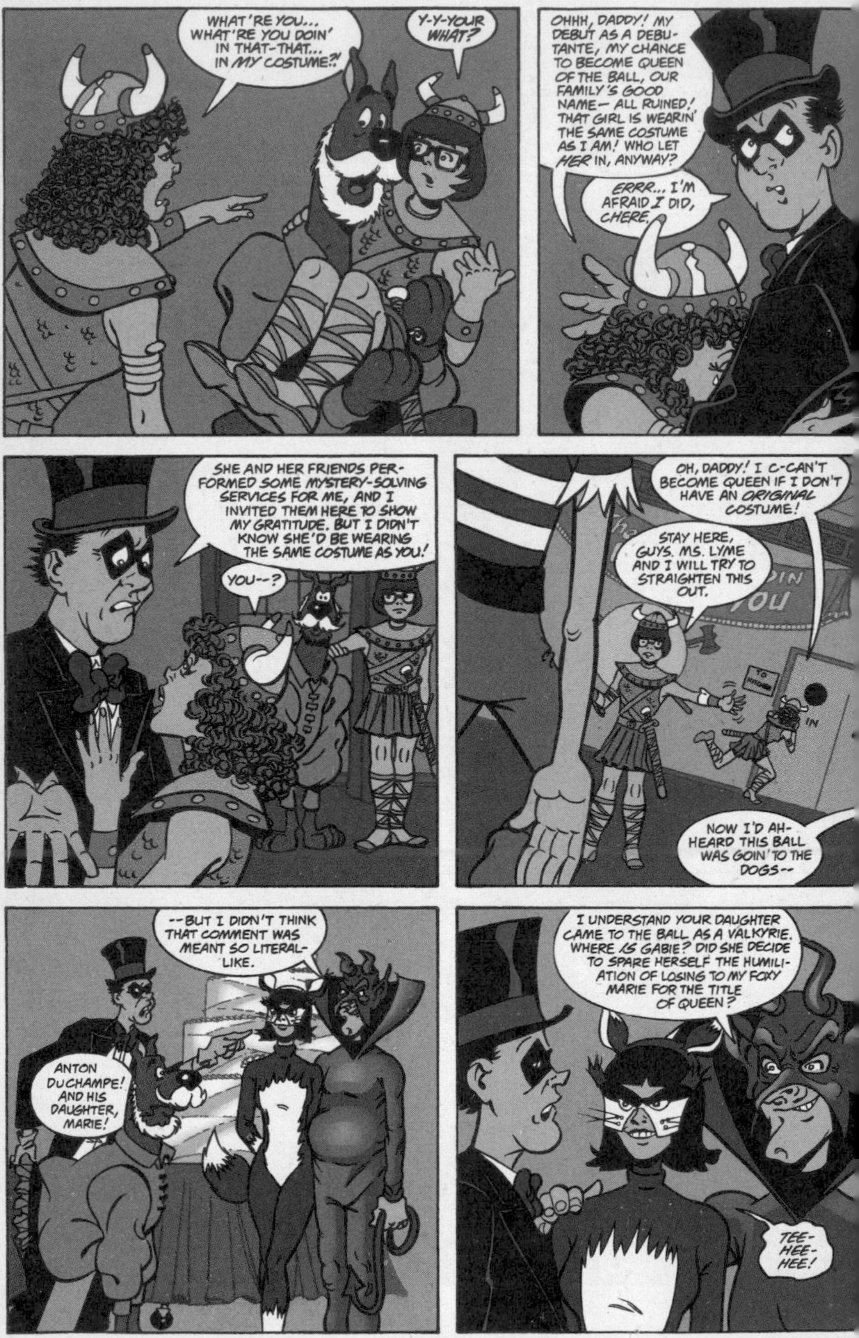
WHAT'RE YOU... WHAT'RE YOU DOIN' IN THAT-THAT... IN MY COSTUME?!
Y-Y-YOUR WHAT?
OHHH, DADDY! MY DEBUT AS A DEBUTANTE, MY CHANCE TO BECOME QUEEN OF THE BALL, OUR FAMILY'S GOOD NAME— ALL RUINED! THAT GIRL IS WEARIN' THE SAME COSTUME AS I AM! WHO LET HER IN, ANYWAY?
ERRR... I'M AFRAID I DID, CHERE.
SHE AND HER FRIENDS PERFORMED SOME MYSTERY-SOLVING SERVICES FOR ME, AND I INVITED THEM HERE TO SHOW MY GRATITUDE. BUT I DIDN'T KNOW SHE'D BE WEARING THE SAME COSTUME AS YOU!
YOU--?
OH, DADDY! I C-CAN'T BECOME QUEEN IF I DON'T HAVE AN ORIGINAL COSTUME!
STAY HERE, GUYS. MS. LYME AND I WILL TRY TO STRAIGHTEN THIS OUT.
NOW I'D AH-HEARD THIS BALL WAS GOIN' TO THE DOGS--
--BUT I DIDN'T THINK THAT COMMENT WAS MEANT SO LITERAL-LIKE.
ANTON DUCHAMPE! AND HIS DAUGHTER, MARIE!
I UNDERSTAND YOUR DAUGHTER CAME TO THE BALL AS A VALKYRIE. WHERE IS GABIE? DID SHE DECIDE TO SPARE HERSELF THE HUMILIATION OF LOSING TO MY FOXY MARIE FOR THE TITLE OF QUEEN?
TEE-HEE-HEE!

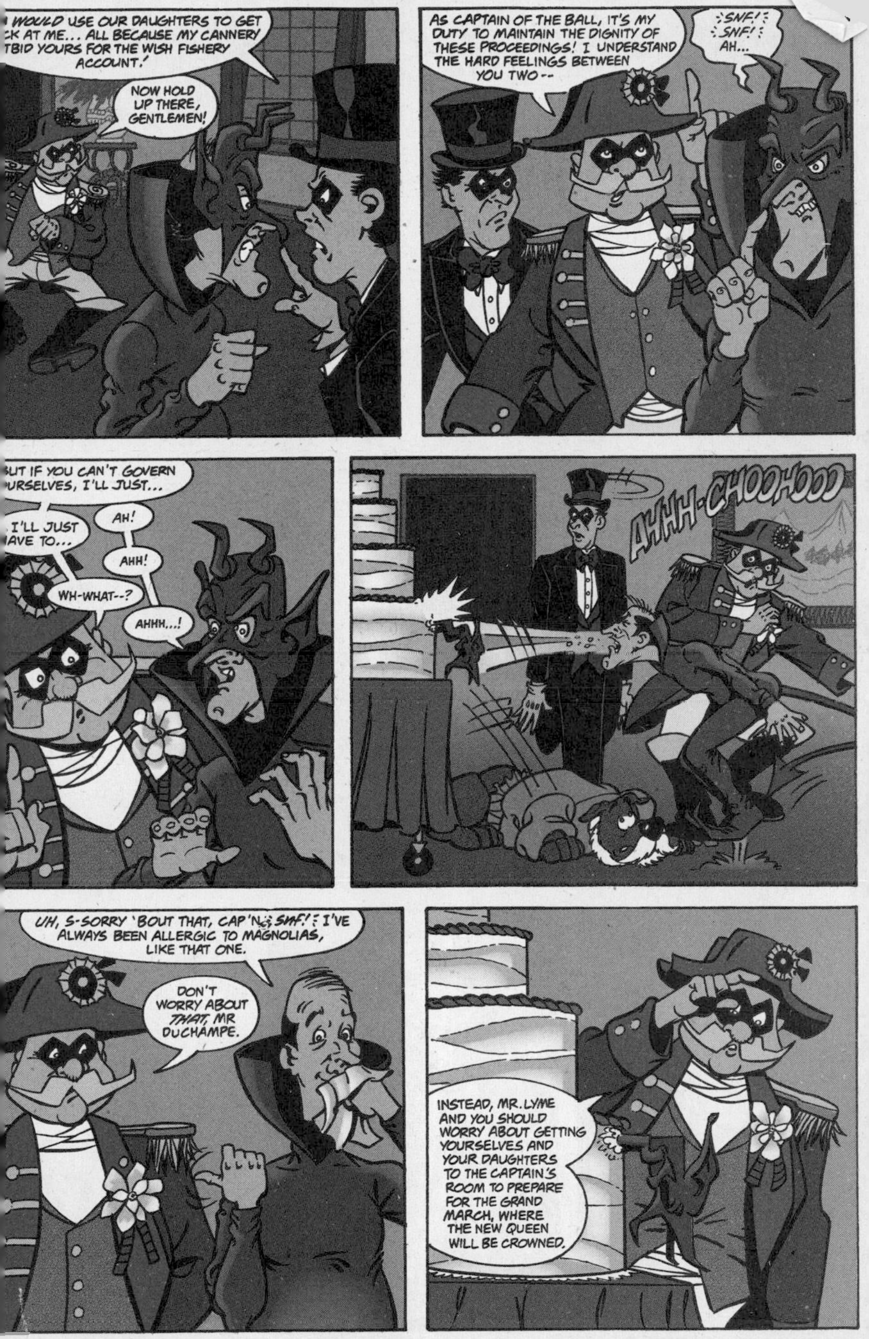
WOULD USE OUR DAUGHTERS TO GET
CK AT ME... ALL BECAUSE MY CANNERY
TBID YOURS FOR THE WISH FISHERY
ACCOUNT.'
NOW HOLD UP THERE, GENTLEMEN!
AS CAPTAIN OF THE BALL, IT'S MY DUTY TO MAINTAIN THE DIGNITY OF THESE PROCEEDINGS! I UNDERSTAND THE HARD FEELINGS BETWEEN YOU TWO--
SNF! SNF! AH...
UT IF YOU CAN'T GOVERN
URSELVES, I'LL JUST...
I'LL JUST
AVE TO...
AH!
AHH!
WH-WHAT--?
AHHH...!
AHHH-CHOOHOOO
UH, S-SORRY 'BOUT THAT, CAP'N SNF! I'VE ALWAYS BEEN ALLERGIC TO MAGNOLIAS, LIKE THAT ONE.
DON'T WORRY ABOUT THAT, MR DUCHAMPE.
INSTEAD, MR. LYME AND YOU SHOULD WORRY ABOUT GETTING YOURSELVES AND YOUR DAUGHTERS TO THE CAPTAIN'S ROOM TO PREPARE FOR THE GRAND MARCH, WHERE THE NEW QUEEN WILL BE CROWNED.

THE CORONATION WILL TAKE PLACE. DESPITE THESE AFFRONTS. OUR KREWE, THE SONS OF ODIN, *MUST* HAVE ITS QUEEN!

EVERYONE'S SEEN OUR PRIDE AND JOY, THE LARGEST KING CAKE OF ANY KREWE. LET'S KEEP IT IN THE KITCHEN UNTIL AFTER THE CORONATION... TO PREVENT ANYTHING *ELSE* FROM HAPPENING TO IT.

OH, SCOO-HOO-HOOOB! THERE GOES THAT BEAUTIFUL CAKE!

ROH, RHE RUMANITY!

YOU KNOW, YOUNGSTERS, THE KING CAKE IS AN IMPORTANT TRADITION. INSIDE *ONE PIECE* IS A PLASTIC BABY--

--AND WHOEVER FINDS IT IS RESPONSIBLE FOR HOSTING NEXT YEAR'S KREWE BALL.

HUH. I MUST BE SQUARE: I THOUGHT CAKES WERE FOR *EATING!*

AHEE HEE HEE HEE!

I KEEP HEARING THE TERM, "KREWE." WHAT'S THAT MEAN, ANYWAY?

WHY, THE KREWES ARE THE MASKING AND PARADING CLUBS THAT HAVE, OVER THE YEARS, *MADE* MARDI GRAS IN NEW ORLEANS!

I COULDN'T FIND MS. LYME ANYWHERE. I HOPE SHE'S ALL RIGHT.

WHAT'S *THAT?*

POOOOFS!

IT'S *NOT A MYSTERY.* REPEAT AFTER ME: "*IT'S NOT A MYSTERY.*"

RIT'S RO, A RYSTER, RIT'S.

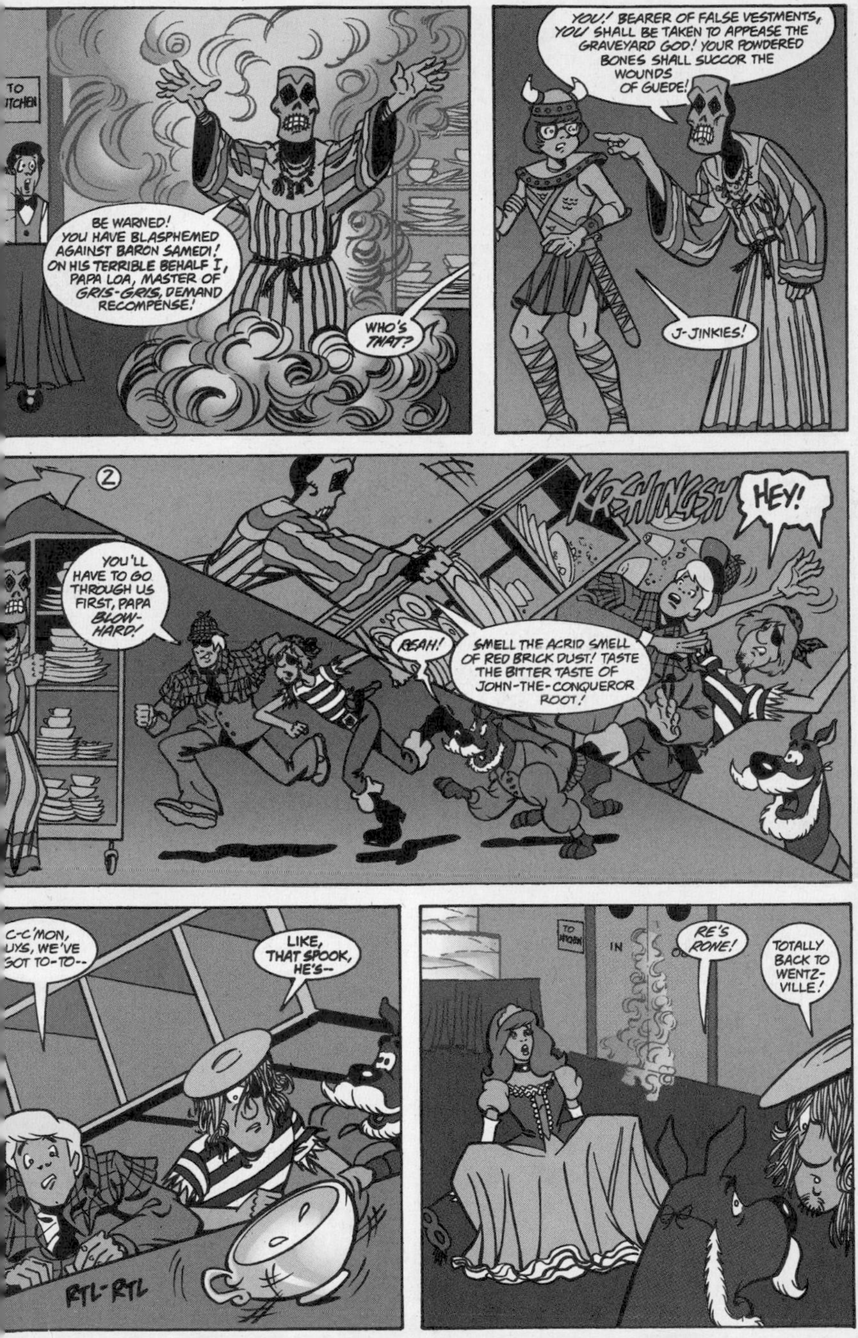
TO KITCHEN
BE WARNED! YOU HAVE BLASPHEMED AGAINST BARON SAMEDI! ON HIS TERRIBLE BEHALF I, PAPA LOA, MASTER OF GRIS-GRIS, DEMAND RECOMPENSE!
WHO'S THAT?
YOU! BEARER OF FALSE VESTMENTS, YOU SHALL BE TAKEN TO APPEASE THE GRAVEYARD GOD! YOUR POWDERED BONES SHALL SUCCOR THE WOUNDS OF GUEDE!
J-JINKIES!
YOU'LL HAVE TO GO THROUGH US FIRST, PAPA BLOW-HARD!
KRSHINGSH
HEY!
REAH!
SMELL THE ACRID SMELL OF RED BRICK DUST! TASTE THE BITTER TASTE OF JOHN-THE-CONQUEROR ROOT!
C-C'MON, GUYS, WE'VE GOT TO-TO--
LIKE, THAT SPOOK, HE'S--
RTL-RTL
TO KITCHEN
IN
RE'S RONE!
TOTALLY BACK TO WENTZVILLE!

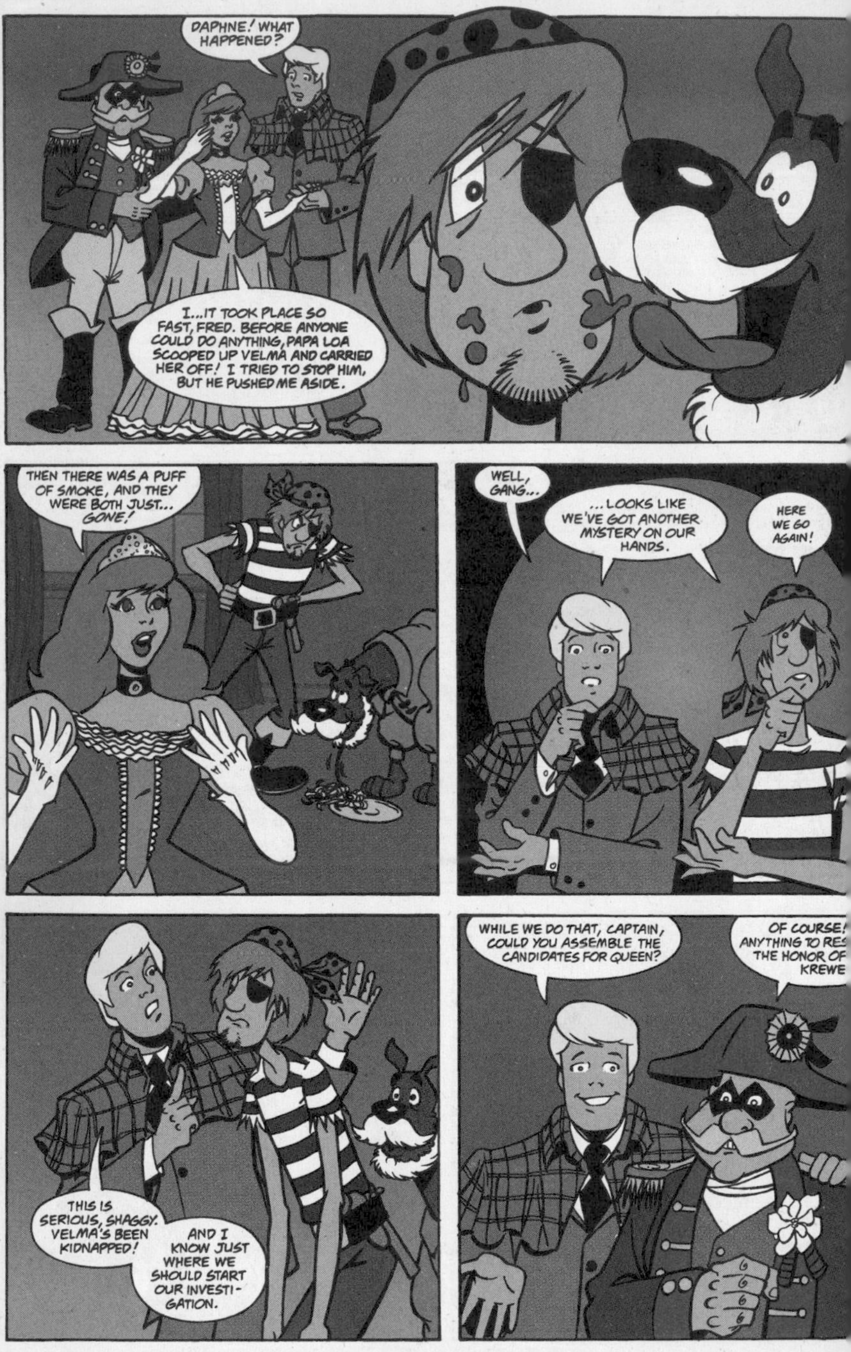
DAPHNE! WHAT HAPPENED?
I...IT TOOK PLACE SO FAST, FRED. BEFORE ANYONE COULD DO ANYTHING, PAPA LOA SCOOPED UP VELMA AND CARRIED HER OFF! I TRIED TO STOP HIM, BUT HE PUSHED ME ASIDE.
THEN THERE WAS A PUFF OF SMOKE, AND THEY WERE BOTH JUST... GONE!
WELL, GANG...
...LOOKS LIKE WE'VE GOT ANOTHER MYSTERY ON OUR HANDS.
HERE WE GO AGAIN!
THIS IS SERIOUS, SHAGGY. VELMA'S BEEN KIDNAPPED!
AND I KNOW JUST WHERE WE SHOULD START OUR INVESTI-GATION.
WHILE WE DO THAT, CAPTAIN, COULD YOU ASSEMBLE THE CANDIDATES FOR QUEEN?
OF COURSE! ANYTHING TO RES
THE HONOR OF
KREWE

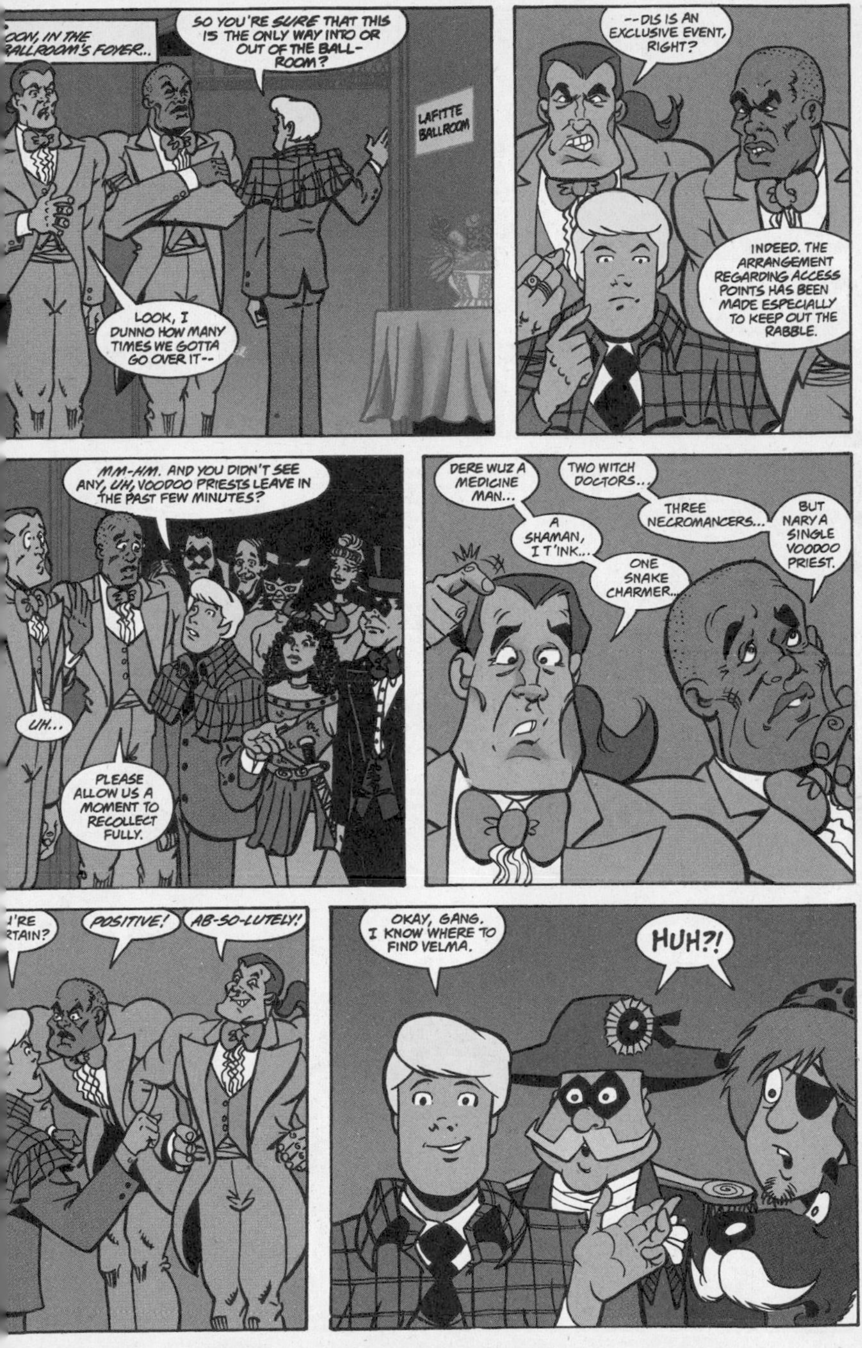
...OON, IN THE BALLROOM'S FOYER...
SO YOU'RE SURE THAT THIS IS THE ONLY WAY INTO OR OUT OF THE BALLROOM?
LAFITTE BALLROOM
LOOK, I DUNNO HOW MANY TIMES WE GOTTA GO OVER IT--
--DIS IS AN EXCLUSIVE EVENT, RIGHT?
INDEED. THE ARRANGEMENT REGARDING ACCESS POINTS HAS BEEN MADE ESPECIALLY TO KEEP OUT THE RABBLE.
MM-HM. AND YOU DIDN'T SEE ANY, UH, VOODOO PRIESTS LEAVE IN THE PAST FEW MINUTES?
UH...
PLEASE ALLOW US A MOMENT TO RECOLLECT FULLY.
DERE WUZ A MEDICINE MAN...
TWO WITCH DOCTORS...
A SHAMAN, I T'INK...
THREE NECROMANCERS...
ONE SNAKE CHARMER...
BUT NARY A SINGLE VOODOO PRIEST.
...'RE ...TAIN?
POSITIVE!
AB-SO-LUTELY!
OKAY, GANG. I KNOW WHERE TO FIND VELMA.
HUH?!

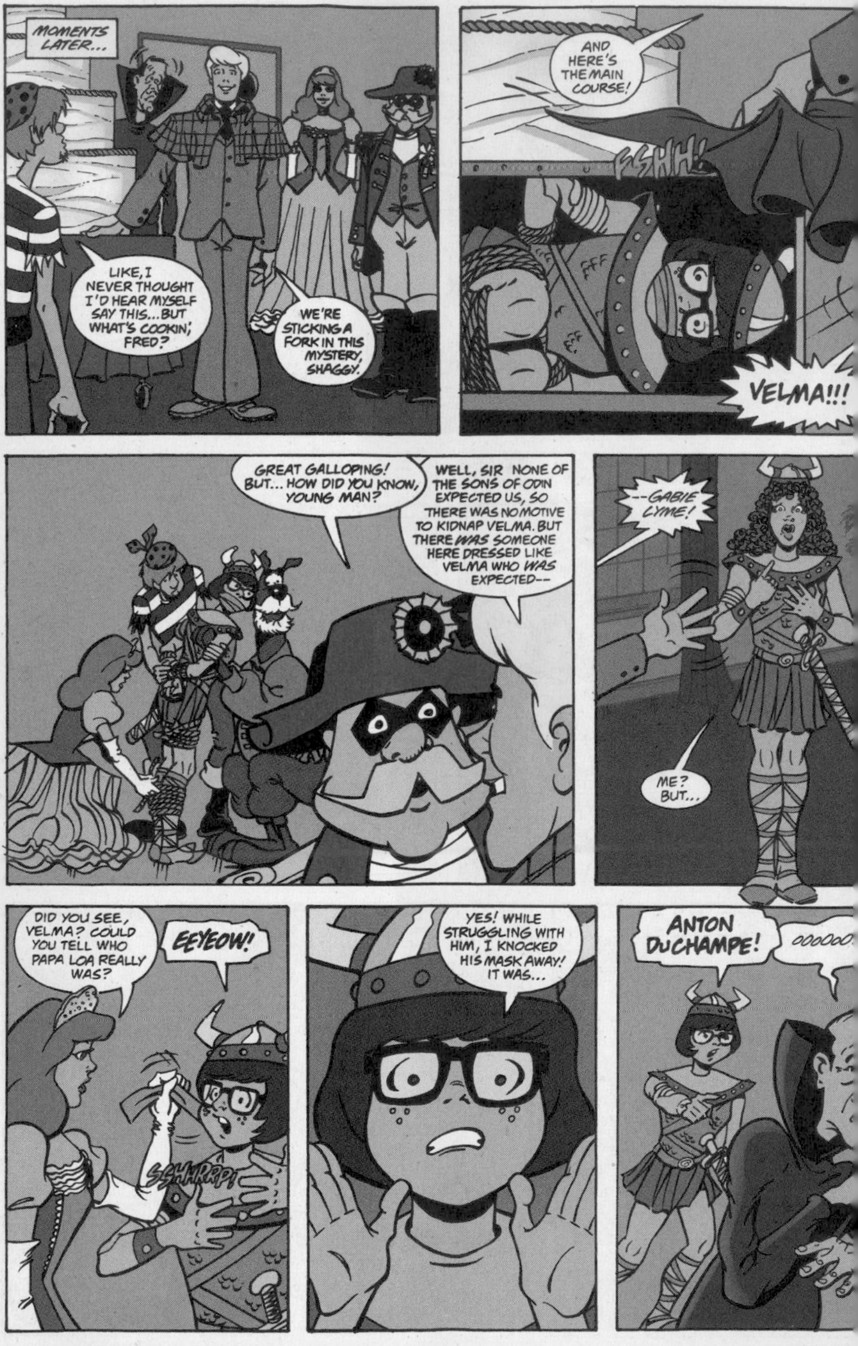
MOMENTS LATER...
LIKE, I NEVER THOUGHT I'D HEAR MYSELF SAY THIS... BUT WHAT'S COOKIN', FRED?
WE'RE STICKING A FORK IN THIS MYSTERY, SHAGGY.
AND HERE'S THE MAIN COURSE!
FSHH!
VELMA!!!
GREAT GALLOPING! BUT... HOW DID YOU KNOW, YOUNG MAN?
WELL, SIR NONE OF THE SONS OF ODIN EXPECTED US, SO THERE WAS NO MOTIVE TO KIDNAP VELMA. BUT THERE WAS SOMEONE HERE DRESSED LIKE VELMA WHO WAS EXPECTED--
--GABIE LYME!
ME? BUT...
DID YOU SEE, VELMA? COULD YOU TELL WHO PAPA LOA REALLY WAS?
EEYEOW!
SSHHRRP!
YES! WHILE STRUGGLING WITH HIM, I KNOCKED HIS MASK AWAY! IT WAS...
ANTON DUCHAMPE!
OOOOOO

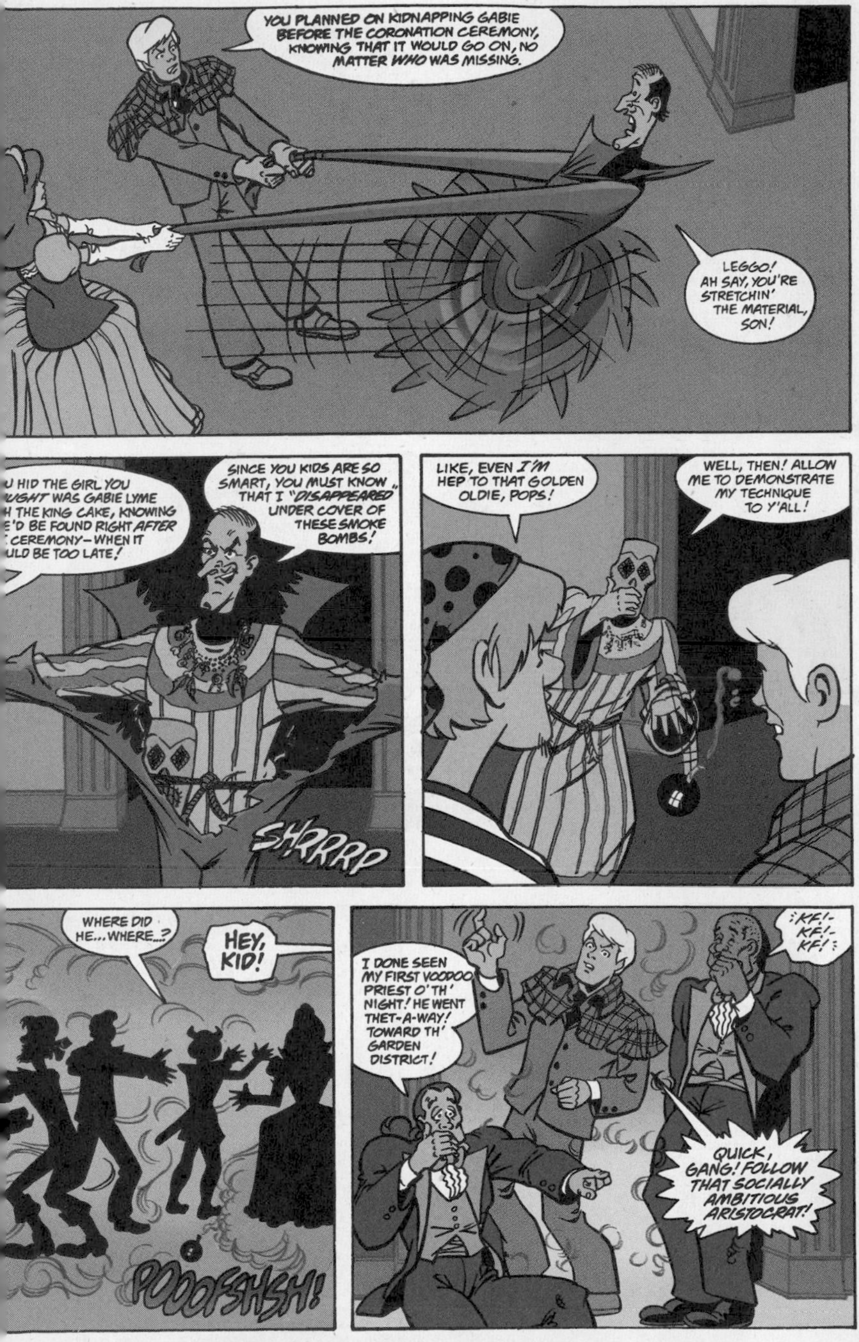
YOU PLANNED ON KIDNAPPING GABIE BEFORE THE CORONATION CEREMONY, KNOWING THAT IT WOULD GO ON, NO MATTER WHO WAS MISSING.
LEGGO! AH SAY, YOU'RE STRETCHIN' THE MATERIAL, SON!
U HID THE GIRL YOU UGHT WAS GABIE LYME H THE KING CAKE, KNOWING E'D BE FOUND RIGHT AFTER CEREMONY—WHEN IT ULD BE TOO LATE!
SINCE YOU KIDS ARE SO SMART, YOU MUST KNOW THAT I "DISAPPEARED" UNDER COVER OF THESE SMOKE BOMBS!
SHRRRP
LIKE, EVEN I'M HEP TO THAT GOLDEN OLDIE, POPS!
WELL, THEN! ALLOW ME TO DEMONSTRATE MY TECHNIQUE TO Y'ALL!
WHERE DID HE... WHERE...?
HEY, KID!
POOOFSHSH!
I DONE SEEN MY FIRST VOODOO PRIEST O' TH' NIGHT! HE WENT THET-A-WAY! TOWARD TH' GARDEN DISTRICT!
KF!-KF!-KF!
QUICK, GANG! FOLLOW THAT SOCIALLY AMBITIOUS ARISTOCRAT!

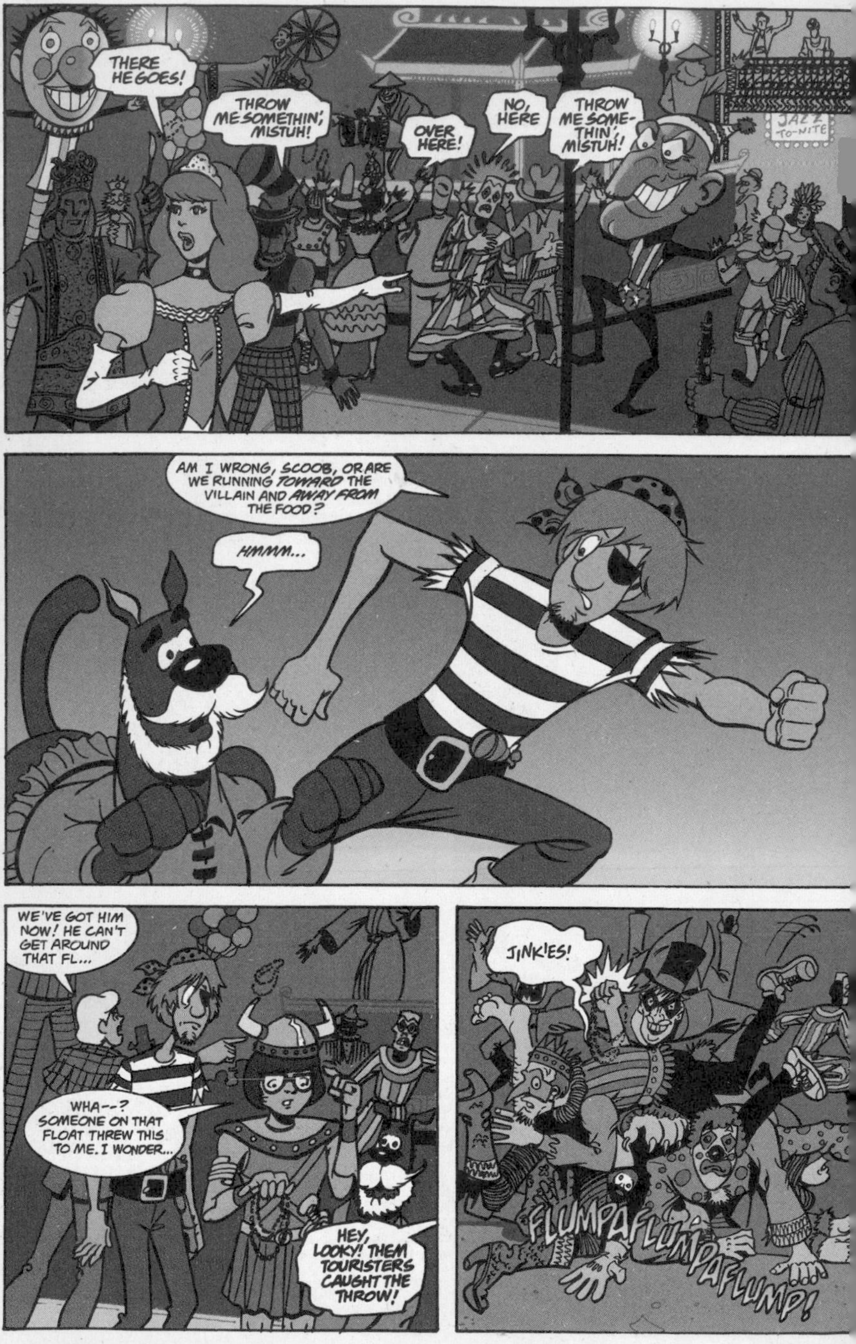

THERE HE GOES!
THROW ME SOMETHIN', MISTUH!
OVER HERE!
NO, HERE
THROW ME SOMETHIN', MISTUH!
JAZZ TO-NITE
AM I WRONG, SCOOB, OR ARE WE RUNNING *TOWARD* THE VILLAIN AND *AWAY FROM* THE FOOD?
HMMM...
WE'VE GOT HIM NOW! HE CAN'T GET AROUND THAT FL...
WHA--? SOMEONE ON THAT FLOAT THREW THIS TO ME. I WONDER...
HEY, LOOKY! THEM TOURISTERS CAUGHT THE THROW!
JINKIES!
FLUMPAFLUMPAFLUMP!

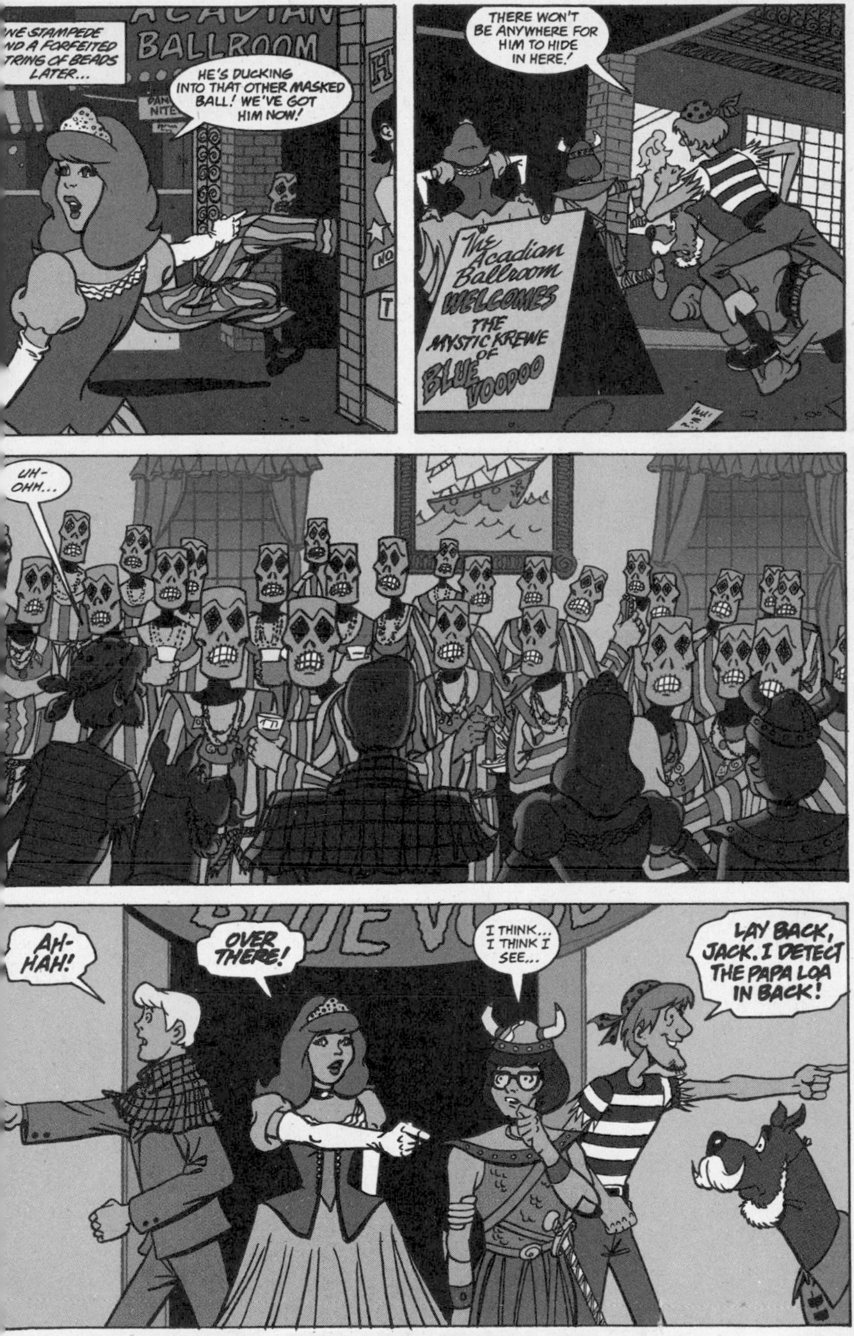
NE STAMPEDE
ND A FORFEITED
TRING OF BEADS
LATER...
BALLROOM
HE'S DUCKING INTO THAT OTHER MASKED BALL! WE'VE GOT HIM NOW!
THERE WON'T BE ANYWHERE FOR HIM TO HIDE IN HERE!
The Acadian Ballroom WELCOMES THE MYSTIC KREWE OF BLUE VOODOO
UH-OHH...
AH-HAH!
OVER THERE!
I THINK... I THINK I SEE...
LAY BACK, JACK. I DETECT THE PAPA LOA IN BACK!

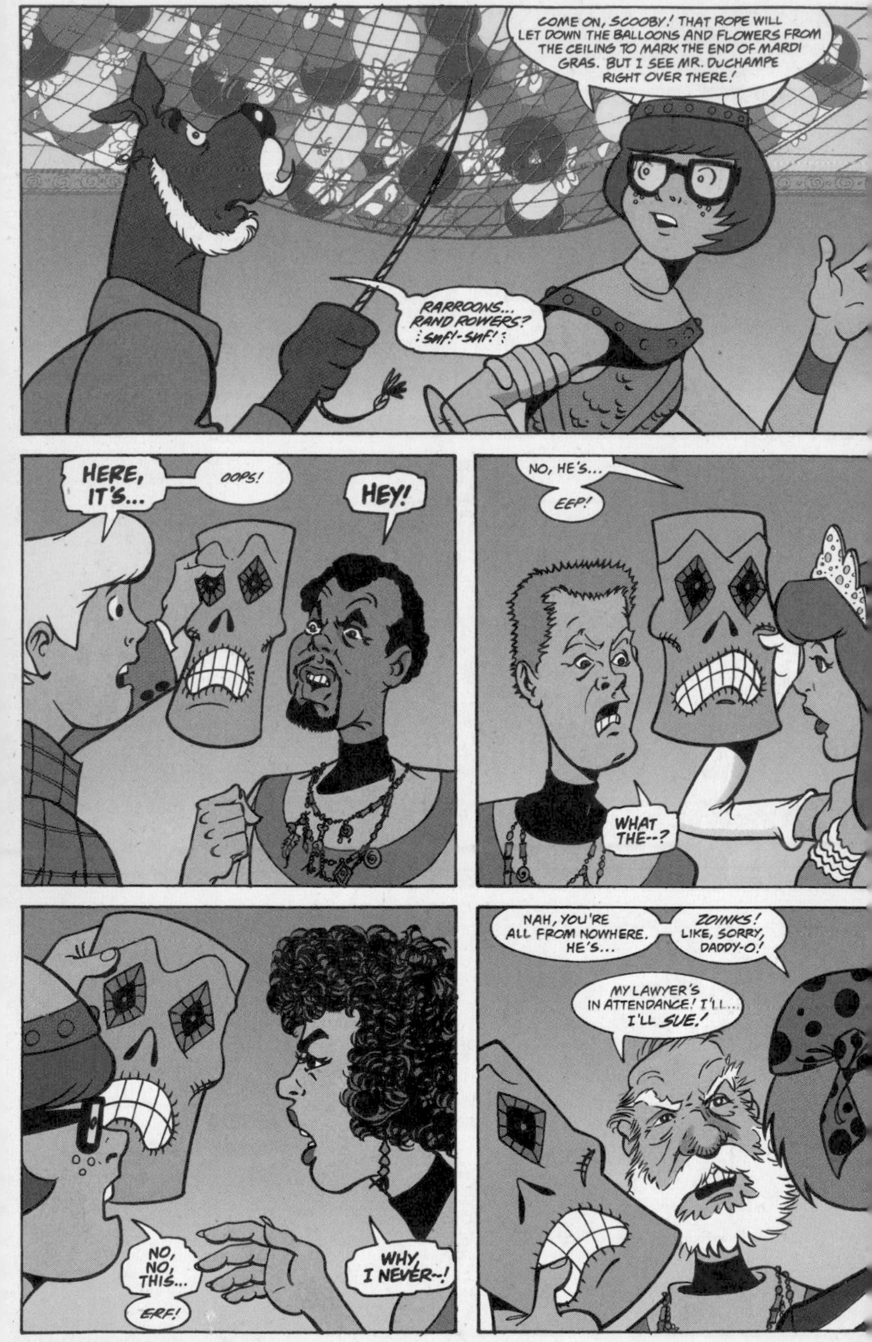
COME ON, SCOOBY! THAT ROPE WILL LET DOWN THE BALLOONS AND FLOWERS FROM THE CEILING TO MARK THE END OF MARDI GRAS. BUT I SEE MR. DUCHAMPE RIGHT OVER THERE!
RARROONS... RAND ROWERS? snf!-snf!
HERE, IT'S...
OOPS!
HEY!
NO, HE'S...
EEP!
WHAT THE--?
NO, NO, THIS...
ERF!
WHY, I NEVER--!
NAH, YOU'RE ALL FROM NOWHERE. HE'S...
ZOINKS! LIKE, SORRY, DADDY-O!
MY LAWYER'S IN ATTENDANCE! I'LL... I'LL SUE!

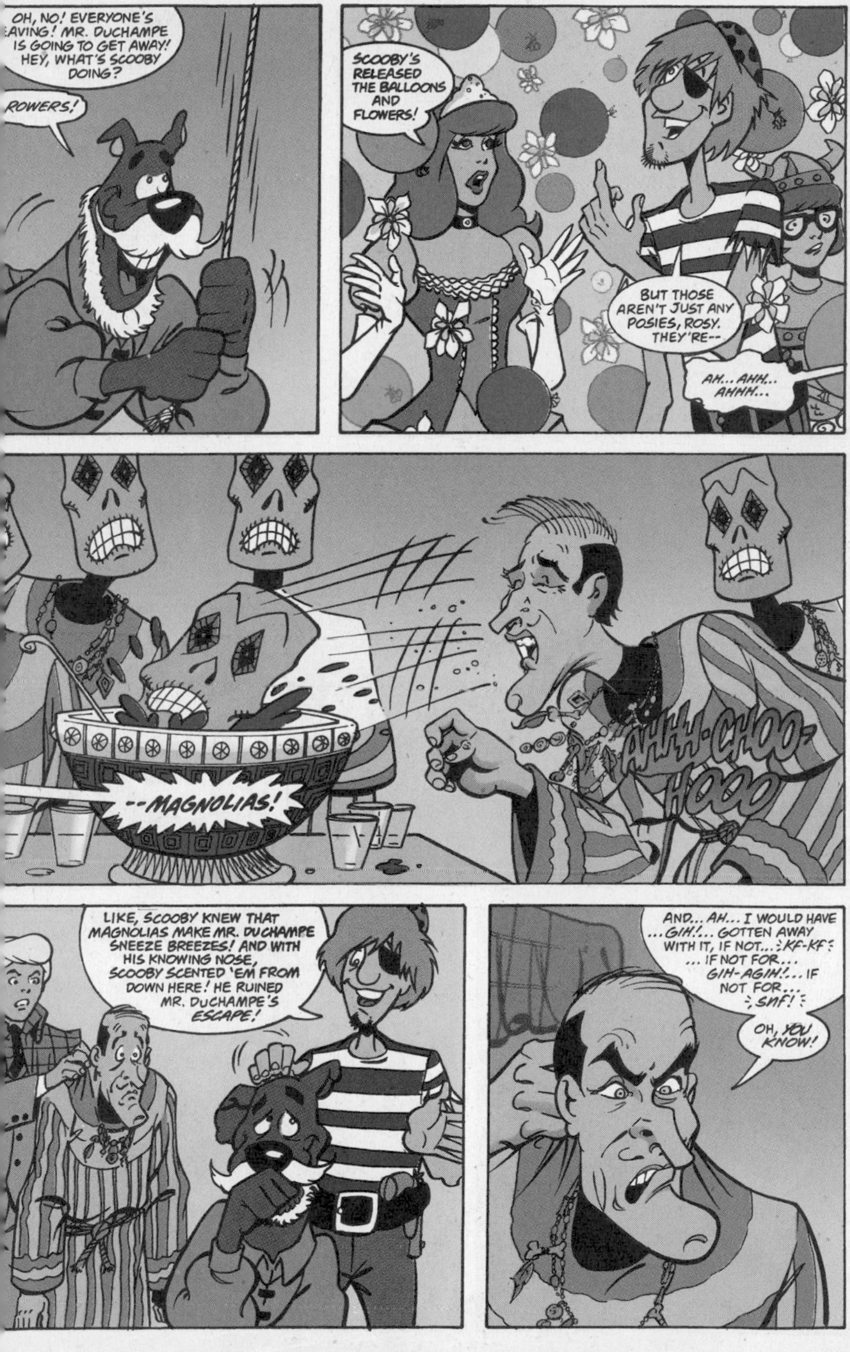
OH, NO! EVERYONE'S LEAVING! MR. DUCHAMPE IS GOING TO GET AWAY! HEY, WHAT'S SCOOBY DOING?
ROWERS!
SCOOBY'S RELEASED THE BALLOONS AND FLOWERS!
BUT THOSE AREN'T JUST ANY POSIES, ROSY. THEY'RE--
AH... AHH... AHHH...
--MAGNOLIAS!
AHH-CHOO-HOOO
LIKE, SCOOBY KNEW THAT MAGNOLIAS MAKE MR. DUCHAMPE SNEEZE BREEZES! AND WITH HIS KNOWING NOSE, SCOOBY SCENTED 'EM FROM DOWN HERE! HE RUINED MR. DUCHAMPE'S ESCAPE!
AND... AH... I WOULD HAVE ...GIH!... GOTTEN AWAY WITH IT, IF NOT... KF-KF ... IF NOT FOR... GIH-AGIH!... IF NOT FOR... SNF!
OH, YOU KNOW!

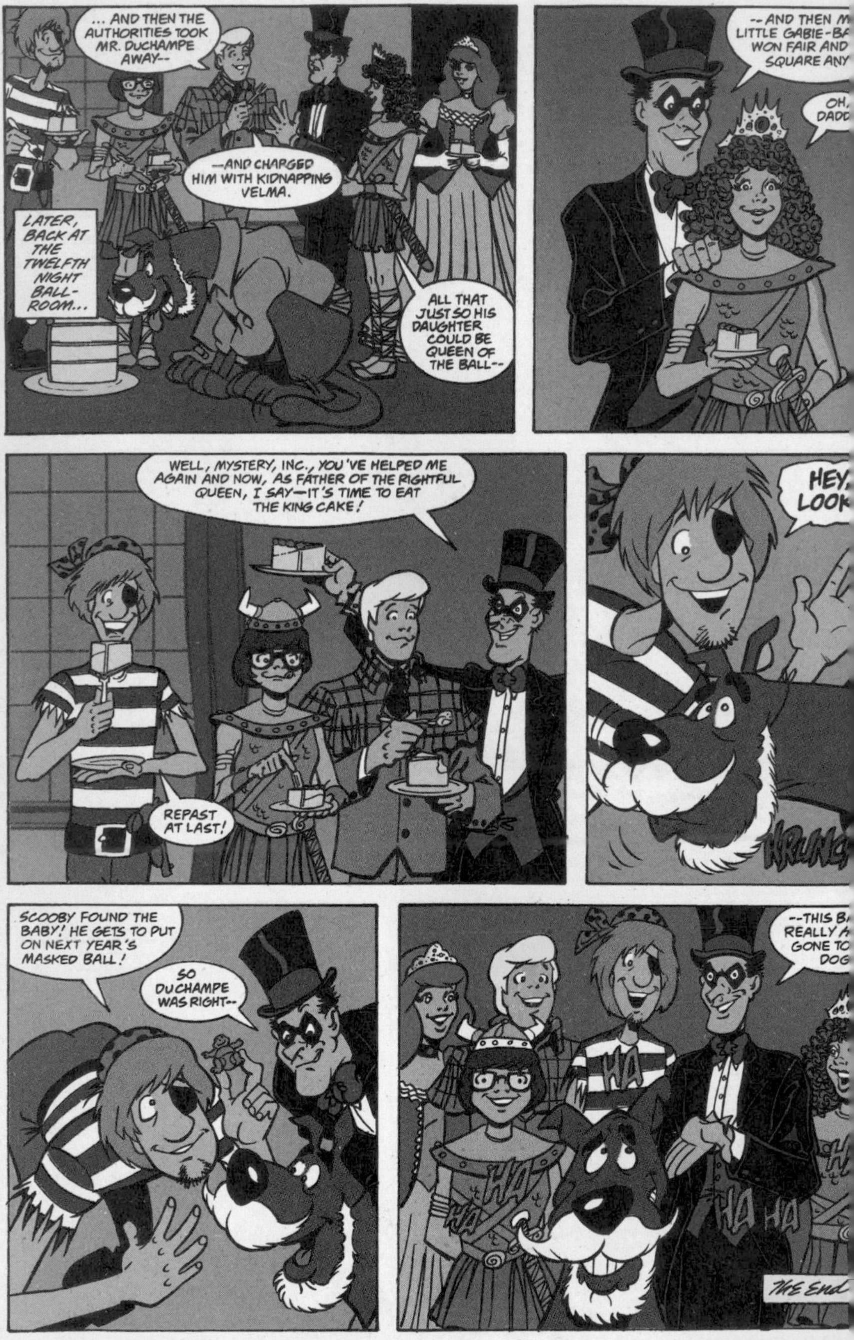
LATER, BACK AT THE TWELFTH NIGHT BALL-ROOM...
... AND THEN THE AUTHORITIES TOOK MR. DUCHAMPE AWAY--
--AND CHARGED HIM WITH KIDNAPPING VELMA.
ALL THAT JUST SO HIS DAUGHTER COULD BE QUEEN OF THE BALL--
-- AND THEN M LITTLE GABIE-BA WON FAIR AND SQUARE ANY
OH, DADD
WELL, MYSTERY, INC., YOU'VE HELPED ME AGAIN AND NOW, AS FATHER OF THE RIGHTFUL QUEEN, I SAY—IT'S TIME TO EAT THE KING CAKE!
REPAST AT LAST!
HEY, LOOK
SCOOBY FOUND THE BABY! HE GETS TO PUT ON NEXT YEAR'S MASKED BALL!
SO DUCHAMPE WAS RIGHT--
--THIS B REALLY GONE TO DOG
HA HA HA HA HA
THE End

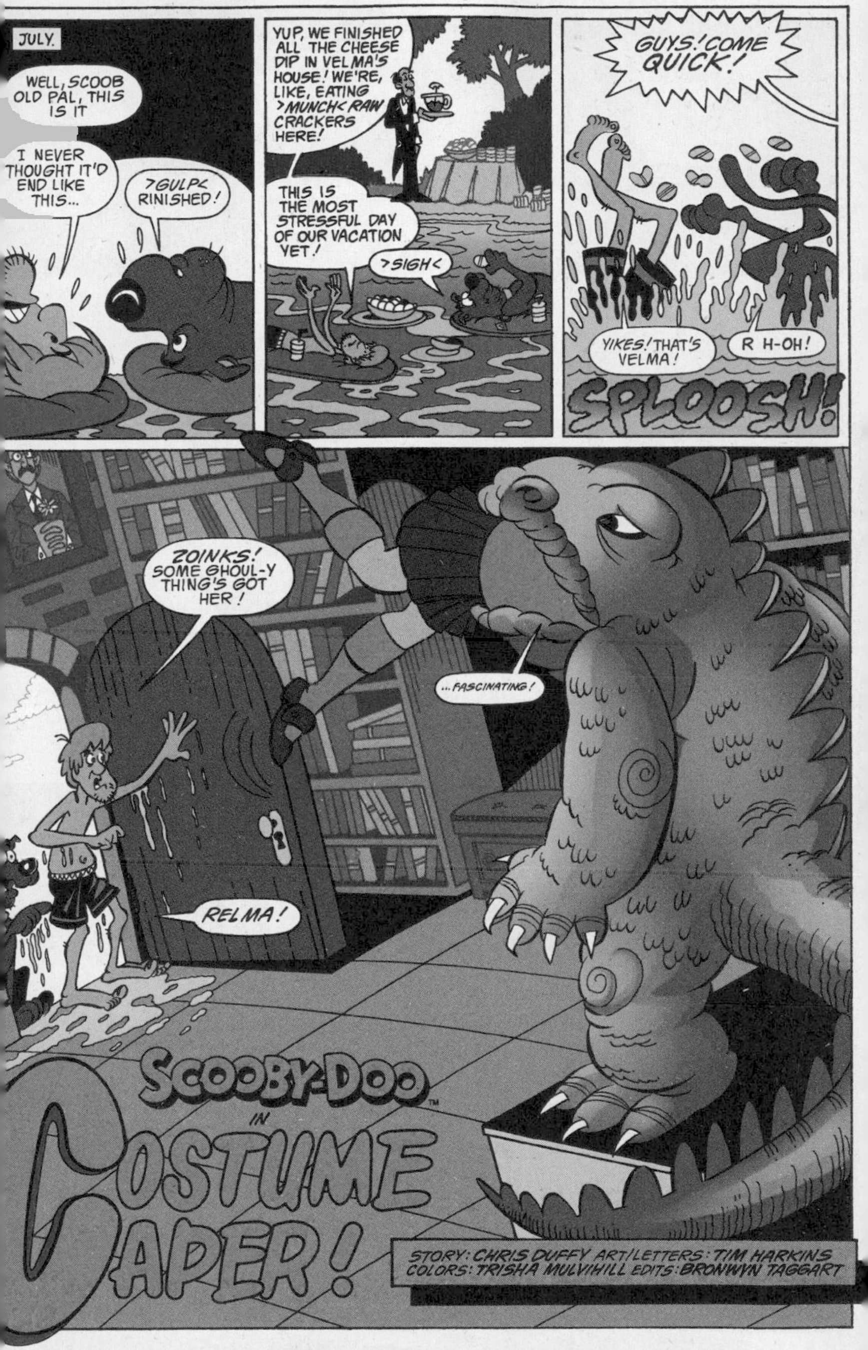
JULY.
WELL, SCOOB OLD PAL, THIS IS IT
I NEVER THOUGHT IT'D END LIKE THIS...
>GULP< RINISHED!
YUP, WE FINISHED ALL THE CHEESE DIP IN VELMA'S HOUSE! WE'RE, LIKE, EATING >MUNCH< RAW CRACKERS HERE!
THIS IS THE MOST STRESSFUL DAY OF OUR VACATION YET!
>SIGH<
GUYS! COME QUICK!
YIKES! THAT'S VELMA!
R H-OH!
SPLOOSH!
ZOINKS! SOME GHOUL-Y THING'S GOT HER!
...FASCINATING!
RELMA!
SCOOBY-DOO™
IN
COSTUME CAPER!
STORY: CHRIS DUFFY ART/LETTERS: TIM HARKINS
COLORS: TRISHA MULVIHILL EDITS: BRONWYN TAGGART

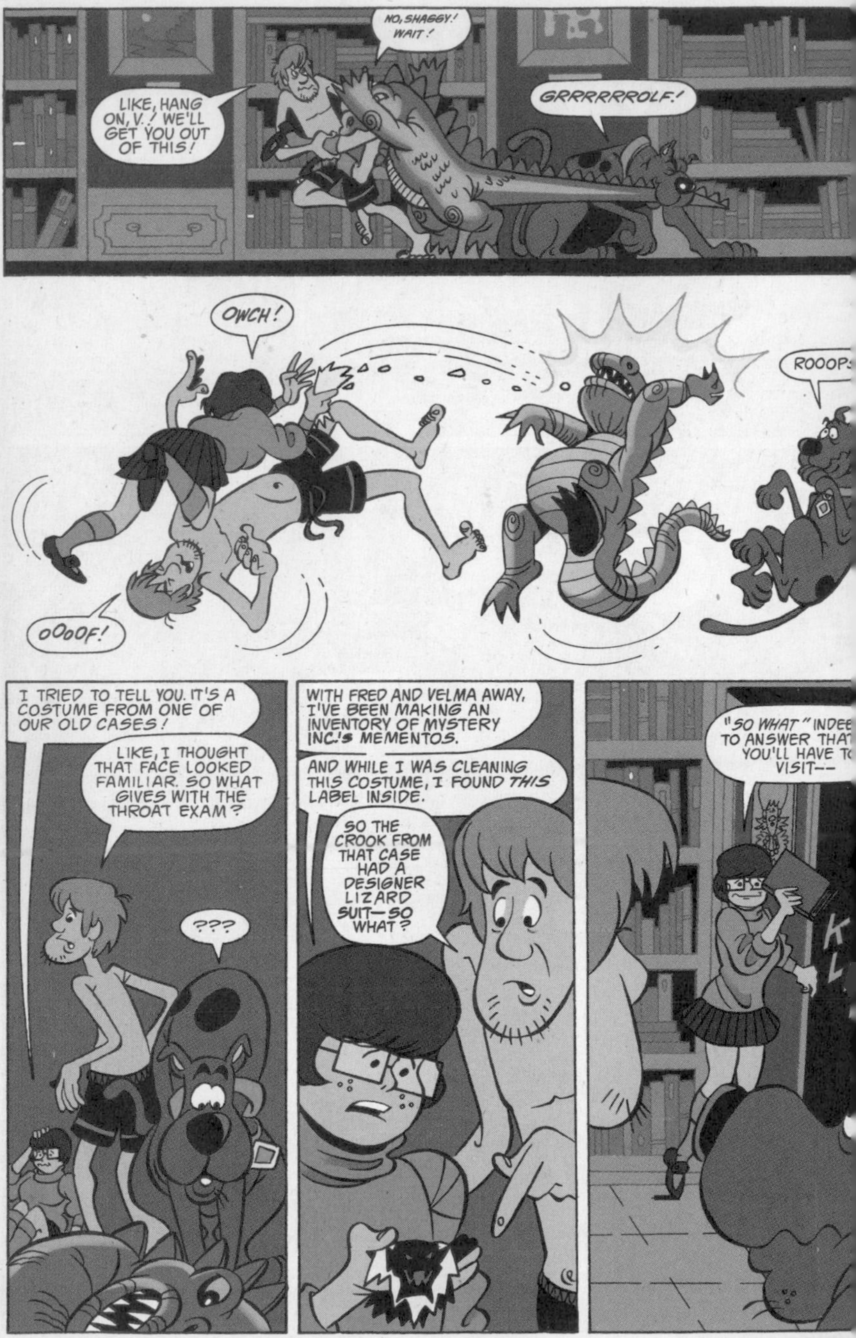
NO, SHAGGY! WAIT!
LIKE, HANG ON, V.! WE'LL GET YOU OUT OF THIS!
GRRRRRROLF!
OWCH!
ROOOPS
OOOOF!
I TRIED TO TELL YOU. IT'S A COSTUME FROM ONE OF OUR OLD CASES!
LIKE, I THOUGHT THAT FACE LOOKED FAMILIAR. SO WHAT GIVES WITH THE THROAT EXAM?
???
WITH FRED AND VELMA AWAY, I'VE BEEN MAKING AN INVENTORY OF MYSTERY INC.'S MEMENTOS.
AND WHILE I WAS CLEANING THIS COSTUME, I FOUND THIS LABEL INSIDE.
SO THE CROOK FROM THAT CASE HAD A DESIGNER LIZARD SUIT—SO WHAT?
"SO WHAT" INDEE TO ANSWER THAT YOU'LL HAVE T VISIT--

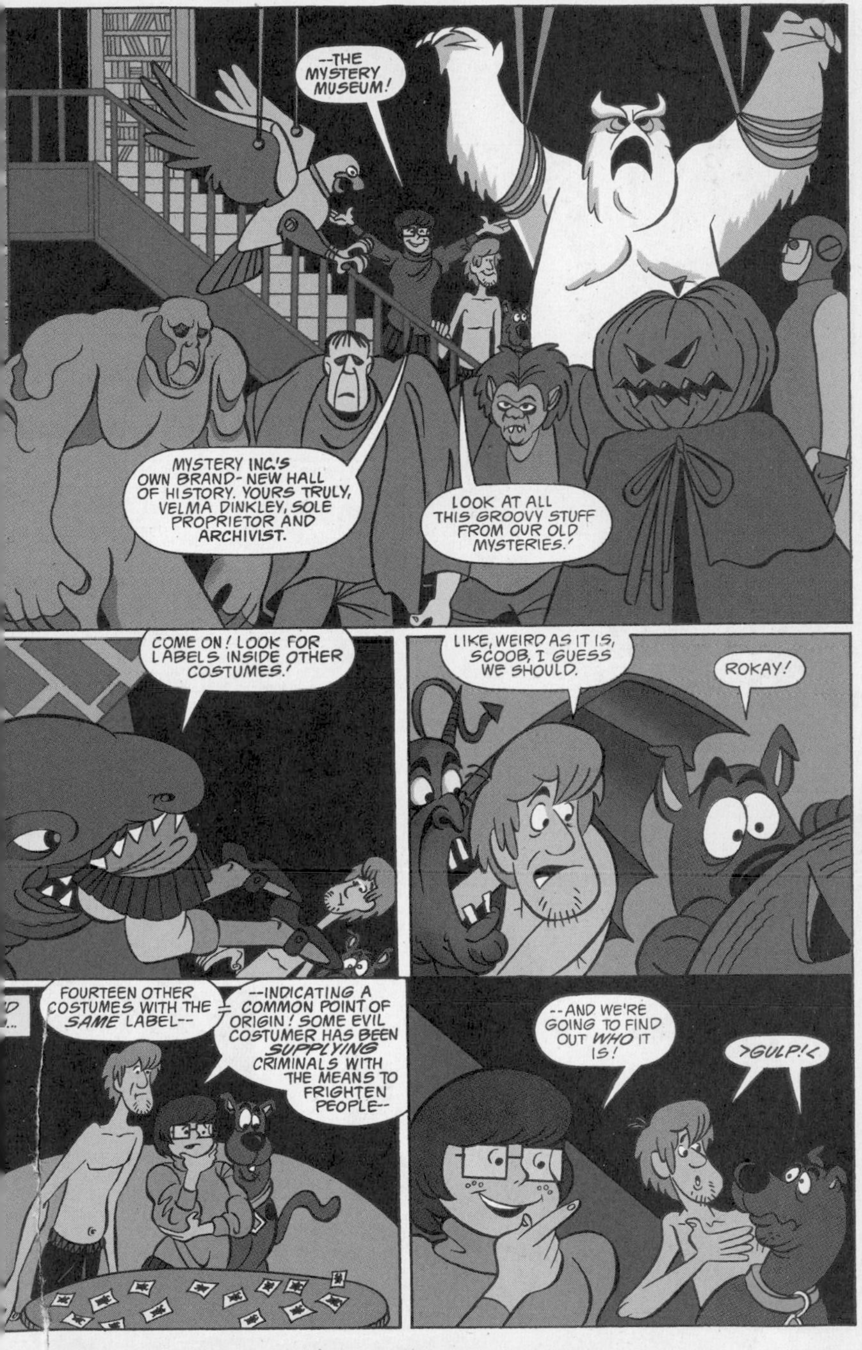
--THE MYSTERY MUSEUM!
MYSTERY INC.'S OWN BRAND-NEW HALL OF HISTORY. YOURS TRULY, VELMA DINKLEY, SOLE PROPRIETOR AND ARCHIVIST.
LOOK AT ALL THIS GROOVY STUFF FROM OUR OLD MYSTERIES!
COME ON! LOOK FOR LABELS INSIDE OTHER COSTUMES!
LIKE, WEIRD AS IT IS, SCOOB, I GUESS WE SHOULD.
ROKAY!
FOURTEEN OTHER COSTUMES WITH THE SAME LABEL--
--INDICATING A COMMON POINT OF ORIGIN! SOME EVIL COSTUMER HAS BEEN SUPPLYING CRIMINALS WITH THE MEANS TO FRIGHTEN PEOPLE--
--AND WE'RE GOING TO FIND OUT WHO IT IS!
>GULP!<

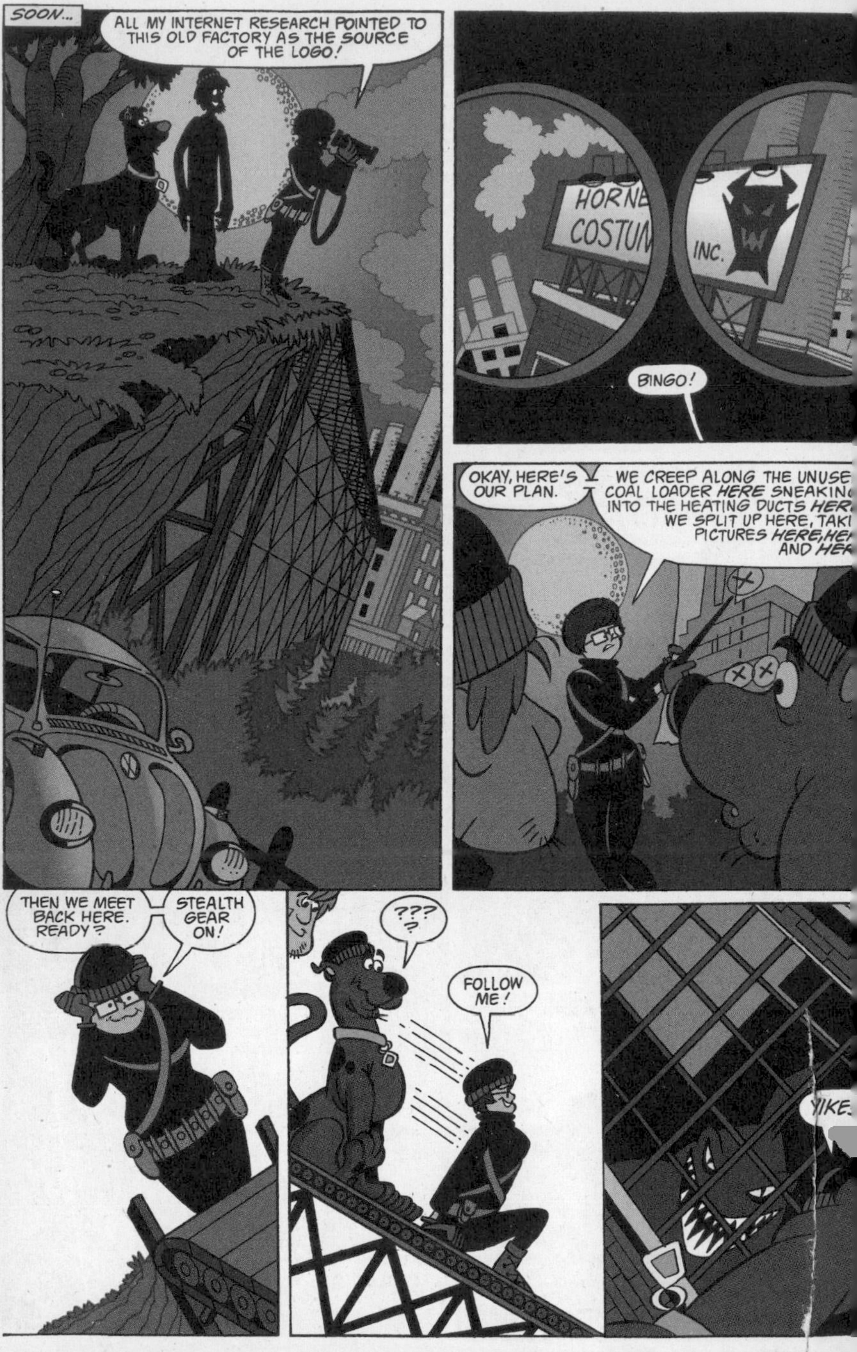
SOON...
ALL MY INTERNET RESEARCH POINTED TO THIS OLD FACTORY AS THE SOURCE OF THE LOGO!
HORNE
COSTUM
INC.
BINGO!
OKAY, HERE'S OUR PLAN.
WE CREEP ALONG THE UNUSE COAL LOADER HERE SNEAKIN INTO THE HEATING DUCTS HER WE SPLIT UP HERE, TAKI PICTURES HERE, HE AND HE
THEN WE MEET BACK HERE. READY?
STEALTH GEAR ON!
???
?
FOLLOW ME!
YIKE

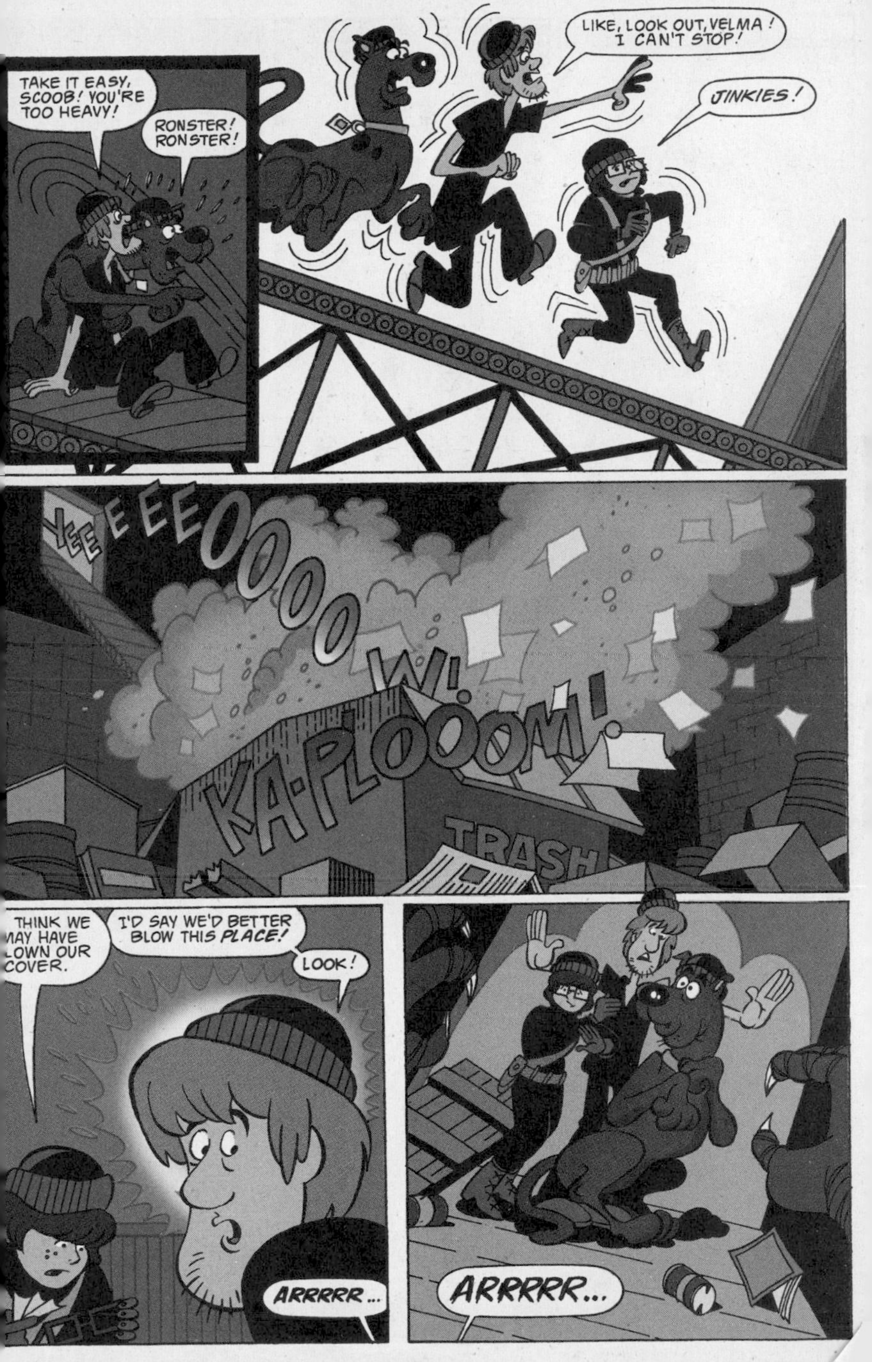
TAKE IT EASY, SCOOB! YOU'RE TOO HEAVY!
RONSTER! RONSTER!
LIKE, LOOK OUT, VELMA! I CAN'T STOP!
JINKIES!
YEE EEEOOOOOW!
KA-PLOOOOM!
TRASH
THINK WE MAY HAVE LOWN OUR COVER.
I'D SAY WE'D BETTER BLOW THIS PLACE!
LOOK!
ARRRRR...
ARRRRR...

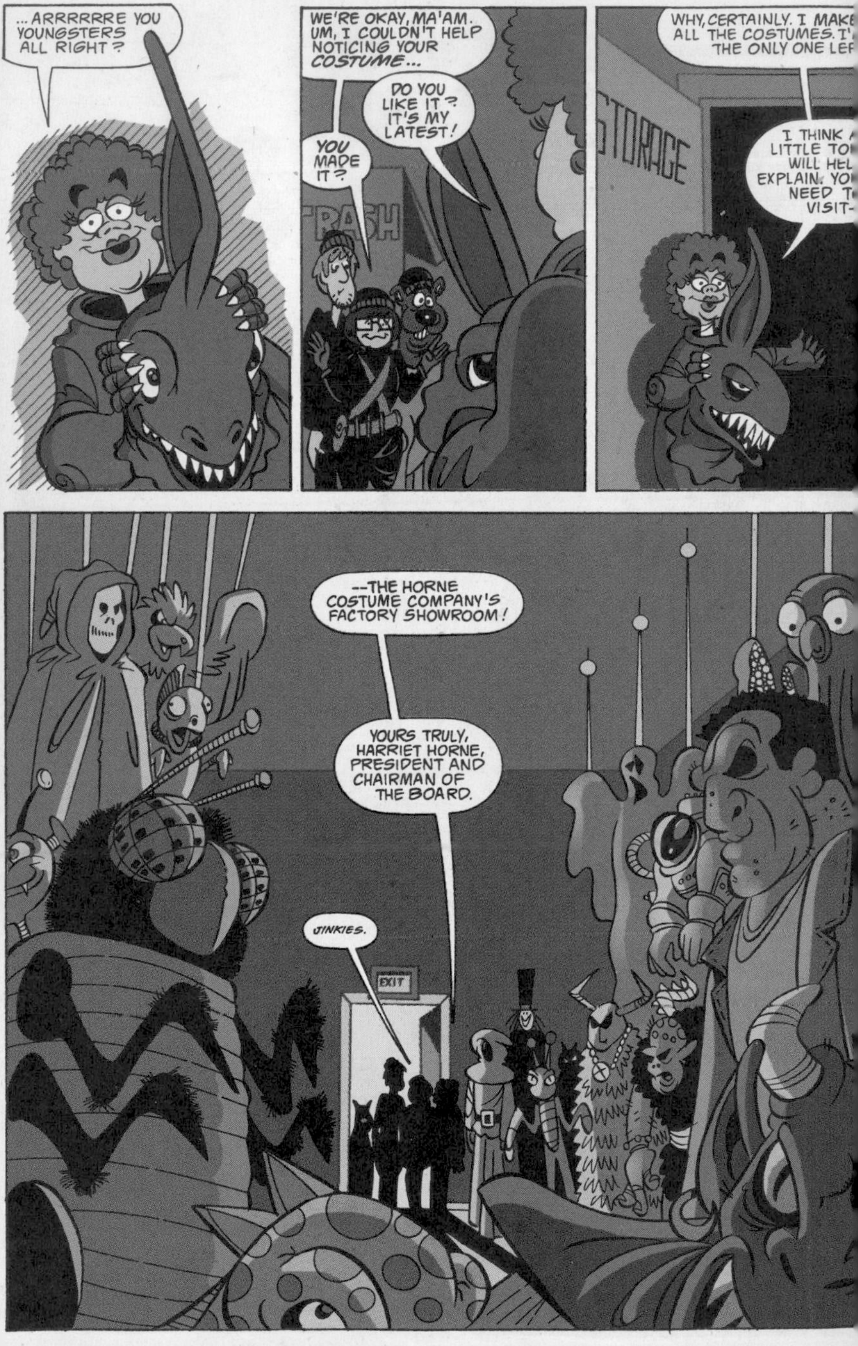
...ARRRRRRE YOU YOUNGSTERS ALL RIGHT?
WE'RE OKAY, MA'AM. UM, I COULDN'T HELP NOTICING YOUR COSTUME...
DO YOU LIKE IT? IT'S MY LATEST!
YOU MADE IT?
TRASH
STORAGE
WHY, CERTAINLY. I MAKE ALL THE COSTUMES. I'
THE ONLY ONE LEF
I THINK A LITTLE TO WILL HEL EXPLAIN. YO NEED T VISIT-
--THE HORNE COSTUME COMPANY'S FACTORY SHOWROOM!
YOURS TRULY, HARRIET HORNE, PRESIDENT AND CHAIRMAN OF THE BOARD.
JINKIES.
EXIT

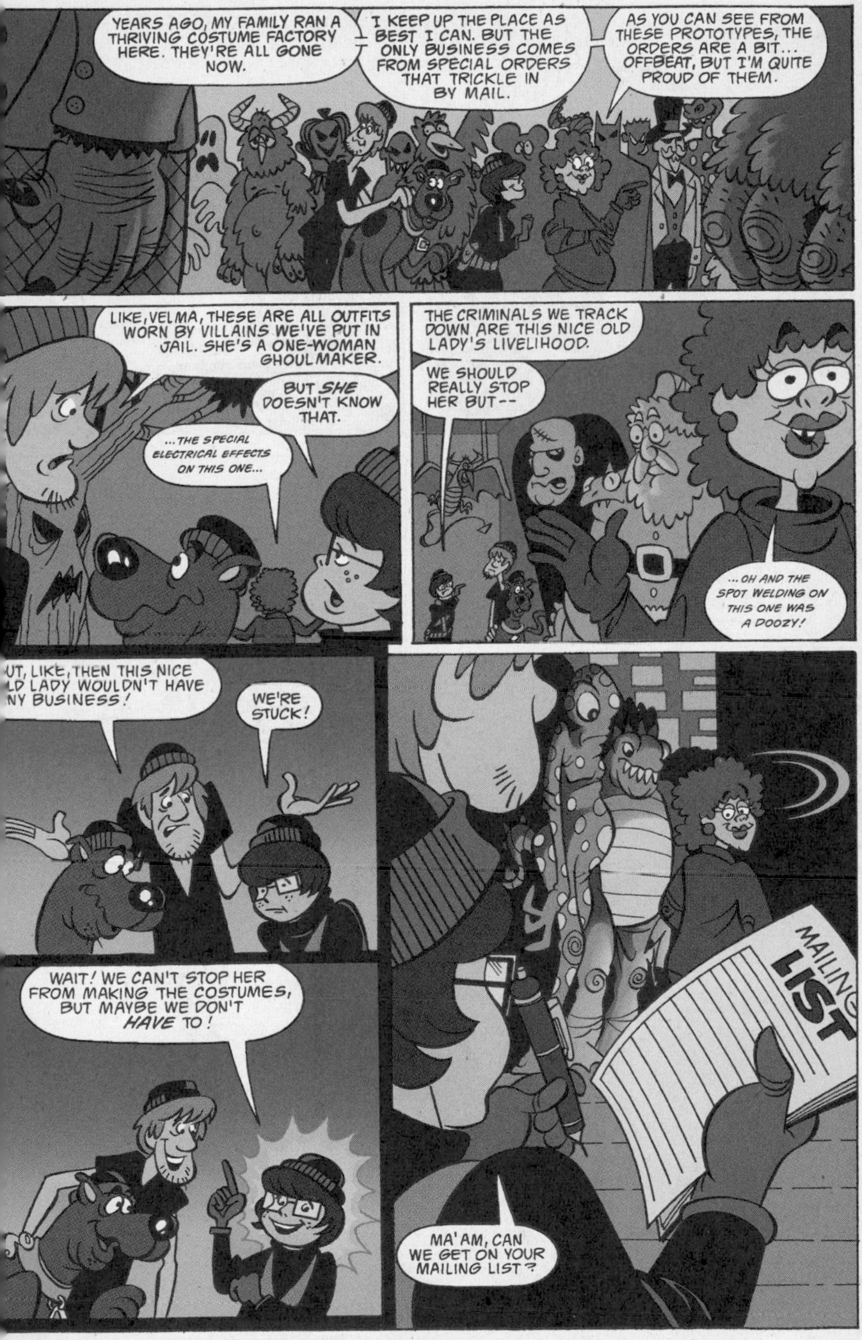
YEARS AGO, MY FAMILY RAN A THRIVING COSTUME FACTORY HERE. THEY'RE ALL GONE NOW.
I KEEP UP THE PLACE AS BEST I CAN. BUT THE ONLY BUSINESS COMES FROM SPECIAL ORDERS THAT TRICKLE IN BY MAIL.
AS YOU CAN SEE FROM THESE PROTOTYPES, THE ORDERS ARE A BIT... OFFBEAT, BUT I'M QUITE PROUD OF THEM.
LIKE, VELMA, THESE ARE ALL OUTFITS WORN BY VILLAINS WE'VE PUT IN JAIL. SHE'S A ONE-WOMAN GHOULMAKER.
BUT SHE DOESN'T KNOW THAT.
...THE SPECIAL ELECTRICAL EFFECTS ON THIS ONE...
THE CRIMINALS WE TRACK DOWN ARE THIS NICE OLD LADY'S LIVELIHOOD.
WE SHOULD REALLY STOP HER BUT--
...OH AND THE SPOT WELDING ON THIS ONE WAS A DOOZY!
UT, LIKE, THEN THIS NICE
LD LADY WOULDN'T HAVE
NY BUSINESS!
WE'RE STUCK!
WAIT! WE CAN'T STOP HER FROM MAKING THE COSTUMES, BUT MAYBE WE DON'T HAVE TO!
MAILING LIST
MA'AM, CAN WE GET ON YOUR MAILING LIST?

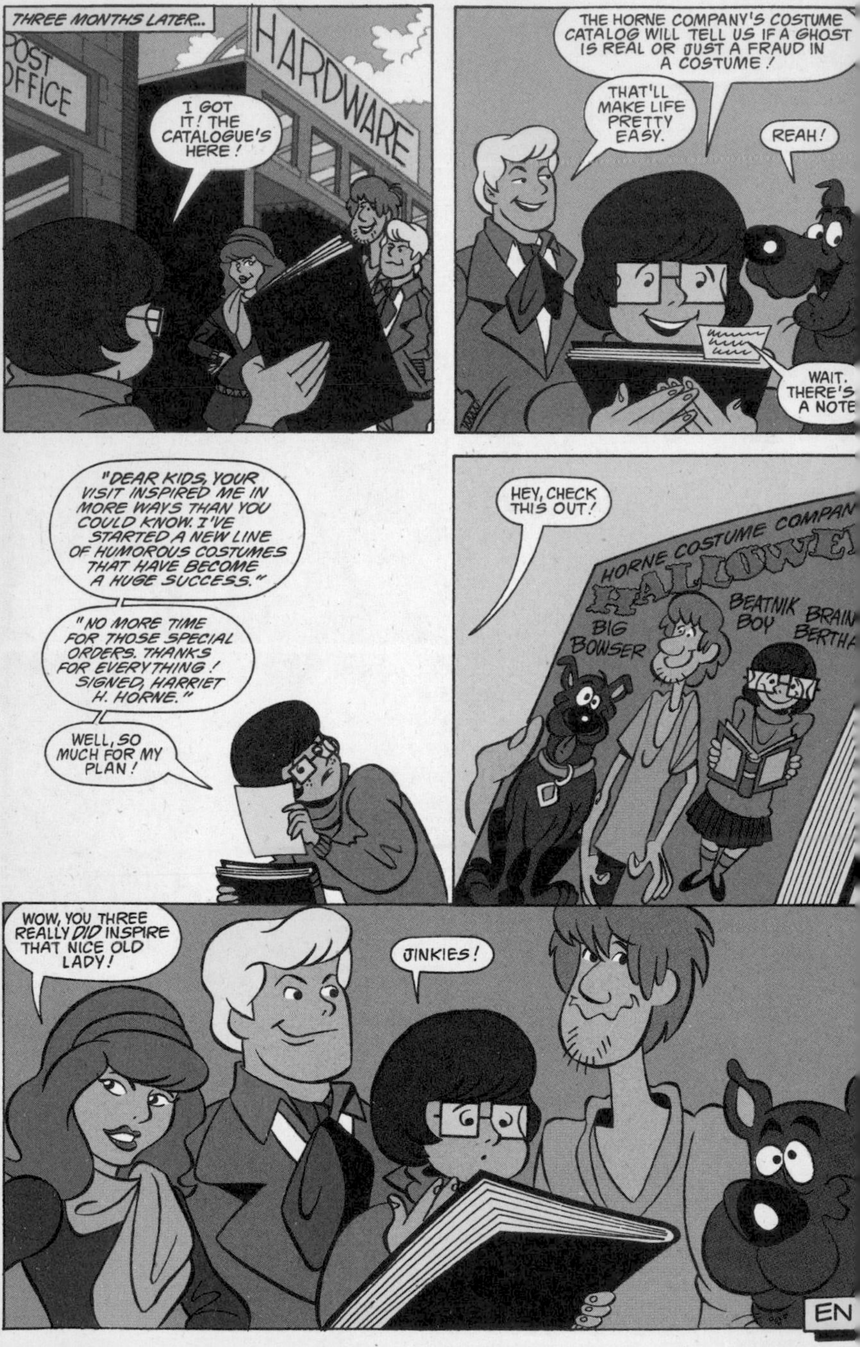
THREE MONTHS LATER...
POST OFFICE
HARDWARE
I GOT IT! THE CATALOGUE'S HERE!
THE HORNE COMPANY'S COSTUME CATALOG WILL TELL US IF A GHOST IS REAL OR JUST A FRAUD IN A COSTUME!
THAT'LL MAKE LIFE PRETTY EASY.
REAH!
WAIT. THERE'S A NOTE
"DEAR KIDS, YOUR VISIT INSPIRED ME IN MORE WAYS THAN YOU COULD KNOW. I'VE STARTED A NEW LINE OF HUMOROUS COSTUMES THAT HAVE BECOME A HUGE SUCCESS."
"NO MORE TIME FOR THOSE SPECIAL ORDERS. THANKS FOR EVERYTHING! SIGNED, HARRIET H. HORNE."
WELL, SO MUCH FOR MY PLAN!
HEY, CHECK THIS OUT!
HORNE COSTUME COMPAN
BIG BOWSER
BEATNIK BOY
BRAIN BERTHA
WOW, YOU THREE REALLY DID INSPIRE THAT NICE OLD LADY!
JINKIES!
EN

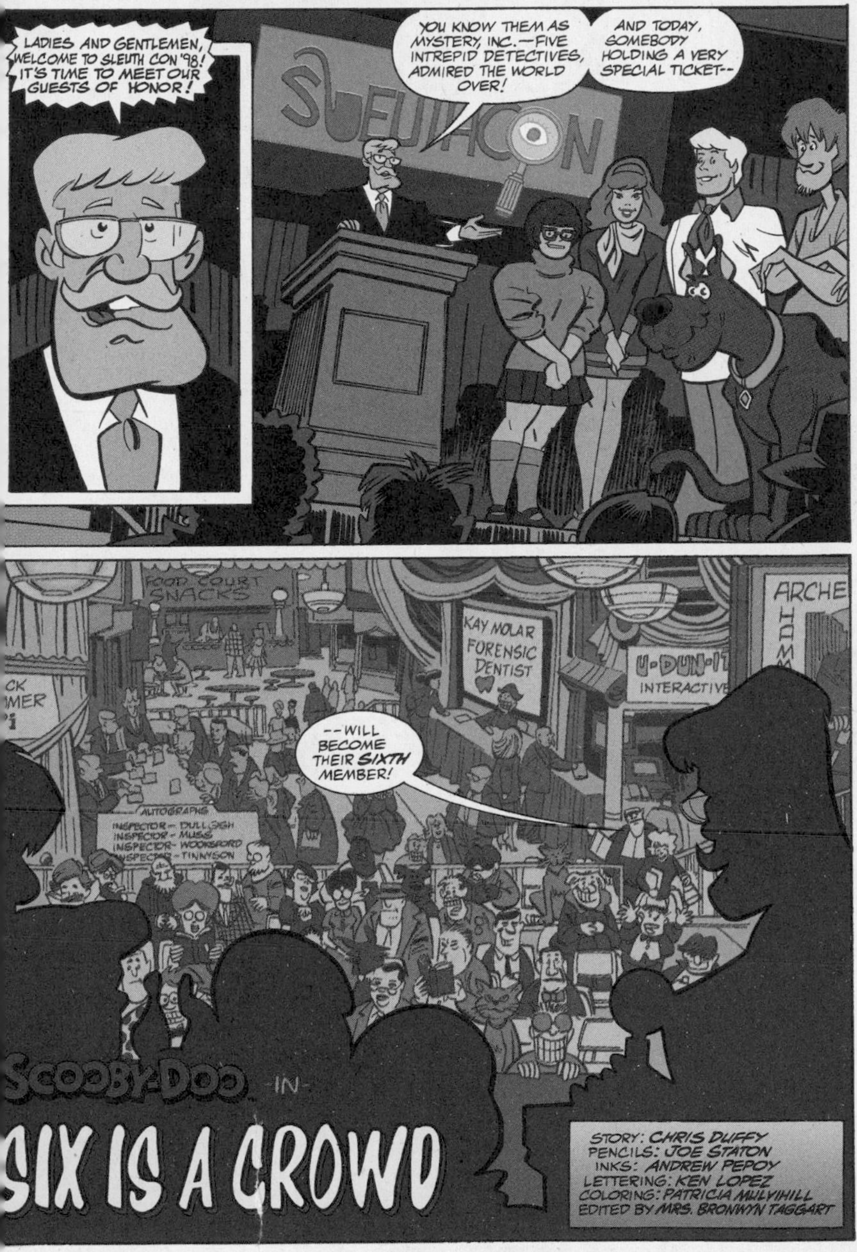
LADIES AND GENTLEMEN, WELCOME TO SLEUTH CON '98! IT'S TIME TO MEET OUR GUESTS OF HONOR!
YOU KNOW THEM AS MYSTERY, INC.—FIVE INTREPID DETECTIVES, ADMIRED THE WORLD OVER!
AND TODAY, SOMEBODY HOLDING A VERY SPECIAL TICKET--
SLEUTHCON
FOOD COURT SNACKS
KAY MOLAR FORENSIC DENTIST
U-DUN-IT INTERACTIVE
--WILL BECOME THEIR SIXTH MEMBER!
AUTOGRAPHS
INSPECTOR - DULLSIGH
INSPECTOR - MUSS
INSPECTOR - WOOKSFORD
INSPECTOR - TINNYSON
SCOOBY-DOO IN
SIX IS A CROWD
STORY: CHRIS DUFFY
PENCILS: JOE STATON
INKS: ANDREW PEPOY
LETTERING: KEN LOPEZ
COLORING: PATRICIA MULVIHILL
EDITED BY MRS. BRONWYN TAGGART

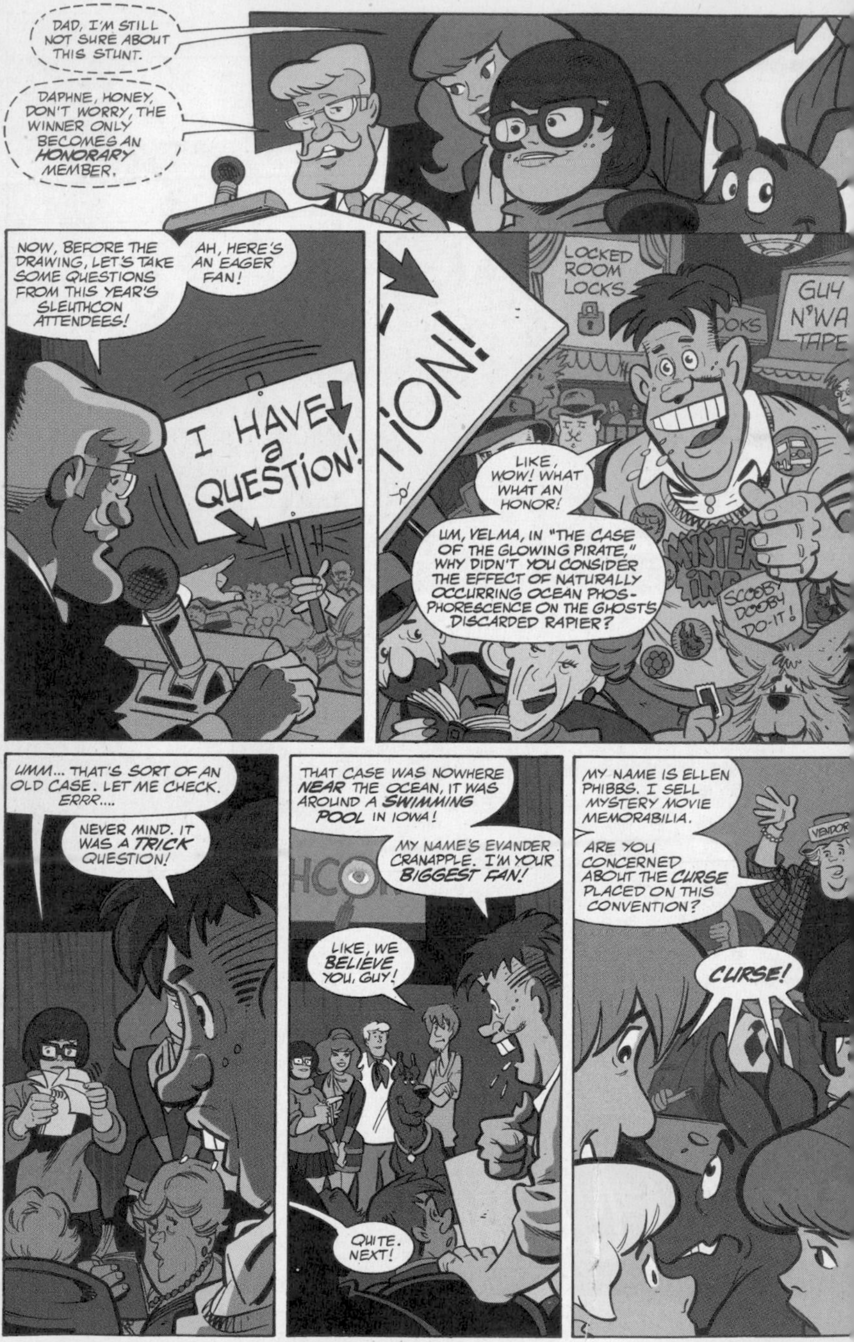
DAD, I'M STILL NOT SURE ABOUT THIS STUNT.
DAPHNE, HONEY, DON'T WORRY, THE WINNER ONLY BECOMES AN HONORARY MEMBER.
NOW, BEFORE THE DRAWING, LET'S TAKE SOME QUESTIONS FROM THIS YEAR'S SLEUTHCON ATTENDEES!
AH, HERE'S AN EAGER FAN!
I HAVE a QUESTION!
TION!
LOCKED ROOM LOCKS
GUY N'WA TAPE
LIKE, WOW! WHAT WHAT AN HONOR!
UM, VELMA, IN "THE CASE OF THE GLOWING PIRATE," WHY DIDN'T YOU CONSIDER THE EFFECT OF NATURALLY OCCURRING OCEAN PHOS-PHORESCENCE ON THE GHOST'S DISCARDED RAPIER?
MYSTERY INC
SCOOBY DOOBY DO-IT!
UMM... THAT'S SORT OF AN OLD CASE. LET ME CHECK. ERRR....
NEVER MIND. IT WAS A TRICK QUESTION!
THAT CASE WAS NOWHERE NEAR THE OCEAN, IT WAS AROUND A SWIMMING POOL IN IOWA!
MY NAME'S EVANDER CRANAPPLE. I'M YOUR BIGGEST FAN!
LIKE, WE BELIEVE YOU, GUY!
QUITE. NEXT!
MY NAME IS ELLEN PHIBBS. I SELL MYSTERY MOVIE MEMORABILIA.
ARE YOU CONCERNED ABOUT THE CURSE PLACED ON THIS CONVENTION?
VENDOR
CURSE!

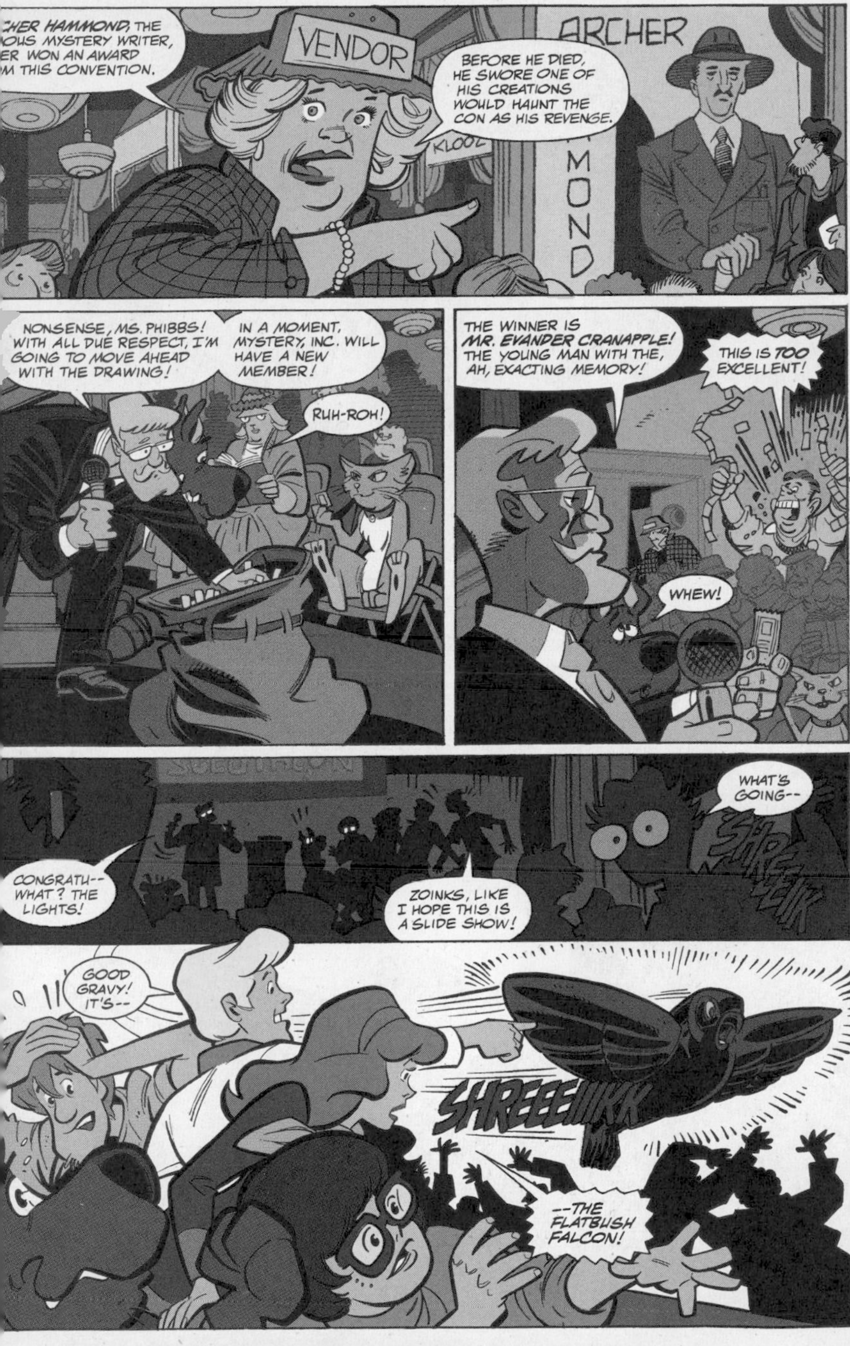
CHER HAMMOND, THE
OUS MYSTERY WRITER,
ER WON AN AWARD
M THIS CONVENTION.
VENDOR
BEFORE HE DIED, HE SWORE ONE OF HIS CREATIONS WOULD HAUNT THE CON AS HIS REVENGE.
ARCHER
MOND
NONSENSE, MS. PHIBBS! WITH ALL DUE RESPECT, I'M GOING TO MOVE AHEAD WITH THE DRAWING!
IN A MOMENT, MYSTERY, INC. WILL HAVE A NEW MEMBER!
RUH-ROH!
THE WINNER IS MR. EVANDER CRANAPPLE! THE YOUNG MAN WITH THE, AH, EXACTING MEMORY!
THIS IS TOO EXCELLENT!
WHEW!
CONGRATU-- WHAT? THE LIGHTS!
ZOINKS, LIKE I HOPE THIS IS A SLIDE SHOW!
WHAT'S GOING--
SHREEK
GOOD GRAVY! IT'S--
SHREEEIIIKK
--THE FLATBUSH FALCON!

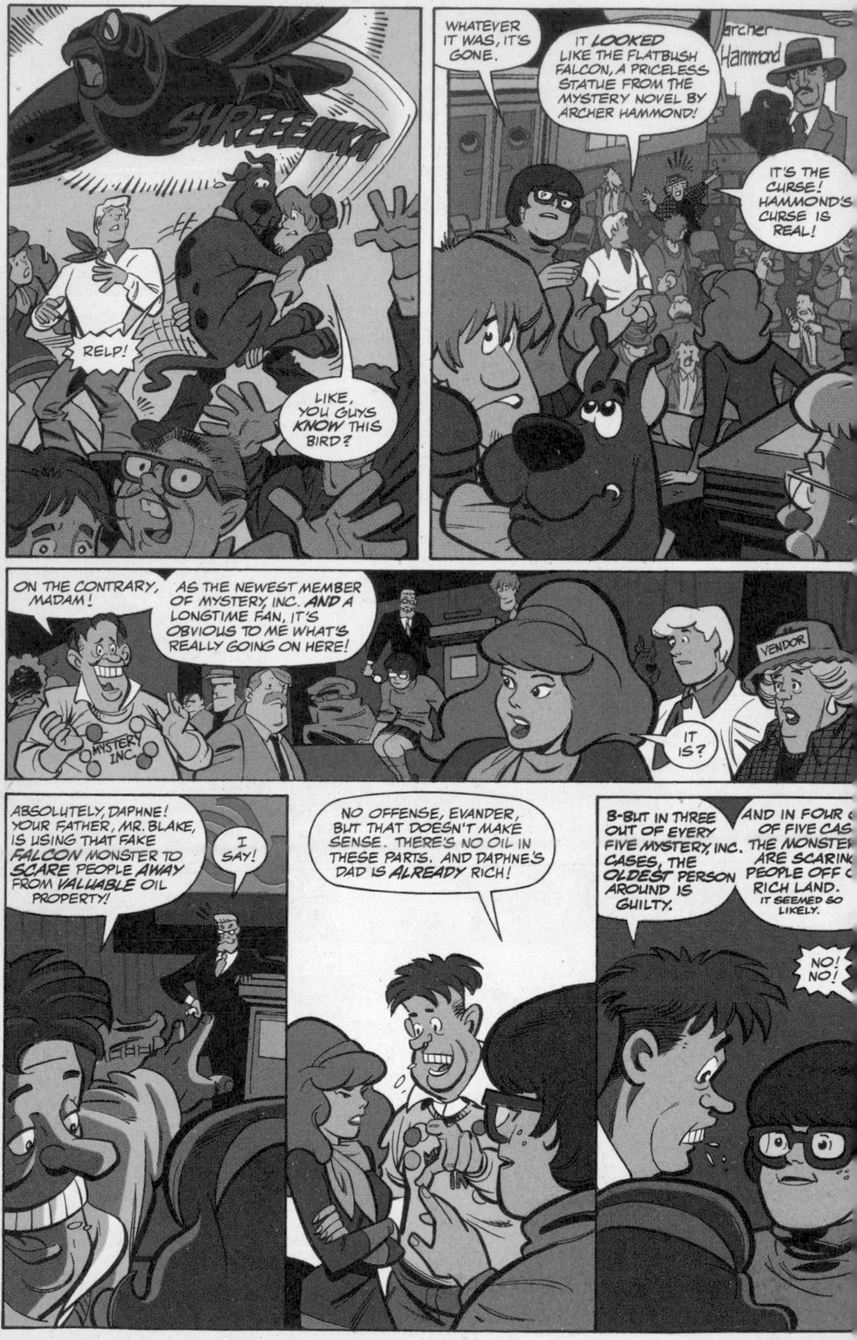
SHREEEIIIKK
RELP!
LIKE, YOU GUYS KNOW THIS BIRD?
WHATEVER IT WAS, IT'S GONE.
IT LOOKED LIKE THE FLATBUSH FALCON, A PRICELESS STATUE FROM THE MYSTERY NOVEL BY ARCHER HAMMOND!
Archer Hammond
IT'S THE CURSE! HAMMOND'S CURSE IS REAL!
ON THE CONTRARY, MADAM!
AS THE NEWEST MEMBER OF MYSTERY, INC. AND A LONGTIME FAN, IT'S OBVIOUS TO ME WHAT'S REALLY GOING ON HERE!
MYSTERY INC.
VENDOR
IT IS?
ABSOLUTELY, DAPHNE! YOUR FATHER, MR. BLAKE, IS USING THAT FAKE FALCON MONSTER TO SCARE PEOPLE AWAY FROM VALUABLE OIL PROPERTY!
I SAY!
NO OFFENSE, EVANDER, BUT THAT DOESN'T MAKE SENSE. THERE'S NO OIL IN THESE PARTS. AND DAPHNE'S DAD IS ALREADY RICH!
B-BUT IN THREE OUT OF EVERY FIVE MYSTERY, INC. CASES, THE OLDEST PERSON AROUND IS GUILTY.
AND IN FOUR OF FIVE CAS THE MONSTE ARE SCARIN PEOPLE OFF RICH LAND. IT SEEMED SO LIKELY.
NO! NO!

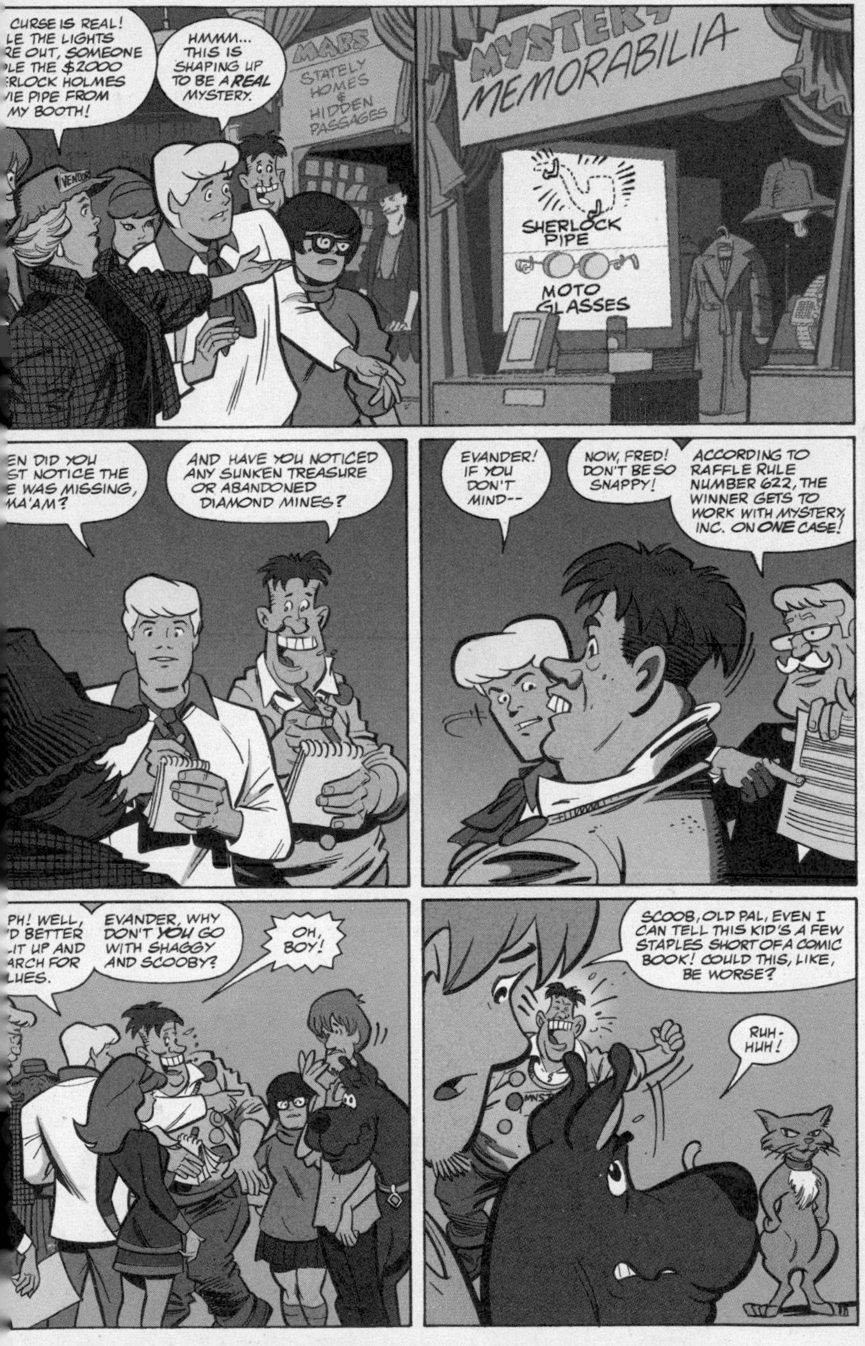
CURSE IS REAL!
LE THE LIGHTS
RE OUT, SOMEONE
PLE THE $2000
ERLOCK HOLMES
VIE PIPE FROM
MY BOOTH!
HMMM...
THIS IS
SHAPING UP
TO BE A REAL
MYSTERY.
MARS
STATELY
HOMES
&
HIDDEN
PASSAGES
VENDOR
MYSTERY
MEMORABILIA
SHERLOCK
PIPE
MOTO
GLASSES
EN DID YOU
ST NOTICE THE
E WAS MISSING,
MA'AM?
AND HAVE YOU NOTICED
ANY SUNKEN TREASURE
OR ABANDONED
DIAMOND MINES?
EVANDER!
IF YOU
DON'T
MIND--
NOW, FRED!
DON'T BE SO
SNAPPY!
ACCORDING TO
RAFFLE RULE
NUMBER 622, THE
WINNER GETS TO
WORK WITH MYSTERY,
INC. ON ONE CASE!
PH! WELL,
'D BETTER
-IT UP AND
ARCH FOR
LUES.
EVANDER, WHY
DON'T YOU GO
WITH SHAGGY
AND SCOOBY?
OH,
BOY!
SCOOB, OLD PAL, EVEN I
CAN TELL THIS KID'S A FEW
STAPLES SHORT OF A COMIC
BOOK! COULD THIS, LIKE,
BE WORSE?
RUH-
HUH!

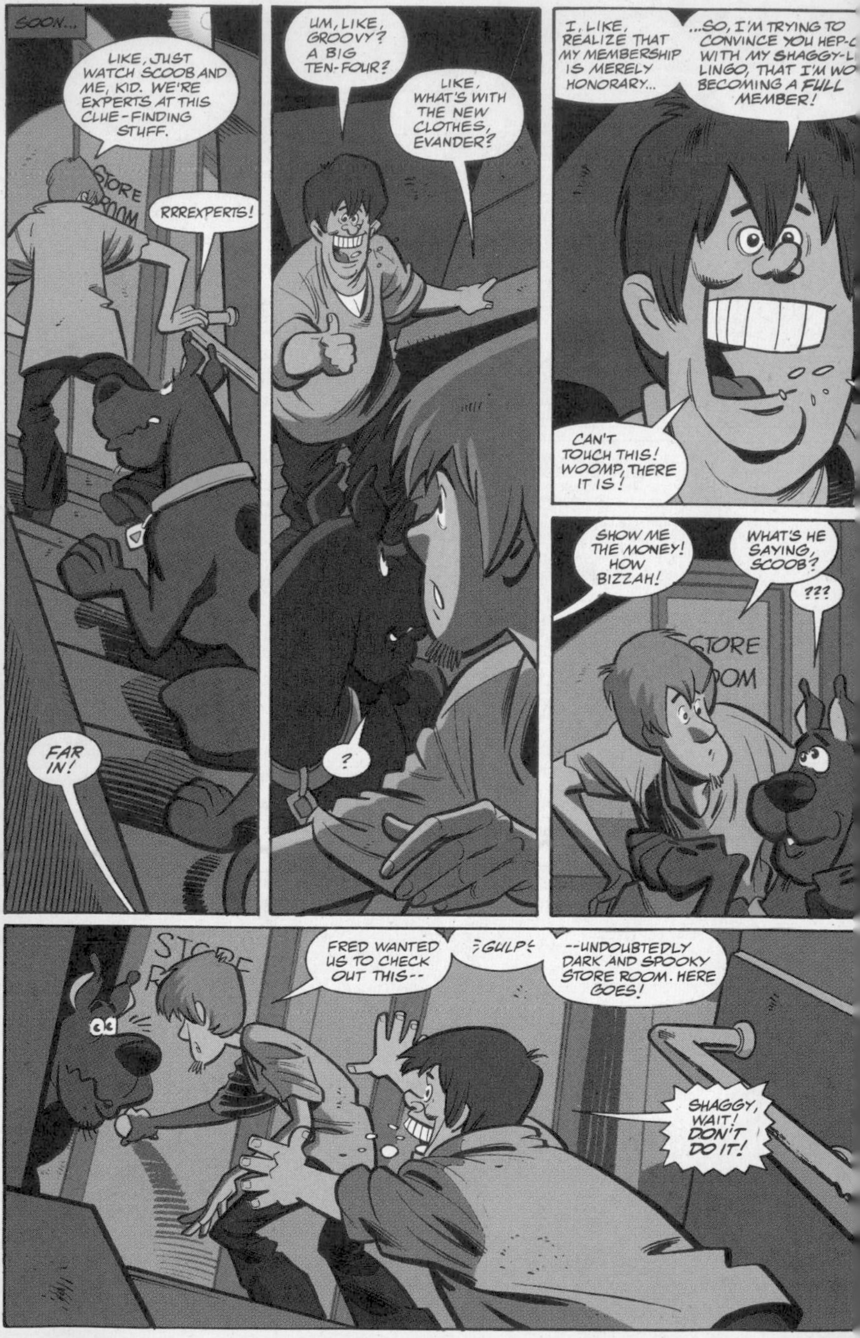
SOON...
LIKE, JUST WATCH SCOOB AND ME, KID. WE'RE EXPERTS AT THIS CLUE-FINDING STUFF.
STORE ROOM
RRREXPERTS!
FAR IN!
UM, LIKE, GROOVY? A BIG TEN-FOUR?
LIKE, WHAT'S WITH THE NEW CLOTHES, EVANDER?
?
I, LIKE, REALIZE THAT MY MEMBERSHIP IS MERELY HONORARY...
...SO, I'M TRYING TO CONVINCE YOU HEP-C WITH MY SHAGGY-L LINGO, THAT I'M WO BECOMING A FULL MEMBER!
CAN'T TOUCH THIS! WOOMP, THERE IT IS!
SHOW ME THE MONEY! HOW BIZZAH!
WHAT'S HE SAYING, SCOOB?
???
STORE ROOM
FRED WANTED US TO CHECK OUT THIS--
GULP
--UNDOUBTEDLY DARK AND SPOOKY STORE ROOM. HERE GOES!
SHAGGY, WAIT! DON'T DO IT!

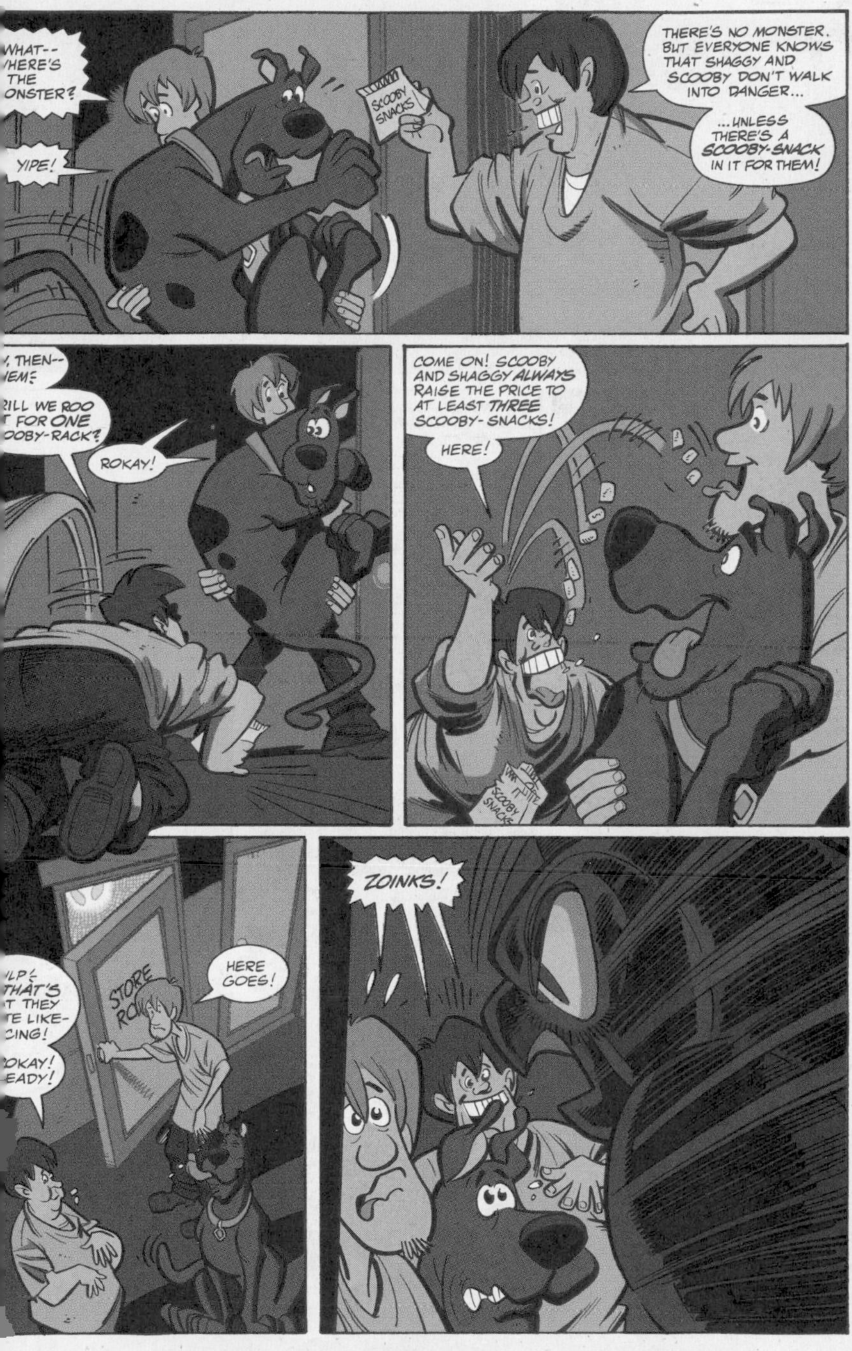
WHAT--
HERE'S
THE
ONSTER?
YIPE!
SCOOBY SNACKS
THERE'S NO MONSTER. BUT EVERYONE KNOWS THAT SHAGGY AND SCOOBY DON'T WALK INTO DANGER...
...UNLESS THERE'S A SCOOBY-SNACK IN IT FOR THEM!
, THEN--
IEM?
RILL WE ROO
T FOR ONE
OOBY-RACK?
ROKAY!
COME ON! SCOOBY AND SHAGGY ALWAYS RAISE THE PRICE TO AT LEAST THREE SCOOBY-SNACKS!
HERE!
SCOOBY SNACKS
LP!
THAT'S
T THEY
TE LIKE-
CING!
OKAY!
EADY!
STORE
HERE GOES!
ZOINKS!

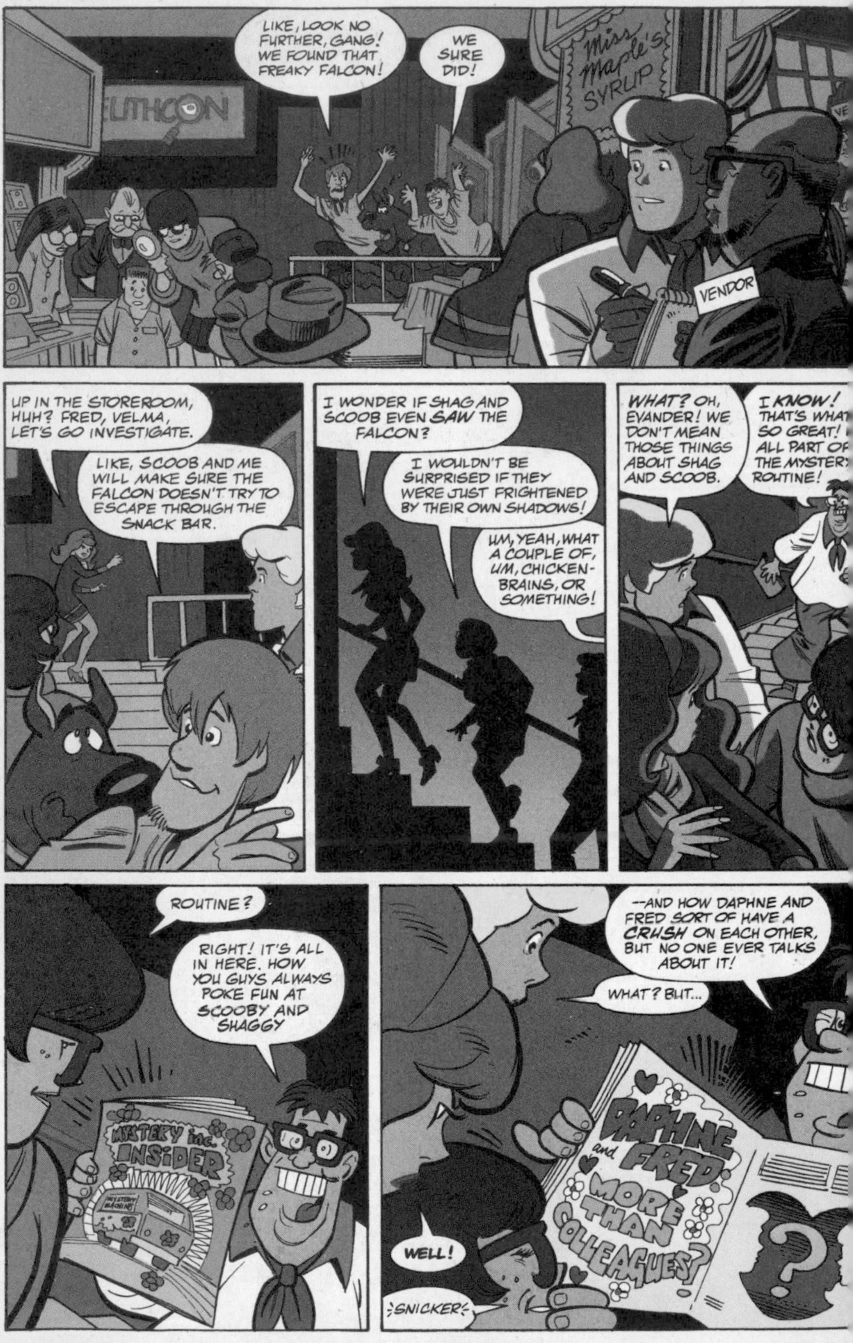

LIKE, LOOK NO FURTHER, GANG! WE FOUND THAT FREAKY FALCON!
WE SURE DID!
Miss Maple's SYRUP
VENDOR
UP IN THE STOREROOM, HUH? FRED, VELMA, LET'S GO INVESTIGATE.
LIKE, SCOOB AND ME WILL MAKE SURE THE FALCON DOESN'T TRY TO ESCAPE THROUGH THE SNACK BAR.
I WONDER IF SHAG AND SCOOB EVEN SAW THE FALCON?
I WOULDN'T BE SURPRISED IF THEY WERE JUST FRIGHTENED BY THEIR OWN SHADOWS!
UM, YEAH, WHAT A COUPLE OF, UM, CHICKEN-BRAINS, OR SOMETHING!
WHAT? OH, EVANDER! WE DON'T MEAN THOSE THINGS ABOUT SHAG AND SCOOB.
I KNOW! THAT'S WHAT SO GREAT! ALL PART OF THE MYSTERY ROUTINE!
ROUTINE?
RIGHT! IT'S ALL IN HERE. HOW YOU GUYS ALWAYS POKE FUN AT SCOOBY AND SHAGGY
MYSTERY inc. INSIDER
--AND HOW DAPHNE AND FRED SORT OF HAVE A CRUSH ON EACH OTHER, BUT NO ONE EVER TALKS ABOUT IT!
WHAT? BUT...
DAPHNE and FRED MORE THAN COLLEAGUES?
WELL!
SNICKER

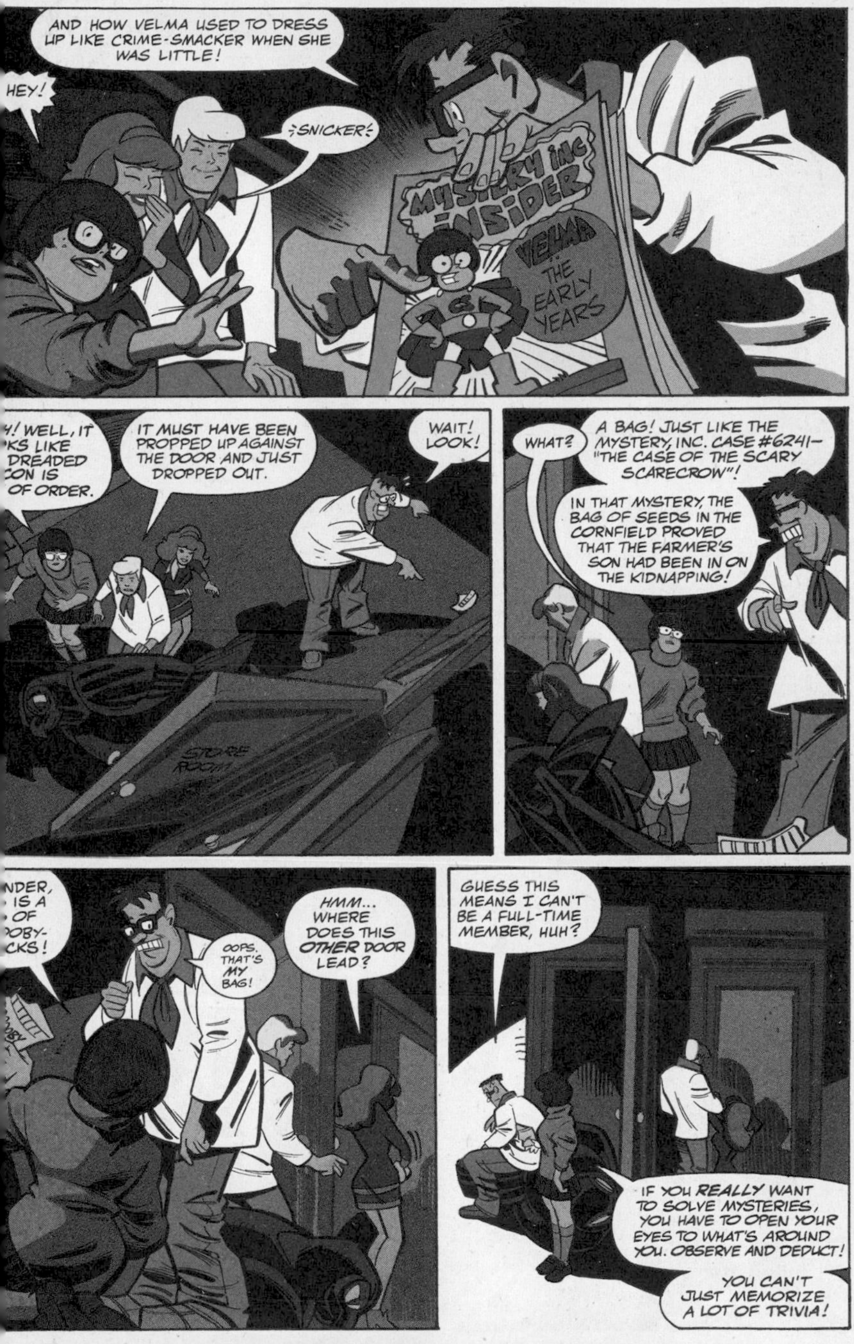
AND HOW VELMA USED TO DRESS UP LIKE CRIME-SMACKER WHEN SHE WAS LITTLE!
HEY!
SNICKER
MYSTERY INC INSIDER
VELMA THE EARLY YEARS
WELL, IT KS LIKE DREADED CON IS OF ORDER.
IT MUST HAVE BEEN PROPPED UP AGAINST THE DOOR AND JUST DROPPED OUT.
WAIT! LOOK!
STORE ROOM
WHAT?
A BAG! JUST LIKE THE MYSTERY, INC. CASE #6241— "THE CASE OF THE SCARY SCARECROW"!
IN THAT MYSTERY, THE BAG OF SEEDS IN THE CORNFIELD PROVED THAT THE FARMER'S SON HAD BEEN IN ON THE KIDNAPPING!
NDER, IS A OF OOBY- CKS!
OOPS. THAT'S MY BAG!
HMM... WHERE DOES THIS OTHER DOOR LEAD?
GUESS THIS MEANS I CAN'T BE A FULL-TIME MEMBER, HUH?
IF YOU REALLY WANT TO SOLVE MYSTERIES, YOU HAVE TO OPEN YOUR EYES TO WHAT'S AROUND YOU. OBSERVE AND DEDUCT!
YOU CAN'T JUST MEMORIZE A LOT OF TRIVIA!

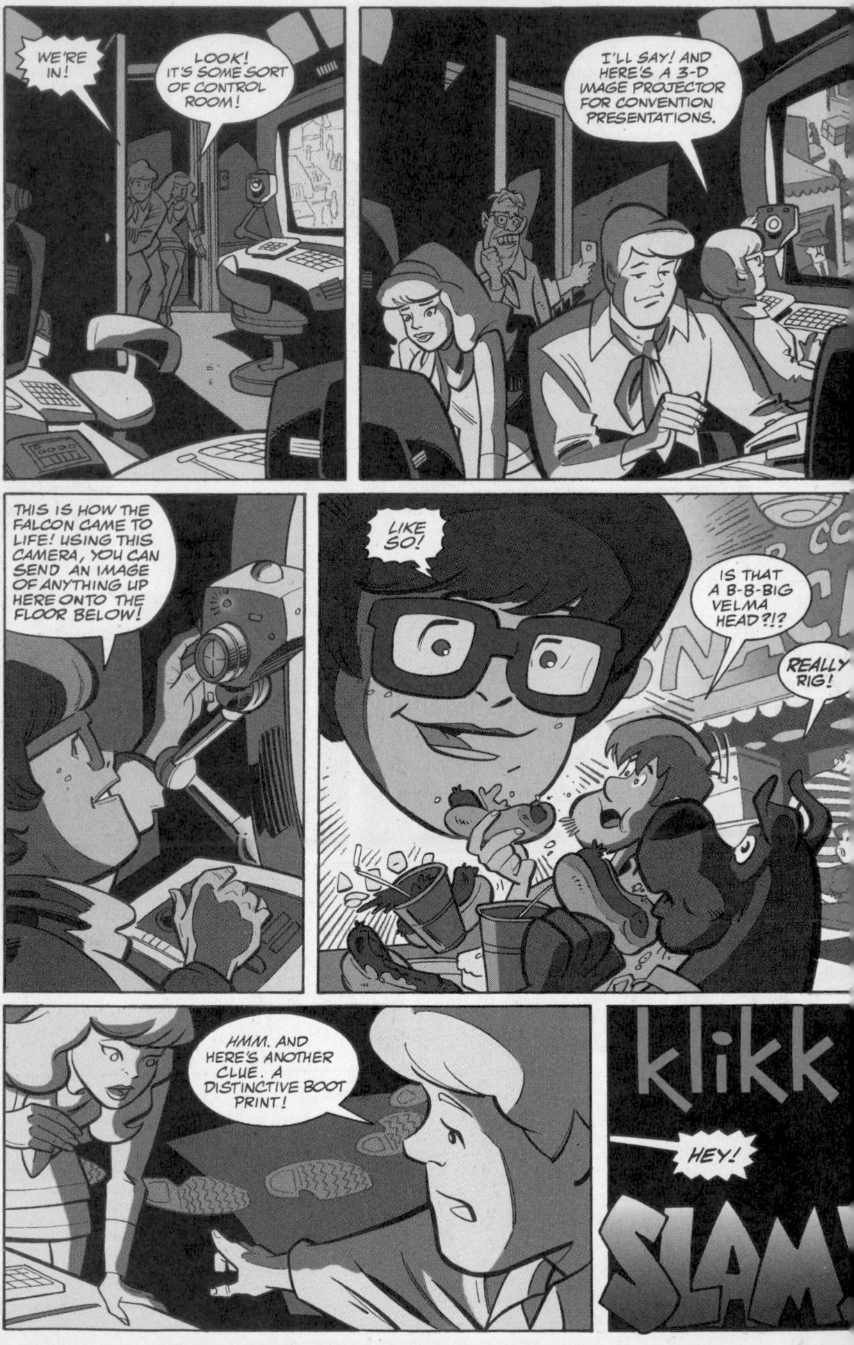
WE'RE IN!
LOOK! IT'S SOME SORT OF CONTROL ROOM!
I'LL SAY! AND HERE'S A 3-D IMAGE PROJECTOR FOR CONVENTION PRESENTATIONS.
THIS IS HOW THE FALCON CAME TO LIFE! USING THIS CAMERA, YOU CAN SEND AN IMAGE OF ANYTHING UP HERE ONTO THE FLOOR BELOW!
LIKE SO!
IS THAT A B-B-BIG VELMA HEAD?!?
REALLY RIG!
HMM. AND HERE'S ANOTHER CLUE. A DISTINCTIVE BOOT PRINT!
klikk
HEY!
SLAM

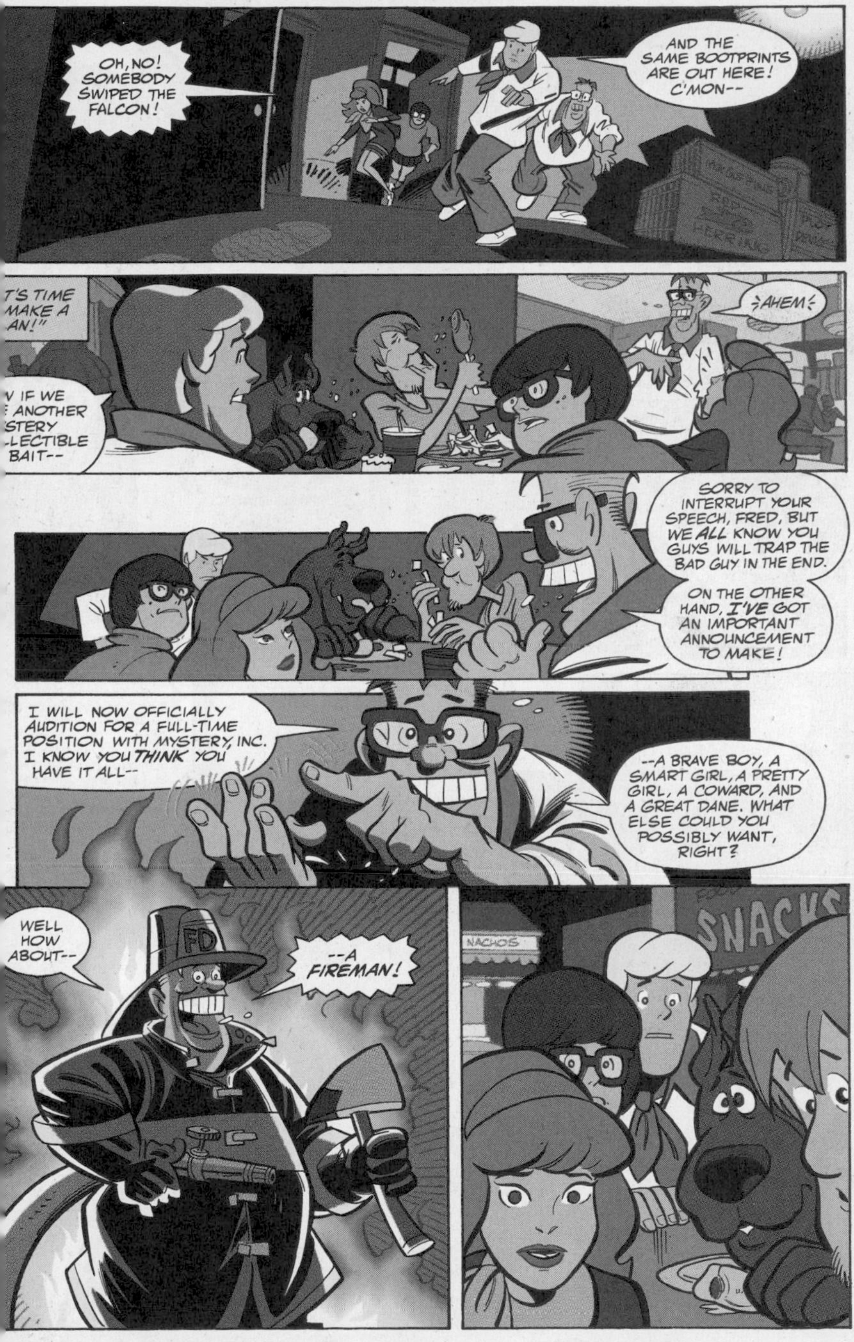

OH, NO! SOMEBODY SWIPED THE FALCON!
AND THE SAME BOOTPRINTS ARE OUT HERE! C'MON--
T'S TIME MAKE A AN!"
V IF WE E ANOTHER STERY LECTIBLE BAIT--
AHEM!
SORRY TO INTERRUPT YOUR SPEECH, FRED, BUT WE ALL KNOW YOU GUYS WILL TRAP THE BAD GUY IN THE END.
ON THE OTHER HAND, I'VE GOT AN IMPORTANT ANNOUNCEMENT TO MAKE!
I WILL NOW OFFICIALLY AUDITION FOR A FULL-TIME POSITION WITH MYSTERY, INC. I KNOW YOU THINK YOU HAVE IT ALL--
--A BRAVE BOY, A SMART GIRL, A PRETTY GIRL, A COWARD, AND A GREAT DANE. WHAT ELSE COULD YOU POSSIBLY WANT, RIGHT?
WELL HOW ABOUT--
--A FIREMAN!
FD
NACHOS
SNACKS

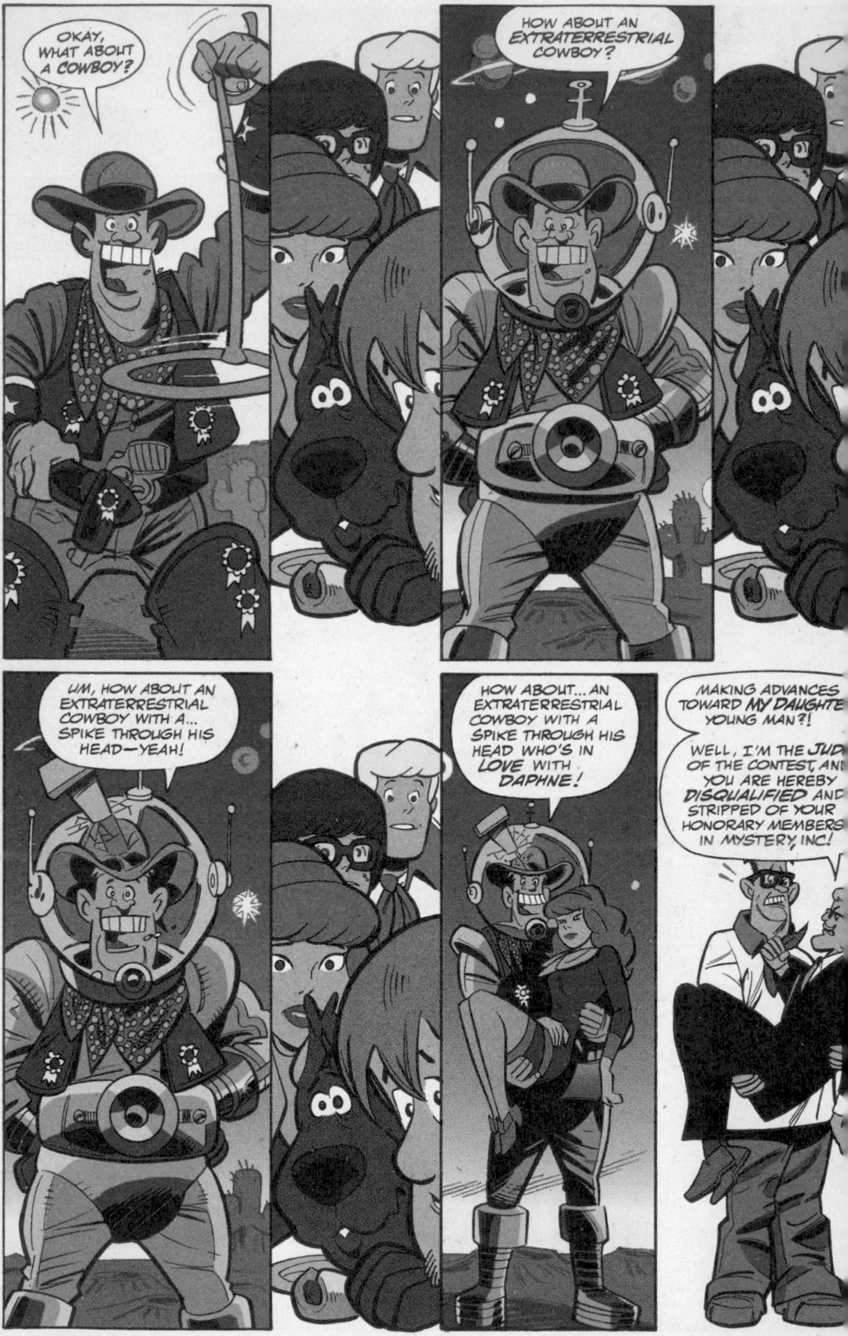
OKAY, WHAT ABOUT A COWBOY?
HOW ABOUT AN EXTRATERRESTRIAL COWBOY?
UM, HOW ABOUT AN EXTRATERRESTRIAL COWBOY WITH A... SPIKE THROUGH HIS HEAD—YEAH!
HOW ABOUT... AN EXTRATERRESTRIAL COWBOY WITH A SPIKE THROUGH HIS HEAD WHO'S IN LOVE WITH DAPHNE!
MAKING ADVANCES TOWARD MY DAUGHTE YOUNG MAN?!
WELL, I'M THE JUD OF THE CONTEST, AN YOU ARE HEREBY DISQUALIFIED AND STRIPPED OF YOUR HONORARY MEMBERS IN MYSTERY, INC!

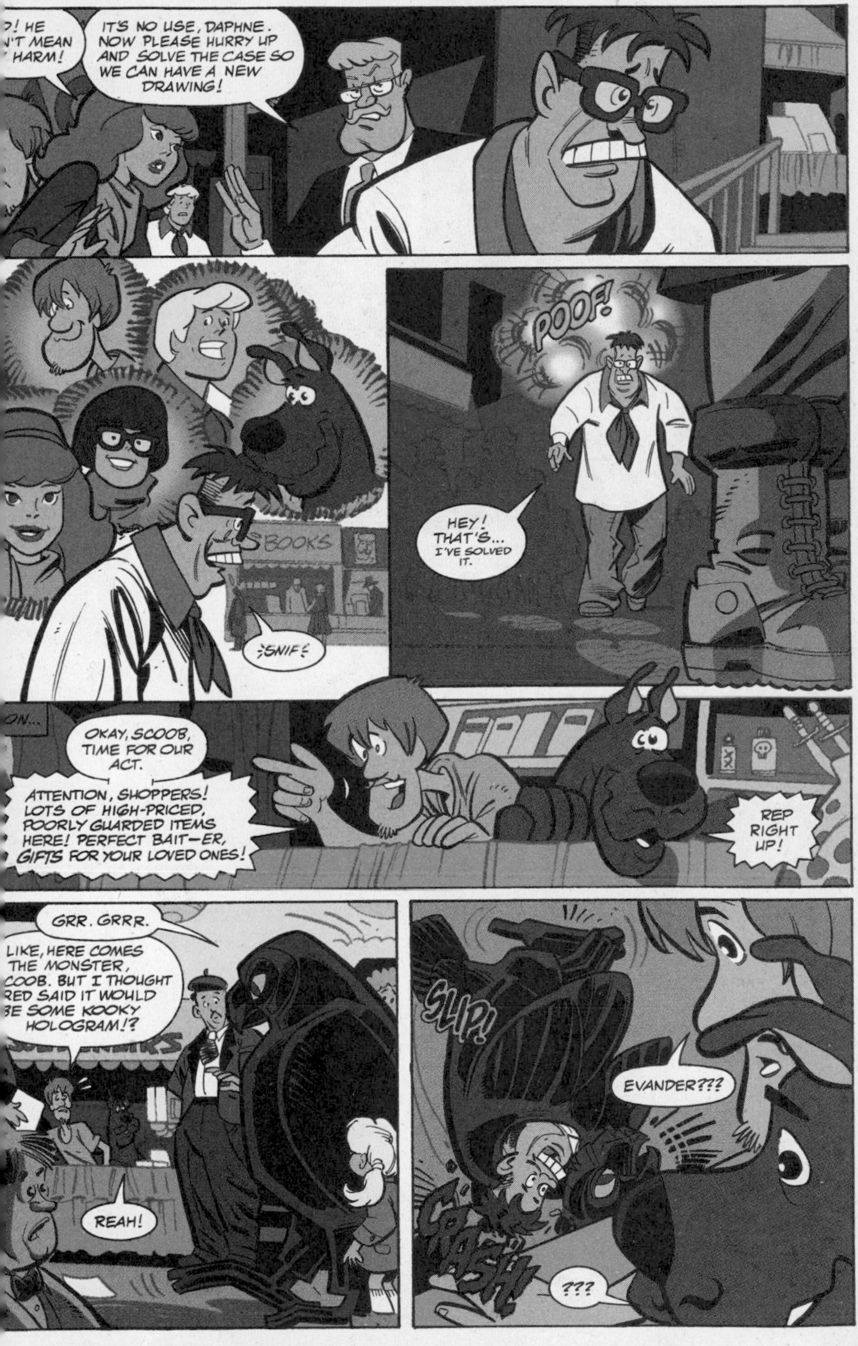
?! HE
N'T MEAN
HARM!
IT'S NO USE, DAPHNE. NOW PLEASE HURRY UP AND SOLVE THE CASE SO WE CAN HAVE A NEW DRAWING!
SNIF
POOF!
HEY! THAT'S... I'VE SOLVED IT.
ON...
OKAY, SCOOB, TIME FOR OUR ACT.
ATTENTION, SHOPPERS! LOTS OF HIGH-PRICED, POORLY GUARDED ITEMS HERE! PERFECT BAIT—ER, GIFTS FOR YOUR LOVED ONES!
REP RIGHT UP!
GRR. GRRR.
LIKE, HERE COMES THE MONSTER, COOB. BUT I THOUGHT RED SAID IT WOULD BE SOME KOOKY HOLOGRAM!?
REAH!
SLIP!
EVANDER???
???

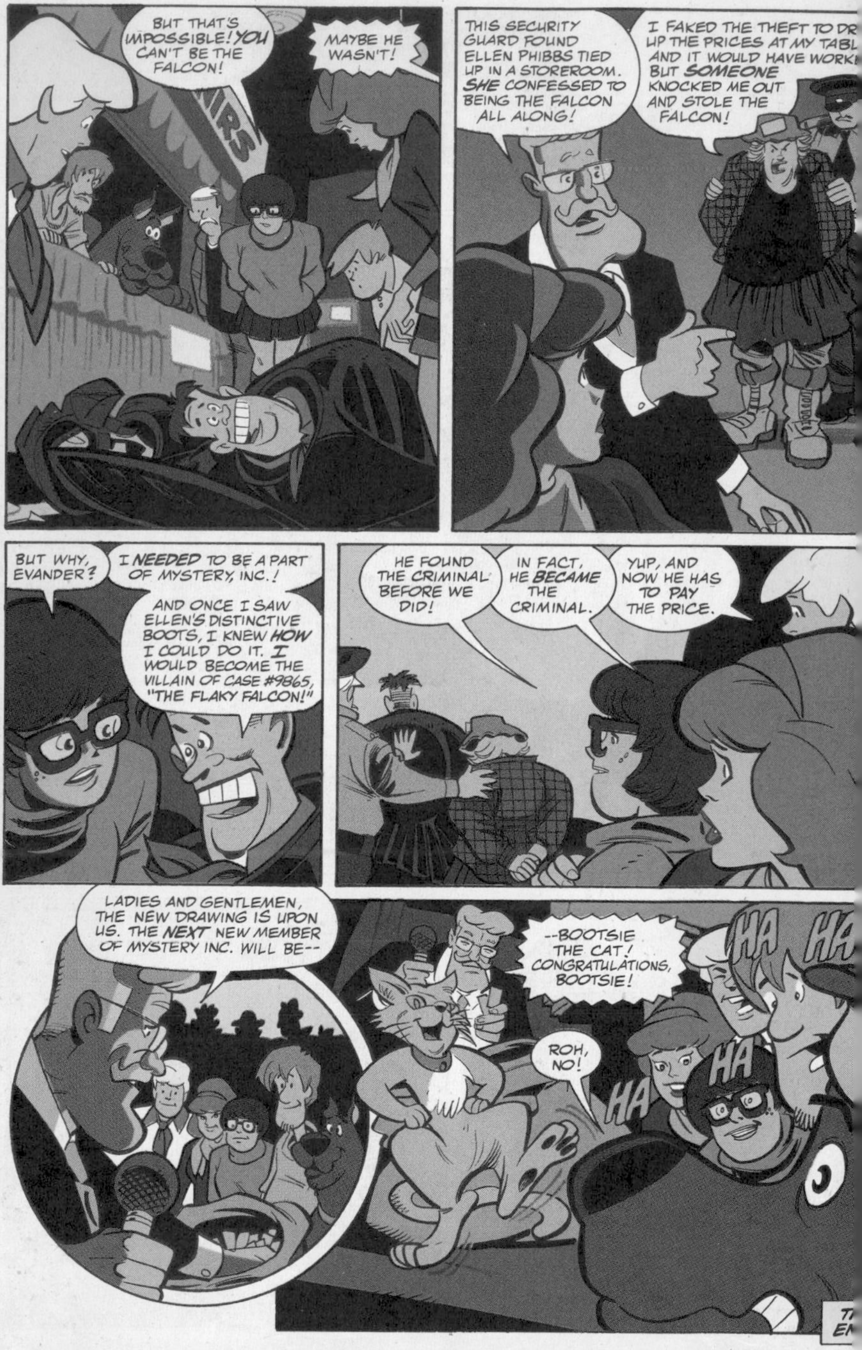

BUT THAT'S IMPOSSIBLE! YOU CAN'T BE THE FALCON!
MAYBE HE WASN'T!
THIS SECURITY GUARD FOUND ELLEN PHIBBS TIED UP IN A STOREROOM. SHE CONFESSED TO BEING THE FALCON ALL ALONG!
I FAKED THE THEFT TO DR UP THE PRICES AT MY TABL AND IT WOULD HAVE WORK BUT SOMEONE KNOCKED ME OUT AND STOLE THE FALCON!
BUT WHY, EVANDER?
I NEEDED TO BE A PART OF MYSTERY, INC.!
AND ONCE I SAW ELLEN'S DISTINCTIVE BOOTS, I KNEW HOW I COULD DO IT. I WOULD BECOME THE VILLAIN OF CASE #9865, "THE FLAKY FALCON!"
HE FOUND THE CRIMINAL BEFORE WE DID!
IN FACT, HE BECAME THE CRIMINAL.
YUP, AND NOW HE HAS TO PAY THE PRICE.
LADIES AND GENTLEMEN, THE NEW DRAWING IS UPON US. THE NEXT NEW MEMBER OF MYSTERY INC. WILL BE--
--BOOTSIE THE CAT! CONGRATULATIONS, BOOTSIE!
HA HA
ROH, NO!
HA
HA

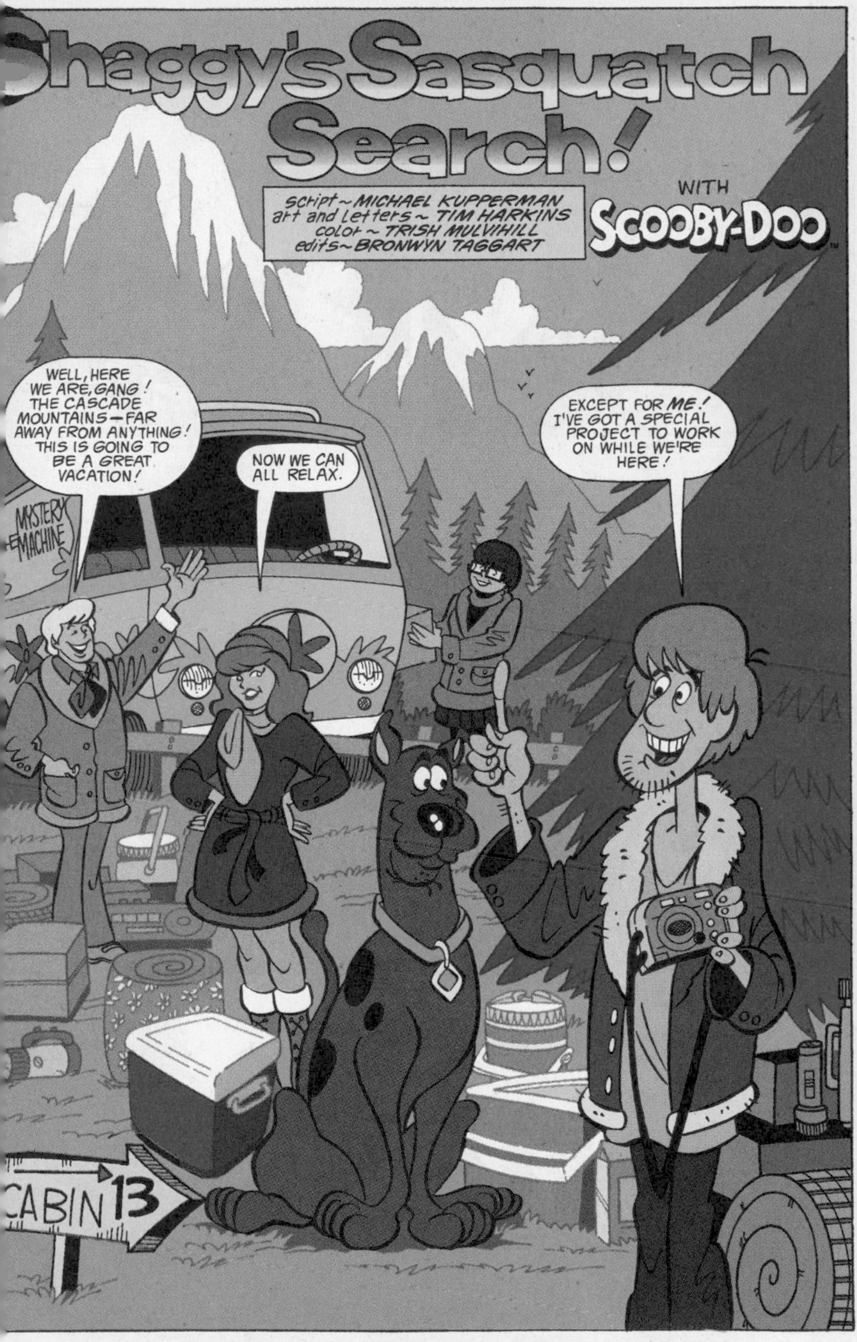
Shaggy's Sasquatch Search!
script ~ MICHAEL KUPPERMAN
art and letters ~ TIM HARKINS
color ~ TRISH MULVIHILL
edits ~ BRONWYN TAGGART
WITH
SCOOBY-DOO
WELL, HERE WE ARE, GANG! THE CASCADE MOUNTAINS—FAR AWAY FROM ANYTHING! THIS IS GOING TO BE A GREAT VACATION!
NOW WE CAN ALL RELAX.
EXCEPT FOR ME! I'VE GOT A SPECIAL PROJECT TO WORK ON WHILE WE'RE HERE!
MYSTERY MACHINE
CABIN 13

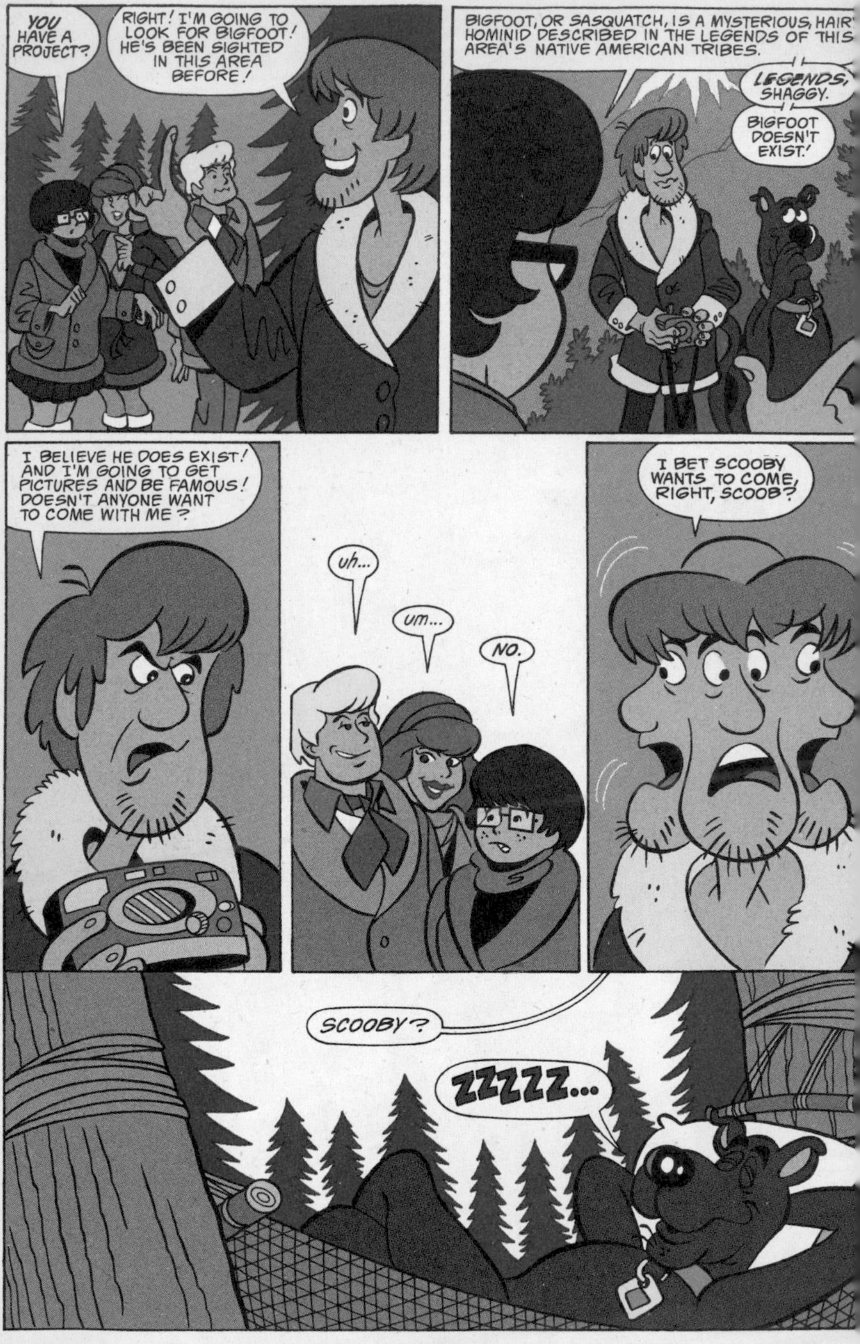
YOU HAVE A PROJECT?
RIGHT! I'M GOING TO LOOK FOR BIGFOOT! HE'S BEEN SIGHTED IN THIS AREA BEFORE!
BIGFOOT, OR SASQUATCH, IS A MYSTERIOUS, HAIRY HOMINID DESCRIBED IN THE LEGENDS OF THIS AREA'S NATIVE AMERICAN TRIBES.
LEGENDS, SHAGGY.
BIGFOOT DOESN'T EXIST!
I BELIEVE HE DOES EXIST! AND I'M GOING TO GET PICTURES AND BE FAMOUS! DOESN'T ANYONE WANT TO COME WITH ME?
uh...
um...
NO.
I BET SCOOBY WANTS TO COME, RIGHT, SCOOB?
SCOOBY?
ZZZZZ...

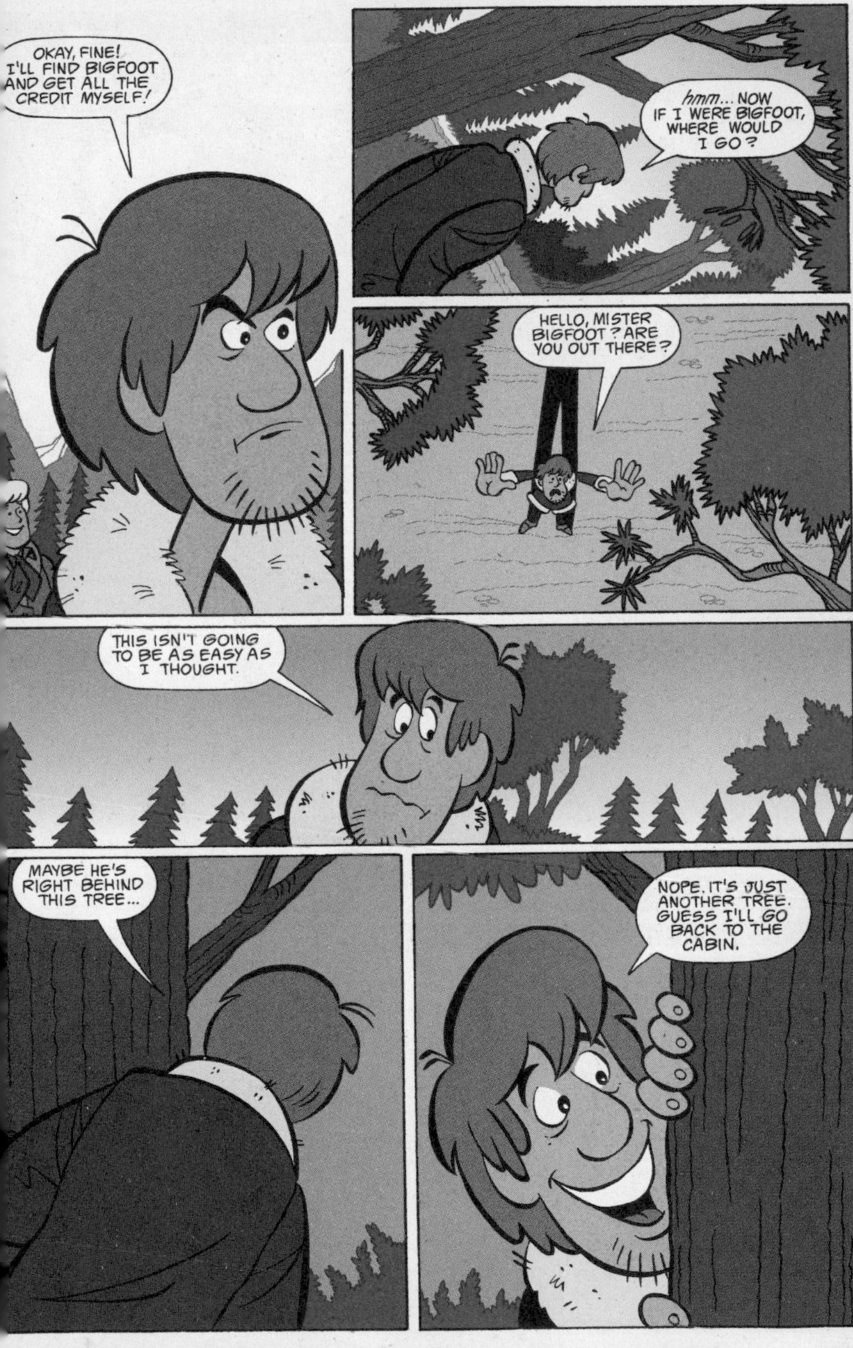
OKAY, FINE! I'LL FIND BIGFOOT AND GET ALL THE CREDIT MYSELF!
hmm... NOW IF I WERE BIGFOOT, WHERE WOULD I GO?
HELLO, MISTER BIGFOOT? ARE YOU OUT THERE?
THIS ISN'T GOING TO BE AS EASY AS I THOUGHT.
MAYBE HE'S RIGHT BEHIND THIS TREE...
NOPE. IT'S JUST ANOTHER TREE. GUESS I'LL GO BACK TO THE CABIN.

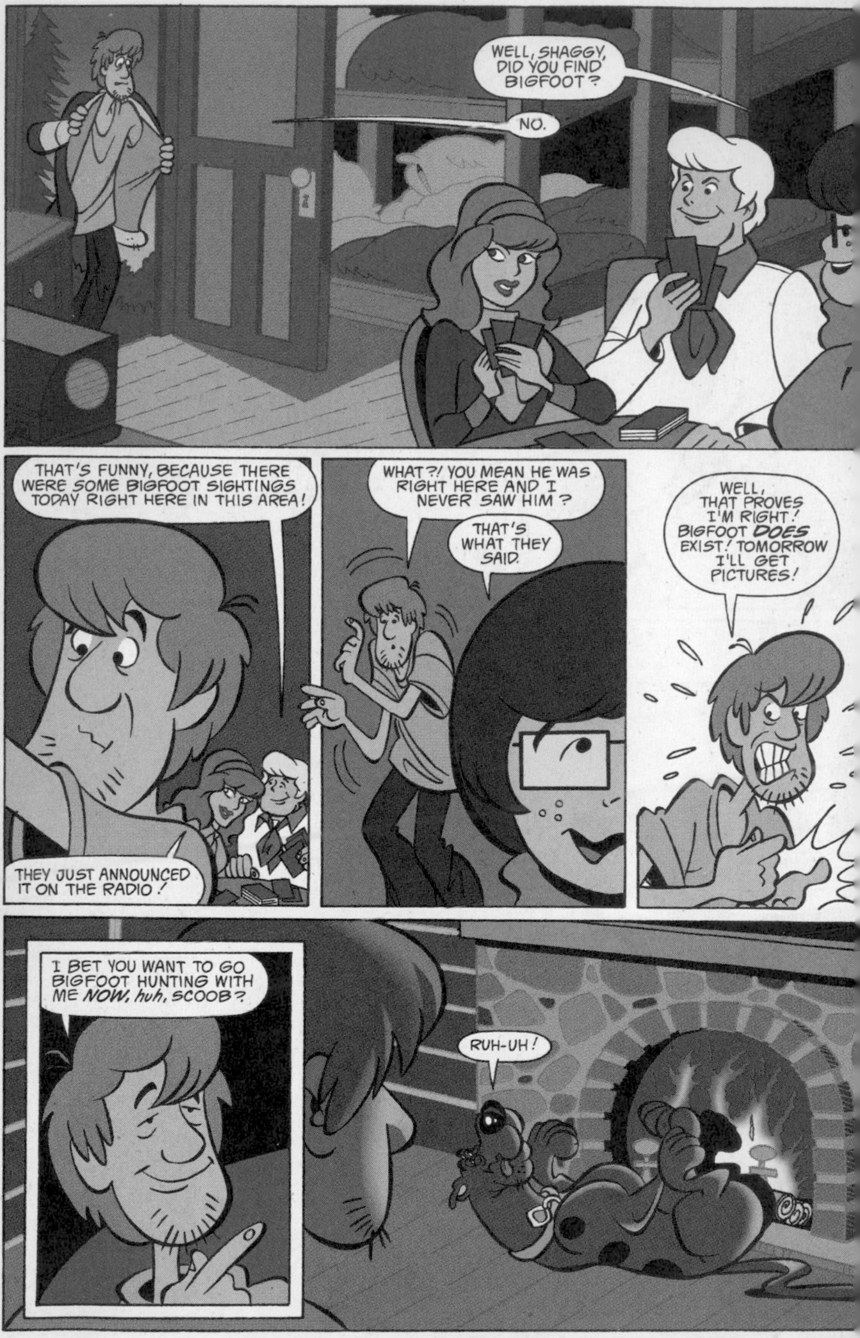
WELL, SHAGGY, DID YOU FIND BIGFOOT?
NO.
THAT'S FUNNY, BECAUSE THERE WERE SOME BIGFOOT SIGHTINGS TODAY RIGHT HERE IN THIS AREA!
THEY JUST ANNOUNCED IT ON THE RADIO!
WHAT?! YOU MEAN HE WAS RIGHT HERE AND I NEVER SAW HIM?
THAT'S WHAT THEY SAID.
WELL, THAT PROVES I'M RIGHT! BIGFOOT DOES EXIST! TOMORROW I'LL GET PICTURES!
I BET YOU WANT TO GO BIGFOOT HUNTING WITH ME NOW, huh, SCOOB?
RUH-UH!

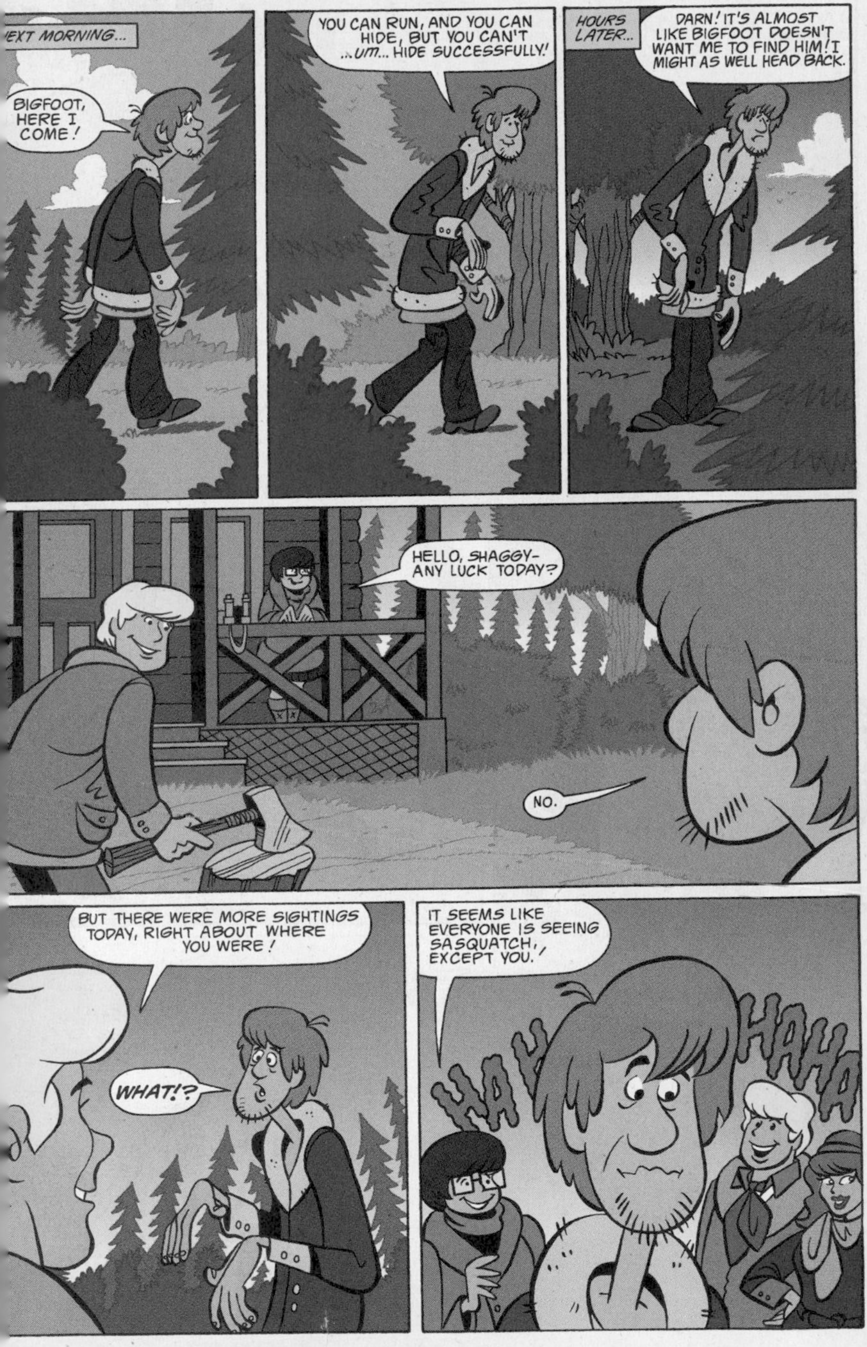

NEXT MORNING...
BIGFOOT, HERE I COME!
YOU CAN RUN, AND YOU CAN HIDE, BUT YOU CAN'T ...UM... HIDE SUCCESSFULLY!
HOURS LATER...
DARN! IT'S ALMOST LIKE BIGFOOT DOESN'T WANT ME TO FIND HIM! I MIGHT AS WELL HEAD BACK.
HELLO, SHAGGY-ANY LUCK TODAY?
NO.
BUT THERE WERE MORE SIGHTINGS TODAY, RIGHT ABOUT WHERE YOU WERE!
WHAT!?
IT SEEMS LIKE EVERYONE IS SEEING SASQUATCH, EXCEPT YOU.
HA HA HAHA HA

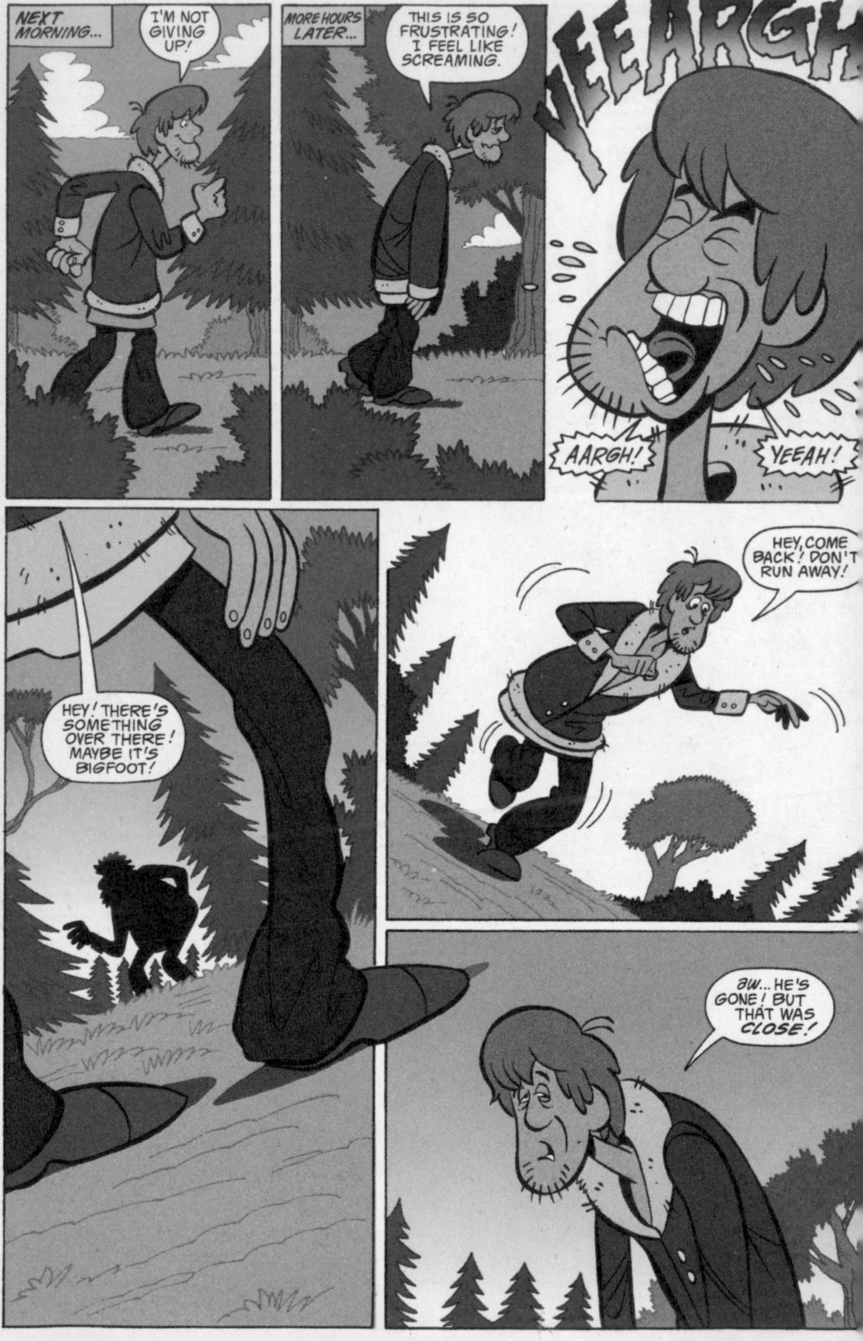
NEXT MORNING...
I'M NOT GIVING UP!
MORE HOURS LATER...
THIS IS SO FRUSTRATING! I FEEL LIKE SCREAMING.
YEEARGH
AARGH!
YEEAH!
HEY! THERE'S SOMETHING OVER THERE! MAYBE IT'S BIGFOOT!
HEY, COME BACK! DON'T RUN AWAY!
AW... HE'S GONE! BUT THAT WAS CLOSE!

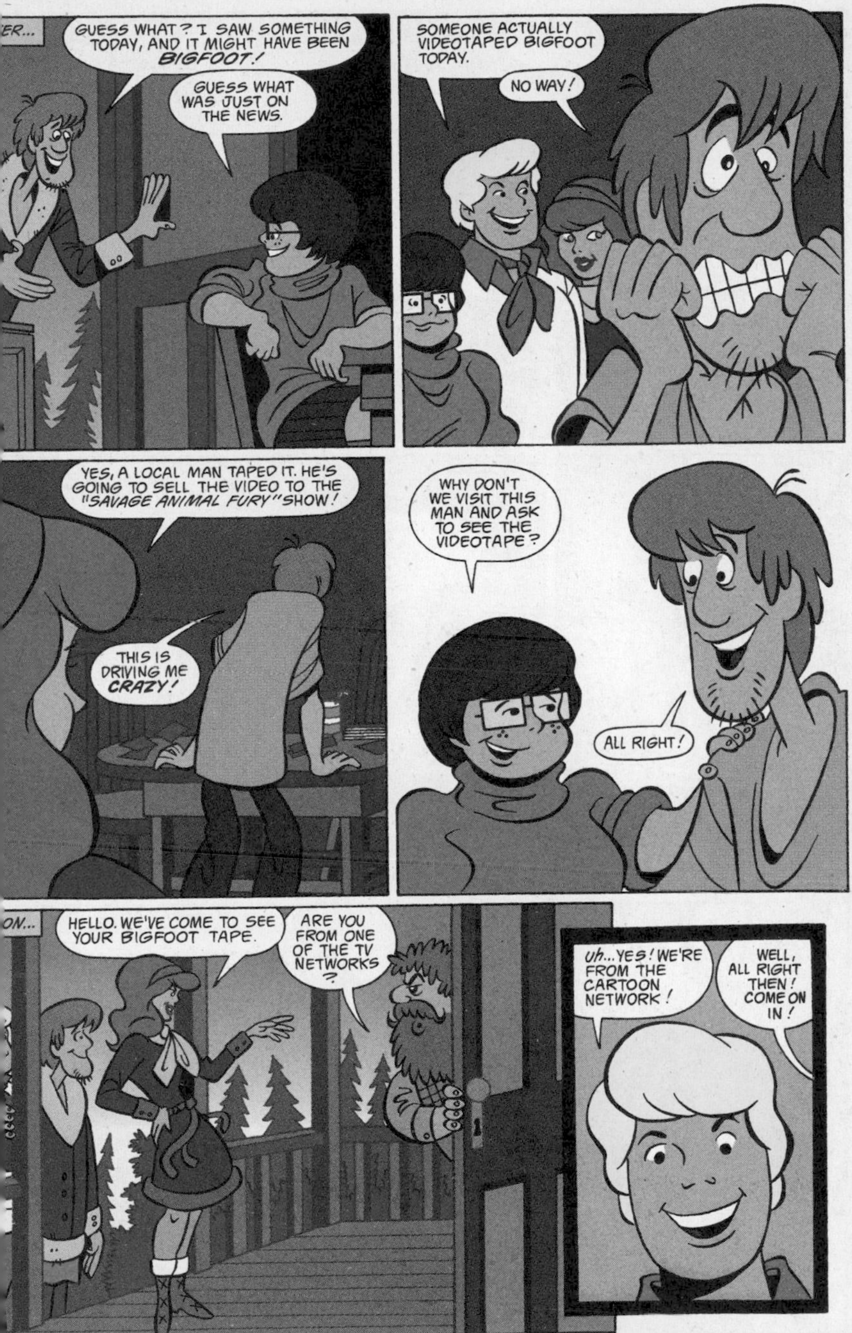

ER...
GUESS WHAT? I SAW SOMETHING TODAY, AND IT MIGHT HAVE BEEN BIGFOOT!
GUESS WHAT WAS JUST ON THE NEWS.
SOMEONE ACTUALLY VIDEOTAPED BIGFOOT TODAY.
NO WAY!
YES, A LOCAL MAN TAPED IT. HE'S GOING TO SELL THE VIDEO TO THE "SAVAGE ANIMAL FURY" SHOW!
THIS IS DRIVING ME CRAZY!
WHY DON'T WE VISIT THIS MAN AND ASK TO SEE THE VIDEOTAPE?
ALL RIGHT!
ON...
HELLO. WE'VE COME TO SEE YOUR BIGFOOT TAPE.
ARE YOU FROM ONE OF THE TV NETWORKS?
Uh...YES! WE'RE FROM THE CARTOON NETWORK!
WELL, ALL RIGHT THEN! COME ON IN!

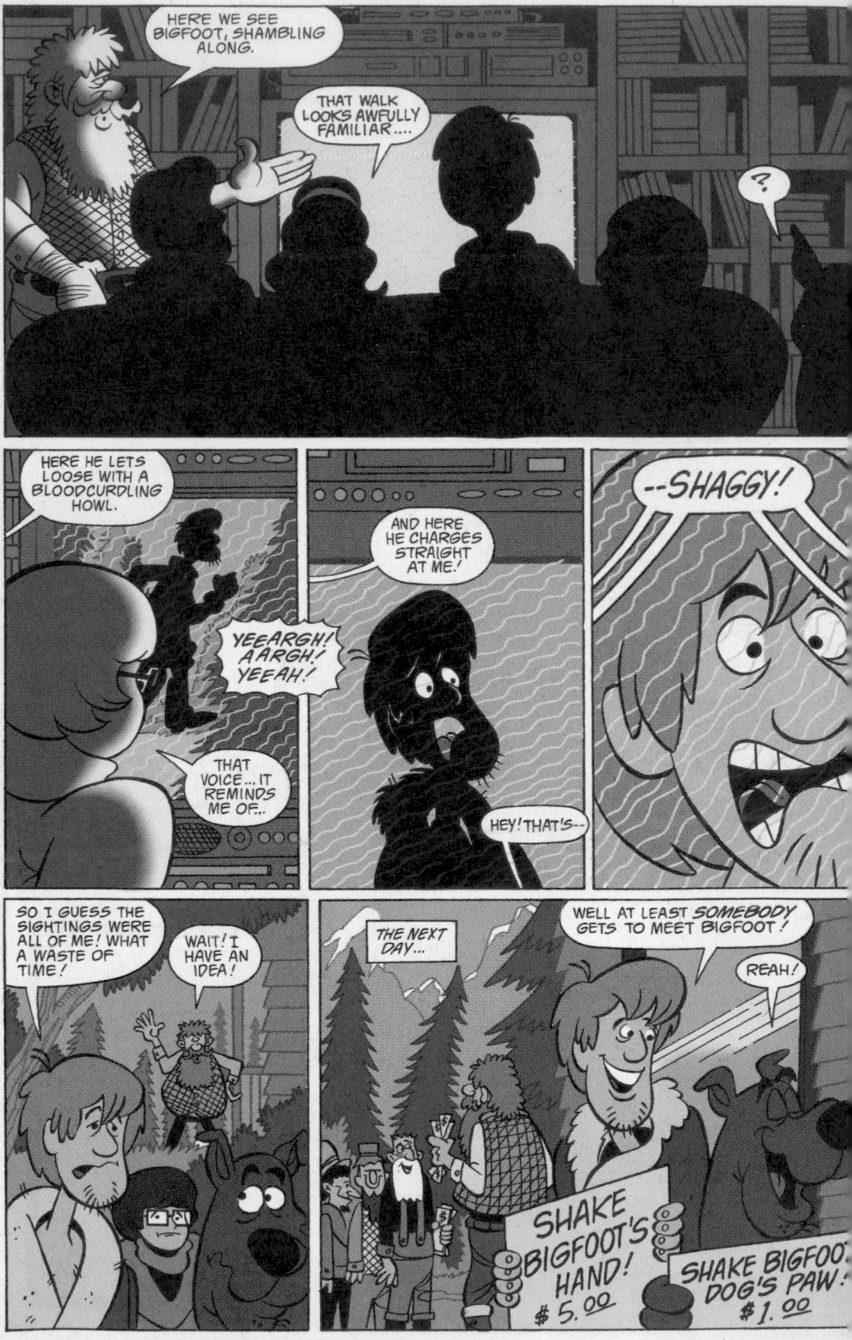
HERE WE SEE BIGFOOT, SHAMBLING ALONG.
THAT WALK LOOKS AWFULLY FAMILIAR....
?
HERE HE LETS LOOSE WITH A BLOODCURDLING HOWL.
YEEARGH! AARGH! YEEAH!
THAT VOICE... IT REMINDS ME OF..
AND HERE HE CHARGES STRAIGHT AT ME!
HEY! THAT'S--
--SHAGGY!
SO I GUESS THE SIGHTINGS WERE ALL OF ME! WHAT A WASTE OF TIME!
WAIT! I HAVE AN IDEA!
THE NEXT DAY...
WELL AT LEAST SOMEBODY GETS TO MEET BIGFOOT!
REAH!
SHAKE BIGFOOT'S HAND! $5.00
SHAKE BIGFOOT DOG'S PAW! $1.00